German Wines

FABER BOOKS ON WINE
General Editor: Julian Jeffs

Bordeaux (new edition) by David Peppercorn
Burgundy by Anthony Hanson
French Country Wines by Rosemary George
Italian Wines (new edition) by Philip Dallas
Port by George Robertson
Sherry by Julian Jeffs
Spirits and Liqueurs by Peter Hallgarten
The Wines of Greece by Miles Lambert-Gócs
The Wines of Portugal (new edition) by Jan Read
The Wines of the Rhône by John Livingstone-Learmonth and
Melvyn C. H. Master
The Wines of Spain (new edition) by Jan Read
The Wines of Australia (new edition) by Oliver Mayo
Drilling for Wine by Robin Yapp

GERMAN WINES

IAN JAMIESON

faber and faber
LONDON · BOSTON

First published in 1991
by Faber and Faber Limited
3 Queen Square London WC1N 3AU

Phototypeset by Intype, London
Printed by Clays Ltd, St Ives plc

A CIP record for this book
is available from The British Library

ISBN 0-571-14154-4
0-571-14155-2 (pbk)

To Ulla with love

Contents

Appendices

Maps

Acknowledgements

Over the years I have greatly appreciated the generosity of many German wine-producers. They have given me tastings galore, much of their time, and without exception have answered my questions with care and patience. To all of them I am indebted, but in particular I would like to thank those with whom I have been in direct contact during the preparation of this book, including:

Wolfgang Graf Castell of the Fürstlich Castell'sches Domänen-amt; Hans and Dr Peter Crusius of Weingut Hans & Peter Crusius; Armin Diel of Schlossgut Diel; Franz Dötsch of the Erzeuger-gemeinschaft 'Deutsches Eck'; Karl Fuhrmann of Weingut Pfef-fingen; Paul Fürst of Weingut Rudolf Fürst; Armin Göring of the Badischer Winzerkeller eG; Garry Grosvenor of G. M. Grosvenor Winebrokers; Heinrich Hillenbrand of the Staatsweingut Berg-strasse; Karl Heinz Hirsch of the Weinbauverband Württemberg eV; Horst Kolesch of the Weingut Juliusspital; Judith Lott of the Winzergenossenschaft Auggen eG; Erwein Graf Matuschka-Greif-fenclau of Schloss Vollrads; Dr Dirk Richter of Weingut Max Ferd. Richter; Thomas Siegrist of Weingut Thomas Siegrist; Andreas Stigler of Weingut Rudolf Stigler; and Christof Tyrell of the Rautenstrauch'sche Weingutsverwaltung.

In addition I am most grateful for the help that I have received from the East German Ministerium für Land-, Forst-, und Nah-rungsgüterwirtschaft in Berlin; Dr Karl Ludwig Bieser of the Wein-absatzzentrale Deutscher Winzergenossenschaften eG; and Dr Franz Michel of the Deutsches Weininstitut GmbH.

I have benefited greatly from the information in the excellent trade magazine published by the Verlag und Druckerei Meininger, *Die Weinwirtschaft*, and my debt to it must be acknowledged. I also have appreciated the friendship of Manfred Völpel of

Deinhard & Co., Koblenz, and the precision of the advice he has given me in my researches into the mysteries of German wine. Rainer Lingenfelder, of Weingut K. & H. Lingenfelder, has assisted and advised me in a number of matters relating to this book and his encouragement and professionalism have been very welcome.

Finally I should like to thank Amanda Howard of Superscript Typing Service for the speed and efficiency with which she converted my manuscript into a readable form.

Introduction

Wine-lovers will be glad to know that the future of German wine is not what it was. In the 1980s it might have seemed that while Germany complimented itself on the individuality and unique qualities of its wines, most of those she was selling abroad were commonplace and cheap. The risk was that the commercial success of these bland and unexciting wines would be so overwhelming that, soon, nobody would give a thought for those of real character and style. As the price of wine depended on the market's assessment of its worth, and not on its quality, good co-operative cellars and the better export houses felt threatened. It became clear that an adequate return was to be found only by producing wines that were above the general run of what was on offer, which could be attractively packaged and sold at a premium, but fair price. Many such have subsequently appeared in Germany as part of a range of superior quality, often based on individual vine varieties. What they nearly all have in common is dryness and the greater concentration of flavour that comes from a restricted grape yield.

As yet few of these enjoyable and welcome wines have been exported, but eventually the most worthwhile will have a place in an offer of German wine which starts to look increasingly convincing. At the bottom of the scale are the cheap and popular medium-sweet wines. Above these are good bottlings by co-operative cellars (particularly those in the Rheinpfalz and Baden regions), of a type to which I have just referred, and then, at the top, the fine wines from the good private and state-owned properties.

For nearly 200 years the Germans have been used to producing their best wines through timely and careful grape selection. This method is particularly suited to the Riesling vine, and can result in some of the most delicate, finely tuned and complex white wines in the world. Its disadvantage is that, while it creates an élite of wine on the one hand, the quality of the rest of the harvest is diminished. Getting the balance right is what the best Riesling estates do year after year, but it is perhaps their achievements in indifferent vintages that really show their professionalism and discipline.

If Riesling remains the glory of the German wine garden, the increasing success of Burgunder (Pinot) wines is a theme that recurs in this book. From the Weisser- and Grauer Burgunder, the white and grey Pinots, wines of a style and flavour are being produced in the middle range that hardly existed ten years ago. If some of the more exotic versions – for example, those with 13 per cent or more of natural alcohol and matured in new untreated casks – are not totally satisfactory yet, there is every reason to expect that their successors will be better, as experience is gained in this type of wine-making. The modern German Spätburgunder (Pinot Noir) is even more surprising as its quality has improved enormously in the last decade. What is so exciting is that now it has moved out of the rut it somewhat smugly occupied for so many years, nobody can yet judge what its full potential is going to be.

Perhaps Germany has one big advantage over other wine-producing countries. She is by far the largest buyer of wine in the European Community, both from member states and from third countries. She is familiar with the making and marketing of wines elsewhere, and can profit from the knowledge. As a performer in the EC wine-market, Germany does well. In spite of variations in the size of her grape harvest far greater than that of other member states, the production, import and sale of wine in Germany are in balance, and any surpluses are proportionately far smaller than they are in France and Italy.

As this book explains, and as Lady Bracknell puts it, in some regions 'land has ceased to be either a profit or a pleasure'. In others, perhaps through greater co-operation amongst wine-producers with varied commercial interests, life is more dynamic and the possibilities for profitable wine-making appear more likely. In general and on balance, the prospects for German wine in the 1990s are rather better than they sometimes seemed in the 1980s.

During the writing of this book, West and East Germany moved towards unification. However, by 'Germany', western Germany only is meant throughout – other than in its extension to include

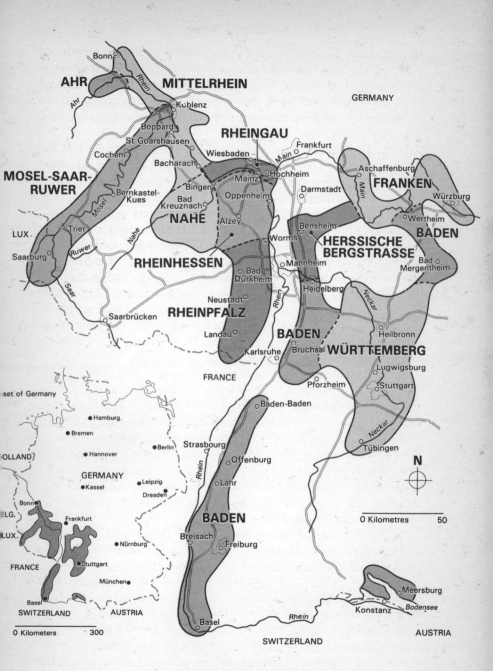

Key to the German vineyards

a short chapter on the wines of eastern Germany, and in historical references.

The German language allows some words to be written in more than one way. I have tried to choose the form which appears to be either officially or commonly used, or which has been selected by those about whom I am writing. Thus, we find '*Gebietswinzergenossenschaft*' as well as '*Gebiets-Winzergenossenschaft*', 'Grauburgunder' and 'Grauer Burgunder', and so on. I apologize to the reader for any confusion this may cause.

Finally, one achievement of the EC was to define precisely certain words which might otherwise be used loosely. Thus 'region' and 'district' have specific meanings in the EC wine world and I have tried to use them, and other terms, in a way that would satisfy the wine-controllers of the European Community. Their German equivalents will be found in the glossary at the end of this book.

I

German Wines since the French Revolution

========

The nineteenth century saw Germany establish itself as one nation and finally abandon the division of so much of its territory into small ineffective states. At the start of the century farming squires, and peasants in the process of being freed from serfdom, were still in the majority, and the urban population was relatively small. The Industrial Revolution arrived late and was initially slow in developing. In 1835 the steam locomotive *Adler* opened the first German railway line by linking the 6 kilometres from Nürnberg to Furth. It had been shipped from Britain in nineteen wooden crates, and on its début was said to 'snort like a great, antediluvian bull'. As a forerunner of an improved public-transport system, it was significant for the trade in wine.

The rivers of Germany have carried freight since the time of the Roman occupation but they are not always easily navigable. As late as the 1960s, until the introduction of the modern road container, high or low water on the Rhein often delayed wine shipments to the overseas markets. To the physical difficulties of river transport was added the imposition of tolls and customs duties. Until the 1830s there were no fewer than thirty-one points on the River Main between Bamberg and Mainz at which duties were levied and transport by boat was, therefore, exceptionally expensive.

Wine had been taxed over the centuries in many ways, but the revenue from customs duties on the Rhein was too alluring not to be milked for all it was worth by the Church and the nobility. As a freight route to the north of Germany, the narrow and steep-sided gorge from Bingen to Koblenz was almost unavoidable, and some Rhein taxes were not finally abolished until 1868. Strangely, they had contributed to the good standard of wine exported to the

United Kingdom, where the British would accept an expensive wine provided the quality was good. A highly taxed poor wine was then of little interest to them.

The German Customs Union of the 1830s signified the end of excessive taxes on wine, and the new ease with which it could be distributed within the homeland benefited the better-quality wines, which now found a wider public.

Political life in Germany was uncertain in the early nineteenth century, but the Rhenish Confederation set up in 1806 under the presidency of Napoleon I was generally well received. The Bavarians feared the powerful Austrians and, although the Rhinelanders had little warmth for the Prussians, they looked favourably at first upon the French, whose revolution had done away with their feudal ties. If Trier-born Karl Marx's mid-century challenge that the proletariat had nothing to lose but its chains had been made forty years earlier, the labourer in the local Mosel vineyard would not have understood. He had recently become free to work without sharing his produce with his overlord and was experiencing a new degree of independence.

With the secularization of the Church-owned properties and vineyards in 1806, the modern era of German wine-production begins, and Stefan Andres, in his *Die Grossen Weine Deutschlands*, identifies two great gifts of the nineteenth century to wine: scientific help and organization.

Since the sixteenth century the overlord's instructions in vineyard and cellar had excused the peasant vine-grower from thinking for himself. On gaining his freedom, how he should prune his vines and when he should pick his grapes became his own decision. Sometimes the necessary knowledge was missing. As the Latin writer on agriculture, Columella, had commented in the first century AD, there were schools for public speaking, music, cooking and even hair crimping, but not for farming. An early viticultural college was founded in 1806 near Meissen in eastern Germany, but the internationally recognized institutes at Weinsberg (Württemberg) and Geisenheim (Rheingau) were not established until 1860 and 1870 respectively.

One of the nineteenth-century scientific achievements, as Bassermann-Jordan pointed out in 1907 in his outstanding *Geschichte des Weinbaues*, was the identification of the various species of insect that attacked the vine, and an understanding of their lifecycles. An efficient defence, however, was not discovered and grape-berry moth, hay worm and sour worm remain today a most serious threat to the vine, second only to the almost invisible *phylloxera*. The European vine, *vitis vinifera*, can be protected from this aphid by being grafted on to American root-stocks, and the first German grafting station was set up at Geisenheim in 1890. Viticultural knowledge had progressed a long way since 1657 when the inhabitants of Amorbach, near the region of Franken, launched a campaign for burning the witches thought to be responsible for frost in the vineyards.

Johann Bronner, a meticulous chronicler of the German wine scene, described in detail in 1833 how hard life was for the vine-growers at Rhodt in the Rheinpfalz. All materials, including stones for paving and wall-building, were either conveyed on the back or by wheelbarrow, there being few horses available in this impoverished village. Food was scarce and the vineyard worker obtained his strength from wine, or so he believed. The difficult jobs were done in daylight and the simpler tasks were completed by the light of the moon. Not all vine-growers were as industrious as the inhabitants of Rhodt, but what they all shared was poverty.

In the early 1830s, a day's wage for a vineyard worker in the Rheinpfalz amounted to 30 Kreuzer plus a ration of wine at midday, or 20 Kreuzer if the employee accepted a 'free' meal. By 1858 the daily rate in the more prosperous Rheingau had risen to 40 Kreuzer, at a time when bread cost 12 Kreuzer per pound. Perhaps a poor return for much hard work encouraged the vine-grower in an increasingly scientific age to study ways of improving the quality of his wine. Be that as it may, the nineteenth century saw the introduction of selective grape-gathering, and the pickers started to bring in the crop only when it was really ripe. They began to pass through the vineyards several times in their search for the sweeter and richer grapes. According to the Rheingau wine-producer H. W. Dahlen, writing in 1896, the first harvest deliberately to be delayed in order to achieve the maximum ripeness was probably about 1820 – not itself, it must be said, an outstanding vintage.

The benefits of 'noble rot' (*botrytis cinerea*), which concentrates the juice of ripe grapes, became more widely appreciated and the habit of gathering various grape varieties individually was introduced. This required more attention than it would today, for, in many cases, vineyards were planted with various sorts of vines in a higgledy-piggledy way. Out of this disorder grew a greater enthusiasm for Germany's two most distinguished vines – the Riesling for white wine and the Spätburgunder (Pinot Noir) for red. Riesling wine is still the best that Germany can produce.

The size of the grape harvest varies considerably from year to year because of the fickle climate. Protection of the vines against pests and diseases was less advanced in the nineteenth century than it is today, which made harvests even more unpredictable. By the 1980s an average crop produced about 100 hectolitres per hectare but, before the planting of so many high-yielding vines in the 1960s, less than half this amount was usually brought in. Records show that in 1830 the whole of the Rheingau produced the equivalent of about 30,000 dozen bottles, whereas the 1834 vintage equalled some 1,181,900 dozen bottles. These fluctuations were an incentive to more scientific vine-growing, but changes were also taking place in the cellar, particularly with regard to the ageing of wine.

When we read of German wine in Britain in the first half of the nineteenth century, what immediately strikes us is the time it spent in cask. According to the British writer Cyrus Redding, 'Hock-heimer' of the 1766 and 1775 vintages was still being offered in 1833 in the 'Ahm' – a barrel of about 155 litres. The wine probably tasted a little like old dry sherry and in its youth would have had a very high level of acidity, as the grapes were picked early in the autumn. Recent experiments at the Bavarian State Institute for Viticulture and Horticulture (Bayerische Landesanstalt für Weinbau und Gartenbau) with vine varieties grown in medieval Germany resulted in acidic wines, described as 'unbelievably awful'. The old comment that if you lie down after drinking such wines you have to be turned over every hour to prevent the stomach being burnt through, becomes understandable. Years in cask would have softened the wines of the past, but perhaps our forefathers tolerated a greater concentration of acid than is acceptable today. Until the middle of the nineteenth century, the usual preference was for wines between ten and twenty years old. Riesling withstood this extended period of ageing and, indeed, was thought to improve through it, but by the early 1900s fine German wine was being served on formal occasions in the modern way, some five or six years after the vintage.

In 1833 Redding characterized German wine as 'generous, dry, finely flavoured' – a description that fits the drier Riesling wines now being produced on good Rheinland estates. The style has varied this century as far as sweetness is concerned but refreshing acidity, particularly tartaric or wine acid as it is known in Germany, has been a regular feature. Not so constant has been the type of name under which wine has been offered.

In the Middle Ages German wine was less varied than it is today, as the characteristics of flavour and bouquet associated with different grape types and soils were little understood. If a wine was given a name it was just as likely to have been that of the place at which it was sold as of the village where the grapes were grown. The link between vineyard, micro-climate and the quality of a wine was recognized more widely from the start of the nineteenth century. Village names were first used to describe a wine in the sixteenth century, and from the seventeenth century the year in which the grapes were gathered began to be quoted as well. What we now call 'varietal' wines (those made from, and sold under the name of, a specific type of grape) first appeared in Germany in the early eighteenth century. From the beginning of the nineteenth century, individual vineyard names (e.g. 'Grain') began to be linked with those of their villages (e.g. 'Deidesheim') to form a composite appellation – Deidesheimer Grain. Previously a vineyard name had simply denoted the vineyard but not the wine made from it.

As Germany moved slowly towards unification in 1871, the trade in wine blossomed, following excellent vintages in 1857, 1862, 1865 and 1868. Later in the century, times were to become much more difficult as the diseases *oidium* and *peronospora*, and the aphid *phylloxera*, struck the vineyards. In his *Geschichte des Weinbaues*, Bassermann-Jordan reflected that beyond the borders of the Rheinpfalz there were always people who liked to buy large quantities of cheap Pfälzer wine, and who therefore had an interest in seeing that the price and reputation of the region's wines were kept as low as possible. To some extent that is true of some of Germany's wine regions a hundred years later, so that fine estate-bottled wines from private or state-owned properties offer the wine-lover the best value for money on the international wine-market.

In 1951, in *The Wines of Germany*, Alfred Langenbach wrote of the rise of what he called the 'gentry estates'. Owned in the second part of the nineteenth century by persons in search of status, they were maintained regardless of cost in opulent, first-class order, subsidized by the owner's wealth derived from other sources. Such properties were roundly condemned by Bassermann-Jordan, whose family had been estate-owners for nearly 200 years. For him they were a cancerous growth which upset the market in fine wine. Today, unfortunately, there are still some producers trading at a loss, but no longer is that through choice. In chapter 8 the costs of earning a living out of making wine in Germany are discussed further.

The reputation for good wine-making in Germany before 1800 was created on the large estates owned by the Church and the nobility, but smaller growers were in the majority. Today they still are, with some 70 per cent of all producers owning less than 1 hectare of vineyard. In the early 1990s, with sales of good estate-bottled wine moving slowly in Britain and even more sluggishly in the USA, producers are forming associations to promote their wines more vigorously.

Co-operation is common in hard times, and so it was in the early nineteenth century. The first recorded growers' association was established in 1799 in Meissen and by the 1830s similar organizations had been set up elsewhere. In the spirit of German unity, wine conferences were held in major towns from 1839 onwards, and these gave growers a rare chance to taste wines from other parts of Germany.

By the middle of the nineteenth century, the German wine trade was in buoyant form. Liberal ideas were abroad, and even if they were later to be stifled by Bismarck, the wine world must have been pleased to hear the future Chancellor declare 'no man should die until he has drunk 5,000 bottles of Champagne'. In those days, 'Champagne' was used as a generic term for all sparkling wine, rather than solely to describe the wine of the Champagne region. Germany's own sparkling wine industry dates from 1826 when G. C. Kessler & Co. of Esslingen began commercial production.

With vintages reduced in size by wine pests and diseases, the circumstances of the small grower deteriorated. Many emigrated, but others formed co-operative cellars, the first being established in the Ahr valley in 1868. The co-operative movement is important in the history of European wine over the last 130 years or so, and today it handles nearly 40 per cent of the German wine harvest.

Whilst life for wine-producers was not easy at the end of the nineteenth century, the wine trade as a whole flourished. According to the magazine the *Deutsche Wein-Zeitung*, there were no fewer than 188 wine-merchants in Mainz in 1885, a great number of whom were Jews. In spite of anti-Semitism in many parts of the world (Russia in particular), the Jews had built up markets for German wine abroad as well as in Germany itself. When celebrating its centenary in 1964, after referring to the 'liberal spirit of these unorthodox and free-thinking, broad-minded and art-loving Jewish businessmen', the *Deutsche Wein-Zeitung* commented: 'It is certainly not exaggerated when we now state that without the Jews with their good foreign connections, the German wine trade would not have become what it is today.'

After 1933 Jews could no longer contribute to life in Germany. They were driven out of all trade associations, and advertising by Jewish firms was forced to stop. Even when they were able to set themselves up as wine-merchants abroad, German Jews were still subject to scurrilous press attacks in their own country. Nevertheless, it was the enforced émigrés to Britain – the Hallgartens, Loebs, Sichels and Thomans to name but a few – who presented a side of the German wine trade that was acceptable after the Second World War, and helped to re-establish German wine internationally.

The language of anti-Semitism in the 1930s had been heard at an infinitely less evil level from the anti-alcohol movement before the First World War. When the Prussian government voted a large sum of money early in the twentieth century to help the needy vine-growers, the monthly *Deutscher Bürger* wondered if brothel-keepers might now expect similar support. It was seriously proposed that the word for a tip, *Trinkgeld* (a literal translation of the French *pourboire*), should be replaced with something less reminiscent of the demon drink. But while the anti-alcohol movement showed how extreme it could be, the British magazine *Home Journal* recommended its female readers to wash in Rhein wine of *Kabinett* quality to improve the skin.

It may seem ironic today that by 1916 some feared in Germany that the wine-makers were concentrating too much on the production of fine wine, rather than offering a drink which the populace could afford. Out of the late 1930s came the Volkswagen, the people's car, but wine as a *Volksgetränk* promoted by the Nazi *Reichsnährstand* (the Reich Food Estate which controlled agriculture) was not a success.

Many large estates have produced wine continuously over the centuries, and some have records going back 500 years or more to prove it. Whether or not the smaller farmer in the less steep parts of Germany grew vines depended on whether grapes or corn was the most profitable crop at that period. Edward Hyams wrote in 1965 in his *Dionysus – A Social History of the Wine Vine* that 'rising cereal prices in the sixteenth century drove back the outposts of the vine in Germany and confined that always ambitious plant to the Rhineland'. The relationship between vine and corn, with the vine coming off second best, continued into the twentieth century and one of the Reich Food Estate's rulings in 1934 was that new vineyards could be planted only if the site was unsuitable for corn or for root crops. In the 1960s meadowland and potato fields along the Mosel were given over to high-yielding vine varieties and by the 1980s low prices were forcing growers to wonder if the expansion of their vineyards was such a good thing.

The economics of vine-growing and wine-making in Germany have always been finely balanced, dependent as they are on a changeable climate. The expressed aim of German wine-makers in the 1970s was to concentrate in the future on producing wines of good quality from restricted yields. In the EC this was the only way to survive and to compete with member states with lower production costs and a steadier climate. Unfortunately, many have not found it possible to follow their own advice and the selling price of wine has often been lower than the true cost.

The cheapest German wine is now sold as a commodity. Without the characteristics of fine wine it can be a pleasant, undemanding drink but it is only a distant relative of the products of the best estates. Cheap wine is always replaceable with that from elsewhere; fine German Riesling wine is not.

Much more often than in the past, today's owners of good estates are going abroad to fight for a share of the international wine market. The high quality of their wines is not in dispute and they have many interesting new ways of presenting them. Every lover of fine wine will wish them success.

2

The Vine in Germany

The notion that profit on wine could be related to its quality spread across Germany during the nineteenth century. Although there were a few vineyards whose wines nearly always stood apart from the rest on account of their particular characteristics, the climate ensured that these were relatively few. The result was that other ways had to be found by which a range of an easily recognizable, enhanced level of quality could be developed in order to make wine-making profitable. The increase in the amount of sugar that a delayed harvest brought with it usually produced a better wine for which a higher price could be expected. Although this was true for Riesling, the twentieth century has bred vine varieties in which increasing sweetness in the grapes has sometimes led to heavier and more clumsy wines. These were designed to make the best of a hierarchical system, largely based on the amount of sugar expected in the Riesling grape.

This remarkable vine, obligingly resistant to cold winter weather, is more demanding when it comes to a choice of site where its grapes will ripen fully in summer. Germany needed, and still needs, a variety of vines to suit the varying soils and micro-climates.

During the early nineteenth century the grape name, which had once been of interest only to the grower, came increasingly to represent certain styles of wine which the consumer could recognize and remember. The influence of vine variety, micro-climate and soil upon the quality and character of wine began to be partially understood. From the nineteenth century onwards, a vine was not to be judged solely by its performance in the vineyard, but by the marketable quality of its wine as well.

In the 1960s the inference in some German cellars was that it did not matter too much if the grapes were not as good as they ought to be, because modern cellar techniques would take care of any deficiencies. Since then, attitudes inside and outside the wine trade have changed, and more respect for nature in cellar and vineyard has brought with it a different approach. Greater importance is now given to the quality of the grape and the art of good wine-production is seen to lie in 'doing as little as possible'. In other words, healthy grapes and hygienic wine-making lead to the best possible product.

Over the centuries the popularity of individual vine varieties has changed from time to time, but perhaps never as much as in the last twenty-five years. The decline of Silvaner has been accompanied by the success of the more prolific Müller-Thurgau, but the latest figures suggest that Silvaner may now be regaining its popularity a little. If so, we should thank those who have led the way back to drier wines since the 1970s. Riesling has undoubtedly benefited from a change in taste in Germany, which has recently reduced the area occupied by some of the rising stars, the 'new crossing' vines. Their flowery, powerfully scented, sometimes inelegant wines are associated with a level of sweetness that is now out of fashion. It must be hoped, however, that the current changes in taste will not be so radical and one-sided that they make it uneconomic to produce excellent, dry Scheurebe, simply because over the last twenty-five years or more, the wine has usually been medium-sweet.

Table 1, based on figures from the Statistisches Bundesamt, shows how the spread of the vine varieties has altered since 1964.

Amongst the traditional white varieties, Elbling in the Obermosel and Gutedel in Markgräflerland enjoy their own particular niches and are well supported in their districts. Ruländer (Pinot Gris) has gone through a period in which the dark-coloured, low-acid wines of the past have been reborn in a much crisper style, selling under the alternative grape name of Grauer Burgunder. Its relative, the Weisser Burgunder (Pinot Blanc), is gaining ground in Baden, where, as a modern dry wine, it is drunk with food.

Of the new white crossings, only Kerner continues to expand its vineyard area significantly, perhaps because its wine is somewhat traditional in flavour and because it can now be a major constituent of Liebfraumilch.

The red-wine scene is excitingly alive and starting to attract attention on the export market. Dry German Spätburgunder can

Table I *The Most Widely Planted Vines in Hectares*

	1964	1982	1988	Change in hectareage	
				1982 compared to 1964	1988 compared to 1982
Traditional White Varieties					
Burgunder, Weisser	465	872	1,009	+407	+137
Elbling, Weisser	1,234	1,122	1,177	−122	+55
Gutedel, Weisser	1,192	1,255	1,295	+63	+40
Riesling, Weisser	17,083	18,791	20,716	+1,708	+1,925
Ruländer	1,283	3,339	2,811	+2,056	−528
Silvaner, Grüner	18,781	8,861	7,562	−9,920	−1,299
Total Traditional White Varieties	40,038	34,240	34,570	−5,798	+330
New White Crossings					
Bacchus	2	3,344	3,573	+3,342	+229
Faberrebe	−	2,197	2,176	+2,197	−21
Huxelrebe	56	1,687	1,684	+1,631	−3
Kerner	5	6,121	7,409	+6,116	+1,288
Morio-Muskat	1,052	2,933	2,222	+1,881	−711
Müller-Thurgau	14,115	24,944	23,881	+10,829	−1,063
Ortega	−	1,169	1,266	+1,169	+97
Scheurebe	342	4,237	4,159	+3,895	−78
Total New White Crossings	15,572	46,632	46,390	+31,060	−242
Other White Varieties	1,169	4,437	4,096	+3,268	−341
Total of All White Varieties	56,779	85,309	85,056	+28,530 (+50.2%)	−253 (−0.3%)

	1964	1982	1988	Change in hectareage	
				1982 compared to 1964	1988 compared to 1982
Traditional Red Varieties					
Burgunder, Blauer Spät	1,839	3,896	5,003	+2,057	+1,107
Limberger, Blauer	365	423	611	+58	+188
Müllerrebe	323	1,168	1,685	+845	+517
Portugieser, Blauer	5,323	3,095	3,508	−2,228	+413
Trollinger, Blauer	1,662	2,079	2,154	+417	+75
Total Traditional Red Varieties	9,512	10,661	12,961	+1,149	+2,300
Other Red Varieties	394	906	1,618	+512	+712
Total of All Red Varieties	9,906	11,567	14,579	+1,661 (+16.8%)	+3,012 (+26.0%)
Total of All Varieties	66,685	96,876	99,635*	+30,191 (+45.3%)	+2,759 (+2.8%)

*Excludes 85 ha of vines on trial

hardly meet the demand and the successful new crossing, Dornfelder, occupies more than half the area of 1,618 hectares shown on the table for 'other red varieties'.

In the EC, where the supply of wine is greater than the demand by about 46 per cent, new vineyards cannot be legally planted except under special circumstances. Expansion of the total area under vine in Germany is, therefore, no longer possible, but the replacement of old vines can continue as before. Because of the reconstruction of the vineyards, as explained in chapter 3, and of the interest there has been in planting new vine varieties, only 13 per cent or so of Germany's vines were over twenty years old at the last census at the start of the 1980s. The corresponding figure for Riesling was 21 per cent, and 38 per cent of the Riesling vines were between ten and twenty years old. If we went back 150 years, we would find that the average age of a Riesling vineyard was between thirty and forty years, according to Johann Bronner writing at the time. Today, in a vineyard such as the Bernkasteler Doctor on the Mosel, the grapes richest in minerals come from old vines growing on their own root stocks.

To conclude that things are not as good as they were would be wrong, for the quality of the vine today is better by far than that of its ancestors in the nineteenth century.

The first deliberate attempts to produce a better race of vine in disciplined circumstances were made by Georg Fröhlich in the Rheinpfalz in 1876. From then on clonal selection was, and continues to be, a strength of German viticulture. Its aim is to retain, and then improve, the characteristics of a particular vine variety, and to establish a supply of vines in which the likelihood of early mutation and degeneration has been much reduced.

Multiplication of vines by the normal sexual process can create completely new varieties, and that is how the famous new crossings of *vitis vinifera* are developed. To produce a clone by propagating from one plant vegetatively (without the sex) is a process which eliminates the variations in offspring that normal reproduction brings with it. The work is usually spread over four phases, which together last for some fifteen to twenty years. Selection follows selection, with perhaps 100 vines being chosen at an early stage from an original 1,000 for further propagation, and even more selection. Not only are vines that show signs of mutating discarded, but resistance to virus diseases is also a decisive factor. At the last phase of selection, the official registration by the controlling body, the Bundessortenamt, takes place. Thereafter, the commercial production of the clone can begin. This description somewhat oversimplifies a process which is complex and rigorously controlled. The work takes place in viticultural institutes and on a small number of private and state-owned estates. It applies to rootstocks as well as to fruit-bearing vines. Better clones have increased average yields from the 20 hectolitres per hectare of 100 years ago to the present 100 hectolitres per hectare, or more. If grape-production is now sometimes said to be too great, that cannot be blamed solely on the stronger vines but on the conditions of the market, discussed elsewhere in this book.

At a time when fashion in wine is asking for a return to the past, new crossings might seem a little out of step. In a sense this is true, but the consumer will decide which are to be retained and which will follow old traditional varieties – like the once widely planted Orléans vine – into oblivion.

For many years the days before the flowering have been very active for the vine-breeding institutes. The miniature grapes destined to be mothers are castrated and the pollen of those which will play the father's role is collected. The result of the mating between two European vines (vitis vinifera) may lead to the official registration of a new crossing twenty years later.

The first important artificial crossing of a vine was made at the Geisenheim viticultural institute in 1882 by Professor Dr Hermann Müller-Thurgau. Riesling was the mother and Silvaner was claimed as father. Subsequent marriages of Riesling and Silvaner have produced a range of other varieties, even including one with red grapes, but Müller-Thurgau resembles none of its presumed relatives.

In the period in which Professor Müller-Thurgau worked, the pest phylloxera and the disease peronospora arrived in Germany and stimulated the early research into new vine varieties. Many years later, in 1971, Professor Dr Alleweldt of the Federal Research Institute for Vine-breeding at Geilweilerhof, explained the aim of his work to the magazine Allgemeine Deutsche Weinfach-Zeitung. 'Each vine-breeder', he said, 'strives to produce the ideal vine.' By 'ideal' he meant resistant to disease and able to produce good quantities of high-quality wine. A vine might be bred that would be perfect as a speciality in suitable viticultural conditions, but a universal wine, for all occasions and sites, was an impossibility. The mood of the time, encouraged by the 'economic miracle', was buoyant and a speaker from the Bavarian State Institute in Würzburg had written in the *Deutsche Wein-Zeitung* in 1964 that the wine world must free itself of the mistaken idea that there was nothing to beat the old vine varieties. Even until the 1960s many growers had been a little reluctant to plant new crossings on any wide scale. Those who sold in bottle directly to the consumer were perhaps the most enthusiastic, for they had the chance to explain their new and sometimes strongly scented wines. When it was realized that new crossings could produce grapes with sufficient sugar in ordinary vintages for their wines to be described as *Spätlese*, or even *Auslese*, enthusiasm spread and the cheap 'supermarket *Spätlese*' was born. Dr Fader of the viticultural institute at Neustadt reported that research had shown that the main reason given by growers for planting new crossings was to make scented wine with a heavier must weight. An increased yield was a less-compelling enticement in the early 1970s. The price of wine in bulk was now determined by its legally established quality category and not by its true quality. The new crossings had enabled wines of *Spätlese* and *Auslese* weight to be sold as commodities, and the meaning of the quality structure for German wine had been destroyed. The move to drier wine from traditional vine varieties that is a characteristic of the late 1980s will perhaps re-establish the worth of the system.

For too long the great deceiver, residual sugar, was allowed to wrap indifferent wine in a cloak of sweetness, best worn by the finest Rieslings in good years.

Although loud praise is now rightly lavished on the Riesling grape, maturation in cask and other symbols of German wine tradition, the official tasting competitions still regard at least some of the new crossings with an eye of favour. Table 2 compares their performance in the Rheinhessen in the years 1982 and 1989 with that of long-established vine varieties. It shows in percentage terms the number of first prizes (*Grosse Preise*) that were won at the national wine competition (DLG competition – see chapter 7), and relates them to the area under vine.

There is no absolute standard for judging wine and therefore, to some extent, the results of the DLG competitions reflect the

TABLE 2 *Rheinhessen*

	Riesling		Silvaner		Müller-Thurgau		Huxelrebe		Scheurebe		Kerner	
	1982	1989	1982	1989	1982	1989	1982	1989	1982	1989	1982	1989
Percentage of all first prizes in the DLG competition	18	39	—	8	16	5	26	25	11	8	21	9
Percentage of total area under vine	5	7	15	13	25	23	4	4	9	9	7	9

subjective opinions and expectations of the judges. Nevertheless, it seems that in the Rheinhessen, Riesling and Silvaner wines have gained in popularity since 1982, Huxelrebe retains its place, whilst Müller-Thurgau and Kerner had slipped as top prizewinners by 1989.

The success of new-crossing vines in the 1960s and 1970s was based on economic factors, with the approval of the German wine-drinker. A continuing demand for drier wines in the 1980s, and the approach of the open market in 1992, has concentrated the minds of many producers. Quality, based on a sharper selection of the grapes at harvest time, is improving. On the best estates yields, which are already relatively low, are declining further, so that wines are becoming more intense in flavour. Riesling, supported by other traditional vines, and the best of the new crossings, is once more properly recognized as King of the White Wines.

TRADITIONAL WHITE VINE VARIETIES GROWING IN 1988

Burgunder, Weisser

1,009 hectares, of which 54.1 per cent is in Baden, 24.6 per cent in the Rheinpfalz and 13.2 per cent in the Rheinhessen. This mutation of Ruländer is better known outside German-speaking countries as Pinot Blanc, where it usually produces sound, attractive dry wine, without any extreme flavours. The best of German Weisser Burgunder (sometimes written as Weissburgunder) can achieve high quality as *Spätlesen* with over 12 per cent of alcohol or more. The steady increase in the plantation of the vine has doubtless been encouraged by the recently found interest in Germany in drinking wine with food, for which Weisser Burgunder is particularly suitable. Its structure is less Germanic than that of Riesling, and the wine is less fine.

Weisser Burgunder needs a good site to reach a minimum of 11 per cent of alcohol or so, and sufficient body for the wine to taste balanced. Normally, the harvest is late (just before that of Riesling), as growers wait for sugar levels in the grape to rise.

Elbling, Weisser

1,177 hectares, of which 93.6 per cent is in the Mosel-Saar-Ruwer region. Ancient vine variety producing a high yield, once widely grown but now found mainly in the Bereich Obermosel (upstream from Trier) and in the Bereich Zell. Ripens late. The wine has good acidity, is light and rather rustic. Mosel Elbling is now being professionally marketed, principally as dry or medium-dry wine. Perhaps at its best as sparkling wine.

Gutedel, Weisser

1,295 hectares, of which 99.8 per cent is in Baden (Bereich Markgräflerland). Allegedly originating in Asia Minor, Gutedel reached Baden in 1780. Its grapes are used for the table as well as for winemaking. Yield can be as high as 150 hl/ha. The wine is pleasant to drink, fairly low in acidity, a café wine much appreciated in south-west Germany.

Riesling, Weisser

20,716 hectares, of which 34.1 per cent is in the Mosel-Saar-Ruwer region, 18.9 per cent in the Rheinpfalz, 11.8 per cent in Württemberg and 11.4 per cent in the Rheingau. It is an indigenous vine that has spread to most of the important vine-growing countries of the world, but whose wine reaches a peak of quality in Germany. It can shine on the Mosel with as little as 8 per cent of alcohol, but in the Rheinpfalz, fully fermented and therefore dry *Spätlese* wines achieve over 12 per cent. This, in a sense, is immaterial, for it is the total impression rather than the technical achievement that admirers of German Rieslings enjoy.

The area under Riesling is increasing again at the expense of other vines, but its further expansion will be limited by the number of suitable sites. Riesling flourishes in a variety of soils, but requires a sunny position to ripen its grapes. The harvest can last for five weeks or more, as the sweetest, noble-rotted grapes may be picked at a different time to the rest of the crop and sometimes before the main harvest has even begun. A characteristic of Riesling is its good amount of acidity (particularly the stylish tartaric as opposed to the unripe malic acid). No matter how full-bodied and alcoholic it may be, it should still remain a fresh and interesting wine.

Riesling is versatile and is at home in all the German wine categories from simple quality wine to *Trockenbeerenauslese*. With maturation in well-seasoned casks of not less than 500 litres, it takes on a bigger dimension, longer in flavour and more intense in bouquet.

The history of Riesling is the history of German wine. It includes the understanding of the benefits of noble rot, and the development of late harvesting, which ultimately led to the making of the first *Eiswein*.

Riesling has fathered, or mothered, many of today's successful new crossings but none, so far, has quite measured up to its parent in terms of flavour or sheer high quality. Perhaps the best are yet to come.

Ruländer

2,811 hectares, of which 58.0 per cent is in Baden, 17.9 per cent in the Rheinpfalz and 14.5 per cent in the Rheinhessen. A mutation of Spätburgunder (Pinot Noir), also known as Grauer Burgunder (sometimes Grauburgunder), and as Pinot Gris outside Germany, Ruländer is perhaps at its best in the hot climate of the Bereich Kaiserstuhl, across the Rhein from Alsace. Confusingly, it is also grown as far north as Luxembourg, but until recently it was thought to need at least 10.5 per cent of natural alcohol from the grape to avoid tasting thin.

Ruländer grapes are dull red in colour (some would say 'grey'), and often the wine, sold as Ruländer, is more highly coloured than a Riesling or a Silvaner. It is relatively low in acidity and broad of flavour. Wine sold as Grauer Burgunder has a powerful flavour, and can surprise by its elegance even when it contains over 12 per cent of alcohol.

In both forms, Ruländer and Grauer Burgunder, the wine is full of character, which can be a little excessive.

Silvaner, Grüner

7,562 hectares, of which 42.3 per cent is in the Rheinhessen, 23.5 per cent in the Rheinpfalz and 14 per cent in Franken. Silvaner is ready for its renaissance. Once it was the most widely planted vine in Germany, but, having replaced Elbling in many vineyards in the nineteenth century, it was pushed aside by the more prolific Müller-Thurgau. Where Silvaner is taken to the limits of production, ordinary wine is the result. On the other hand, dry Silvaner wine from a restricted yield is firm, concentrated, fairly neutral in flavour but unmistakably 'classy'. Like wines from Rülander, Silvaner is now being produced in a much fresher style, with acid levels at the harvest being as important as sugar content. In general, the best dry Silvaner wines come from Franken, the village of Ihringen in the Bereich Kaiserstuhl in Baden, and from certain growers in the Rheinhessen. Dry Franken Silvaner is sometimes cited as the German wine that is most easily appreciated by the French and Italians.

NEW WHITE VINE VARIETIES GROWING IN 1988

Bacchus

3,573 hectares, of which 54.7 per cent is in the Rheinhessen, 14.6 per cent in Franken and 13 per cent in the Rheinpfalz. A highly successful crossing of (Silvaner × Riesling) × Müller-Thurgau, which can produce large quantities of coarse, soft wine, or a small yield (say 60 hl/ha) of stylish wine, a little reminiscent of Sauvignon Blanc. If a minimum alcohol content of about 10 per cent is reached, the wine develops a bouquet rather like that of Scheurebe. Although Bacchus is not known for its ability to age, a dry 1982 *Kabinett* wine from Weingut Fürst Lowenstein in south Franken still tasted young and fresh in 1989.

Faberrebe

2,176 hectares, of which 75.8 per cent is in the Rheinhessen and 16.4 per cent in the Rheinpfalz. A crossing of Weisser Burgunder and Müller-Thurgau, the wine has more acidity than Müller-Thurgau but a lower yield. In areas where Riesling cannot grow satisfactorily, Faberrebe will produce similar, but less distinguished, wines. It has the advantage of being able to ripen its fruit longer in the season than Silvaner or Müller-Thurgau and therefore the harvest can often be late-picked (*Spätlese*). A good-quality crossing whose wine wins medals.

Huxelrebe

1,684 hectares, of which 54.4 per cent is in the Rheinhessen and 41 per cent in the Rheinpfalz. A crossing of Weisser Gutedel × Courtillier Musqué which, when suitably restrained, can produce *Auslese* wine in average-to-good sites in poor vintages. Huxelrebe has more acidity than Müller-Thurgau and a higher concentration of sugar in its grape juice. The wines win many prizes in the state and national competitions and can offer very good value for money – without having the elegance of Riesling.

Kerner

7,409 hectares, of which 34.5 per cent is in the Rheinpfalz, 28.5 per cent in the Rheinhessen, 11.8 per cent in Württemburg and 11.7 per cent in the Mosel-Saar-Ruwer. This crossing of Trollinger × Riesling has been widely planted in Germany in the last twenty-five years but has probably reached its peak of popularity. The leaves have some resistance against late autumn frosts and therefore the crop can be picked late in the season, shortly before Riesling. The wine is considered to be similar to, but lacks the aristocratic style of, a good Riesling.

Morio-Muskat

2,242 hectares, of which 59.8 per cent is in the Rheinpfalz and 37.2 per cent in the Rheinhessen. A Silvaner × Weisser Burgunder crossing, which produces a high yield of scented wine, destined mainly to add interest to cheap and thin commercial blends. The increased body that comes from a lower yield improves the wine considerably, but as a single vine wine the Muskat bouquet and flavour can quickly cloy. Now becoming much less popular, as it has been left behind by the return in taste to traditional, less-scented vine varieties.

Müller-Thurgau

23,881 hectares, of which 23.5 per cent is in the Rheinhessen, 22.4 per cent in Baden, 21.2 per cent in the Rheinpfalz and 11.9 per cent in the Mosel-Saar-Ruwer region. None of the German vineyard areas is without this crossing dating from 1882. Its parents were at first declared to be Riesling and Silvaner, but some experts today doubt the involvement of Silvaner. The point is perhaps academic, as the vine is now so widely established that it is regarded as 'traditional'. As a named variety, Müller-Thurgau made its début in a Franken wine (from the viticultural college at Veitshöchheim) at an exhibition in Koblenz in 1925. There were then, in the whole of undivided Germany, 4 hectares planted in Müller-Thurgau, all in Franken. Today it is easier to find a high-quality Müller-Thurgau wine from that region than from any other.

The tremendous increase in the area planted in Müller-Thurgau in the 1960s and 1970s was stimulated by the vine's high yield and its gentle, medium-sweet wine, which pleases so many undemanding 'occasional-drinkers'. Unfortunately, the concept of a large yield of inexpensive wine is not good for economic health in Germany, and Müller-Thurgau has been allowed to damage all sides of the German wine trade. That it can produce concentrated, characterful wine when the yield is as low as 33 hl/ha has been shown by Weingut Dr Loosen on the Mosel. A limited crop on other quality-conscious estates is also producing thoroughly worthwhile results with which the breeder of the crossing, Professor Müller-Thurgau, would doubtless have been pleased.

In order to get away from the image of mass production, some producers are now using the name Rivaner as a synonym for Müller-Thurgau.

Ortega

1,266 hectares, of which 52.9 per cent is in the Rheinhessen, 29.2 per cent in the Rheinpfalz and 11.3 per cent in the Mosel-Saar-Ruwer. A crossing of Müller-Thurgau x Siegerrebe (Madeleine Angevine × Gewürztraminer), producing wines from high must weights (over 14 per cent of alcohol if all the sugar is fermented out) and low acidity – not typically German. In spite of this, Ortega wins medals at all quality levels and remains an interesting addition to the list of German vine varieties. The grapes ripen early and therefore attract wasps.

Scheurebe

4,159 hectares, of which 54.6 per cent is in the Rheinhessen and 31.7 per cent in the Rheinpfalz. In terms of quality, Scheurebe (Silvaner × Riesling) is the most successful of all the new-crossing wines in wide commercial production. The acidity level is usually only a little below that of Riesling, whilst the concentration of sugar in the grape juice is greater. The strong, blackcurrant bouquet tends to become less predominant as the wine ascends the quality scale. Some of the fullest and best Scheurebe wines come from the Rheinpfalz, where Weingut K. & H. Lingenfelder regularly demonstrates their great potential both as dry and as sweet wines up to the *Trockenbeerenauslese* level.

TRADITIONAL RED WINE VARIETIES GROWING IN 1988

Spätburgunder, Blauer

5,003 hectares, of which 68.9 per cent is in Baden. Spätburgunder, more widely known as Pinot Noir, has been grown in Germany since the fourteenth century and possibly even earlier. In the recent past, the best of German Spätburgunders have been surprising wine-tasters outside Germany by their colour and depth of flavour.

Once the vine was grown much more widely than it is today, but even in areas where a particularly Germanic form of Spätburgunder has been produced (a little sweet and with a noticeably low level of tannin) wines are now being made that can be compared easily with those of, say, the Hautes Côtes de Beaune. However, on good estates in good vintages, they have a natural alcohol content (without the addition of sugar) of 13 per cent or more that would amaze many Burgundians.

Clonal selection has been very important in improving Spätburgunder, and the clone from Weinsberg called Mariafeld is particularly successful when its crop is restricted.

Spätburgunder needs a good site, and the removal of all rotten grapes (which can be used for *Weissherbst*, or rosé wine) before the harvest for red wine begins. At the start of the 1990s the prospects for the increasingly planted Spätburgunder are no longer merely rosé, but full-blooded red. Quality is improving constantly and excitingly.

Limberger, Blauer

611 hectares, of which 98.4 per cent is in Württemberg. A vine known to have reached Germany from Austria, where it is widely planted, under the name Blaufränkisch. It is now one of Württemberg's most interesting red wines. The grapes ripen before those of Spätburgunder, but, not being sensitive to rot which would destroy their colour, they can be left to produce excellent *Spätlese* wine with over 12.5 per cent of natural alcohol, or more. The wine is 'serious', dark coloured, with a good amount of tannin and a backbone of acidity, but without the quality of Spätburgunder at its best.

Müllerrebe

1,685 hectares, of which 85.9 per cent is in Württemberg. Known in France as Pinot Meunier (where it covers over one-third of the Champagne region), Müllerrebe, to add to the confusion, is often sold in Germany as 'Schwarzriesling'. Compared to Spätburgunder, Müllerrebe is less demanding of site and soil and the wine is not so distinguished. Sometimes blended with Trollinger.

Portugieser, Blauer

3,508 hectares, of which 57.6 per cent is in the Rheinpfalz and 28.9 per cent in the Rheinhessen. A vine brought to Germany in the nineteenth century from Austria, of uncertain nationality in spite of its name. It is often regarded as a red-wine counterpart to Müller-Thurgau. The vine is undemanding and ripens a large crop early. From high yields a light, drinkable red or rosé (*Weissherbst*) simple-quality wine ('QbA', or *Qualitätswein eines bestimmten Anbaugebietes* – quality wine from a specified region) is produced. A smaller crop improves the wine noticeably.

Trollinger, Blauer

2,154 hectares, of which 99.7 per cent is in Württemberg. If ever you wish to visit Stuttgart, say not a word against Trollinger. It is to the city what Guinness is to Dublin. To outsiders, Trollinger is a vine that in Germany requires a well-situated vineyard and ripens its luxuriant grapes late in the season. Its future seems secured by a high yield and a totally committed Schwabian following. The wine is light in colour, a pleasant drink, but in no way a serious red wine. As a constituent of *Schillerwein*, a rosé made exclusively in Württemberg, Trollinger has a successful, secondary role.

3

Growing Vines

If the northern climate gives German wine a common style, the wine-producers, an independent-minded body of people, seem to respond by trying to make it as varied as possible. The nineteen vines described in chapter 2 cover 94 per cent of the total vineyard area, but in the remaining 6 per cent no fewer than a further eighty or so registered vines are growing. The grapes are gathered at different times, from September onwards, resulting in a range of wines in the official quality categories, which are bottled with varying amounts of residual sugar, from bone dry to lusciously sweet.

Every grower has his own idea of how to manage a vineyard, determined by the type, quantity and quality of grapes he wishes to grow, by his financial circumstances, and by his experience and training. In this somewhat anarchic world where each is his own master, there are points at which the growers share a common vine-growing aim. Perhaps none is taken more seriously in the early 1990s than the wish to protect the environment. It is seen not just as socially desirable but as economically necessary. The land needs to be treated with respect and intelligence if it is to continue to produce good-quality fruit regularly.

The modern grower trains his vines in such a way that they receive the maximum amount of light needed to ripen a modest crop of healthy grapes. Management of the leaf growth is important for photosynthesis to be as efficient as possible, as, of course, is a good supply of water. When it is scarce in summer, the rate at which sugar is created in the grape slows down and the vine can become stressed. Riesling, with its roots deep in the soil, is equipped to withstand long, dry spells, as in 1985, but Müller-Thurgau is not and suffers accordingly.

Herbicides are used sparingly, if at all, and 'green manuring' is widespread. It has been a common practice since the 1960s to sow a crop between the rows of vines, to be turned into the soil and so improve the structure. Swaths of vetch, clover or rye give the wine garden an unkempt appearance, but besides adding to the humus they also permit tractors to travel between the vines without compacting the soil. To what extent and for how many months of the year German orderliness in the vineyard is allowed to be lost under the weed growth depends on the moisture in the soil. In the steep vineyards, green manuring has the further function of reducing the risk of erosion.

It seems as though the diet of the vine should, ideally, be as balanced and regulated as that of a human being. Whereas there was a tendency twenty years ago to overfeed on the 'add a bit for luck' principle, well-informed growers today provide only what is needed according to the appetite of the vine and the fertility of the soil, with emphasis being laid on organic manures.

The change from the prophylactic chemical spraying with fungicides and insecticides, which eventually led in a number of countries to wines that developed 'off' smells with age, has been enthusiastically supported in Germany. The attitude now is that the care of the vine begins with a healthy, strong plant, based on the layout of the vineyard, the management of the soil, the control of leaf growth, and the pruning and training of the vine. Perhaps the battle against insects in their various forms will be fought in future by farm-reared ladybirds and their relatives, rather than by the chemical methods which, so far, have not been totally replaced.

Another aspect of viticulture which would absolutely accord with 'green' thinking would be the planting of crossings of the European *vitis vinifera* with American vines, upon which much work is being carried out at the Geisenheim viticultural institute. These new hybrids are resistant against the diseases *oidium* and *botrytis cinerea*, and therefore require less spraying than standard *vitis vinifera* varieties. However, according to the present law, their wines cannot be sold as 'quality wine', which places them at a commercial disadvantage.

If the main and very understandable wish of the German vine-grower is to make a profit, in the more ordinary vineyards of the Mosel-Saar-Ruwer, the Rheinhessen and the Rheinpfalz it is one that was often unfulfilled in the 1980s, particularly when growers sold their wine in bulk, rather than in bottle. However, the depressed lot of the producer would be far worse were it not for the modernization of the vineyards that has been promoted by the Federal State and the individual *Länder*. The aim of *Flurbereinigung*, as it is called, is to reduce labour costs and lighten the work in the vineyard, to produce a more consistent yield, and to improve the quality of the fruit. It is achieved in a number of ways, including:

– reallocation of land to create a smaller number of larger holdings;
– the construction of a road network in the vineyards with stopping and turning places;
– improvement of the drainage systems to reduce soil erosion;
– improvement of vineyard layout (length of rows, distance between rows, etc.) to make the best use of sunlight, and occasionally the complete alteration of the contours of a vineyard;
– improving the micro-climate and reducing the risk of frost by planting trees in well-chosen sites;
– the avoidance of labour-intensive ways of training vines;
– the use of the most suitable root-stocks and the best clones for the fruit-bearing vines.

In some areas, as in parts of Kaiserstuhl in Baden, much of the shaping of the landscape as part of *Flurbereinigung* has been visually unsuccessful, to say the least, but generally, and particularly in recent years, the work has been undertaken elsewhere with sensitivity and great care for the environment. Labour costs, including those arising from travelling time for the workers, have been cut by up to half. Some 7 per cent of the total German viticultural area in production cannot physically be reconstructed, but 60 per cent has already been improved – almost entirely since the 1950s.

Many who have visited Germany will recall its steep vineyards, particularly those of the Mosel-Saar-Ruwer and the Mittelrhein. They attract tourists, their beauty is often praised, and much of their Riesling wine is magnificent, but to make any other than the most famous vineyards profitable is not easy, and in many instances possibilities of improvement through *Flurbereinigung* are restricted by the very difficult and steep terrain. However, even where the vineyard has an incline of up to 60 per cent, mechanization of the work is still possible if the vine rows are 2 metres or more apart.

In the steepest sites mechanical harvesting is, of course, out of the question, but in Germany as a whole one-third or more of the crop in 1989 was picked by 800 harvesting machines. Their help, and that of short-term Polish immigrants, is increasingly appreciated.

Whenever possible, work takes place in the vineyards from the back of a tractor, but the pruning largely remains one of those occasions when man, or woman, meets vine face to face, often assisted nowadays by mechanical shears. The aim of pruning is to build up the root-stock, to balance yield with quality, and to ensure a long and active life for the vine. If winter pruning is seen as the main way of producing a limited but better-quality crop, many good growers also remove any excessive bunches of grapes after the vines have flowered. This is an expensive process which it is difficult to justify on strict economic grounds. It is not easy to move away from the arithmetical fact that there is often more money to be made from producing a larger amount of a less-good-quality wine than a small yield of something rather special, particularly as far as the trade in bulk wine is concerned.

Wine-production exceeds consumption in the EC and the surplus is too great for the export markets of the world. Responding to the requirement of the European Community, the state of Rhein-land-Pfalz introduced limitations on yield expressed in hectolitres per hectare shortly before the 1989 harvest. Baden-Württemberg, Bayern and Hessen followed suit in time for the 1990 vintage. The good private and state-owned properties in Rheinland-Pfalz already produce considerably less than the allowed maximum amounts, and they will not be directly affected by the official restrictions, but the new regulations should reduce the supply of the cheapest wine in bulk to the trade. Whether they will noticeably improve quality remains to be seen, and is perhaps hardly relevant given the fact that consumers seem perfectly happy with the present quality of cheap German wine. If, on the other hand, the new regulations help to create a market in which better-quality wines receive better prices, they will have done much for the health of the whole German wine trade.

For all its ancient estates and large, modern wine-merchants' cellars, German grape-growing remains mainly a part-time occupation. Of the total regular labour force at the start of the 1980s, only 15 per cent was employed for more than 100 days per year, and the lighter but time-consuming jobs in the vineyard, including the picking of the grapes, are largely left to the 'casual woman', without whom the wine trade of Europe would soon come to a halt.

4

The Harvest

Of all the events in the vineyard there is none more testing than the harvest. Although it would be wrong to write that a grower is only as good as his last vintage, a few misjudgements can dent a reputation that has taken hundreds of years to build. The world's interest in bad news of all sorts ensures that reports of an error spread with a speed that increases with the importance of the estate, and with an inaccuracy that grows in the retelling.

The harvest offers not only the birth of a new wine but drama, hyperbole and all the excitement of a major sporting event with an uncertain outcome. To wine-makers and estate-owners it is a time for clear-headed planning and detailed organization, and in Germany the critical decisions that have to be made are difficult and numerous, thanks to the weather. The cooler the climate, the more important the micro-climate is a rule that applies particularly to vines, as a glance at the slopes of the Mosel will show, where the hardy gorse and the vine claim adjacent parcels of land for themselves.

Differences in wines from neighbouring sites can be significant but, as the Director of the Domänenweingut Schloss Schönborn puts it, 'Nature has not given us the individuality of our wines for it to be lost in a large blend. It is there to be expressed, not suppressed.' This is a view with which some now disagree because of the marketing difficulties it creates, but for 200 years a characteristic of good German wine has been that its style reflects the vineyard and the vine, and its quality the vintage and the point in the autumn when the grapes were picked.

Over the centuries the Rheingau region, with its concentration of aristocratic estates, has been a leader in the field of German wine and its achievements have been carefully recorded. In 1896

H. W. Dahlen wrote that before the nineteenth century good vintages were gathered relatively early. Only in poor years were grapes left hanging on the vine until late in the season in the hope that they would eventually ripen. Schloss Johannisberg began harvesting the two outstanding vintages of 1727 and 1728 on 25 September and 4 October respectively, but by the end of the nineteenth century Rheingau ideas had changed completely so that picking often started early in November, and sometimes not before the middle of the month. Since 1822 growers had begun to realize that in a good year with a fine autumn the noble rot (*botrytis cinerea*) might arrive, spread and improve the ratio of sugar to water in the grapes. There were risks involved in the late harvest, but it was thought that the rewards for patience and daring were sufficiently great to make them worthwhile.

Nowadays, on many estates 80 per cent of the production is of dry or medium-dry wines. Avant-garde growers, such as Schlossgut Diel in the Nahe valley, who concentrate on good dry white wine, look for a crop free of rot of all sorts, with high acidity. Even on a property as aristocratic and as full of tradition as that of the Domänenweingut Schloss Schönborn in the Rheingau, with its cellar dating from the fourteenth century, noble rot is now avoided for *Spätlese* wines whenever possible. Ideally, a Schloss Schönborn *Spätlese* of the 1990s will be clean as a whistle, and produced from ripe grapes with over 12° of potential alcohol. Any grapes affected by noble rot are likely to have been picked in advance, perhaps to make a wine of *Auslese* quality. The old notion that in Germany better wine meant sweeter wine, or that the best grapes were gathered late in the season, does not always hold true today. It is difficult in this time of rapid transition to understand how the range of German wine is formed, now that some of the rules of the game appear to have been changed. Suffice it to say that if the graph of quality in German wine no longer ascends exactly in parallel with that of increasing sweetness, what the world regards as the very finest German wines remain the *botrytis*-affected Rieslings, with much residual sugar, that can be harvested only once in a decade or so.

Botrytis cinerea is no friend of the strawberry-grower, and if it appears on the grapes when they have less than 9° of potential alcohol it is equally unwelcome. At the right time and place, it causes important changes in the chemical composition of the grape and, in particular, increases the sugar content. However, the amount of liquid in grapes attacked by noble rot may be reduced by 40 per cent or more – a loss for which compensation must be sought in the selling price of the wine. The production costs of Riesling *Auslese* wines with *botrytis* are usually also much increased by the extra time and care that has to be spent on selection of the grapes. In 1976 the crop was so ripe that the harvesting of Riesling *Auslese* grapes in the Rheingau could be carried out directly from the vine, without a further selection being made in the press-house, but in an average year matters are different. Then a laborious and keen selection is made of the few grapes with noble rot before the start of the main harvest. Disappointment can follow, as it did on the Rheingau Mumm estate between 1976 and 1988. The sweetest grapes were picked separately in several intervening vintages, but each time, although the wines could legally have been sold as Riesling *Auslese*, the quality was not up to the estate's own standards.

The arrival of *botrytis* at the moment when the grapes are sufficiently ripe to benefit is uncertain. Humidity and warmth are needed for it to develop, but even when conditions seem technically correct, it does not always appear, as, for example, was the case in the autumn of 1985. At Bernkastel on the Mosel in 1988, grapes from the upper third of the vines trained on the vertico system up a single pole were covered with *botrytis*, while those on the lower part of the vine, sheltered from the breezes, were rot free. It is controversially assumed that the wind carried the *botrytis*, but the explanation for its behaviour is often less simple.

Botrytis in some circumstances is welcome, but where it is always a curse is in red-wine production, as it reduces the colour in the skins of the grape. To avoid this happening, any *botrytis*-affected red grapes are harvested separately, and with luck the rest of the crop will remain free of rot and ripen further. To reduce the risk of an onset of rot, a number of growers have planted clones (such as the Spätburgunder clone called Mariafeld) whose bunches are loosely packed so that infection spreads more slowly.

So far, in this chapter, the Rheingau has been taken as the main point of reference from which to comment on the German wine harvest. Together with the Rheinpfalz, the Nahe, and the Mosel-Saar-Ruwer, it can produce the most elegant *botrytis*-affected Riesling wines in the world, as competitive tastings have shown.

Their complexity and intense flavour, which takes at least ten years to reach a plateau of excellence (only lesser wines 'peak'), make them unique and rare.

When grapes ripen depends on the vine variety, the vineyard site, the climate and the micro-climate. Examination of weather records throughout the German vineyards shows that there is a cocktail of varying factors that result in different styles and qualities of vintage. Ideal conditions are seldom achieved, and the hopes of growers can be frustrated by cold weather during the flowering of the vines in June and early July, or by too little or too much rain in summer and autumn. The result is that good German wines vary greatly from vintage to vintage, but with the cheapest wines, which are blended to suit a particular taste, vintage characteristics are much less noticeable.

It is a generally accepted working principle that a higher sugar content in the grapes should produce a better wine, other factors being equal. To put this in an understandable framework a scale has been created which, by measuring the specific gravity of the must in 'degrees Oechsle', links the sweetness of the grape to the possible official quality of the future wine.

When Christian Ferdinand Oechsle died in 1852, he left behind a large number of inventions, many for use in the pharmaceutical industry. Unfortunately, virtually all of the remaining examples of the work of his creative mind were destroyed in the Second World War, and today, in Germany and elsewhere, he is best remembered for the Oechsle scale.

The lowest quality of wine in Germany and in the rest of the EEC is called 'table wine'. There is a superior sub-category, *Landwein* (*vin du pays*), which is followed up the official scale by 'quality wine from a specified region', or *Qualitätswein eines bestimmten Anbaugebietes*, understandably shortened to 'QbA'. These three categories can be picked in Germany at any time during the harvest – on a good estate from about 10 a.m. onwards, once the dew has evaporated. The minimum levels of must weight, laid down in law for Riesling wines, will be found in Appendix IV, p. 221.

German table wine (*Deutscher Tafelwein* or 'DTW'), *Landwein* and QbA will normally be 'enriched', as the EC describes the addition of sugar to wine. As always, there are exceptions, amongst which is the Rheinpfalz estate of Weingut Oekonomierat Rebholz, south of Neustadt, all of whose wines are made to stand on their own solid legs, without enrichment. On the other hand Schlossgut Diel in the Nahe valley believes that its dry wines must have a very firm structure to be drunk with food, so that even its late-picked wines with up to 11.4°of potential alcohol (85°Oechsle) or more are automatically enriched and thereby downgraded in the eyes of the law.

Continuing up the scale from QbA, we come to *Kabinett* wine, the lightest white wine in the world and the lowest of the quality wines of distinction (*Qualitätswein mit Prädikat* or 'QmP'). As with all QmP, no enrichment is allowed, which means that a good-quality Riesling *Kabinett* from the Mosel-Saar-Ruwer may contain less than 7.5° of actual alcohol, plus a certain amount of unfermented sugar. Grapes of potential *Kabinett* quality may be picked at any time during the harvest, but, in the natural order of things, are seldom gathered late in the season.

Probably the best known, and certainly the most copied of the QmP outside Germany, are the late-picked, the *Spätlese* wines. Their grapes may not be gathered until seven days after the start of the main harvest, but their lateness is only relative to the particular vintage. In 1989, for example, the *Spätlese* crop was picked on the Mumm Rheingau estate from 9 October onwards, eleven days earlier than the average starting date for the main harvest in previous years.

As we have seen, the *Auslese*, or selected crop, can be gathered at any time in the autumn, providing the grapes are sufficiently sweet. The law states that all diseased and unripe grapes must be eliminated, so if an *Auslese* is being gathered it follows that the picking must be by hand, rather than by the generalized method of the harvesting machine. In practice, the quantity of *Auslese* wine from the traditional vine varieties on the Rhein is so small that nothing but hand-picking comes into question, but a mechanical harvesting of grapes of *Auslese* weight from the new white crossings would sometimes be possible.

Beerenauslese and *Trockenbeerenauslese* wines from very concentrated musts, are rare for Riesling and can be produced only in exceptional vintages. Amazingly, the Rheinpfalz estate Weingut Dr Bürklin-Wolf picked a Wachenheimer Luginsland Riesling Trockenbeerenauslese as early as 27 September in 1989. On most estates the harvesting of a Riesling *Beerenauslese* takes place under the personal supervision of the administrator or owner, with the participation of the most experienced grape-pickers. It involves the particularly keen selection of the sweetest, individually gathered grapes, resulting in a wine with some 4.5° (depending on the region) of potential alcohol more than that required for a Riesling *Auslese*. Like the even sweeter Riesling *Trockenbeerenauslesen*, which are made from noble-rotted grapes that have dried and become more concentrated on the vine, these sweet dessert wines are quite incomparable and immensely expensive. In spite of their high selling prices, because of the reduction of liquid and the production costs, they bring the grower little direct financial profit, but great prestige.

From other vines, such as Ruländer, Scheurebe, and Gewürztraminer, *Beerenauslese* and *Trockenbeerenauslese* of outstanding quality can also be harvested on occasions, but the best of Riesling is the finest of them all.

If Riesling *Beerenauslese* and *Trockenbeerenauslese* are rarities, *Eiswein* is a wine of similar concentration but different structure, which can be produced more frequently. It is made from grapes gathered at a temperature of −8°C or so, and taken in their frozen state to the press-house for immediate pressing.

One of the great specialists in this type of harvesting, Weingut Max Ferd. Richter at Mülheim on the Mosel, was able to make *Eiswein* in 1983, 1985, 1986, 1987 and 1988 with like frequency in the 1970s. In so doing the estate took risks. Cold weather, sufficient to freeze the grapes, seldom arrives before mid-November and, on occasion, not for a month or more after that. When grapes left on the vine for *Eiswein*-production deteriorate, the loss is almost total. Weingut Richter's attempts failed in 1980, 1981, 1982 and 1984.

As in the making of wine, there are regulations controlling the grape harvest which are laid down by the wine-producing states of Rheinland-Pfalz, Hessen and Bayern. (Baden-Württemberg, where most of the crop is processed by co-operative cellars, has its own arrangements.)

A committee in each wine-producing community, headed by the mayor, decides when the various stages of the harvest (the *Lese*) should start. Sometimes there is a *Vorauslese*, a pre-main harvest special gathering of rotten grapes, or, perhaps, a simple *Vorlese* of grapes that have fallen to the ground. That is followed by the main harvest (the *Hauptlese*) and then by the *Spätlese*. During the period of the harvest the vineyards are officially out of bounds, except at certain specific times. Each producer is required to maintain a daily record of what has been picked, a detailed extract of which must be given to the authorities by 15 December each year. Additional reporting systems operate for wines of *Spätlese* quality and upwards. One association of some eighty-eight growers, the Erzeugergemeinschaft Deutsches Eck on the Mosel and in the Mittelrhein, invites an official daily control of the harvest in each of its members' cellars in its determination to maintain the high standards needed to develop its considerable reputation further.

Since the 1950s the changes in the layout and organization of the vineyards, as described in chapter 3, have been aimed at greater efficiency, a reduction in costs and better wine-making. Mechanical harvesting began in the 1960s and may eventually lead to grapes being pressed in the vineyards. Where the terrain and training of the vines permit the use of harvesting machines, exhaustive tests have shown that they do a satisfactory job, economically. Of course, if a special selection of the grapes is the aim, machine-picking is out of the question, but for a standard-quality wine its speed and reduction in labour costs are attractive. An important precondition for mechanical harvesting is that the machinery for transporting and processing the grapes should be able to handle a supply of 4–7.5 tons of fruit per hour. Experiments in the Cognac region of France have shown that white wine grapes can deteriorate rapidly within the first hour of picking, so the speed of the large output of the harvesting machine can be a blessing, but only if the organization of the press-house is good. Although harvesting machines are not normally associated with the highest-quality wines, their use is legal and technically possible in *Eiswein*-production, as the large Rheinhessen vineyard-owners Weingut Louis Guntrum of Oppenheim have successfully shown.

Consideration has mainly been given in this chapter to the standards set by the best producers of Riesling wine, rather in the same way that in thinking of Bordeaux we turn first to the classified growths of the Médoc. The volume of wine they produce is not large, but as they own the best parcels of vineyard their proportion of QmP is greater than that of the regions as a whole.

As it is, the official quality categories do not represent very high

37

standards, so *Spätlese* and sometimes *Auslese* wine from grapes other than Riesling may be bought quite cheaply. Table 3 shows the production of QbA, *Kabinett* and *Spätlese* in the main exporting regions, expressed as a percentage of the total average crop in each region from 1984 to 1988.

TABLE 3

	QbA %	Kabinett %	Spätlese %
Baden	77.4	16.4	2.1
Mosel-Saar-Ruwer	72.1	12.8	8.0
Rheinhessen	68.1	15.2	15.1
Rheinpfalz	70.9	15.1	6.7
Rheingau	59.2	29.6	6.1

Everywhere, the largest part of the average harvest is of QbA quality, which from good producers can be truly distinguished and full of character. The minimum must-weight levels for Baden wine (see Appendix IV, p. 221) are generally higher than those of regions further north and the demand in Baden is for QbA and *Kabinett* wines, often sold in litre bottles to local restaurants. The Rheingau is known for its Riesling *Kabinett* wine, which appears in good commercial quantities in most vintages, at prices from which the producer can make a profit but which are acceptable to the consumer.

Germany expects that the 1990s will bring more competition on its home market, where 70 per cent or more of its wine is sold. To face this situation many bottlers are simplifying their range of wines, but nature is not so easily controlled. To make the best of an unstable climate, a staggered harvest will continue to be characteristic of German wine-making, with all the risks, additional work and, sometimes, great rewards to which the growers have long been accustomed.

5
Wine-making

Changes in wine-making are brought about by technical invention and market forces. Louis Pasteur's discovery, that yeast caused alcoholic fermentation, led to filters, designed for cleansing water in the First World War, being developed to remove yeast from wine. Large-scale production of light-in-alcohol, medium-sweet wines, best represented on the export market by Liebfraumilch, was the eventual result. The German liking for sweetness in wine after the Second World War is still shared by millions of un-demanding wine-drinkers abroad. As we have seen, in Germany itself the taste is now for drier wine, which is popularly thought to be 'better', and even 'healthier'. In truth, 'sweet' and 'dry' define flavour and not quality.

Perhaps many German consumers associate the concept of dry-ness with the *Naturweine* of the past and forget that the quality of these natural wines was superior, not because they were free of added sugar, but simply because they were made from riper and better grapes. However, if a sensible addition of sugar does not make an ordinary wine distinguished, it will not make a basically good wine ordinary, as the *châteaux* of Bordeaux frequently demonstrate.

The Germans have a selective nostalgia for the past, as is clear from the number of 'old' wine bars, built in the last twenty years and filled with reproduction, rustic fittings and furniture; but were the broad range of wines of grandfather's day to be served in their pristine condition in the 1990s, only the very best would meet with wide approval. Recently, the wine-maker has had to be nimble of foot and wit to keep up with a changing market and yet the general quality of his wine is better than ever before. As always, deeply serious wine is being produced on the good estates, but what is just as exciting in a way is the high quality of the middle-of-the-road wines at DM 5.00 per bottle or so from the better co-operative cellars.

If the cry of the 1970s and 1980s was for *Reductiver Ausbau* (wine-making and maturation with the minimum of oxygen), that of the 1990s is *Zurück zur Natür* – back to nature. Vineyard and cellar are seen as an entity and the effects of spraying the vines and manuring the soil, and the need for healthy, undamaged grapes, are more widely understood than before. As Weingut Dr Loosen of Bernkastel explains, ordinary wine can be made according to a formula and a fixed timetable, but the best wines are the sum of refinements in cellar technique. Given the high standards in the training of all trades in Germany, perhaps the most important additional requirement for the wine-maker is a passion for excellence. Good cellars today treat their wine as little as possible and as much as necessary, and order and cleanliness remain compulsory.

Timing is a significant element in fine wine-making. The basic processes of alcoholic fermentation are the same everywhere, but Weingut Loosen's refinements often simply mean doing what needs to be done at exactly the right moment, and there is a 66 per cent chance that that will be outside the eight hours of a normal working day. A large cellar that depends on an hourly paid staff does not have quite the same flexibility as the small producer and must paint with a broader brush.

All good wine-makers value what the French call *typicité*. They aim to produce wines that are typical of site, vine variety and region, and in the changing world of German wine-making some estate-owners are asking themselves, 'What is a German Spätburgunder?' or 'What is a Nahe, dry white wine?' This introspection seems very positive, and it is realized that answers must be found in preparation for a more competitive and wider European market. An open mind is needed to see beyond the end of your nose and into the future.

The good, modern wine-makers are well aware of the styles of wine from other countries, and there is a continuous exchange of ideas amongst them. The tendency in the 1990s will be for wines to become a little more alike, but still, it is hoped, retaining their *typicité*. Nearer the source of the Rhein, by avoiding their traditional malo-lactic fermentation which softens the sharp taste of a wine, the Swiss have introduced a style resembling that of the

Baden region. Further north, where the acidity is naturally higher, Germany has been experimenting with the limited use of malo-lactic fermentation in white wine-making, and the exporting house of Sichel has launched a branded wine, *Novum*, showing what can be done at the risk of threatening German *typicité*.

How a wine is made depends on different factors, but on good estates the routine is broadly similar. Unless speciality *botrytis*-affected wines are being produced, the first requirement in wine-making is for healthy, clean grapes. Those from the oldest vines contain more flavour-imparting minerals, although their content of acid and sugar may not be noticeably higher than the crop from young vines. The individual approach of each producer becomes obvious when the grapes arrive at the press-house. They will usually be partially or wholly separated from the stalks, crushed and gently pressed. In a poor vintage it is important that the pressure is kept low, otherwise the sour juice from unripe grapes could taint the wine. The must may now be left in a sealed vat for twelve hours or so to clarify. In some large cellars a similar effect can be achieved by a centrifuge or filtration. White wines are more often fermented in vat than in wood, at a temperature of 15–20°C, with the help of cultured yeast. Some producers prefer to rely on the natural yeasts on the grapes for a spontaneous fermentation, but this is a more uncertain path to follow. It can result in an increase in unwanted lactic and volatile acids, and in less alcohol. Trials carried out in Franken suggested that wine made with cultured yeast, particularly that called 'Champagne Epernay', was the most successful.

To increase the alcohol content, sugar may be added to must, or later to young wine, destined to be table or simple-quality wine. Where acid levels are high, chemical de-acidification is also allowed, although, other than for cheaper wines, the practice is somewhat out of favour. The main fermentation will be over in five days or less, and the young wine will be left on the yeast, perhaps for one or two months.

Other than in a vintage with many rotten grapes, sulphurous acid will not be added until some ten to twenty-one days after the main fermentation has stopped. This acid, which gives wine a harsh smell and flavour when present in too great a concentration, protects it from oxidation, and, incidentally, is itself a by-product of alcoholic fermentation. It is not important if must becomes a little oxidized, but the aim in good wine-making is by the use of cultured yeast, and the fermentation of clean must at a controlled pace and temperature, to be able to add only the minimum of sulphurous acid. By storage at a cool temperature and with the appropriate protection of sulphurous acid, a malo-lactic fermentation will be avoided. Perhaps the real value of making light wine with as little sulphurous acid as possible is that in so doing a very high overall standard of cellar technique is required if disaster is not to result.

On many estates wines with relatively high acidity are matured in old wooden casks of not less than 500 litres (a *Halbfuder*) or 610 litres (a *Halbstück*). There are exceptions to this use of wood, amongst which is the famous 18-hectare, largely Riesling estate of Bürgermeister Anton Balbach Erben in Nierstein, where the wines mature in vat and bottle only. In general, apart from allowing wine to develop more depth of flavour, cask maturation is considered to be part of the German cellar tradition which is as valuable today as it ever was. The storing of wine in new wooden *barriques* of 225 litres which impart a flavour is practised, but in Germany it seems best suited to wines from Burgunder or Pinot grapes. For German wine-making as a whole, it remains only an interesting side issue, perhaps because it is thought that the flavour of Riesling needs no additives.

To mature wine in old, seasoned casks is to increase its individuality for reasons that are not wholly understood. Some estates allot the same casks each year to wine from a particular vineyard, presumably hoping for a certain consistency of style. When wine has developed sufficiently in wood, and if bottling is not to follow immediately, it may well be transferred to a vat of stainless steel or some other inert material. Here it can rest, with few signs of further maturation, until the convenient time for bottling has arrived. The cold of winter will have precipitated in the form of crystals any non-soluble salts of the acids. With large-scale, merchants' bottlings, the young wine is artificially chilled in order to stabilize it. If a crystal deposit forms later in bottled wine, it is only a visual blemish but nevertheless one that bottlers try to avoid. The German wines in which it is most likely to appear are those of *Beerenauslese* or *Trockenbeerenauslese* quality. Normally the deposit will rest happily at the bottom of the bottle until the last drop is served. If there seems to be a risk that the crystals will be disturbed by the process of pouring, the wine should be treated like a mature red wine and decanted.

On 19 June 1663, the English diarist Samuel Pepys drank 'a pretty wine' at the Rhenish Wine-House in London, a 'red Rhenish wine called Bleahard'. Like many German red wines 'Bleichert', to allow its correct name, was probably more rosé in colour than red. According to Bassermann-Jordan, the habit of fermenting the grapes with their colour-transmitting skins did not reach Germany from France until the eighteenth century. It was probably the growing German interest in the link between wine and food in the late 1970s, which encouraged dry white-wine production, that also revitalized the German red-wine market. From having been a wine that the rest of the world found itself unable to take seriously, German red wine is improving with the speed of change which is characteristic of modern Germany.

The new-style red wine, of which the best examples are usually from Spätburgunder, is made *à la française*. Alcoholic fermentation on the skins is accompanied or followed, by a malo-lactic fermentation. This leads into maturation in cask, often of 225 litres and sometimes of new wood. As in so many cellars of the world, French Allier and Limousin oak is frequently used, but Schloss Schönborn is patriotically and interestingly experimenting with German Hunsrück and Spessart oak. Spätburgunder wines reared in this way, from a low grape-yield, have good colour and the tannin one expects of a well-made wine of the Côte d'Or.

Other German red wines relate to these well-structured, new-style wines in much the same way as a Côtes du Rhône made by carbonic maceration does to one produced by the traditional methods of fermentation in an open vat. In other words, the older style of German wine is fruitier and softer, and an essential part of its vinification in recent years has been the heating of the must for a few minutes, perhaps to a temperature of 85°C, or to a lower temperature for rather longer. The results are pleasant, lack character, but normally have the commercial advantage of being ready for consumption immediately after bottling.

Some people in the German home market simply do not like noticeably tannic wines. Their tastes can be met at a high but rather expensive level of quality by the State Cellars at Assmannshausen in the Rheingau, whose wines are totally serious but fermented on the skins for a short time only.

The mechanical handling of grapes, must and wine has improved continuously since the 1970s, and in the 1980s the 'green' thinking behind vine-growing and wine-making has also been beneficial. Perhaps in the next ten years the value of lower grape-yields will become not only further appreciated but also more widely practised. The deciding factor in this and in other ways of improving the general run of wines will be the consumer's willingness to pay for the higher production costs.

6

Living with the Law

Erwein Graf Matuschka-Greiffenclau, owner of Schloss Vollrads and past-President of the prestigious association of estate bottlers, the Verband Deutscher Prädikatsweingüter, described the German Wine Law to me in 1989 as 'total marketing nonsense'. To the overseas customer, the complications of German wine names are inexplicable, and they are only partially understood by those who live in the wine-producing regions.

There seems to be a tradition in Germany for the wine-producers to do two things in times when trade flows slowly. They envy the French and they blame the Wine Law. As the *Deutsche Wein-Zeitung* put it in 1891, 'The French are practical people, who do not write themselves down, but take care to praise themselves immoderately.' Asked what the opinion was in France about the falsification of wine in the 1890s, a French legal expert replied, '*On ne discute pas cela chez nous.*' To which one might perhaps now reply, '*Plus ça change . . .*'.

Serious infringements of the Wine Law occur infrequently in Germany, but when they do today the guilty are severely punished. Unfortunately, so are all wine-producers, for the very public debate that follows a wine 'scandal' damages the reputation of German wine as a whole – but that is the price a country has to pay when it takes its wine law seriously.

In *The History of the Wine Trade in England*, André Simon wrote of the seventeenth century that 'The evil of misrepresentation appears to have been far greater as regards German wines than those of any other country.' The problem of the German wine-producer today is not falsification or fraud, but how to live with a national law that is so very different to that which covers the remaining 97.5 per cent of the world's wine-production.

The first national law dealing with the sale of wine dates from 1892, and was later to be amended and replaced as the regulations became more comprehensive and as new cellar techniques made alterations necessary. In 1951 the Deutsche Weinbauverband (German Wine Growers' Association) began work on a new wine law, which was finally published eighteen years later in 1969. It never came into force, as it was overtaken by the EEC regulations for the organization of the wine market, Numbers 816 and 870 of April 1970. Hurriedly, the 1969 German Wine Law had to be redrafted to meet the requirements of the Common Market, and the new law became effective on 19 July 1971. Since then it has been revised and amended many times – in fact, so often that it is now so complex that it is almost beyond the grasp of the wine trade and sometimes even of the civil servants who administer the trade. Instructions from Brussels pass to the Federal Government in Bonn, which then requires the state governments concerned to issue implementing regulations – all of which takes time. In the intervening period different legal interpretations can result. Those involved would wish the flow of new legislation to stop, and then for the law to be codified in such a way as to be easily accessible, but the European Community changes and develops continuously, and so it appears wine law must do likewise.

When the 1970 EEC wine regulations were being drafted, the tendency was simply to adapt the French *Appellation contrôlée* legislation of 1935, which had proved its worth in controlling the market for quality wine in France. However, at that time it was not thought suitable for wine-production in the cooler German climate. At Germany's instigation, the EEC was divided into a series of zones to cope with climatic differences between the Rhineland and Sicily. All of Germany's eleven wine regions except Baden are included in Zone A, but the minimum must-weight levels may vary from one region or one vine variety to another (see Appendix IV, p. 221). Baden is proud of its hotter summer and shares its Zone B with regions such as Champagne, Alsace, the Loire Valley, and perhaps in the near future Burgundy as well.

One of the most important aspects of the 1971 law, which has been criticized but not amended, are the smaller geographical units into which the wine-growing *Anbaugebiete*, or regions, are broken down. The largest of these is the *Bereich*, or district, followed in decreasing order of size within the *Bereich* by the *Grosslage*, or collection of individual vineyard sites, and then by the *Einzellage*, the single vineyard site itself. A *Gemeinde*, or community, name is always attached to that of an *Einzellage* or *Grosslage*, and occasionally a wine will be sold under the community name only, as is the case with the Deinhard *Heritage* range. Objections to this division of the vineyards mainly concern the use of *Bereich* and *Grosslage* names, and the excessive number of *Einzellagen*.

Many of the *Bereiche* bear names such as Bernkastel or Nierstein, in order to link wines from little-known villages within the *Bereich* with the name of a more famous village. This seems a sad admission of lack of marketing ability, but it was presumably supported in the early 1970s by the Deutsche Weinbauverband which participated in the drafting of the 1971 Wine Law. If nothing else, it is misleading for the consumer. For example, the Bereich Bernkastel covers about 75 per cent of the 12,760 hectares of the Mosel-Saar-Ruwer region, and the blending regulations could allow 25 per cent of a wine called 'Bereich Bernkastel' to consist of base wine and unfermented grape juice (i.e. *Süssreserve*) from elsewhere in the region, outside the Bereich Bernkastel. Of course, this does not mean that the quality of the wine would necessarily be lowered as a result, but, whatever the law may say, it is a misuse of the name of the village of Bernkastel.

As far as they can, wine-producers ensure that the popular idea is correct, that the smaller the geographical unit from which a wine originates, the better it should be. A wine sold under a *Bereich* name can, therefore, be expected to be sound and true to type, but hardly a fine wine.

A similar criticism can be made, with slightly less force, of the use of *Grosslagen*, which again has the effect of allowing wines from unknown villages to be sold under famous names. This means, for example, that a wine from the *Grosslage* Bernkasteler Kurfürstlay can originate from about 1,800 hectares of vineyard in eleven different villages (including Bernkastel). The main complaint must be that there is no way of telling from the label if the wine in the bottle is from a single site, and should therefore have characteristics peculiar to that site, or if it is a blend from a sizeable portion of the region's vineyards. Inexpensive wines which are available in large quantities need broadly based names, but they should surely be able to be found without the use of appellations associated with wines of higher quality. A start has been made by the introduction of specific types of QbA sold under names such as *Moseltaler*. Some would say that the offer of cheaper wine would seem more credible if *Bereich* and *Grosslage* names were to be abolished altogether.

There are nearly 2,600 *Einzellagen*, or single vineyard sites. Allowing for some noteworthy exceptions, the differences in wine they represent at the QbA level are frequently not sufficiently pronounced to justify the use of their names. Discussion on the proliferation of individual site names dates back to the start of the twentieth century. As it is, until the majority of those involved in grape-growing and the production of wine agree, or are forced by the market to agree, that the time has come to reconsider the structure of German wine names, change is unlikely. Politicians who depend on their constituents' support for their livelihood would sooner see nothing altered than risk losing popularity. This enervating inactivity increases further the debt of the whole of the German wine trade to those good estate bottlers who set their own high standards, and thus make plausible the country's claim to produce the finest white wine in the world. This theme is discussed further in chapter 8.

Judging by their approach to wine, the Germans are a very statistically minded people, and anybody visiting the vineyards and cellars will find the need for figures infectious. At most tastings details of acid, sugar and alcohol levels, not to mention the original must weights and the date when the grapes were picked, will be supplied without asking. Where there is the possibility of comparing a wine with others, this information is of interest, but for most consumers statistics taken in isolation are probably as meaningless as is the knowledge of the niacin content of cornflakes. In spite of the fact that a heavier must weight does not automatically mean a better wine, there is within any one vine variety in any one region a close connection between the two, as was mentioned in chapter 4. If it were to be left to the law to improve the quality of cheap German wine, all that would be necessary would be to increase the basic minimum must-weight levels for QbA appropriately. The short-term effect of this would be a loss of income for many grape-growers, as heavier must weights would be mainly the result of a lower yield, so little progress can be hoped for in that direction.

Suggestions have also been made that having done away with *Bereiche* and *Grosslagen*, the use of *Einzellage* names should be reserved for QmP from certain higher-class vines (Riesling, Sil-vaner, Gewürztraminer, the Burgunder (Pinot) family, Scheurebe and a few others). This, together with a severe reduction in the number of single vineyards, would undoubtedly lead to a more understandable wine offer. German wine as a generic style is unique amongst the wines of the world. The best does not need the accretion of complicated names that has gathered during the twentieth century, and the lesser wines would benefit from simple but meaningful appellations.

In France 'quality wine' can be produced only by certain vine-yards responsible for about 25 per cent of the country's total wine harvest. This system does not take into account changes in wine quality brought about by the weather in different vintages. The German Wine Law takes the view that all vineyards are theoreti-cally capable of producing all qualities of wine in the official categories from *Tafelwein* to *Trockenbeerenauslese*. Under what geographical name a German wine may be sold depends to some extent on its quality as seen by the law.

According to Dr Friedrich Bassermann-Jordan in his *Geschichte des Weinbaues*, the first recorded addition of sugar and water to wine in Germany was in 1745 in Württemberg. It has always been a process which has aroused mixed opinion. Some have denounced it as a falsification of wine, but the second German Wine Law of 1901 made it permissible as long as the aim was to improve a wine rather than simply to add to its volume. Today, wet sugaring, as it was called, is no longer allowed but, as has been mentioned, table wine and QbA may have sugar (saccharose) added to them to increase the alcohol content. That QmP cannot be treated in the same way shows that the German Wine Law still reflects an attitude of slight disapproval of any sugar in wine other than that from the grape itself. At a cost of DM 960,000, Rheinland-Pfalz has installed a nuclear magnetic resonance spectrometer which can determine whether sugar has been illegally put into a QmP or added in excess to a QbA. It must be said that the enthusiasm to ensure that wine is made only in accordance with the law is notice-ably stronger in Germany than it is in some regions nearer the Mediterranean.

If the main influence on the German Wine Law until 1971 was that of the needs of production and the health of the consumer, the requirements of the market are likely to become a more decisive force in the 1990s. 'Green' thinking has already made an impact on wine-making, and the opening up of the European Community and the concentration of ownership within the whole of the international drinks industry are unlikely to allow important questions affecting the sale of wine to be decided at grower level. At the end of the 1970s, the General Secretary of the Deutsche Weinbauverband wrote in his contribution to a book called *Der Deutsche Wein* that the entry of Britain, Eire and Denmark into the EC had made no difference to wine-making, as they were not wine-producing countries. In recent years matters have changed, and the consumer is listened to more attentively in the 1990s. The large wine-importer can now dictate his needs, and the biggest importer of wine in the world is West Germany. In matters of wine law she is potentially more strongly represented within the EC than is perhaps realized.

7

Testing the Wine

Some 95 per cent of the German wine vintage falls into the EC category of quality wine which can be either still or sparkling. Every German quality wine is officially examined to ensure as far as possible that it is typical in all respects of what it ought to be and that, at the moment of tasting, it shows no faults. Three samples of the wine to be tested are sent to one of nine control centres spread throughout the vineyard area, together with a chemical analysis carried out by an officially recognized laboratory. This analysis shows the alcohol, total acid, sulphurous acid and sugar content of the wine, as well as the level of sugar-free extract (the sum of substances such as minerals, tannin, acids, etc.).

Tasting wines professionally demands concentration, and a session at a control centre may last up to three hours, with as many as sixty wines being examined. Compared to young red Bordeaux wine, which is usually more alcoholic and more tannic, German wine is less tiring to taste. Nevertheless, stamina and the right mental and physical ability are needed by all professional tasters, and those who wish to judge wines at a control centre in Germany are themselves tested before being awarded a tasting certificate. When a wine has been officially approved, it is given a reference number – the *Amtliche Prüfungsnummer* – which appears on the label of the bottle. About 3–4 per cent of all wines fail their official test, more often because of a fault picked up by the tasters, such as slight oxidation, than because of an inadequacy shown by the chemical analysis. *Amtliche Prüfung* ('AP') centres do not have the resources to examine the history of each wine in detail, or to be present at its various stages of production from the harvest onwards. What they are competent to assess is simply whether a wine appears to meet the minimum requirements of the law at the time when it passes through the control centre. It is possible for unwelcome flavours or faults in the bouquet to develop as the wine matures further in bottle, once it has been granted its AP number. If this happens, the control authorities can compare the wine that may by now be on sale with the samples that were retained for such a purpose after the control examination, and then take whatever action is appropriate. The AP system has been criticized for being too lenient in its judgements, but it is still the most thorough examination of wine on a national scale within the EC.

The AP centres have a useful subsidiary function in that they publish detailed summaries of the results of their official tastings. These show in which categories wines were tested, whether they were dry, medium-dry and so on, and with other information they offer a clear picture of trends in wine-drinking.

The marking system used by the AP authorities, and by those responsible for wine competitions in Germany, is based on a scale of 5 whole and 5 half marks which are used in the following way:

1.5 to 2.0 marks = adequate
2.5 to 3.0 marks = good
3.5 to 4.0 marks = very good
4.5 to 5.0 marks = excellent

The scent, taste and harmony of a wine are each allocated marks out of 5. The total marks, which will then be out of 15, are divided by 3. A minimum of 1.5 marks is needed for a wine to be granted an AP number, and with 2.5 marks a wine can win a *Deutsches Weinsiegel*, a 'German Wine Seal'. At the regional and national competitions, 3.5 marks will earn a bronze medal, 4 marks a silver medal and 4.5 marks the *Grosser* or top prize. Each wine is judged within its category so that a simple QbA may be awarded a *Grosser* prize and an *Auslese* wine, for example, may come away from the competition with no prize at all.

In principle, a wine must have been successful at a regional competition before it may be entered for the *DLG-Bundesweinprämierung*, the national competition. The DLG, the Deutsche Landwirtschafts-Gesellschaft, or German Agricultural Society, which dates from 1885, is the oldest testing institute in the world, although its work was interrupted between 1934 and 1947. Today about 1–2 per cent of the wine harvest is entered for the national competition. In 1989, when 4,223 wines were examined, 10 per cent failed to win an award, 17 per cent won a bronze medal, 38 per cent a silver medal, and 35 per cent a *Grosser* prize, with Baden winning more awards than any other region. The rules controlling the national competition are very precise and strict, so ensuring that the samples of wine submitted are backed by certain minimum stocks. The cost of entering each wine for the competition is DM 85.00 – a substantial sum for a small estate.

Producers have varying views about the value of wine competitions and many well-known estates take no part in them. On the other hand, faced with the large and complicated range of German wine, the virtual guarantee of high quality from a silver or *Grosser* prizewinner can be a great help to the overtaxed consumer.

8

The Estates in the 1990s

In thinking of the best German wines we turn automatically to the private and state-owned properties, whose influence is much greater than their size. A few measure up to the mental picture we have of a palace or castle, built in the eighteenth century or earlier, overlooking a courtyard where the grapes are brought each year for pressing and transformation into wine in the cellars below. Schloss Vollrads in the Rheingau, Schloss Staufenberg in Baden, and Burg Hornberg, the eleventh-century Württemberg home of the adversarial peasant leader Götz von Berlichingen, fulfil this role with style. The glow that shines from such long-established estates should reflect on the whole of the German wine trade. In the early 1990s it is somewhat overshadowed by the brasher light emitted by the large bottling establishments of the *Weinkellereien*, as they turn out container loads of cheap, ordinary wine to the profit of few, and to the detriment of the good name of German wine. But the old estates, centred as they are in mid-Europe, have survived many things worse than a temporary period in the wilderness. Their loss of proper recognition is mainly confined to an export market dominated by wine travelling under debased names such as 'Liebfraumilch' or 'Niersteiner Gutes Domtal'. The problem is that German wine has a hierarchy of notional quality, based on the sugar content of the grapes, which ignores the other constituents of wine or the impact of the wine-maker. Analysable minimum standards have become targets for those wishing to claim a particular level of quality for a product that is sold in enormous volumes at the cheapest possible price.

On all good estates, wines are produced to standards stricter than those laid down in law. The result is that a basic wine from a good estate will be of much higher quality than a *Kabinett* or

Spätlese wine bottled by a merchant, who sells large amounts of wine that has only just made the legal grade.

While a number of German wine estates are architecturally and historically interesting, many are more modest establishments. Amongst the terraced houses in the wine villages the notice '*Flaschenweinverkauf*' ('wine sold in bottle') is usually an indication that here an 'estate' has its headquarters. Of the over 80,000 vine-growers in Germany, only about 30 per cent make wine themselves, and, of these, perhaps a quarter sell their wine exclusively in bottle.

Throughout the EC, the ownership of the vineyards is very fragmented, and this results in an imbalance of commercial strength in favour of the large distributors of wine, the big supermarkets and chains of grocery stores. Other than in a general sense, however, the estate bottlers and the large outlets for wine are not in direct competition in Germany, as they play to different audiences.

Most estates like to have a variety of customers, which may include a number of good restaurants, for reasons of prestige rather than profit. As an alternative to the restaurant trade, estates also sell directly, or via brokers, to wine-merchants, to exporting houses, to the board rooms of industry and to the consumer.

In spite of signs of greater co-operation amongst estate-owners, they still very much make their own marketing decisions and in recent years many have chosen to trade with private customers. In fact, it was suggested in an article in *Der Deutsche Weinbau* in 1983 that over two-thirds of German estate-bottled wine was sold in this way. In his dealings with an estate, the consumer usually has the chance to taste before placing his order, and probably buys about twenty to forty bottles at a time. The transaction may take a little longer than the estate-owner would like, but there is a reasonable profit on the sale and the wine is paid for at once.

Most of the countryside in which the vineyards are set is attractive and much is quite beautiful. A visit to a wine estate is often linked to a weekend break, particularly by the many Germans who are urban dwellers, living in apartments without gardens.

A brief study of life on an estate can make you wonder why anybody should involve himself in such hard, unrelenting and financially not very rewarding work. Since 1970 the cost of wine in Germany is said to have increased by less than 50 per cent, whilst the average hourly wage of an industrial worker has risen by nearly 170 per cent. How German wine, in general, has been left behind by prosperity is shown even more clearly on the export market, where the average price per litre of wine exported in 1988 of DM 2.52 was lower than in any year since reliable figures became available in 1972. Although the low figure of DM 2.52 reflects the large volume of cheap wine sold overseas, there was no significant compensating export of higher-price wine to improve upon it.

The motivations of the estate bottler are not simply financial and include a desire for independence and freedom of choice, and, above all, a love of good wine. In his book *Life beyond Liebfraumilch*, Stuart Pigott identified the impact that the younger generation of energetic estate-owners was having on the quality of wine now being produced. If it is true that out of hard times come good wines, we can expect outstanding wines in the 1990s. It seems likely that not only will some estate names become much more familiar, but that the standing of individual wine-makers will be internationally recognized.

Interestingly, while some marketing directors expect the financial health of the German wine trade to deteriorate yet further in the 1990s before it recovers, Japan, in the form of Suntory and Sanyo, has begun to involve herself in the production of estate-bottled wines in the Rheingau and in the Rheinpfalz. The investment must be made for good reason.

In the recent depressed years, the selling price of vineyard land has dropped significantly, and in some instances has been halved, while difficult to work vineyards have become unsaleable. When the time has come for the vineyard-owner to hand over to his children, they have often decided that grape-growing is not for them and have looked for a more profitable source of income. He who makes wine and has the necessary expertise to bottle and sell it as 'estate-bottled' is in a better position than the vineyard-owner who sells his grapes for processing. Dr Zerbe of Schloss Rein-hartshausen in the Rheingau has shown, however, that even the great and famous estates feel the pinch. Having defined in an article in *Die Weinwirtschaft* in 1985 his fixed and variable costs, he explained that in a big vintage such as 1982 or 1983 the total production costs per bottle amounted to about half of that in vintages such as 1980 or 1981. Indeed, in these small vintages with few QmP wines, production costs could not be covered. This was particularly true in the less-distinguished vineyards such as the

Erbacher Michelmark, where little QmP was harvested. Even on the best estates, where as a matter of policy the yield per vine is kept low, the pressure to produce more grape juice is always present. It is resisted, but will remain until the market price for good-quality German wine reaches a fair and acceptable level.

Many of today's trends in German wine-making, such as the move from medium-sweet to medium-dry or dry wines, have been led by private estates. The lengthy names given to German wine are now proving too complicated for some, such as Schlossgut Diel in the Nahe valley, or Wegeler-Deinhard with vineyards in the Rheingau, Rheinpfalz and the Mosel-Saar-Ruwer regions. They, and others besides, are restricting the use of vineyard names and laying more emphasis on their own estate names. The result is a reduced offer of wine names which might ultimately lead, in the manner of Bordeaux, to one or two wines per estate per year, plus an additional *Beerenauslese* or *Trockenbeerenauslese* wine in the rare and great vintages. Such a move, with fewer bottlings as a result, has obvious appeal to a cost-conscious wine-maker, and could help the consumer.

Logically, there is no reason for wines to bear individual village or vineyard names unless the characteristics derived from these locations can be clearly discerned on the palate or in the bouquet. At present, the wine-drinker has the right to complain that German wine names are unnecessarily complicated. The number of people who can identify the differences in wines from, say, all of the eighteen different single vineyards at Nierstein, which are solely attributable to soil and site, can probably be counted on two hands. In those circumstances, to emphasize the factors of grape variety and the name of the estate bottler is to give importance in terms of style and taste where it is due. If that is true of a fine wine-producing village like Nierstein, how much more should it apply to less-distinguished vineyards elsewhere.

The late 1980s have seen estates working hard to improve the way in which they present their wines. The concept of a label designed by an artist rather than a printer has been borrowed from France, to the surprise of traditionalists. Since 1979 the excellent Rheingau estate of Balthasar Ress has each year commissioned a different artist to design a label for a selected bottling. It is a practice which attracts the attention and links fine wine with art, to the benefit of all involved. While some estates look for eye-catching new labels and unusual bottle shapes, others prefer to remain with charming labels from the nineteenth century. Schloss Johannisberg, in particular, has some very pretty old label designs, as does the Aschrott estate at Hochheim.

Attempts have been made by journalists in the 1980s to classify the best wine estates, but the task is immensely difficult. Bordeaux managed to establish an order of precedence for its leading *châteaux* in 1855, but the number of candidates was relatively small and, of course, each property sold one blend of wine per vintage only. In Germany the number of potential candidates for classification is far larger and their bottlings, running into many thousands, defy regimentation. Although it is easy to understand the attraction of a neat estate classification, it really is neither practical nor necessary. More difficult still is the idea of a vineyard classification. It might serve as a device to control the market, as in France, but would have little to do with the quality of the wine in the bottle.

It is not difficult to discover from books or from merchants' lists the names of a few of the best estates, and, having done so, you should look for the Riesling grape; in the main exporting regions in the north, it provides the best wine. Stylish estate-bottled wines are also made from other grapes, particularly in Franken, Württemberg, Baden and the Rheinpfalz. Most of the new-crossing vines, except Scheurebe and, some might add, Kerner, are not signposts to fine wine, but the long-established varieties of Grauer Burgunder and Weisser Burgunder (the grey and white Pinot), and Silvaner and Gewürztraminer all have areas where they excel.

Even after radical rationalization, the range of estate-bottled German wine is likely to remain far wider than any of us can expect to comprehend and that may be a weakness, but combined with its quality it is also its attraction.

9

The Co-operative Cellars

It has sometimes been the pipe-dream of those who live in cooler climates to own a vineyard, to tend grapes and to make wine. This idyll takes us back to imaginary days of rustic simplicity and golden sunshine, leading to the inevitable mellow fruitfulness of autumn. Unfortunately, it ignores the realities of vine-growing, which were particularly pressing in the nineteenth century in much of Germany. The competition was strong from foreign wine and falsified wine made from anything other than grapes, and to the commercial difficulties of the wine-makers was added the severe reduction in crop, caused by the *phylloxera* pest, the powdery mildew of *oidium* and the downy mildew of *plasmopara viticola*.

Charitable help was welcome but self-help was even better, as the economist Friedrich Wilhelm Raiffeisen understood when he established the first agricultural co-operative bank. 'One for all and all for one' was the maxim of those who relied primarily on themselves and improved education to sort out their problems, but early attempts at co-operatives did not last. In the 1820s co-operative associations of growers were established in Baden and Württemberg, and others followed suit, but none was entirely successful. Most foundered on the discrepancy between the price of grapes and that of wine.

How to run a co-operative cellar was better understood by the 1860s, and the Prussian Co-operative Law of 27 March 1867 provided the right legal framework. The direct result, thirteen months later, was the registration in Koblenz of the Winzerverein Mayschoss in the Ahr valley – Germany's first, modern co-operative cellar. Others were established in neighbouring villages, in 1871 at Walporzheim, in 1873 at Dernau, in 1874 at Ahrweiler and in 1893 at Marienthal. The little Ahr valley, with its half-timbered

59

houses and rocky, steep vineyards, led the rest of Germany in forming the new co-operative cellars, known as *Winzergenossenschaften* or *Winzervereine* or, in Württemberg, as *Weingärtnergenossenschaften*.

Today there are 317 co-operative cellars, including the six central cellars in the regions of Baden, Württemberg, Rheinhessen, Franken, Mosel-Saar-Ruwer and Nahe. Only 171 actually make wine. The rest either operate as pressing stations, passing on the must to other cellars for vinification, or simply as delivery points for grapes to be processed elsewhere later. The function of the central cellars is to receive the harvest in one form or another from smaller cellars or from individual vineyard owners.

The membership of approximately 70,000 consists of growers who, for any number of reasons, are either unwilling or unable to involve themselves in the business of wine-making. Once the member has paid his joining fee, the co-operative cellar guarantees to buy his grapes. To this end, the national storage capacity of the co-operatives is sufficient to hold up to three average-size vintages in bulk, two-thirds in expensive stainless steel and nowadays less than 2 per cent in the traditional wooden casks.

Payment for the member's crop is based on the sugar content, the grape variety, the vineyard site and the type of harvest (e.g. late-picked or not), amongst other factors. Bonuses are awarded for better-quality grapes, but the level of payment, of course, has to be related to the likely market price of the future wine. In some cases, it may inevitably be up to two years after the vintage before the member receives the final payment on the grapes he has supplied – particularly if they were of the highest quality, destined to become slow-selling, fine wines.

Unlike their Italian counterparts, the German co-operatives buy grapes solely from their members and do not obtain must or wine on the open market. Neither do they follow the custom of some French co-operative cellars, which allows the names of individual members to appear on the bottle label in the form equivalent to 'Estate Bottled by Mr Dubois', simply because Dubois is the supplier of the grapes. In fact, the Germans usually play the game of selling wine with a straighter bat than most, and the books of a co-operative cellar are subject to a particularly thorough, independent audit.

Over the years, the co-operatives have much increased the

amount of wine they sell in bottle, as opposed to that which is sold in bulk. At the end of the 1980s, 83 per cent of the sales by volume and 93 per cent of the financial turnover lay in bottled wine. Since 1960 the number of co-operatives has dropped from 543 to the present 317, but the storage capacity has increased from 1.8 million hectolitres in 1960–1 to 11.9 million hectolitres in 1987–8. The area under vine which supplies grapes to the co-operative cellars has grown by 96 per cent during the last thirty years, but it is unequally divided amongst the eleven wine-producing regions as table 4 shows.

TABLE 4

Region	Grape-bearing area in hectares in 1988	Percentage of area supplying co-operative cellars
Ahr	393	94
Baden	14,762	89
Franken	5,026	44
Hessische Bergstrasse	370	88
Mittelrhein	323	40
Mosel-Saar-Ruwer	12,156	23
Nahe	4,185	12
Rheingau	2,716	17
Rheinhessen	22,749	13
Rheinpfalz	20,847	29
Württemberg	9,251	94

It seems only right that the Ahr valley, having offered such a fruitful soil for co-operative cellars in the nineteenth century, should still be their joint leading suppliers of grapes on a proportional basis, along with the more numerous Württembergers. The wine of Württemberg sold in the 0.25-litre glass reaches almost twice the price of that on the Mosel, and is well supported by an enthusiastic local population.

In the 1970s customers wished to see high-technology cellars. The towering stainless-steel vats and the latest gadgetry are still there to produce the best possible wine from the available material, but the required image has altered. The need for a human scale has returned and, in the spirit of the age, the large Zentralkellerei Mosel-Saar-Ruwer at Bernkastel-Kues has been rechristened 'Moselland'. Similarly in the region with the greatest co-operative throughput, the Zentralkellerei Badischer Winzergenossenschaften is now known under a more homely title: the Badischer Winzer-keller.

To the everlasting frustration of the production directors of co-operative cellars, trade buyers are seen as wishing to make their own customers believe that the inexpensive co-operative wines are individual and hand-crafted, rather than just an agreeable, well-made but unsubtle drink. The result is that even in the largest establishments the economies of scale are confounded by 400 dif-ferent wines being individually bottled, as happens at the Zentral-kellerei Rheinischer Winzergenossenschaften at Gau-Bickelheim. In this impressive cellar in the rolling, rural Rheinhessen, thirty-nine different vine varieties are vinified and bottled separately to meet the demands of customers in a region where profitable trading is not easy. Commercial strength lies too much in the hands of the wine-buyers in western Germany, and the relationship with the producing trade has been out of balance for many years.

The largest single customer for wines from the central cellars or the big, district co-operatives are the supermarkets and cash-and-carry stores. The co-operatives can supply the large bottlings they need, sufficient for their many outlets. These big buyers work on little profit and a fast turnover, so the price to the consumer is as keen as it can be. Faced with this, the traditional wine-merchant, who needs a larger unit of profit to survive, will often buy from a co-operative cellar only if it is willing to supply him with wine bearing a label that will never appear in a supermarket. The mer-chant lives from what are seen as good wines, and supports an image based on personal service and advice, aimed at a loyal clientele.

Research in Germany suggests that in the eyes of two-thirds of the population, co-operative cellars seem every bit as shining bright as private estates. If this is so, it should help them to enlarge their rather small turnover in the important, top-quality restaurant trade. The prestige to be gained in Germany through having a wine listed by a leading restaurant is considerable, but the servicing of such an account is often time-consuming and not very profitable. The restaurant may well expect the cost of its wine list to be met by its suppliers, and reserves of wine to be held free of charge for a year or more, without any commitment to buy. This comes hard to a co-operative cellar with a small unit of profit on its wine, especially when it sees the restaurant selling with a margin of over 300 per cent.

The export market is relatively undeveloped for the co-operative cellars, amounting to less than 5 per cent of their total business. In the Mosel-Saar-Ruwer, Rheinhessen and Rheinpfalz, the share is much larger and the wines of the central co-operative cellar Moselland eG are found all over the world. Their prices relate well to the quality of the wine and can be genuinely described as competitive – which is not to say they are the cheapest.

Comments about wine from a large bottling plant cannot be too precise, but it is fair to write that the consumer is usually well served with co-operative wine, which is expected to be sound and typical of the area and the vine. In the northern regions of Mosel-Saar-Ruwer, Nahe, Rheingau and Rheinhessen, none of the co-operative cellars can compete on quality with the best private estates, whose motivations and constraints are different. Neither is it easy for them to set the limitations on yield essential for producing more concentrated wines. If there is any money to be made in a market whose prices for basic wine are very low, it seems to the member of the co-operative to be through extra litres of wine rather than via enhanced must weight. That an improvement in the quality of a range of wine can be made to pay has nevertheless been shown by the producers' association on the Mosel, the 'Deutsches Eck' (see chapter 15).

The main task of a co-operative cellar is to ensure as good a return as possible for its members. The selling difficulties of the Mosel are not necessarily those of the Rheinhessen, but it is easy to gain the general impression that co-operative cellars in the south of Germany are more successful than those further north. Perhaps communication with the membership in the south is better, so that it is able to understand the needs of the market. Be that as it may, the quality of wine and of its packaging, from some of the co-operatives in Baden and the Bereich Südliche Weinstrasse, is quite excellent. The emphasis is moving away from the endless vineyard names of the past that meant little in terms of differences of character or quality of wine, and is being replaced by a more significant influence on taste – the grape variety.

Some relatively small village co-operatives (supplied by 100 hectares or so of vineyard) are enjoying an increasingly good reputation in Germany for well-made dry red and white wine. As yet, few of these wines are directly exported, although many good bottlings from the Rheinpfalz co-operative cellars in Forst, Deidesheim and Bad Dürkheim have found their way abroad over the years via export houses such as H. Sichel Söhne or Deinhard & Co. The big district co-operative cellars at Rhodt and at Ilbesheim in the Rheinpfalz have also established their names outside Germany, but the best of the co-operative wines from Baden stay in the neighbourhood of the Black Forest. In nearby Württemberg little local wine of any sort crosses the regional boundary.

Co-operative cellars produce wines in all the official quality categories. Their future strength on the export market may well be in supplying really good 'quality wines' (QbA). In the United Kingdom that is already happening through the best supermarket chains, and it is difficult to think of a better introduction to the whole range of decent German wine.

Liebfraumilch

For most of its history Liebfrau(en)milch* has been regarded as a symbol of excellence. In praising the wine many have also referred to its widely known reputation. Amongst the earliest of such comments was the mention of *die berühmte Lieben Frauen Milch zu Worms* (the famous Lieben Frauen Milch of Worms) in *Rhein Antiquarius* published in Frankfurt in 1744. Bronner, that observant commentator on German wine, described in detail the layout of the vineyards by the Liebfrauenstiftskirche (the Collegiate Church of Our Lady) ninety years later, and again refers to its 'famous Liebfraumilch' wine. The best came from vineyards, lying within the 'shadow of the church', and this was genuine Liebfraumilch. If the shadow defined the precise area of the Liebfraumilch vineyards, the stonework of the church protected the 'sensitive site from the raw north and north-east winds and increased the warmth of the sun to a remarkable extent'.

Even at the time of Bronner, the source of Liebfraumilch had spread beyond the precincts of the Liebfrauenstiftskirche, although, as he says, the quality of some of the wines was not as good as that from the original vineyard. In his assessment of Liebfraumilch in 1833 as a 'well-bodied wine, grown at Worms', which 'generally fetches a good price', Cyrus Redding was more sober than some, but the praise, led by Victor Hugo in 1838, was almost constant throughout the nineteenth century and the area of production increased to meet the demand. The wine sold well, even in France where it was known as *lait de la Vierge*. No British visitor to the Rheinland failed to ask for Liebfraumilch, according to a writer in

---

*'Liebfraumilch' is a corruption of 'Liebfrauenmilch' dating from the nineteenth century. The law allows both spellings.

1844, who then went on to explain that much of the Liebfraumilch sold in north Germany and The Netherlands came from the Haardt area (in the Rheinpfalz) and elsewhere. The situation was so worrying that the owners of the original Liebfrauenstiftskirche vineyards felt themselves obliged to announce publicly that they were the sole source of *echte Liebfraumilch* – genuine Liebfraumilch. Amongst them was the name of P. J. Valckenberg, now a leading export house that still retains its share of the Liebfrauenstiftskirchenstück site.

Besides the praise of numerous writers, there are other indications of the quality of Liebfraumilch in the nineteenth century. The original vineyards were planted exclusively in Riesling, usually a promise in Germany of good things to come, and, in 1896, Friedrich Jakob Dochnahl cited Liebfraumilch as one of the best Riesling wines in Germany. According to Bronner, the yield of the Liebfraumilch vines was 25 per cent less than that of the well-known wine villages of Westhofen and Bechtheim, north of Worms. The price of Liebfraumilch remained high and J. B. Sturm wrote in his book *Rheinwein*, published in 1882, that it was clear that a 'large amount of *better* Hessen wine' was sold under the Liebfraumilch name. As sales grew, the origin of the wine became more vague but, in spite of this, even as late as 1931 wine-controllers Josef Rausch and Heinrich Lang wrote that most Germans expected Liebfraumilch to come from the vicinity of Worms and not from the Rheingau, Rheinpfalz, Nahe and Mosel. In fact, it was the Wine Law of 1909 that had made it legally possible for Liebfraumilch to be produced outside the Rheinhessen, and Liebfraumilch became a *Fantasiebezeichnung* – literally, a fantasia designation. This seems an apt description, given that the dictionary defines a fantasia as a 'free musical composition in which the composer follows his fancy rather than any particular musical form'. However, it was understood, according to Dr Eduard Goldschmidt of the *Deutsche Wein-Zeitung*, writing in 1951, that Liebfraumilch should be a Rheinhessen wine of a '*particularly* good, medium-sweet style'.

Under the 1971 Wine Law, Liebfraumilch became a quality wine from grapes grown in the Nahe, Rheinpfalz and Rheinhessen regions. Apart from not being acceptable to the EEC, this concept of Liebfraumilch seems rather dangerous. If the wine did not have to originate in a single region, was not Liebfraumilch simply a style of wine, that could be produced anywhere, even, perhaps, outside Germany? The response of the wine-merchants and export houses was to suggest the creation of one Liebfraumilch region, covering the whole of the Nahe, Rheinpfalz and Rheinhessen. The grape-growers successfully argued that the names of their own regions should appear on the bottle label and, thereafter, the wine could come from any one of the three regions mentioned above or from the Rheingau. Today, about half of all Liebfraumilch is from the Rheinhessen, and almost as much comes from the Rheinpfalz. The contribution of the Nahe is very small and virtually none is produced in the Rheingau. Liebfraumilch must be a quality wine with more than 18 grams per litre of residual sugar but, in practice, it usually contains 25–30 g/l. It can be produced from any vine variety permitted for quality wine but must be at least 70 per cent from Riesling, Silvaner, Müller-Thurgau or Kerner. It is the wish of the Association of German Wine Exporters that this restriction should be increased to 85 per cent by 1991 in an effort to uplift the quality from what most of the wine trade and wine writers feel is a dismally low level.

The quality of Liebfraumilch sold abroad declined in the 1960s along with that of most cheap German wine. It was now produced to the most basic standards and, as Dennis Williams of H. Sichel, the owners of the good *Blue Nun* brand, wrote in the *German Wine Review*, the era of 'is it good enough to pass the official "AP" test? had arrived'. Despite this, millions seem satisfied with what Liebfraumilch offers them today, and it remains the best-selling wine in the United Kingdom. It is the low price at which most Liebfraumilch is sold that concerns the Association of German Wine Exporters, which resisted the suggestion that the wine should be downgraded from quality wine to *Landwein*. (In the event, this would have been difficult as, by law, a medium-sweet wine cannot be a *Landwein*.)

The problem with the indifferent quality of today's Liebfraumilch and other cheap German wines could be solved. The means of improvement are available. Increase the minimum levels of must weight for quality wines, raise the standards of expectations at the official control centres (see chapter 7), and cheap Liebfraumilch would become a better and more expensive wine. A doubling of the bulk price for Liebfraumilch from DM 1.00 to DM 2.00 per litre would probably result in an increase in the retail price in

Britain (Germany's largest export market) of up to 50p per bottle, at the most, but would it be an impossible marketing goal to aim for the present level of sale at a higher price?

The answer may be uncertain, but where much of the German wine trade is relying on a large volume of a cheap product to keep it in business, even a slight decline in exports would be unpopular amongst the grape-growers of the Rheinhessen and the Rheinpfalz, and the wine-merchants and bottlers stationed on the Mosel.

It is likely that as long as the world is happy to drink cheap German wine as it is made at present, Liebfraumilch will remain what it has become – derided by the critics but enjoyed by many.

Buying Wine in Germany

The Germans are modest about their wine, and show little of the loyalty with which Frenchmen pay somewhat uncritical respect to their local *vin de la région*. Without a capital city equivalent to Paris to set trends in wine-drinking, the main influences on taste in wine seem to come from abroad. Germany has an even greater international wine market than the United Kingdom and she is by far the largest importer in the EC of wines from all over the world. Anything French is popular and thought to have a special glamour. Thus a cheap *Spätlese* wine from the Rheinhessen will sell for DM 3.00–5.00 per bottle, and an insignificant Côtes du Rhône for DM 5.00–7.00 or so. Neither will be exciting, but for DM 7.00 a wine of real character and style is directly available from most estates, as well-informed wine-lovers are increasingly aware.

Most wine in Germany is bought by the consumer in supermarkets and various types of grocery outlet, where the co-operative cellars are strongly represented by wines with *Grosslage* names. The cheapest wines, bottled by *Weinkellereien*, or wine-merchants' cellars, will appear on special offers as low as DM 1.70 per bottle or less, but these mainly medium-sweet wines are made important only by their volume of sale. They are otherwise without interest.

Although branded sparkling wines have been hugely successful in Germany, the branded German still wine, with very few exceptions, has not sold so well. According to Dr Franz Werner Michel of the Deutsches Weininstitut, even at the very bottom of the market the German consumer has shown an 'emotional, almost religious, identification of geographical origin with a guarantee of authenticity'. True to their rather broad origins the cheapest wines may be, but at under DM 3.00 per bottle that is no guarantee of quality. For many, prestige is important and research suggests that those who drink wine only occasionally are attracted by the implications of the word *Spätlese* on the bottle. However, they do not realize that it can have a bearing on quality only when the wine is sold at perhaps twice the price at which it appears on the supermarket shelf. The most interesting source of wine remains the estate bottlers, many of whom sell a large proportion of their production directly to the consumer. Often estates have a wine bar, or at least a room set aside, where wines may be tasted. Given the dangers of driving with alcohol in the blood it causes no surprise at a tasting if you ask for a spittoon if more than two or three wines are offered. There is no general rule as to the minimum number of bottles you may buy, but a purchase of twelve bottles of any one wine may bring a rebate, and should please the producer. Because the Germans prefer their better-quality wines (other than the richest) to be dry or medium-dry, the number of medium-sweet wines on offer may be small. Price lists show clearly whether a wine is sweet or dry (sometimes by means of a chemical analysis!), so choosing is not difficult.

Throughout Germany's eleven wine-producing regions there are said to be some 10,000 estates selling directly to the consumer. To these have to be added the co-operative cellars which serve the public in a similar way, offering good wine at value-for-money prices. Many of the best are in Baden, where small village co-operatives have a high reputation, in particular for wines from the Burgunder or Pinot family. Here, and in neighbouring Württemberg, the sale of wine in litre bottles to the consumer is increasing, perhaps as more people realize that the wine in a litre bottle costs 15 per cent less than the same wine in an 0.75-litre bottle. A tasting panel, put together by the magazine *Alles über Wein* in 1988, was pleasantly surprised by the attractiveness of Riesling wines sold by the litre at about DM 4.00–7.00 or so. This was an interesting result, as until recently the litre size was reserved for rather ordinary wine.

With a consumption of 143 litres per head, German adults drink 6 litres more beer per year than the British. Even in the wine-producing regions, the cafés and middle-quality restaurants, with the possible exception of those in Württemberg, seem more interested in selling beer than wine. In most cases the choice of wine by the glass is small and, although vineyards may be immediately adjacent, local wines are frequently not on offer. Large

Weinkellereien control a sizeable proportion of the market in cheap wine. The scale of their operations is shown by the fact that over 40 per cent of QbA whose grapes originated in the Rheinpfalz or Rheinhessen are bottled outside their regions. As a result, as far as the cheapest wine is concerned, the close connection between grape-grower and the café that serves the wine cannot exist, and so it becomes a commodity with no added value.

Aware of a lack of 'image', some regions are now offering sound wines, made to a particular specification, which are sold under such names as *Nahesteiner* or *Der Rheinhess*, and are discussed elsewhere in this book.

For those far removed from the vine-growing area and for whom it is inconvenient to visit a winery, good German wine-merchants offer a range of imported and home-produced estate and co-operative bottled wines. Buying wine from a merchant is more expensive than buying directly from an estate, perhaps by DM 2.00–3.00 per bottle at *Kabinett* or *Spätlese* level, but it is the range that a merchant can offer that attracts those with broad tastes in wine-drinking. If it is the variety of good German wine that you seek, a wine-merchant is often your best source of supply.

12
Sekt

'Neither do men putteth new wine into old bottles: else the bottles break, and the wine runneth out.'

The explosive effect of fermentation was common knowledge in the days of Christ, but, until the use of cork as a bottle-stopper, its exuberance remained untamed. The early history of sparkling wine is sometimes imprecise, with hopeful sentiment editing information to suit a particular purpose. However, it seems to be agreed that the world's first recorded sparkling wine was made about 1540 at Limoux in south-west France, and it is sure that German commercial production began in the 1820s.

It is quite acceptable in Germany to speak of a sparkling wine as having been 'made', and it is officially regarded by the tax authorities as an industrial product. Although some of the early sparkling-wine producers were also vineyard-owners (Burgeff and Mattheus Müller in the Rheingau, for example), the 'manufacturing' aspect of the German sparkling-wine industry has never been denied. What the EC calls 'quality sparkling wine' Germans know as Sekt, and since September 1986 *Deutscher Sekt* has been made exclusively from German wine. Previously the description meant that a wine had been made sparkling in Germany, but not necessarily from German base wine. This interpretation still holds good in eastern Germany, where the old 1930 Wine Law remains in force.

Since the middle of the nineteenth century, *Sekt* producers have bought base wine wherever price and style were appropriate for their blends – particularly in the early days in Alsace and Lorraine. In the 1970s Italy overtook France as the main supplier and today only 10 per cent or so of *Sekt* produced in Germany is made from German wine. Cheap sparkling wine is enjoyed by millions as an uncomplicated, pleasant drink, but it is the finer *Sekt*, especially when made from German Riesling wine, that draws the attention and appeals to the lover of fine, still wine.

With 70 per cent of its output being sold at less than DM 5.00, and a further 26 per cent between DM 5.00 and DM 10.00 per bottle, it is clear that as a whole the German *Sekt* industry is not aiming to produce sparkling wine of the highest quality. Costs will be discussed later, but retail prices were so low in Germany in the late 1980s that it was feared that harmonization of European taxes in 1992–3, could reduce the current tax of DM 2.28 per bottle, inclusive of VAT, to a point at which some *Sekt* would become as inexpensive as mineral water. With the average special offer price for brands such as Faber Krönung already as low as DM 3.84 (annual sale = 45 million bottles), any residual quality image that *Sekt* might have would then finally disappear in the supermarket. However, the gap between the cheapest and the most expensive *Sekt* is now so wide, both in quality and price, that perhaps fine, elegant *Sekt* can no longer be touched by what happens in the bargain basement.

The EC definition of *quality* sparkling wine (94 per cent of the sparkling-wine production in Germany) is based on various technical factors, including the alcohol content of the base wine, the length of fermentation of the sparkling wine, and the time it remains on the yeast after fermenting. These and a minimum maturation period are basic standards upon which the producers of good *Sekt* improve. The sparkle in *Sekt* must be the result of a second alcoholic fermentation, be it achieved in bottle or vat. It is generally held by disinterested parties that the size of the container for the second fermentation does not automatically have a bearing on the quality of the *Sekt* that is produced. Much more significant in this respect are the quality of the base wine, the care put into the fermentation, and the length of maturation.

There are three main systems in Germany through which *Sekt* develops its bubbles. The oldest, and the most favoured on economic grounds where production is small, is known as *Flaschengärung* or 'bottle fermentation'. Here a solution of wine, or must and saccharose, is mixed with selected yeast and added to the dry base wine. After bottling, fermentation inevitably starts, carbon-dioxide gas develops, as does an unsightly brown deposit in the bottle. This must be removed for the wine to be saleable, so after maturation the bottles are placed in slotted 'desks', resembling the capital letter 'A' when seen from the side. The near-vertical bottles are shaken regularly and the deposit slips on to the cork, from where it can be removed with a certain legerdemain after the necks of the bottles have been frozen. Until 1890 this was the only known way by which a sparkle could be developed in a wine through a second fermentation. As a system it has the advantage of being able to be applied commercially to as little as 500 litres of wine at a time and, where labour is cheap or sparkling-wine prices are high, it is still found and much praised (Spain on the one hand, Champagne on the other).

A development of straightforward bottle fermentation was the *Transvasierverfahren*, or 'transfer system', which avoids the expensive hand-shaking of bottles to separate the yeast from the wine. Introduced by *Sekt* producers Kupferberg in 1954, the sparkling wine is emptied under pressure from the bottle into a tank. After filtration, the clear wine is then bottled once more. Although this method is still in use, about 98 per cent of the volume of *Sekt* made in Germany today develops its sparkle in tank by the *Grossraumgärverfahren*, the 'large area fermentation process'.

As early as 1888 attempts had been made by the founders of the *Sekt* house Schloss Wachenheim to produce a sparkling wine in lightly sealed casks, but it was the Frenchmen Charmat and Chaussepied who developed the system in the 1930s that is now so popular in a refined form in Germany. The process of the second fermentation in tank is similar to that in a bottle, except that in a tank the development of the sparkling wine can be more easily controlled.

It is almost true that the more acid the base wine is, the better the future sparkling wine will be. In its raw, pre-second fermentation stage, the taste is pretty severe and to retain a style that is light and refreshing not more than 10–11° of alcohol are needed. Like Riesling, Elbling wine from the Mosel meets this specification well, and yet Elbling *Sekt* has never achieved a nationally recognized identity for itself. As long as foreign base wine can be obtained at 70 Pfennig or less per litre, more expensive German wine is unlikely to attract a *Sekt* house trying to market a product at under DM 4.00 per bottle.

Cheap *Sekt* is big business, and over half of Germany's annual *Sekt* production of nearly 400 million bottles is sold via grocers or supermarkets. Whereas the quality and variety of *Wurst* in a German supermarket is usually very impressive, the wine department is likely to be less so – particularly when it sells *Sekt* at DM 3.99.

The price of such a product is the result of rationalization, huge throughput, and creative accounting. Table 5 shows how it might break down.

TABLE 5

	DM per bottle
Retail price in supermarket	3.99
VAT (14%)	.49
	3.50
Profit for supermarket	.46
(15% on buying)	3.04
Sekt tax	2.00
DM	1.04

Out of the cost to the supermarket of DM 1.04 has to be taken that of the base wine and of the conversion into sparkling wine, of all materials (sugar, bottles, stoppers, labels, etc.), labour, distribution ex-producer, possibly of promotions, theoretically of financing, plus an element of profit for the producer. How ends are made to meet remains obscure, but when better-quality *Sekt* is produced the costings appear much healthier and, indeed, show a profit greater than that which can be expected of most sound-quality still wines.

In the price of an elegant, bottle-fermented Riesling *Sekt* at DM 13.00 per bottle, there will be an element of VAT at DM 1.60 and of *Sekt* tax at DM 2.00, producing a notional tax-free selling price of DM 9.40. The gross cost of the *Sekt* in the producer's cellar might be about DM 6.00, resulting in a respectable profit of DM 3.40 per bottle. The selling price of a wine is largely a matter of what the market will stand, and for top-flight *Sekt* the German consumers will pay DM 16.00 per bottle or more.

There are, in fact, a number of distinguished *Sekte* from prestigious estates at DM 30.00-55.00. Non-vintage Champagne, such as Pommery (DM 29.88) or Charles Heidsieck (DM 24.99), may be bought for less, but the expensive German sparkling wines find loyal customers, for whom the price of Champagne is irrelevant.

Some 85 per cent of *Sekt* is not only cheap but also sweetish in taste. However, EC legislation deceptively allows the description 'medium-dry' to be used for sparkling wines with as much as 50 grams per litre of residual sugar – the approximate equivalent of one heaped teaspoonful per glass. Few *Sekte* are totally dry, but a wine labelled 'extra brut' should not contain more than 6 grams per litre of sugar and will taste very dry, particularly if made from Riesling or Elbling.

Although we think of *Sekt* first as a white wine, 12 per cent or so is red, and increasingly rapidly in sales. In 1879 Henry Vizetelly wrote in *Facts about Champagne and Other Sparkling Wines* that much of the *Sekt* for consumption in Germany was made from the red Spätburgunder grape – still grown as Pinot Noir in Champagne today. Like the Champenois, the Germans used their red grapes to produce a white sparkling wine of full flavour, but Riesling remained the variety preferred by the English for 'Sparkling Hock'.

The branding of *Sekt* began about 100 years ago and names such as Faber Krönung, Söhnlein Brilliant, Rüttgers Club, Deinhard Cabinet and Henkell Trocken now lead the market – all at less than DM 8.00 per bottle. The German *Sekt*-consumer knows his brands and likes the styles, but he is not interested in details that are important to the wine-lover. To satisfy the latter's thirst for varied but clearly defined 'taste experiences', there is a growing number of *Sekte*, sold with the attributes of a good still wine. In other words, beside the vine variety the wine-lover also wishes to know the vintage of his *Sekt*, the region (Mosel-Saar-Ruwer and Rheinhessen being statistically the most popular) and sometimes even the vineyard from which the wine comes.

To encourage wine-drinkers to ask for a *Sekt* with a pedigree derived from the base wine, and because of the poor trading on the still-wine market, a new range of *Sekt* producers appeared in the 1980s. They varied in size from the large *Sekterzeugergemein-schaft* (Sekt Producers' Association) to the small family estate.

As the traditional *Sekt* houses bought less and less base wine in Germany, the wine-producer had to find another channel through which he could dispose of his simplest and somewhat acidic wines.

To this end, two producers' associations were formed – one in the Rheinhessen and another in the Mosel-Saar-Ruwer region.

Flexibility is a characteristic of an *Erzeugergemeinschaft*, both in its structure and in the way it operates. In the Rheinhessen some members sell wine to the Producers' Association, and that is the end of the transaction. Others will supply wine, which will be put into a general blend. They can then draw from the Association's stock in proportion to the amount of still wine supplied. For another category of member, the Association converts the specific wine taken from the member into *Sekt* and returns it to him in its now sparkling form. Finally, there are those who merely buy *Sekt* from the Association, without supplying any base wine at all. No matter what the trading relationship, base wines can be separated, of course, according to vine variety, vintage, vineyard of origin, or in any other way that might be required.

Apart from the obvious economies of scale, a producer's association can also offer the expertise in *Sekt*-making that the small vine-grower may lack. Prices to the consumer from the Erzeuger-gemeinschaft Winzersekt Rheinhessen GmbH, to give the full title, range from DM 9.00 to about DM 15.00. With *Sekt* production costs (materials and labour) of under DM 3.00 per bottle, and allowing for financing and investment costs, producing *Sekt* seems a more interesting activity than selling wine in bulk on the open market for less than DM 1.00 per litre.

Besides the newly formed *Erzeugergemeinschaften*, the *Winzer-genossenschaften* (the co-operative cellars – see chapter 10) are also involved to a limited extent in making sparkling wine. The best-known brand, *Schloss Munzingen*, produced by the unfortu-nately named (to non-German speakers) Gräflich von Kageneck'-sche Erzeuger-Weinvertriebsgesellschaft GmbH, Breisach, is sold mainly in the supermarkets and grocery trade in Germany, but is also found on the export market. The co-operatives in Baden handle some 89 per cent of the crop, and so their near-monopoly allows them to emphasize the region's name without any fear that a serious competitor might benefit from their efforts.

The side of the German sparkling-wine trade with which the wine-lover will most easily be in sympathy is probably that occu-pied by the private estate. To make its still wine sparkle, most estates employ a *Sekt* company which will do the job for about DM 3.50 per bottle, or less. As the amount of base wine will be small, the secondary fermentation will usually take place in bottle, rather than in tank. The result, an individual good-quality sparkling wine, probably *brut*, or *extra dry* (maximum 20 grams per litre of sugar), will please the private customers to whom most estates sell.

A number of estates have taken on the role of *Sekt* manufacturer for themselves, using the bottle-fermentation method. Many are still feeling their way and gaining technical experience as they proceed. It will be interesting to taste the quality of sparkling wine that they produce in the year 2000.

If sales of wine-lovers' *Sekt* from private estates, co-operative cellars and producers' associations are increasing, they are still very small when compared with the turnover of the large *Sekt* houses.

After Georg Christian Kessler, with his sixteen years of experience gained at Champagne Veuve-Clicquot, founded a *Sekt* cellar in 1826, others followed his example. Burgeff, Mattheus Müller, Deinhard and Kupferberg were all in production by 1850, and are still trading nearly a century and a half later. Only Kessler and Deinhard, however, remain in the hands of their founding families.

One of the largest producers of *Sekt* is the Reh Group, based on Trier, with a turnover of 80 million bottles, plus a further 20 million bottles of sparkling wine made in Alsace. Its most important brands are Faber Krönung, and the Feist and Schloss Böchingen ranges.

Henkell and Söhnlein, owned by the Oetker family, enjoy sales of 86 million bottles a year. Nearly 14 million bottles of Henkell Trocken are sold annually at about DM 8.00 per bottle and the sale of 8 million bottles of Fürst von Metternich *Sekt* at DM 12.99 per bottle makes it the most successful of the more expensive, big brands.

Deinhard sells more than 14 million bottles of its Cabinet *Sekt* at about DM 7.00 per bottle, plus a further 2 million bottles of quality Riesling *Sekt* at over DM 10.00 per bottle. For many, Henkell Trocken and Deinhard Cabinet are brands which represent a good compromise between quality and price. They are served at the family festivities which count for so much in Germany. Hardly a birthday goes by without a celebration, and in the largely Roman Catholic Rheinland vast quantities of *Sekt* are consumed during the annual carnival.

According to research by the Ifak-Institut for the magazine *Der*

Spiegel, those with the best formal education buy the more expensive *Sekte*. Presumably, this is another way of saying that people in top jobs drink top-quality products, but in spite of the steady demand for *Sekt* of all types throughout the year, nearly one-third of the total annual sale is made in December.

In the past the restaurant trade in Germany has shown little interest in cheap or middle-price *Sekt*, often preferring to offer more expensive and more profitable Champagne to its customers. This now seems to be changing slightly, perhaps helped by the thought that if drier German still wines taste well with food, there should also be a place for drier, top-quality *Sekt* on a good restaurant list.

The consumption of *Sekt* on the export market has been small for many years, after great success in the last century. Of the total German production in 1873, nearly half was exported to the United Kingdom, according to producers Burgeff. In the late 1980s Britain is still the most important export customer for *Sekt*, taking a little over 2.6 million bottles per year. At an average price of DM 3.90 per litre from the producer's premises, little of the best-quality *Sekt* can reach Britain. Nevertheless, even cheap Riesling *Sekt* should be refreshing and enjoyable, although it is a poor relation of the very best of Germany's sparkling wines. For them, it is probably best to visit Germany itself.

13
Ahr

Area under vine in hectares in 1988: 428 ha, planted 40.4 per cent Blauer Spätburgunder, 23.4 per cent Blauer Portugieser, 13.3 per cent Weisser Riesling, 10.8 per cent Müller-Thurgau, and 12.1 per cent others.

Average temperature during period of vegetation:	13.9°C
Average sunshine hours during period of vegetation:	1,092
Average rainfall during period of vegetation:	420mm
Average annual rainfall:	646mm
Recent vintages in thousand hectolitres:	1985 20.0, 1986 35.0, 1987 32.0, 1988 24.0, 1989 50.0
Average yield in hectolitres per hectare:	1978–87 75.5 hl/ha

The Ahr is one of the most commercially successful of Germany's eleven vine-growing regions. The wines from its co-operative cellars sell for almost twice the price paid for Mosel and the best are often sold out within days of having appeared on the producer's list. Ahr wine is a speciality beloved by the visitor from Cologne, the Ruhr district and the Benelux countries. Judged by international standards, most of it is of little consequence, but amongst the medium-sweet red wines that taste as though they were meant to be white, there are others with true red-wine character and style. These are relatively new arrivals on the scene, which sell for up to DM 32.00 per bottle, and are bought rapidly as soon as they become available.

The viticultural part of the Ahr stretches 25 kilometres from Altenahr, downstream to Heimersheim near the confluence with the Rhein, south of Remagen. The landscape is spectacular, wooded and rocky. Steep, south-facing vineyards climb out of the twisting narrow valley, and enjoy a micro-climate far warmer than

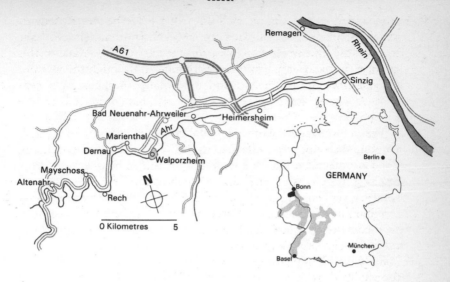

The Ahr Valley

that of the region as a whole. About 10 per cent only of the vines are grown on level ground so that, once again, costs are high, but modernization (*Flurbereinigung* – see chapter 3) has helped to improve net incomes. Five co-operative cellars handle over 90 per cent of the harvest and they, like the private estates, sell enthusiastically to the passing trade. The Winzergenossenschaft Mayschoss-Altenahr, the oldest existing co-operative cellar in the world, claims to receive 500,000 visitors a year, which seems entirely believable given the congestion on the region's roads from 11 a.m. onwards in the summer. With sufficient time, perhaps the best way to visit the Ahr and absorb its individual atmosphere is to follow the official 29-kilometre footpath through the vineyards. If even this proves too busy, there are many other well-marked and less-frequented tracks, with impressive views over the valley below. Wildlife is well protected in Germany (noticeably more so than in France), so that when the weather is good deer are often met on a wood and vineyard walk, and kites and buzzards fly overhead.

The Ahr has been slower than most regions to move to drier wines, perhaps because the customers from Cologne and the north, who combine wine-buying with a day out in the valley, have changed their tastes more slowly than those in the southern half of Germany. Nevertheless, there are many more dry and medium-dry wines being offered in the early 1990s than there were ten years ago, as a glance at the results of the DLG competitions will show.

The A61 motorway that leads south to Koblenz crosses the Ahr on a viaduct near Bad Neuenahr – the largest town in the region, and the home of a well-known private estate Weingut J. J. Adeneuer. Everything in the little Ahr region is on a fairly small scale, so the 5.7 hectares devoted exclusively to red-vine varieties represent quite a sizeable property. Amongst the estate's holdings is one of the smallest registered single vineyards in Europe, the 0.68-hectare Walporzheimer Gärkammer. Here Spätburgunder produces wine up to *Beerenauslese* quality (minimum 15.3 per cent potential alcohol) in a good vintage.

Walporzheim is famous for its ancient Romantik-Restaurant St Peter, with a Michelin Guide star. For centuries the estate which owns the restaurant, Brogsitters Weingut 'Zum Domherrenhof', was the treasured property of the chapter of Cologne cathedral. Today the 15-hectare estate, and a 20-hectare producers' association (*Erzeugergemeinschaft*) attached to it, have a good reputation for 'old-style' Ahr red wines with residual sugar. With the sweetness there is in some German game dishes, a certain amount of unfermented sugar in a wine is often thought appropriate. But argument about the 'correct' structure of red wine is taking place in the Ahr as it is in other regions.

Most still take the view that an Ahr Spätburgunder should be low in tannin, high in acidity, and sometimes a little sweet. This is the type of wine produced by the largest estate in the region, the Staatliche Weinbaudomäne, based on Marienthal. Weingut Meyer-Näkel at Dernau, a kilometre or so away, follows an altogether different but very varied line. All the Meyer-Näkel Spätburgunder wines that I have tasted are serious, individual, and very true to the vine variety. The variations, apart from those of soil and must weight, result from different fermentation techniques (with or without the stalks), malo-lactic fermentation and the partial use of *barriques* for maturation. The average yield for Meyer-Näkel Spätburgunder is about 50 hl/ha, which, together with the work in the cellar, produces wines of a quality and colour that are probably unique in the region. They are snapped up quickly by knowledgeable wine-lovers, but would be of no interest to the average tourist looking for a bottle of typical Ahr wine. Amongst Meyer-Näkel's unusual bottlings, which catch the eye and stay in the memory, is a white wine, placed in the lowest official category of 'table wine'. (This avoids the risk that as a 'quality wine' it would not be given an AP number – see chapter 7 – on the grounds that it was untypical.) This 1989 Weiss von Rot table wine from Spätburgunder has excellent 'Pinot' style and good grip. Even at DM 19.00 per bottle it sells with ease and must help to show other wine-makers in the region what can be achieved. Some will surely follow.

White wine was produced from red grapes in the Ahr in the nineteenth century, as it still is, of course, in Champagne. In his *Facts about Champagne and other Sparkling Wines*, Henry Vizetelly decribed in 1879 the procedure followed by Deinhard, the *Sekt* manufacturers: 'In order that the wine may be as pale as possible, the black grapes are pressed as soon after gathering as they can be, and only the juice resulting from the first pressure is reserved, the subsequently extracted must being sold to the small growers of the neighbourhood.'

Ahr *Weissherbst*, rosé from a single vine variety, is very successful and it has the advantage of a good level of acidity, sometimes with an added flavour from the slatey soil. Before the art of red-wine making was learnt from the French in the eighteenth century (see chapter 5), pale Ahr 'red' wine must have been very similar in colour to modern *Weissherbst*. A tradition of making red wine so pale that most would call it rosé continues in many German and Alsatian cellars.

To deepen the colour of Spätburgunder in the Ahr, a little Dornfelder is sometimes added, but this is not necessary for the better-quality wines. Apart from Spätburgunder, Portugieser shows again that, where the crop is restricted, wines of character can result. In the very large 1989 vintage the average Portugieser yield in the Ahr reached 130 hl/ha, whereas in the Bereich Südliche Weinstrasse in the Rheinpfalz it rose to 160 hl/ha. Generally speaking, overcropping in the Ahr is not a problem and, because of the high prices paid for the region's wine, better and less wine can be made.

Some recommended producers in the Ahr

Weingut J. J. Adeneuer, 5483 Bad Neuenahr-Ahrweiler, Max-Planck-Strasse 8: exclusively red wines or *Weissherbst*. Cask matured, many dry.

Weingut-Sektkellerei Brogsitters 'Zum Domherrenhof', 5483 Bad Neuenahr-Walporzheim, Walporzheimer Strasse 125: well-made white and red wines from restricted yields.

Weingut Meyer-Näkel, 5487 Dernau, Hardtbergstrasse 20: exciting high-quality wines, mainly dry. Many innovations.

Staatliche Weinbaudomäne, 5487 Marienthal, Walporzheimer Strasse 48: traditional Ahr wines up to *Trockenbeerenauslese* quality.

14

Mittelrhein

Area under vine in hectares in 1988: 731 ha, planted 74.8 per cent Weisser Riesling, 10.4 per cent Müller-Thurgau, 5.8 per cent Kerner, and 9.0 per cent others.

Average temperature during period of vegetation:	15.0°C
Average sunshine hours during period of vegetation:	1,204
Average rainfall during period of vegetation:	385mm
Average annual rainfall:	591mm
Recent vintages in thousand hectolitres:	1985 50.0, 1986 61.0, 1987 57.0, 1988 51.0, 1989 90.0
Average yield in hectolitres per hectare:	1978–87 78.9 hl/ha

The Mittelrhein is the only region in Germany where the vineyard area has not increased in size over the last forty years. To put it more precisely, it has shrunk by over one-third since 1950 and continues to do so. Although labour costs have been reduced by rationalization, they still remain high as so many of the vines are planted in sloping and difficult terrain. According to Helmut Prössler, an authority on the region, the vineyards had been established on the flat land near Andernach, north of Koblenz, by AD 400 and by about AD 1000 vines slowly started to move up on newly created terraces on the steep slopes above the River Rhein. Later, when explosives became available, the expansion continued with the rocky landscape being blown into a workable shape.

The proportion of Riesling grown today is almost as high as that in the neighbouring Rheingau and the average annual yield is among the lowest in Germany. At the same time, the retail price for good Mittelrhein Riesling remains DM 1.50–2.00 or so less than that of Rheingau wine of similar quality. In these circumstances, grape-growing and wine-making can often be profitable in the Mittelrhein only when sales are made directly from the producer to the consumer, and so it is a great region for signs reading *Flaschenweinverkauf* – wine sold in bottle. The passing tourist is important to the wine-producers, who are helped enormously by some of Germany's best-known, most dramatic and most romantic scenery. Given Queen Victoria's predilection for the beautiful but sometimes gloomy 'Stag at Bay' Scottish Highlands, it is easy to understand how she was captivated by the sight of the castles above the slate-covered slopes, which climb to a height of 200 metres above the Rhein.

Many Mittelrhein wines are destined to be sold by the glass in the riverside cafés. A recent visit showed Mittelrhein Müller-Thurgau being sold at DM 1.60 for the 0.2-litre *Römer*, and tea at DM 1.80 the cup. Unfortunately, some of the local cafés not owned by vine-growers seem quite happy to offer wine from the Rheinhessen (presumably because it is the cheapest they can buy), rather than support their own regional wine industry *à la française*. There is a not very large trade in Mittelrhein wine in bulk, centred in particular on the Viertälergebiet, a district of four valleys branching off the Rhein near Bacharach. Here the Riesling wines convert excellently into fresh-tasting sparkling wine, as the Koblenz *Sekt* producers, Deinhard & Co., discovered over a century ago. Bacharach has had its own, respected *Sekt* manufacturer in Georg Geiling since the 1890s. This small firm, founded in the Champagne region, shows on its list from where the base wine for its *Sekt* originates, and this can be either Bordeaux, the Loire or a German wine-producing region.

The heyday of Bacharach as a wine town was before 1700, when it was one of the most important markets for wine in Germany. According to Bassermann-Jordan, the fifteenth-century Pope Pius II had a *Fuder* (a cask equivalent to a little over 1,300 750-ml bottles) of Bacharacher sent to Rome each year. The Pope's wine would have been one that was bought at Bacharach, but not necessarily from one of the town's vineyards. Wines were often named according to the place at which they were sold, rather than after the name (if any) of the vineyard in which the grapes were grown (see chapter 1). The Mittelrhein has a few high-quality private estates, with six at Bacharach being members of the regional branch of the VDP (an association discussed in chapter 19). In

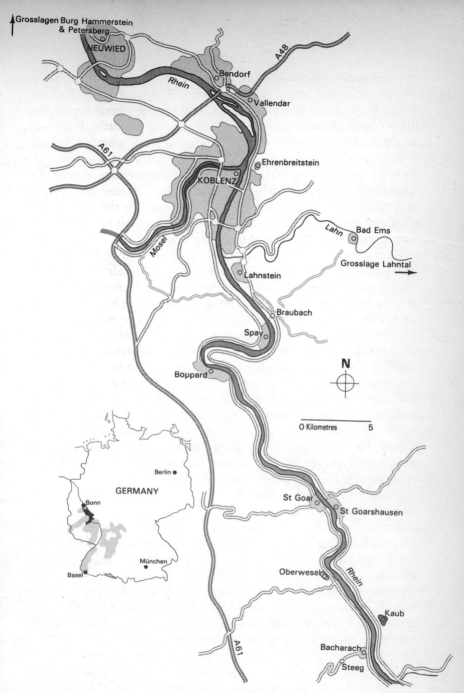

Mittelrhein: southern section

87

general, their Riesling wines are similar in structure to those of the Rheingau – particularly, of course, to those of Lorch, just over the Mittelrhein border. They have their own clearly defined, steely flavour, but they usually lack the refinement of the best of the Rheingau. Their appeal is perhaps similar to that of a good Alsatian Riesling, if lighter in weight.

After Bacharach, moving downstream, there are a number of attractive villages or small towns on both sides of the Rhein. Boppard, once one of ten customs posts between Mainz and Andernach at which duty was levied on the river traffic, is known as a tourist centre. It was here, incidentally, that Humperdinck composed *Hänsel und Gretel*, and the Rheinland has inspired many writers and composers, from Achim von Arnim to Richard Wagner. The Boppard Hamm forms one sweep of steep, continuous and curving vineyard. Its wines are well thought of locally, but they are seldom found elsewhere.

The most important vineyards of the Mittelrhein overlook the river, but there are a number of side valleys which also form part of the region, including that of the Lahn. It is a peaceful river, which has lost some of the rural charm that it had forty years ago, and many of its vineyards as well. The area under vine is now very small and the wines must be sought out on the spot.

The Mühlental at Koblenz is a delightful, steep-sided valley, whose wine is sold as Ehrenbreitsteiner Kreuzberg. In the nineteenth century the red wine was made into *Sekt* but today the valley is best known for its earthy Riesling, as well as for a host of wines from other vine varieties.

North of Koblenz there is a gap until serious vine-growing starts again at Leutesdorf. This small town with its 'wine atmosphere', its well-maintained half-timbered houses and reconstructed vineyards, has an air of prosperity, but the most interesting town in this stretch of the Rhein is Linz, parts of which seem to be a set for *Die Meistersinger*. These northern outposts of the German vineyard, which were once at its geographical centre, are all carefully preserved or restored and well worth a visit. Their hold on wine is tenuous and abandoned vineyards are easy to find. If their evident civic pride could be stretched to include viticulture, its future might be more secure.

Some recommended estates in the Mittelrhein

Weingut Toni Jost, 6533 Bacharach, 'Hahnenhof', Oberstrasse 14: good Riesling wines from low yields. Holdings also in Rheingau.

Weingut August Perll, 5407 Boppard, Oberstrasse 81: a full range of Riesling wines from dry to luscious.

Weingut Walter Perll, 5407 Boppard, Ablassgasse 11: prizewinning, mainly Riesling estate.

Weingut J. Ratzenberger, 6533 Bacharach-Steeg, Blücherstrasse 167: dry, cask-matured firm Rieslings, and Spätburgunder.

Weingut Klaus Wagner, 5400 Koblenz-Ehrenbreitstein, Mühlental 23: wines as individual and characterful as the estate-owners.

15

Mosel-Saar-Ruwer

Area under vine in hectares in 1988: 12,760 ha, planted 55.3 per cent Weisser Riesling, 22.2 per cent Müller-Thurgau, 8.6 per cent Weisser Elbling, 6.8 per cent Kerner, and 7.1 per cent others.

Average temperature during period of vegetation:	14.4°C
Average sunshine hours during period of vegetation:	1,157
Average rainfall during period of vegetation:	448mm
Average annual rainfall:	727mm
Recent vintages in million hectolitres:	1985 1.2, 1986 1.4, 1987 1.3, 1988 1.3, 1989 2.0
Average yield in hectolitres per hectare:	1978–87 109.9 hl/ha

---

For almost all of the 240 kilometres from the French border to its confluence with the Rhein at Koblenz, the Mosel flows in sight of vineyards. Passing downstream from Trier and under the motorway bridge at Schweich, the river has carved its way through the Rheinische Schiefgebirge, the Rheinland Slate Mountains. Perhaps mountain is rather a dramatic description for the surrounding hills, but nobody would quarrel with the mention of slate. It is everywhere and, as our faithful chronicler Bronner wrote in 1834, while slate was used in other areas to decorate palaces, on the Mosel it covered the roof of every peasant's dwelling and, of course, his vineyards as well. Large quarries were excavated at the top of the steep vineyards from which small slabs of slate could be scattered amongst the vines. Bronner suspected that the blue-black slate contributed to the minerals in the soil, and was rightly certain that it retained and later reflected the warmth of the sun. So generously and so frequently was it distributed that the natural earth of the vineyard could no longer be seen, and so it is in many of the best and oldest sites to this day.

Under the influence of the Gulf Stream, the Mosel climate is mild. Over half the region's vineyards lie on slopes of more than 26 per cent inclination, with the sun's rays being at their most effective on a south-facing slope of 30 per cent. In the side valleys of the river the micro-climate is more continental and here the Riesling comes into its own in hot, dry summers, when the vines in the best sites of the Bereich Bernkastel are sometimes stressed through lack of water.

Along the Mosel the vines are protected by the woods of the Eifel to the north and of the Hunsrück to the south (the setting of the epic film *Heimat*). It is an area for unusual wildflowers, and predatory birds circle in the warm air rising from the vineyards. Fishing has increased on the river since it finally became navigable in 1964, and now shipping up to 1,500 tons can move from France, along the Saar and down the Mosel to Koblenz and beyond.

In spite of the activity on the river and the half a million visitors to the Bernkastel district alone each year, the Mosel-Saar-Ruwer retains its identity as one of the prettiest of Germany's vine-growing regions. Every writer, from Decius Magnus Ausonius in the fourth century onwards, has praised the beauty of the river, and the quality of the wine at its best lives up to the standard set by the scenery. It seems only logical that some of the least-interesting, non-Riesling Mosel wines should come from dull-looking, flat, agricultural land in the *Grosslagen* Bernkasteler Kurfürstlay or Piesporter Michelsberg, while so many of the best wines are born in the steep sites of great natural beauty, which start almost in the suburbs of Koblenz.

BEREICH ZELL

Between Koblenz and Trier, the vineyards are divided into two *Bereiche*, or districts. The first, somewhat overshadowed in the world of wine by the much larger Bereich Bernkastel, is the Bereich Zell. To the visitor the two districts look very similar, but there are a number of reasons, some more to do with the structure of the wine trade than anything else, why the better wines of the Bereich Zell have been undervalued. The unexpected thing is that

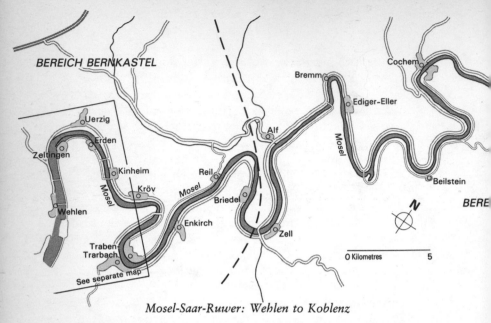

Mosel-Saar-Ruwer: Wehlen to Koblenz

on a check-list of standard requirements for fine wine-making in Germany, the smaller district would compare so well with its larger neighbour. The Bereich Zell has a higher proportion of Riesling vines and also of steep, south-facing vineyards. On average its yield per hectare is lower and its grapes have a greater must weight than those of the Bereich Bernkastel – all of which, perhaps rightly, leaves wine-merchants and brokers unmoved. The most commercially successful wine of the district is the Zeller Schwarze Katz, from a *Grosslage* of a little over 600 hectares around the town of Zell itself. Its label, bearing the *Schwarze Katz* or black cat, is well known in Germany and in some countries abroad, at a slightly lower price than a Piesporter Michelsberg.

Moving up the Mosel from Koblenz, the first important village is Winningen. Its Riesling wine is steely and related in flavour and style to that of the Mittelrhein. It enjoys a good local reputation which is being further improved by the work of the Erzeuger-gemeinschaft Deutsches Eck. This is an association of some ninety producers who observe a self-imposed standard of vine-growing, far higher than that required by law, and similar to what one would find on a good private estate in the top wine villages of the

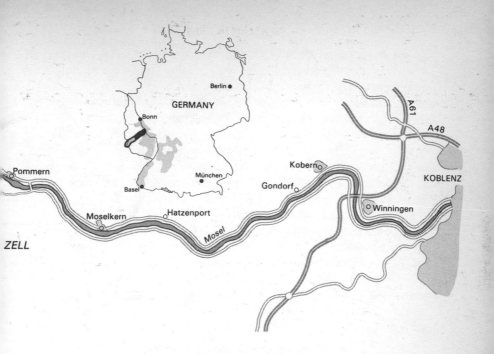

Mosel. Only Riesling wines from a maximum yield of 80 hectolitres per hectare can be sold under the Deutsches Eck name. In the view of the President of the association, good Riesling wine can be harvested at 100–120 hl/ha, but eventually the strain is too much for the vine and, two years in ten, the quality of the wine will suffer. The value of this association to the German wine world as a whole is that, after some difficulty, it has demonstrated that QbA in a not very fashionable part of the Mosel can be sold at a minimum price of DM 5.00 per bottle, if the quality is both good enough and consistent.

In the villages near Winningen many of the steep vineyards, abandoned in the 1970s, which are ideal for ripening Riesling, could well be replanted if the success of the Deutsches Eck association continues.

Producing the best possible wine in Germany requires technical expertise and total dedication. With little alcohol to fortify its structure, a light Mosel *Kabinett* wine can be almost ethereal in its delicacy, but without due care its charm goes, leaving it thin and ordinary. The expectation of a fair selling price for the successful wine is the best encouragement any wine-producer can have.

In the early 1990s it is still more profitable for most journeymen-growers to harvest larger quantities of Müller-Thurgau grapes than smaller amounts of Riesling from sloping vineyards, so, for them, the incentive to improve is missing. As a result Christoph Tyrell, of the Karthäuserhof estate in the Ruwer valley at the opposite end of the region, foresees a two-tier trade in Mosel wine developing. In his opinion there will be top wines which will be appreciated by the increasing number of quality-conscious Germans, and there will be the basic wines. In between, a vacuum will wait to be filled, perhaps by well-made QbA from good but not outstanding sites.

After Winningen there follows a succession of wine villages whose wines are seldom exported. They are usually cheaper than those of the Bereich Bernkastel and much is sold to passing tourists and loyal, private customers. The narrow village streets are attractive in summer, but space is short and gardens are small, and often immediately adjacent to vineyards. A road follows both banks of the river for most of the way, and it is intended that the existing cycle path should eventually run without a break from Koblenz to Trier.

Once the Mosel was known for its red wine and in recent years Spätburgunder and other red-grape varieties have been planted in some 21 hectares in a number of villages, including Pommern in the Bereich Zell. To be successful on the Mosel, Spätburgunder really needs to occupy a site that would suit Riesling well, and there is no doubt which vine produces the better wine in this northern climate. On the other hand, if a Mosel Spätburgunder can be sold as a curiosity at DM 8.00 per bottle or more, it could be an interesting sideline for a producer selling to the consumer.

Cochem, 51 kilometres from Koblenz, may have only 7,000 inhabitants, but a great inflow of well-behaved tourists from spring to late autumn keeps the cafés busy. There is much to see, besides the Burg or castle that overlooks the town, and the romantic Burg Eltz is not far away near Moselkern. Beilstein, upstream, is a charming, half-timbered village which lost a little of its rusticity to road construction and the replacement of orchards on the opposite bank of the Mosel by rather ordinary vineyards. Much of the wine from the new vineyards is sold under the *Grosslage* name of Ellenzer Goldbäumchen.

A few kilometres further along the Mosel, the composite village of Ediger-Eller enjoys a good reputation for its Riesling wine, and is also known for the sixteenth-century relief of *Christus in der Kelter* (Christ in the wine-press) in the Kreuz Kapellchen, the Chapel of the Cross, above the vineyards. The theme of Christ treading 'the wine-press alone' (Isaiah 63:3) recurs in German art from the twelfth century onwards.

Entering yet another of the Mosel's sharp bends, Germany's steepest vineyard, the Calmont, shared between the villages of Bremm and Eller, rises 200 metres above the river. A little further on, from the Marienberg, high above Alf on a pear-shaped promontory around which flows the Mosel, there are spectacular views of Zell and its *Bereich* and at Briedel, nearby, the Bereich Bernkastel begins.

BEREICH BERNKASTEL

The Bereich Bernkastel, also known as the Mittelmosel, shares with the Rheingau the distinction of having the greatest concentration of top-quality estates in Germany. In 1825 Anton Jordan of the export house of Deinhard wrote that it would be easy to acquire 'an excellent reputation' for Mosel wines, 'but only the best examples with fine aroma and taste are suitable for the British market'. Where cheap wines were required, Jordan's advice was to look to the Rheinpfalz. Today the way to find the best Mosel wine with 'aroma and taste' is to identify the top growers. The point here is that whereas every Brauneberger wine from an estate such as Weingut Fritz Haag will be good, not every wine sold as Brauneberger will be of the same standard. The geographical origin supplies the outline of the wine, but the estate is responsible for its quality.

Given a choice, and depending on the occasion, most wine-drinkers in Germany would probably select a medium-dry Mosel Riesling rather than a dry version. In spite of this, dry *Auslese* wines from good estates sell well, perhaps because they are still a novelty.

Although the good Weingut Selbach Oster at Zeltingen has been producing dry *Auslesen* since 1979, Carl von Schubert in the Ruwer valley points out that they are a recent invention. In the past such wines were probably sold as *Naturrein*, which meant that the alcohol in the wine derived solely from the grape. Recent invention or not, with the new-found German interest in drinking

95

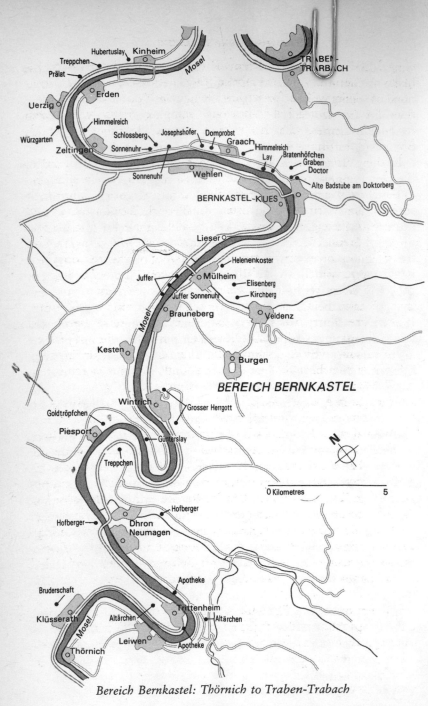

Bereich Bernkastel: Thörnich to Traben-Trabach

wine with food, the production of dry Mosel Riesling *Auslesen* is likely to continue – weather permitting. They have a greater likelihood of selling well, according to Weingut Dr Loosen at Bernkastel, than do the wonderfully luscious, complex, fruity wines with residual sweetness that have been associated with the Bereich Bernkastel for many years.

In their *Atlas van Rijn & Moezel Wijnen*, published in 1986, the Dutch authors Leenaers and Jorissen suggested a classification of the Mosel-Saar-Ruwer vineyards in three categories; four of the seven Grand Cru A came from the Bereich Bernkastel, as did thirteen of the eighteen Grand Cru B, and eighteen of the forty in the third Premier Cru category. Inevitably, some will disagree with the selection, or even with the idea of trying to classify vineyards in Germany, which are not themselves always homogeneous, but probably those without any commercial involvement would say that, the task being set, the Dutchman's choice was broadly fair. If there are thirty *Einzellagen* names in the Bereich Bernkastel worth classifying, perhaps that leaves the remaining sites to provide sound reasons why theirs should continue to be used for anything other than the best of their Riesling QmP. As was suggested in chapter 6, it is not only vines that need pruning.

Amongst the large wine-producing villages or small towns on the Mosel with the most land under vine are the Protestant enclaves surrounded by a Roman Catholic community, of Traben-Trabach and Reil. This unusual circumstance dates back to the sixteenth century when the Reformation arrived in villages under the control of the Protestant Sponheim family from the Hunsrück. The influence of the Roman Catholic Church on the wine of the Mosel is probably most often remembered by the edict of the Elector of Trier in 1787 that required inferior vines to be replaced by Riesling. Before the French Revolution, Benedictines, Carthusians and Dominicans all owned extensive vineyards between Graach and Trier, as site names such as Abtsberg* and Karthäuserhofberg† remind us.

The first of the villages with a reputation for world-class wine, passing upstream from Traben-Trabach, is Erden with its best vineyards on the opposite bank of the river. By the large and good

---

* 'The hill of the abbot'.
† 'The hill of the Carthusian estate'.

Erdener Treppchen there is the tiny Erdener Prälat *Einzellage*, one of the many exceptions to the EC rule that every named site should be at least 5 hectares in size. Erdener Prälat is one of the best *Einzellagen* in the Mosel-Saar-Ruwer, producing wines with 7–8° Oechsle (over 1° of alcohol) more than its neighbouring vineyards. It is often sold, unfortunately, under a colourful label in the worst *kitschig* tradition, depicting a prelate holding a glass of wine up to the light. Although the wine is expensive it does not suffer from the occasional inflationary tendencies of the even more famous Bernkasteler Doctor site.

At neighbouring Uerzig, the red soil from the Eifel combines with slate and clay to give a particular flavour to wines from its Würzgarten site. Between Zeltingen-Rachtig and Bernkastel-Kues the non-stop sweep of vines includes the best of Wehlen, and the slopes of Graach.

The Wehlener Sonnenuhr was officially registered as a 10-hectare site in 1913, but there is documentary evidence to show that vines were growing in Wehlen in the ninth century. Since 1913 Wehlener Sonnenuhr has spread to include parts of inferior vineyards, making a nonsense of the concept that wines from one *Einzellage* should be of similar quality. The growers in the best and original part of this outstanding site include, firstly, J. J. Prüm, then S. A. Prüm, Dr Loosen, and Wegeler-Deinhard.

At Bernkastel-Kues the population of 7,500 is probably enlarged by more visitors than any other town on the Mosel, and it is easy to understand why. Here spectacular vineyards, ancient half-timbered buildings, and generations of wine-making fulfil every expectation of what a wine town should be. The dominating vineyard is the 3.2-hectare Bernkasteler Doctor that rises directly from the rear of the town, the most important owners of which are Wegeler-Deinhard, the two Dr Thanisch estates, and Weingut Lauerburg. Doctor wines need time, perhaps ten years or more at *Kabinett* level, and longer still for *Auslesen* and above. When they are fine they are very, very fine, but when they are not, much cheaper wines from other sites can be more enjoyable.

A walk across the 210-metre bridge over the Mosel takes us firmly out of the time of the Brothers Grimm and into the world of the Zentralkellerei Bernkastel-Kues, otherwise known as Moselland eG. It is estimated that 40–5 per cent of wine from the Mosel-Saar-Ruwer is sold in bottle by the grower, 35–40 per cent by wine-merchants (who buy grapes, must and wine in bulk), and 20–5 per cent by Moselland eG, the central co-operative cellar for the region. In 1987 Moselland took in grapes from 5,200 of the 12,000 growers in the Mosel-Saar-Ruwer. It therefore has a heavy responsibility to the whole of the region to show the outside world how good its cheaper wines can be, notwithstanding Anton Jordan's preference for inexpensive Pfälzer wine mentioned earlier. Most of Moselland's wines are sold under *Grosslage* names and 40 per cent of its annual production is sent abroad. The need to export is pressing as the image of Mosel wine – not with the wine trade but with the consumer in Germany – is poor.

The cheapest end of the Mosel wine trade is represented by the *Weinkellereien* – the wine-merchants' cellars – which compete with Moselland. There is on the river a greater concentration of these large merchants' cellars than anywhere else in Europe. The size of the local harvest makes it understandable that, of a turnover of 61 million litres of a large *Kellerei* in Bernkastel-Kues in 1988, only 14 million litres came from the Mosel-Saar-Ruwer – the balance being made up largely of whatever was available cheaply elsewhere.

Leaving behind Bernkastel with its fine vineyards, and Kues across the river with its mammoth bottling lines, the top wine villages become more widely spaced out. Virtually all the good estates have holdings in more than one village and those of Weingut Max Ferd. Richter, for example, stretch from Traben-Trabach downstream, via Wehlen, Graach, Bernkastel, to Brauneberg, and back to the home village of Mülheim, and on to neighbouring vineyards at Veldenz and Burgen. Once one turns to the large estates based on Trier, the spread of vineyards becomes wider still.

The best-known *Einzellagen* on the stretch of river after Bernkastel are the Brauneberger Juffer and the Brauneberger Juffer Sonnenuhr, which have absorbed the Falkenberg, Bürgerslay and Hasenläufer sites.

Coming from a *Grosslage* of nearly 1,400 hectares, most Piesporter Michelsberg will have little to do with the great vineyards of Piesport, so to taste a top wine from the village itself try a Piesporter Goldtröpfchen from any of three Trier-based estates – Kesselstatt, Bischöfliche Weingüter, or Vereinigte Hospitien. The wine should be 'classy', well structured and 100 per cent Riesling. Unlike so many fine estate-bottled Mosels, amongst the fine wines of the world, Piesporter Goldtröpfchen is correctly priced and expensive, but it is possible to buy wines from other Mosel vineyards of similar value more cheaply.

After Piesport, Neumagen-Dhron can produce top-quality wine, and Trittenheimer Apotheke Riesling Kabinett, from the admirable Friedrich Wilhelm Gymnasium estate, offers high-class Mosel at a very reasonable price of less than DM 8.00 per bottle. If that part of the Bereich Bernkastel which is famous for fine wine starts to come to an end when Trittenheim is passed, there can always be surprises from steep vineyards at Klüsserath, Thörnich, Mehring or Longuich. Without Bernkastel, Wehlen and others in that rarefied circle, the 'lesser' villages of the Mosel would be better known. As Michelin would say, they are worth a détour.

BEREICH SAAR-RUWER

It would be easy to overlook the Ruwer valley. The river, hardly more than a small stream, carries the water from the high ground of the Hunsrück, through meadows bordered by steeply ascending vineyards, down to the Mosel. In the last twenty years some of the vines have given way to housing development, but the fine vineyards, and they really are of the highest quality, remain intact. Having found the minor road that leads up the valley, one comes to two of Germany's best-known estates: the Rautenstrauch'sche Weingutsverwaltung Karthäuserhof at Eitelsbach and the C. V. Schubert'sche Gutsverwaltung. Both produce wines that might be described as 'finely tuned', with an intense bouquet and the firm structure from the good acidity of ripe grapes.

Since the 1986 vintage, all the Karthäuserhof vineyards which previously sold their wines under five different site names have been combined into one 19-hectare *Einzellage*, the Eitelsbacher Karthäuserhofberg. Besides the marketing advantage that follows from having a simplified range to sell, producing wines from one composite site also helps the wine-maker. An estate can pick and process grapes only at a certain pace, so that the first of the crop may be too high in acid and the last too low. By blending the two together when necessary, Karthäuserhof can produce a balanced wine without having to consider chemical de-acidification.

In the thesis for which he was awarded a doctorate in agriculture, Dr Carl von Schubert examined the methods by which vines are grown on steep slopes. He concluded that training vines on wires, grown horizontally across terraces, offered an economically interesting alternative to the usual German practice of rows running vertically up the slopes. In the mid-1970s, 76 per cent of all vines in the Mosel-Saar-Ruwer were supported by individual posts, but von Schubert admitted that modern methods were often not introduced until a younger generation took over the vineyards. When this happened on the Karthäuserhofberg estate, every third row of vines was removed. The remaining vines – many of which were growing on their original root-stocks, as *phylloxera* has not progressed quickly in the region's slate soil – benefited at once. The amount of shade was reduced, the soil became warmer, and the air circulated more freely to produce a healthier crop. Elsewhere in the region other ways of training vines are on trial with an eye for economic and ecological advantages and a gain in quality.

If Karthäuserhof and von Schubert come to mind first when we think of Ruwer wine, the village of Kasel draws our attention thereafter. The Bischöfliche Weingüter, von Kesselstatt and Wegeler-Deinhard estates all have holdings in the Kaseler vineyards which can produce superb wines in good vintages. This is a comment which has often also been made about the best sites in the larger part of the *Bereich* near the River Saar.

In the archives of the Karthäuserhof there is an official opinion dated 1861, which was quoted by the authors Sauerwald and Wenzel in their *Könige des Riesling*. The Saar vineyards 'produce wines in very good vintages which surpass those of the Mosel'. Their style is positive, powerfully flavoured, with a strong backing of steely acidity, almost reminiscent of a top quality Alsatian Riesling from the Clos Ste-Hune. They have a similar pure, long-lasting flavour. In feeble vintages, Saar wine converts well into *Sekt* and Saar Riesling Sekt has enjoyed a good following for many years. To develop the market further a local *Sekt* producers' association, the Sekterzeugergemeinschaft Saar-Mosel, was formed in 1984. It is supplied with base wine by small vineyard owners in the Bereiche Saar-Ruwer and Obermosel, and makes Riesling and Elbling Sekte which sell successfully at over DM 12.00 per bottle.

The River Saar flows into the Mosel with some style and a wide sweep of water a few kilometres upstream from Trier. Apart from being an administrative centre for a quarter of the state of Rheinland-Pfalz, since the time of the Roman occupation, Trier has been

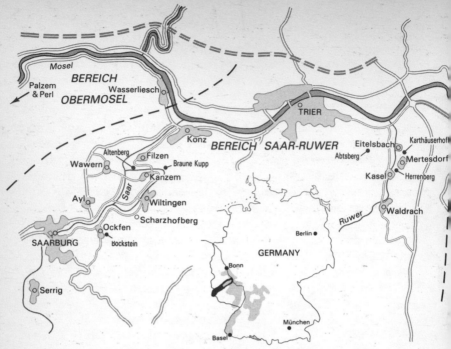

Mosel-Saar-Ruwer: Palzem to Erden

associated with the making and selling of wine – particularly, in the more recent past, on the export market. In 1983 the Chamber of Commerce and Industry reported that it had handled over 19,000 export documents covering 27.6 million bottles of wine, figures which arouse mixed feelings in non-bureaucrats, and which will certainly have increased in the intervening years.

The big estates of Trier have holdings on all three rivers, Mosel, Saar and Ruwer, as do the members of the *Grosser Ring*. This association of leading Riesling estates, dating from 1908, auctions its wine in Trier and has recently held an annual tasting in London. A high proportion of its estates are based on the Saar, whose scattered vineyards begin near Konz.

The first of the better-known villages moving upstream are Filzen and Kanzem with the steep Kanzemer Altenberg being one of the most famous sites. Wiltingen, with its particularly good Braune Kupp and Gottesfuss sites, has another outstanding vineyard that sells simply under its own name. The Scharzhofberg lies in a side valley away from the Saar. It is classified as an *Ortsteil*, a part of a larger community, and is sold without the usual accompanying

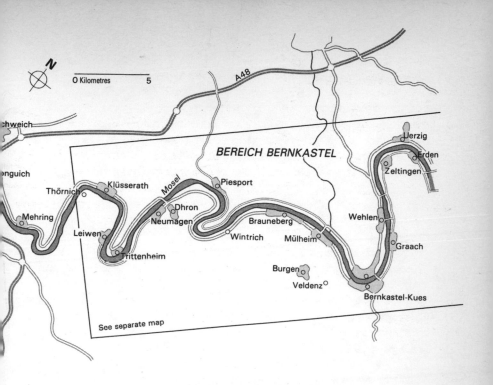

community name. Care has to be taken here, for the *Grosslage* covering the vineyards near the River Saar is 'Scharzberg' and a wine sold as Wiltinger Scharzberg should be sound, but a far cry from the glories of Wiltingen's *Ortsteil*, Scharzhofberg.

As usual, there are a number of estates with holdings in the Scharzhofberg vineyard, but the best known of them all, and probably the first amongst equals, is Weingut Egon-Müller-Scharzhof. The wines from the heart of the enlarged Scharzhofberg, owned by Egon Müller, have won prizes at international competitions for well over 100 years, but their distinction is far greater than that might imply. Like all good Saar wines, they are 100 per cent Riesling, concentrated, often with a slight sparkle. The long flavour from the decomposed Devonian slate, and the high acidity, is intense and truly impressive.

Ayl and Ockfen, on either side of the Saar, and Wawern up a side valley, produce great wines whenever the opportunity occurs, and after the hilly town of Saarburg, Serrig is the last top-quality wine-producing village on the Saar.

BEREICHE OBERMOSEL AND MOSELTOR

In the lower reaches of the Saar modern living has the upper hand over ancient rusticity, and Konz is described in *Das Deutsche Stadtlexikon*, published in 1981, as 'an aspiring, young, industrial town'. Here representatives of textile, building machinery and floor-tile manufacturers are more obvious than the labourer in the vineyard. Vine-growing is not a prosperous part-time occupation and so it is the upwardly mobile of industry who support one of the Mosel's few good restaurants with a worthy wine list – the Scheid at Wasserliesch.

Leaving the bustle behind and continuing up the River Mosel one enters the Bereich Obermosel. The countryside is rolling and rural and, above the vineyards, agricultural. Cocks still crow, and the midden is a feature of villages, put together again after the Second World War. One of the few wine properties of note is the ancient Schloss Thorn which, on 20 February 1945, was the site of a pitched battle between the advancing US 94th Reconnaissance Troop and the resisting Germans. A history of events at that time records that 'the Americans poured shells into the château and the surrounding buildings' in the morning, and 'at 2200 hrs the Germans deluged Thorn with a 120mm barrage' in reply. Restoration of the buildings may be completed by 1995 and, with humour, the owner, Freiherr von Hobe-Gelting, describes the Schloss as the 'biggest Elbling château in the world'. Usually Elbling in the Bereich Obermosel is the most unaristocratic of wines. H. Goethe (not to be confused with the earlier J. W. Goethe) described Elbling wine in his *Ampelographisches Wörterbuch* in 1876 as 'light, watery, and without bouquet' and Georg Scheu (the breeder of Scheurebe) characterizes the wine as 'poor, sour, thin, and without aroma'. Bearing in mind that Elbling produces a very large yield, one can imagine that without the benefit of modern wine-making it could be worth avoiding. As it is, Elbling today is a pleasant, honest, ordinary wine, a mini-Riesling without the style and quality of the 'King of the White Wines'.

An attempt has been made in the late 1980s to develop sales of a wine from the Mosel-Saar-Ruwer, based on Riesling, Müller-Thurgau, Elbling or Kerner. With a residual sugar content of 15–30 grams per litre and at least 7 g/l of total acid, *Moseltaler*, as it is called, is an alternative to Liebfraumilch, aimed at the under-forties. So far their response has been weak, and another 'concept' wine, *Riesling Hochgewächs*, is also selling slowly. This is a 100 per cent Riesling, quality wine with 10° more must weight (over 1.5°of potential alcohol) than a standard Riesling QbA, and which has to achieve at least 3 points at the examination at the official centre (see chapter 7). The Mosel-Saar-Ruwer produces 83 per cent of *Riesling Hochgewächs*. As 36 per cent of applications for *Hochgewächs* at the control centres fail, it suggests that the examination is severe and those that do reach the market should be well made, attractive wines. Whether there is a need in Germany for yet another category of wine is open to question.

The Bereiche Obermosel and Moseltor face Luxembourg across the river. The difference in the commercial success of vineyards separated by a few hundred metres of water is remarkable. The Luxembourgeois vineyard of a little over 1,300 hectares is similar in size to the Piesporter Michelsberg *Grosslage*. In general, its wines appear to have a little more sugar added to make them more alcoholic than is usual in Germany. They are dry and are bought by the Grand Duchy's polyglot inhabitants and visitors at comparatively high prices. With an annual Luxembourgeois wine consumption of over 50 litres per head per year (more than twice that of West Germany), there may be a lesson to be learnt by the hard-pressed *Moselle Allemande*.

It is curious that while most of the Mosel-Saar-Ruwer lies in the state of Rheinland-Pfalz, the tiny Bereich Moseltor forms part of the Saarland. It has a few estate bottlers, but the crop is processed mainly by Moselland eG in Bernkastel-Kues. In eastern Germany, where the annual wine consumption is roughly 9 litres per head, every fifth bottle comes from the Bereich Moseltor via Moselland, and this connection with Eastern Europe is being widened to include other countries. The export market is important to all producers of inexpensive Mosel wine.

Some recommended producers in the Bereich Zell

Weingut Eduard Bremm, 5581 Neef, Moseluferstrasse 4: a source of fully fermented, 100 per cent Riesling wines.

Edward Theod. Drathen GmbH & Co. Kg, 5584 Alf, Postfach 41: important export house with annual turnover in excess of 16 million bottles. Own good estate-bottled wines.

Weingut Josef Friedrich, 5583 Zell-Kaimt, Marientaler Au 50: prize winning estate bottlers and merchants.

Weingut Reinhold Fuchs, 5593 Pommern, Bahnhofstrasse 37: cask-matured Riesling from steep vineyards.

Weingut von Heddesdorff, 5406 Winningen, Haus Heddesdorff: 100 per cent Riesling wines. Mainly dry or medium-dry.

Weingut Heyman-Löwenstein, 5406 Winningen, Bahnhofstrasse 10: 100 per cent Riesling estate, rapidly gaining fame.

Weingut Freiherr von Landenberg, 5591 Ediger-Eller, Moselweinstrasse 60: Part-owners of the Eller Calmont. 95 per cent Riesling.

Weingut Heinrich Mayer, 5583 Zell, Jakobstrasse 64: 80 per cent Riesling, small, family-run estate.

Freiherr von Schleinitz'sche Weingutsverwaltung, 5401 Kobern-Gondorf, Kirchstrasse 15–17: leading Bereich Zell estate. 98 per cent Riesling.

Zimmermann-Graef GmbH & Co. Kg. 5583 Zell, Marientaler Au, Postfach 1128: very large wine-merchants with vineyard holdings in Zell.

Some recommended producers in the Bereich Bernkastel

(R) = additional holdings on the Ruwer
(S) = additional holdings on the Saar

Verwaltung der Bischöflichen Weingüter, 5500 Trier, Gervasiusstrasse 1, Postfach 1326: famous combination of several estates with ecclesiastical origins covering over 100 hectares, almost 100 per cent Riesling. (R) (S)

Stiftung Staatl. Friedrich-Wilhelm-Gymnasium, 5500 Trier, Weberbach 75: an important source of marvellously true-to-type Riesling wines. (S)

Weingut Grans-Fassian, 5559 Leiwen, Römerstrasse 28: excellent seventeenth-century family estate. Showing the 'green' thinking of many modern wine-makers.

Weingut Fritz Haag, 5551 Brauneberg, Dusemonder Hof: small, but absolutely top-quality estate. Elegant, distinguished wines.

Weingut Reichsgraf von Kesselstatt, 5500 Trier, Liebfrauenstrasse 10: vast combination of several estates of the highest quality with holdings in leading villages. (R) (S)

Weingut St Johannishof, Dr Loosen, 5550 Bernkastel, Postfach 1308: family estate run with total dedication. Outstanding wines.

Weingut Mönchhof–Robert Eymael, 5564 Uerzig: 100 per cent Riesling estate. Top-quality wines.

Weingut Dr Pauly-Bergweiler, 5500 Bernkastel-Kues, Gestade 15: beautifully fresh, often slightly *spritzig* wines.

Weingut Joh. Jos. Prüm, 5550 Bernkastel-Wehlen, Uferallee 19: medium-size but absolutely top-quality estate. Possibly the finest wines in the Bereich Bernkastel.

Weingut S. A. Prüm Erben, 5550 Bernkastel-Wehlen, Uferallee 25–6: 100 per cent Riesling estate. First-class wines.

Weingutsverwaltung Richtershof, 5556 Mülheim, Hauptstrasse 81–3: excellent wines, 90 per cent Riesling.

Weingut Max Ferd. Richter, 5556 Mülheim, Hauptstrasse 37; top-quality, well-differentiated wines of character.

Weingut Geschwister Selbach-Oster, 5553 Zeltingen, Uferallee 23: 100 per cent Riesling well-made wines of character and style.

Verwaltung der Staatlichen Weinbaudomänen, 5550 Trier, Deworastrasse 1: four estates produce wines to very high standards. (S)

Vereinigte Hospitien, 5500 Trier, Krahnenufer 19: great estate, with holdings in top sites in many villages. (S)

Gutsverwaltung Wegeler-Deinhard, 5550 Bernkastel-Kues, Martertal 2: source of good, firm Riesling wines, relishing bottle age. (R)

Some recommended estates in the Bereich Saar-Ruwer

RUWER

Weingut Karlsmühle, 5501 Mertesdorf: family-run estate and hotel. Excellent value-for-money Rieslings.

Rautenstrauch'sche Weingutsverwaltung Karthäuserhof, 5500 Trier-Eitelsbach Karthäuserhof: estate of ancient origins once more producing great wines.

C. v. Schubert'sche Gutsverwaltung, 5501 Grünhaus bei Trier: very distinguished property. Outstanding Riesling wines.

Additional Ruwer estates are listed under Bereich Bernkastel.

SAAR

Weingüter Dr Fischer, 5511 Ockfen – Wawern, Bocksteinhof: steely, well-structured, elegant wines.

Weingut Forstmeister Geltz Zilliken, 5510 Saarburg, Heckingstrasse 20: fine, firm wines, typical of the Saar

Weingut von Hövel, 5503 Konz-Oberemmel, Agritiusstrasse 5–6: characterful, fine wines of outstanding quality.

Weingut Egon Müller-Scharzhof, 5511 Wiltingen-Scharzhof: probably best-known Saar estate. Powerful, fine wines live up to their reputation.

Weingut Oekonomierat Piedmont, 5503 Konz-Filzen, Saartal 1: 100 per cent Riesling estate. Top-quality wine-making.

Weingut Edmund Reverchon, 5503 Konz-Filzen, Saartalstrasse 3: interesting wines from a range of vineyards. Largely dry or medium dry.

Weingut Schloss Saarstein, 5512 Serrig: steely excellent-quality Riesling wines.

Weingut Bert Simon, 5512 Serrig über Saarburg: large estate. Outstanding Saar wines. Further holdings on the Ruwer.

16
Nahe

Area under vine in hectares in 1988: 4,579 ha, planted 25.9 per cent Müller-Thurgau, 23.2 per cent Weisser Riesling, 12.0 per cent Silvaner, 8.3 per cent Kerner, 6.9 per cent Scheurebe, and 23.7 per cent others.

Average temperature during period of vegetation:	14.6°C
Average sunshine hours during period of vegetation:	1,206
Average rainfall during period of vegetation:	343mm
Average annual rainfall:	520mm
Recent vintages in million hectolitres:	1985 0.26, 1986 0.36, 1987 0.36, 1988 0.34, 1989 0.49
Average yield in hectolitres per hectare:	1978–87 82.9 hl/ha

It is perfectly possible to persuade yourself that the River Nahe produces the finest Riesling wines in the Rheinland and, therefore, in the world. The best are exquisitely tuned and a sheer delight, quite different to the robust wines of southern lands, which can seem gross and unrefined in comparison. That is a biased view which comes from the daily and exclusive tasting of fine Nahe Riesling, with no other wine to balance the judgement. Introduce the best of the Rheingau, and the perspective alters somewhat, for if the Nahe pins its reputation on its delicacy, the Rheingau wine, at its finest, has a little more substance and is probably, therefore, the better wine.

The River Nahe, 116 kilometres long, rises in hilly country below Birkenfeld and the A62 motorway. After flowing through Idar Oberstein and Kirn, on the edge of the Hunsrück, the first vine-yards begin at Martinstein. Thereafter they are scattered through-out a wide area, both north and south of the river, with the better-known sites being closest to its banks. At Bingen in the

Rheinhessen, the Nahe joins the Rhein directly opposite the vine-yards of Rüdesheim in the Rheingau.

The Nahe is a dry region; in some years even too dry. The clouds from the west rise over the heights of the Hunsrück and, having done so, release their rain on the woods below. Here the annual rainfall is double that of the neighbouring Nahe valley, where the vineyards have been planted not in any orderly, continuous pattern, but wherever the soil and micro-climate have shown that grapes are a good crop to grow. Roughly a quarter of the vineyards have an inclination of more than 20 per cent, and many, such as the Schlossböckelheimer Kupfergrube, are considerably steeper. Ries-ling tolerates drought better than most vines and excels in the steep slopes, where the reputation of the best Nahe wine has been made.

A glance at the figures at the start of this chapter shows that Riesling does not occupy even a quarter of the vineyard area and, as in the Rheinhessen, the top wines represent a very small proportion of the total production. On average, about 70 per cent of Nahe wine is sold as QbA, which, of course, can range from rather ordinary quality to excellent, stylish wines from good pro-ducers. Much is sold under *Grosslage* names, with that of Rüdes-heimer Rosengarten (not to be confused with the Rüdesheim in the Rheingau) being the best known. As in many places in Ger-many, and elsewhere in this book, the use of *Grosslage* names has been criticized, but it must be said that the present structure for naming German wines is an improvement on its predecessor, which was current until 1971. In those days, before the creation of EEC Wine Law, the *Gattungslage* name for a wine had an even wider base than that offered by the *Grosslage*. Taking an historical view we can see the *Grosslage* as a stage in the slowly increasing control in the identification of German wine. The process will continue but the present situation remains unsatisfactory when a Burg Layer Schlossberg comes from an *Einzellage* in the Nahe of some 21 hectares, and a Burg Layer Schlosskapelle is a wine from a *Gross-lage* of over 700 hectares. Life was indeed simpler when wine was named after the market at which it was sold. This, in the Nahe valley, would usually have been Kreuznach.

Basic Nahe wine tastes rather like its opposite number in the Rheinhessen. The very cheapest, such as the 1987 Bereich Kreuznach offered at a retail price of DM 1.98 per bottle before Christmas 1989, cannot be expected to taste of anything very

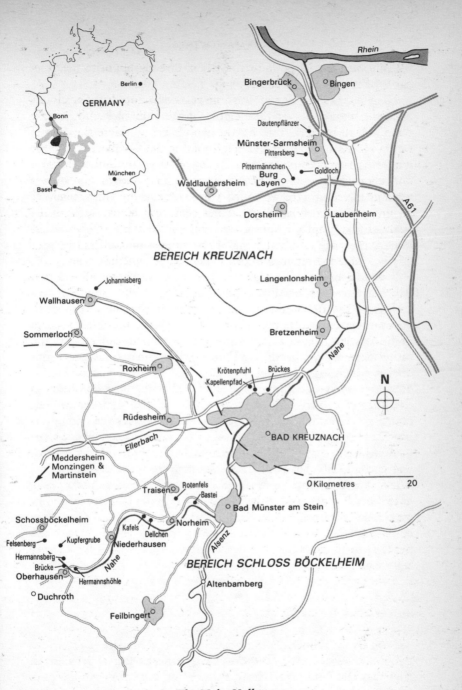

The Nahe Valley

III

much. However, a sound, medium-sweet Rüdesheimer Rosengarten QbA, made from Silvaner and Müller-Thurgau, should have some of the flavour that comes from the varied soils. Wine of this quality can make respectable Liebfraumilch, although the amount of wine from the Nahe sold under this name (perhaps 3 per cent of the whole) is minute compared to that produced in the Rheinhessen and Rheinpfalz.

The very cheapest wines lack the body and flavour to be sold without the improving effect of some sweetness, but, in general, the consumer who likes his wine dry, or thinks he does, is willing to pay a more sensible (i.e. slightly higher) price for it. At present, some 21 per cent of the volume of the Nahe wine harvest of about 4 million dozen bottles is offered as 'dry'. The better versions can only come from a low yield, but that is not difficult to achieve in the relatively rainless local climate.

In 1834 Johann Bronner wrote flatteringly of the intelligence of the vineyard-owners in the area of Kreuznach, the principal town of the region. (This was not routine flattery, for Bronner found the Mosel vine-growers distinctly backward, if not bone-headed, and he was critical of their performance.) Some of the descendants of the wise men of Kreuznach (the 'Bad', indicating a spa, was added later) are still in business and a number of wine-making families can trace their origins back to the eighteenth century or even earlier. In 1990 the seven members of the Nahe branch of the Verband Deutscher Prädikatsweingüter, all with important estates, feel that good Nahe wine is undervalued and underpriced, compared to equivalent wine from the Rheingau. This would appear to be so, and outside Germany little of the best Nahe wine is found other than that from Bad Kreuznach and from a few villages further upstream. The Untere Nahe, or, as it is officially called, the Bereich Kreuznach, starts at Bingerbrück and from this point it is not long before we come to top-quality vineyards.

BEREICH KREUZNACH

Nearly twenty years ago, the Nahe valley ceased to be a relatively unknown backwater. As it dives down from the eastern side of the Hunsrück and into the flatter land of the Rheinhessen, the new A61 motorway gives a fleeting glance of the Nahe. Seen from the

A61 and travelling in the direction of Ludwigshafen, the first vines appear at Waldlaubersheim. Burg Layen follows, and then the two important Dorsheim vineyards of Goldloch and Pittermännchen. Perhaps the best way to discover the taste of the good wines of this part of the lower Nahe is to visit the Staatliche Weinbaudomäne at Niederhausen in the Bereich Schlossböckelheim. Here a direct comparison can be made with those from other parts of the region, in which the state cellars also have holdings. The wines of Dorsheim and Münster-Sarmsheim are less refined than those of Niederhausen, but they fill the mouth with flavour.

At Burg Layen there is the substantial 34-hectare estate of Dr J. Höfer, whose wines are found outside Germany, and Weingut Michael Schäfer, a name well established in the United Kingdom. Also, there is the 12-hectare estate of Schlossgut Diel, now one of the best-known addresses in Germany for dry white wine.

Armin Diel operates in a manner similar to that of a private estate in Alsace, offering his wines simply as 'Schlossgut Diel', followed by the grape name. Although its constituents may come from different sites, the standard range is blended into one cuvée, according to the vine variety. Only the finest wines from the best vineyards are vinified individually and kept apart. All wines, other than those from the sweetest grapes in great vintages, are enriched (have sugar added to them in the French manner) and, having been fermented until they are dry, they are sold as QbA or as table wine. Their selling prices the estate would doubtless describe as 'good'. Where necessary wines are matured in new wood, in casks of 220 or 300 litres made in Cognac from Allier oak. In spite of the many innovations at Schlossgut Diel – perhaps 'revolutions' would be a better word – the estate does not indulge in outré labels or unusually shaped bottles, and its estate-bottled Riesling wine has been particularly successful in the restaurant trade in Germany. The ultimate and probably unachievable aim of Armin Diel is to produce one wine only each year. Other Nahe growers have moved a little in the same direction by simplifying their wine lists, but many of the conservative private customers prefer to buy wines with the individual site names to which they have long been accustomed.

In *Die Nahe*, published by the Seewald Verlag in 1979, we can read that 'the late picking of the grapes is a precondition today for the production of Germany quality wine'. Just over ten years later, German wine has seemingly gone through a U-turn in order to produce clear, crisp, dry wine, and Diel tells its customers that 'the longer one leaves the grapes on the vine, the greater is the danger of a natural breakdown of acidity and the development of unwanted rot'. In fact, a fruity, cleanly flavoured ripe acidity has long been a characteristic of good Nahe wine, as samples from the past can demonstrate. It is perhaps surprising that from apparently contradictory ideas so many high-quality wines emerge.

The vineyards adjacent to the river are easy to find, but to track down the outlying wine villages to the north, the *Nahewein Strasse* is helpful. It can be picked up at Burg Layen near the A61 motorway and, followed in an anti-clockwise direction, it will take you into country where, without its help, you would risk becoming lost.

The clockwise direction, parallel to the Nahe, leads directly to Bad Kreuznach, passing through Laubenheim, Langenlonsheim and Bretzenheim on the way. At Laubenheim, the small Weingut Michael Klören sells most of its wines under the village and grape name only. Unlike Schlossgut Diel, Klören leaves the young wines on the yeast from the fermentation, to gain flavour until after Christmas. They are matured in bottle for at least a year before being offered to the private clientele. At Langenlonsheim, Weingut Erbhof Tesch, now in its ninth generation, is one of the largest owners of vineyards and agricultural land in the region. Three-quarters of the 38 hectares under vine are planted in Riesling, and tended on biological lines, with the minimum use of insecticides and fungicides. The largest share of sales goes directly to the consumer, with 70 per cent of the cleanly made, fresh white wines being dry.

At Bretzenheim on the outskirts of Bad Kreuznach are the central cellars of the co-operative movement (the Nahe-Winzer Kellereien), which receive grapes, or wine from other co-operative cellars, throughout the whole of the Nahe region. The share of Riesling and Silvaner amounts to 20 per cent each, and although the grocery stores in Germany are its largest customer, the United Kingdom and The Netherlands also take considerable quantities of its inexpensive wines.

Much of the area in which the vineyards of the Bereich Kreuznach lie is given over to general farming or forestry. The villages to the north, linked by the *Nahewein Strasse*, are attractively rustic.

There are few large wine estates, but the Prinz zu Salm-Dalberg'sches Weingut in the village of Wallhausen is a member of the Verband Deutscher Prädikatsweingüter. The Salm wines are mainly dry, about two-thirds are Riesling, and the holdings are scattered throughout Dalberg, Roxheim, Sommerloch and Wallhausen itself.

The relatively small size of the Nahe makes it possible to gain an oversight of the region quickly, even if the outer edges obstinately refuse to come into focus. Detailed information about the many estates which welcome visitors is available from Weinland Nahe eV in Bad Kreuznach. They are found throughout the region, but it is the central part of the Nahe which attracts the attention of most people. Here the greatest volume of world-class wine is made and it begins in Bad Kreuznach, where vines have grown since the ninth century.

If the region as a whole was less known before it was connected to the motorway system via the A61, Bad Kreuznach has attracted visitors, searching for health and relaxation, since the eighteenth century. Most of the town lies on the right bank of the Nahe where the vineyards meet their neighbours in the Rheinhessen. Although these sites on the edge of the region are south to south-west facing, their reputation does not stand so high as that of the best vineyards on the opposite bank of the river, where Riesling predominates.

Bad Kreuznach and its suburbs have over 1,100 hectares under vine with some of the top sloping sites, such as Brückes, Kahlenberg, Krötenpfuhl or St Martin, being nearest to the town. Kreuznacher Brückes, a steep site of about 19 hectares, is well known for its ability to produce 'classic' Kreuznacher wines – in other words, fresh Rieslings, with a pronounced fruity bouquet. This natural, invigorating style is encouraged by slow fermentation at a low temperature, followed by a period in well-seasoned oak casks – minimum size, 600 litres. In 1947, the state-owned viticultural institute at Bad Kreuznach, which has 22 hectares under vine, developed the technique of controlling the progress of white-wine fermentation in tank by the use of carbon dioxide. Apart from making it easier to produce wines with a predetermined amount of their own natural sugar, the carbon dioxide emphasized their inherent freshness. Nowadays sweetness is less in demand in Germany, but a very slight prickle from the fermentation, provided it is not too obtrusive, can be most attractive in good wines of QbA or *Kabinett* quality from the Nahe and other northern wine regions. An essential element in the style of *spritzig* German wine is a good level of acidity, as is found in Rieslings. Where a wine is medium-sweet and the acidity is low, it is not necessarily improved by the marked liveliness of carbon dioxide. Contrariwise, a dry white wine with little character or acidity, such as a basic Swiss wine from the Chasselas grape, can be more appealing through being slightly *spritzig*.

Bad Kreuznach has many private estates within its boundaries, with three of the largest being amongst the best. The 51 hectares of Weingut Reichsgraf von Plettenberg concentrate on Riesling (60 per cent) and on the Burgunder varieties, the Pinot family of vines. In 1989 von Plettenberg held a tasting of *Spitzenweine*, top wines, going back to the 1921 Winzenheimer Rosenheck Riesling Trockenbeerenauslese. On some German occasions there is a tendency to overpraise old wines, a form of *vieillesse oblige* perhaps, but if so, this was not one of them, and Riesling showed its near immortality.

The Anheusers form the greatest wine dynasty in Bad Kreuznach. Since 1869, in other words in its relatively recent history, it has run two separate estates, Weingut Paul Anheuser and Weingut Oekonomierat August E. Anheuser. Both produce excellent wine, and confusingly have separate holdings in at least eight of the same Kreuznacher sites. The Paul Anheuser estate is the largest in the Nahe, with 55 of a total 76 hectares of vineyard in production. The holdings stretch as far upstream as Monzingen and most are on south-facing slopes. Paul Anheuser exports a larger share of its production than most Nahe estates and only 10 per cent is bought by private customers 'from the cellar door'.

Weingut Oekonomierat August E. Anheuser has 52 hectares under vine, including the sole ownership of the 3-hectare Kreuznacher Steinberg, near the village of Winzenheim. Via its merchant business, Anheuser & Fehrs, it has been selling wines from other regions of Germany for over 100 years.

Both Anheuser estates are members of the Verband Deutscher Prädikatsweingüter (the 'VDP') which holds an auction in Bad Kreuznach every June. As always in Germany, only brokers may bid, and before a wine is put for sale it is tasted by all present. The auction lost support some years ago, but the VDP now sees it as a public platform around which other events to promote Nahe wine can be created.

Minor differences between wines are usually more interesting to the enthusiast than those that result from different vine varieties grown under varied climatic conditions. That is the attraction of a large tasting devoted to wines from one small region, as the Bad Kreuznach wine auction regularly shows.

BEREICH SCHLOSS BÖCKELHEIM

Five kilometres upstream from Bad Kreuznach is the small and attractive spa of Bad Münster am Stein-Ebernburg, overlooked by three massive outcrops of porphry rock. The Rheingrafenstein and the Gans are on the right bank of the Nahe and across the river the Rotenfels rises a sheer 214 metres. As the guidebooks never fail to tell us, it is the highest rock face in Germany north of the Alps. At its foot there is the small Traiser Bastei vineyard, littered with fragments from the rockface above. In this site Weingut Hans & Peter Crusius produces steely Riesling wines with great depth of flavour from a low yield. They have an unmistakable but hard-to-define stamp of authority, and the demand for the 1989 Traiser Bastei Riesling Auslese Trocken at DM 19.00 per bottle is so great that Crusius is obliged to ration the wine amongst the regular, private customers. Demand does not often exceed supply so convincingly in Germany.

All the most famous villages of this stretch of the Nahe fall within the *Grosslage* Burgweg, including some less well known in the valley of the Alsenz which joins the Nahe at Bad Münster. Were it not for the holdings of the State Cellars, the wines of Altenbamberg would probably be as unfamiliar as those of so many of the villages away from the proximity of the Nahe. The state's 7 hectares of Altenbamberger Rotenberg produce characterful Riesling wines that have improved their position in the price lists of the Weinbaudomäne over the years.

Turning back to the Nahe, the Weinstrasse passes through Norheim, where the bend of the river repeats the scenery of the Rotenfels in a less dramatic way. Norheimer Kirscheck, Dellchen and Kafels are all good Riesling sites, with firm, slightly earthy, full-bodied wines.

With the move to less residual sugar in all wines, the grower has to guard against losing his sense of direction and even his identity. His problem is that his experiments, which take place in public, can also be an inevitably delayed reaction to what may be only a whim of fashion. In the past the idea has been accepted that Riesling wines improve with bottle age, and so they do. Unfortunately, increased age has not been accompanied by a simultaneous appreciation in the market price, although improvement in quality has not been disputed. The drier versions of today reach their peak of quality as quickly as do most dry wines elsewhere in the world. For dry Riesling QbA, this means two years or so after the vintage, while dry Riesling *Spät-* or *Auslesen* should normally be drunk within eight years of the vintage, if they are not to lose their elegance. How long a wine stays at its best is not of direct commercial interest to many good Riesling estates selling to the consumer, as within eighteen months of the grapes being gathered the vintage will have been sold.

For Nahe wines, ancient and modern – in other words medium-sweet, medium-dry or dry – the Staatliche Weinbaudomäne at Niederhausen is still an outstandingly good source. Some would go further and say it is the finest wine estate in Germany. When it was founded in 1902 the territory on the left bank, the Niederhausen side, of the Nahe, belonged to Prussia. The land to the south, on the right bank, was Bavarian, as a plaque by the Oberhausen bridge across the Nahe below the Domäne makes clear. The Königlich-Preussische Weinbaudomäne Niederhausen-Schlossböckelheim is today owned by the state of Rheinland-Pfalz. Its wines bear a label showing a stylized Prussian eagle, as do other cellars formerly in Prussian state-ownership, such as the Staatliche Weinbaudomäne at Eltville (Rheingau), now in the state of Hessen.

The setting for the Domäne Niederhausen on its promontory looking up the Nahe is perfect and peaceful. The woods above the vineyards on both sides of the river are filled with game and for those better informed than the writer there are interesting examples of flora and unusual fauna. Many of the smaller estates in this area, which sell directly to the consumer, still produce more medium-sweet than drier wines. An exception is Weingut Hermann Dönnhof at Oberhausen which has a reputation for dry wines of a very high standard from a wide variety of soils.

Looking at a vineyard map of 1901 there is a gap between

Niederhäuser Steinberg and Schlossböckelheimer Felsenberg, where in the early part of this century convicts were used to clear the steep, rocky scrubland as well as the site of an old copper (*Kupfer*) mine. This became the Kupfergrube vineyard, the best parts of which are owned by the State Cellars.

Beyond Oberhausen and the Domäne, the Schlossböckelheimer Felsenberg, Mühlberg and Königsfels *Einzellagen* run down steeply to the Nahe and the railway that leads eventually to Saarbrücken. No other villages or vineyards upstream from Schlossböckelheim are widely known but Monzingen, an old village of half-timbered houses, and Meddersheim have a good local reputation for their wines. At Meddersheim there is the Winzergenossenschaft Rheingrafenberg, a co-operative cellar receiving grapes from about 150 hectares which include some distant vineyards in the Kreuznacher Kronenberg *Grosslage*. These cellars have a history of success in the DLG national wine competitions and were amongst the first in recent times to produce dry wines. They are also a good source of Nahe sparkling wine.

If the proposed motorway is built, linking the Rheinhessen with the Mosel and beyond, the western end of the Bereich Schloss Böckelheim, the Obere Nahe, will become less isolated. Perhaps the loss of rural charm will be offset by interested wine-buying visitors from the central Rhein area.

Some recommended producers in the Nahe

Weingut Oekonomierat August E. Anheuser, 6550 Bad Kreuznach, Brückes 53: justly famous, 80 per cent Riesling estate.

Weingut Paul Anheuser, 6550 Bad Kreuznach, Stromberger Strasse 15–19: large estate. Excellent, fresh, slowly fermented wines.

Weingut Reinhard Beck, 6553 Meddersheim, Oberer Winkel 1: mainly medium-sweet wines. Very successful in DLG tastings.

Weingut Bischof-Klein, 6551 Bretzenheim, Naheweinstrasse 62: known for wines with natural residual sugar. Dry wines also win prizes.

Weingut Hans & Peter Crusius, 6551 Traisen, Hauptstrasse 2: high-quality estate. Famous for well-differentiated Riesling wines.

Schlossgut Diel, 6531 Burg Layen, Hauptstrasse: well-publicized source of a restricted range of top-quality Nahe dry wines.

Weingut Hermann Dönnhoff, 6551 Oberhausen, Bahnhofstrasse 11: outstanding dry wines, but medium-sweet Rieslings also win prizes.

Weingut Emrich-Schönleber, 6557 Monzingen, Naheweinstrasse 10: good Riesling estate, mainly supplying the German consumer.

Weingut Carl Finkenauer, 6550 Bad Kreuznach, Salinenstrasse 60: many wine varieties. Proportion of Riesling increasing. Dry, cask-matured wines up to *Auslese* level.

Weingut Dr J. Höfer, 6531 Burg Layen, Schlossmühle, Naheweinstrasse 2: 34-hectare estate concentrating on Riesling and Silvaner, offering a wide range of wine and *Sekt*.

Weingut F. W. Jung. 6539 Waldalgesheim, Ernst-Esch-Strasse 4: interesting range from a variety of wine-making methods.

Weingut Klören, 6531 Laubenheim, Am Steinkreuz 17: new and very successful estate. Many vine varieties in addition to Riesling.

Weingut Kruger-Rumpf, 6538 Münster-Sarmsheim, Rheinstrasse 47: a rapidly increasing reputation for true-to-type but individual wines.

Weingut Adolf Lötzbeyer, 6767 Feilbingert, Kirschstrasse 6: highly successful, prizewinning medium-sweet wines.

Weingut Reichsgraf von Plettenberg, 6550 Bad Kreuznach, Winzenheimer Strasse: leading Nahe estate. Classic Rieslings and Burgunder (Pinot) wines.

Weingut Alfred Porr, 6551 Duchroth, Schlosstrasse 1: excellent, inexpensive, Riesling, Silvaner, and Müller-Thurgau wines.

Winzergenossenschaft Rheingrafenberg eG, 6553 Meddersheim, Naheweinstrasse 63: co-operative cellar selling all its well-made wine in bottle.

Prinz zu Salm-Dalberg'sches Weingut, 6511 Wallhausen, Schloss: ancient estate in an outlying area, likely to become much better known.

Weingut Michael Schäfer, 6531 Burg Layen, Hauptstrasse 15: vines from many different vine varieties, made to last.

Weingut Jakob Schneider, 6551 Niederhausen, Winzerstrasse 15: 96 per cent Riesling estate. Well-made wines from good sites.

Weingut Bürgermeister Willi Schweinhardt Nachf. 6536 Langenlonsheim, Heddesheimer Strasse 1: important, marketing-oriented estate. High-class, prizewinning wines.

Verwaltung der Staatlichen Weinbaudomänen Niederhausen-Schlossböckelheim, 6551 Oberhausen: superb, large, mainly Riesling estate, selling to the wine trade and the consumer.

Staatsweingut, 6550 Bad Kreuznach, Rüdesheimer Strasse 68: teaching institute with many vine varieties, selling 90 per cent to the consumer.

Weingut Erbhof Tesch, 6536 Langenlonsheim, Naheweinstrasse 99: ancient estate with modern ideas. Clean, well-defined, top-quality wines.

17
Rheingau

Area under vine in hectares in 1988: 2,904 ha, planted 81.7 per cent Weisser Riesling, 6.7 per cent Blauer Spätburgunder, 4.5 per cent Müller-Thurgau, and 7.1 per cent others.

Average temperature during period of vegetation:	14.7°C
Average sunshine hours during period of vegetation:	1,316
Average rainfall during period of vegetation:	343mm
Average annual rainfall:	536mm
Recent vintages in million hectolitres:	1985 0.18, 1986 0.24, 1987 0.19, 1988 0.22, 1989 0.32
Average yield in hectolitres per hectare:	1978–87 77.2 hl/ha

All the vineyards of the Rheingau are in the Bereich Johannisberg. Thus the region and the district cover the same area on the ground.

To a tidy mind it may seem a pity that the Rheingau is severed by the conurbation of Wiesbaden and Mainz. East of the dividing line there is the diaspora of the Rheingau and one of the region's largest wine villages. Hochheim, beloved, like most things Rhenish, by Britain's Queen Victoria, is surrounded at a discreet distance by the spread of industry and commerce. The vineyards, running down to the River Main, are nearer the centre of Mainz than they are to the main body of the Rheingau, and the pastoral scene of nineteenth-century engravings is tarnished by urban development. As a compensation, the 2.6 million people living in the Rhein-Main area provide a solid base of customers for Rheingau wine.

Good producers take an individual approach to their wine-making, based on the differences that start in the vineyard, but when it comes to selling, many in the Rheingau share a common policy. From the prosperous business world of Mainz, Wiesbaden and Frankfurt, the 'collecting private customer' fills his car at the cellar door and some estates look for no other outlets for their wines. The consumption in the region itself may be restricted by the laws on drinking and driving, but the 'take-home' trade is formidable. For those who are free to enjoy the wine away from the safety of their homes, the *Amt für Fremdenverkehr des Rheingau Taunus-Kreises* recommends forty-nine wine bars not yet 'discovered by the tourists', where a good range of wines can be tasted.

Besides Hochheim, the villages best known for their wines outside Germany lie in a consolidated middle section of the region, between Walluf and Rüdesheim. The vineyards stretch 3 kilometres or so from the Rhein, starting at a height of about 80 metres above sea-level and climbing up to a little over 200 metres at the edge of extensive woods.

The Rheingau lies in the state of Hessen, while the Rheinhessen across the river belongs to Rheinland-Pfalz. It is no surprise to learn that Hessen is the most wooded of all the *Länder* (states), and the forests date from the end of the Ice Age. If the 1,900-year-old vineyards seem relatively new in comparison, the conifers did not reach the Rheingau woods until the 1820s, perhaps in anticipation of the demand for Christmas trees. In all events, the appeal of the woods to the Germans is even greater than that of the vineyards, as the nineteenth-century poet Julius Hammer realized when he wrote 'O Wald . . . *wie gleichst du den deutschen Gemüt*' – 'Oh forest, how like you are to the German spirit'. Soulmates of the estate-owners or not, the woods often make an impact on the vines, protecting them, by chance or design, from the winds of middle Europe. As J. B. Sturm wrote in his book *Rheinwein* in 1882, nobody understands how to use what nature has given them better than the Rheingauers. The efficiency of their green fingers, however, was somewhat reduced at the harvest by the viscosity of overripe grapes, which could only be eased from the vine with the aid of a fork. This picture of sticky fruitfulness ignores the years when extreme weather (which today would be associated with the greenhouse effect) upset the growers' calculations. A booklet produced by the village of Walluf to mark its 1,200th anniversary in 1979 tells of waggons, loaded with 2.5 tons of goods, being hauled across the frozen Rhein in 1845 and 1848. (The absence of bridges over the Rhein, both then and now, would make this less of a pointless exercise than it might seem.) On 18 April 1847

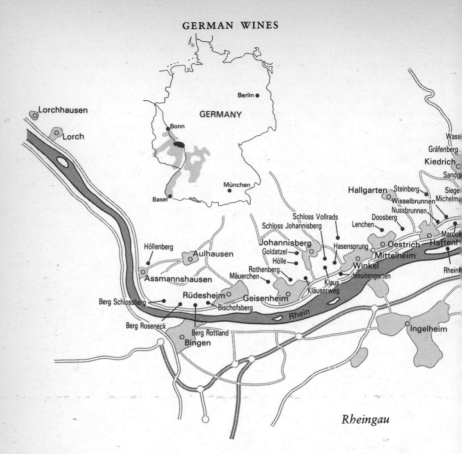

Rheingau

the snow lay two 'shoes' deep, but the weather improved so rapidly that vines were flowering on 30 May – some three weeks ahead of schedule. Often the variations in the pattern of weather overrode the beneficial effects of micro-climate, and the differences in the size and quality of the nineteenth-century Rheingau vintages were marked. Since the Second World War the Rheingau has gathered commercial quantities of rich Riesling *Beerenauslesen* and *Trockenbeerenauslesen* in 1947, 1949, 1959, 1964, 1967, 1971, 1976 and 1989. Although great vintages remain infrequent, the crop, larger than it was in the past, can still vary considerably from year to year – from 0.48 million hectolitres in 1982 to 0.16 million hectolitres in 1984. This is in spite of the levelling effect of the high proportion of Riesling vines (82 per cent as opposed to 54 per cent a century ago, and now much improved by clonal

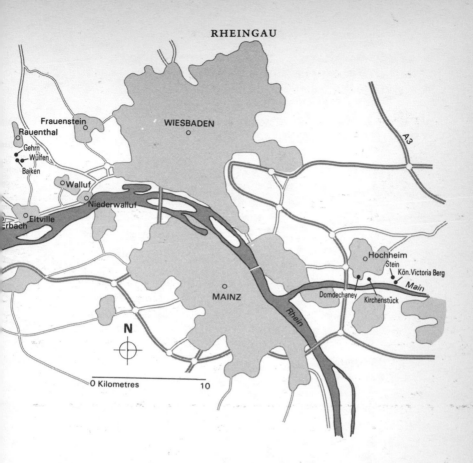

selection). As it is, the average yield in the Rheingau is well below
that of Germany as a whole. From the 1990 vintage, the grower
will not be able to sell more than the equivalent of a production
of 88 hectolitres per hectare in any one year. This will make no
difference to most of the estates which sell their wine in the bottle,
as their yields usually range between 55 and 70 hectolitres per
hectare. Nevertheless, compared to the amounts that may be legally
produced in some of the other wine regions, 88 hectolitres per
hectare is low.

An examination of the world's wine lists would suggest that
Rüdesheim marks the eastern end of the Rheingau. Indeed, the
vineyards of the Rüdesheimer Berg, overlooked by the 12.38-metre
statue of Germania (a lady similar to Britannia and of equally
noble proportions), would bring the Rheingau to a fitting,

fortissimo finale. However, the region carries on, round the bend of the river and into the Rhein gorge for another 13 kilometres, giving way to the Mittelrhein only at Lorchhausen.

LORCHHAUSEN TO RÜDESHEIM

Lorchhausen and neighbouring Lorch are not the greatest names of the Rheingau, but any Riesling wine coming from slopes with an incline up to 48 per cent is going to be worth tasting. The soils vary, as they always do, but the decomposed slate and quartzite add flavour to wines that, not surprisingly, lie somewhere in style between those of the central Rheingau and those of the Mittelrhein. The annual costs of cultivation in the difficult terrain of the Rhein gorge can rise to DM 40,000 per hectare or more and, at a yield of 75 hectolitres per hectare, the expenses in the vineyard will then amount to DM 3.00 per bottle, according to the Rheingauer Wine Growers' Association. Since 1968 the largest Lorch estate, the thirteenth-century Weingut Graf von Kanitz, has followed a strictly biological system and the vines are untouched by artificial fertilizers, herbi- and fungicides. The tone in which such a regime is described may sometimes sound a little sanctimonious, but the intentions are admirable.

Between Lorch and Rüdesheim, and backed by a valley of vineyards, is Assmannshausen, probably the best-known village in Germany for supple Spätburgunder wine.

The Rheingau was producing red wine long before it turned to white-vine varieties, and since the nineteenth century Assmannshäuser Spätburgunder has reached prices at auctions as high as those of the finest white Marcobrunner or Steinberger wines. It still holds its price well and on the State Cellars' 1989–90 price list, 1987 Assmannshäuser Höllenberg Spätburgunder Kabinett Trocken (dry) is offered at DM 17.70 per bottle and the 1988 Steinberger Riesling Kabinett Trocken at DM 11.40. Their Assmannshäuser Höllenberg, with a slightly sweet flavour and little tannin, is not really to the international taste, but a 1954 Spätburgunder Kabinett from the State Cellars, opened by the London wine-merchants Bibendum in 1989, was astoundingly good, soft and gentle and still alive. This was all the more surprising for, as S. F. Hallgarten wrote in *Rhineland Wineland*, 'If wine is captured sunshine, there can be no "wine" in 1954.' Not all the wine from Assmannshausen's green manured, violet-blue phyllite slate vineyards has little more than local appeal. Apart from the State Cellars there are other producers who offer dry Spätburgunder, partially matured in 225-litre *barriques*, and of considerable force and depth of flavour. They can be compared with the new and serious Spätburgunders from the Rheinpfalz and Baden, wines for which no explanations are needed.

Perhaps the real speciality of the State Cellars are the sweet Spätburgunder *Auslesen* and *Beerenauslesen*, but these are so rare and made in such limited quantities as to be more image-builders than profit-earners. The *Weissherbst* (rosé) *Eisweine*, on the other hand, are produced in most years and seem to be priced very much according to their quality, so they can be much cheaper than Riesling *Eisweine* from great Rheingau vineyards such as the Steinberg or the Rauenthaler Baiken. To harvest Riesling *Auslese* in anything other than the best vintages is immensely time-consuming and costly, and on economic grounds some consider it is better to aim to produce *Eiswein*. This is to gamble on the weather, but at least only one picking of the grapes is normally involved and, even in the mild winters, the temperature often drops low enough before Christmas to make *Eiswein*-harvesting possible.

At Rüdesheim, moving upstream, the Rhein takes on the dimensions that it maintains until the outskirts of Wiesbaden. In some places it is a kilometre wide and the warming effect on the region's vineyards is quite believable, particularly at Rüdesheim which shares with Hochheim the reputation for powerfully flavoured, full-bodied wines. In *The Great Vintage Wine Book* Michael Broadbent reports a 1653 Rüdesheimer tasted from cask in Bremen in 1977 as being 'starbright, madeira-like, but not madeirized; dry, intense, powerful' and adds 'ten stars for a rare experience'. Bassermann-Jordan describes 1653 as a 'fruitful year. Much and good wine. Harvested in September.' Although it might have been a better wine still if the picking had been delayed until October, it is clear that good wine-makers were at work in Germany at a time when Oliver Cromwell ruled England. The evidence is there to be tasted by the lucky few.

Rüdesheim has a little over 300 hectares of vineyard and the best sites stretch across the Berg, or hill, to the west of the town. As so often, the boundaries of the individual vineyards have expanded and contracted over the years, but have finally settled down into four *Einzellagen*, each between 29 and 37 hectares in size. All are good, but some would say that Berg Schlossberg produces, on average and marginally, the best wines. Perhaps the greater variety of soil types in the Berg Rottland, Berg Roseneck and Bischofsberg sites means that their range of wine is wider, but remembering the other factors that influence how a wine tastes and smells, dogmatic statements based solely on the vineyard of origin are very unsafe.

In a booklet the Association of Charta estates has reproduced a section of an 1896 price list from the London wine-merchants Berry Bros & Rudd which includes an 1862 Rüdesheimer Hinterhaus. The wine from this vineyard, which was absorbed by Rüdesheimer Bischofsberg in 1971, was offered at 200/- per dozen bottles. Château Lafite 1878 (a vintage which the *régisseur* or wine-maker of the day described as '*assez abondante. Très bonne*') is listed at 140/-, and Pommery Champagne at 96/-. The Charta association, a group of dedicated Rheingau estates, has set its sights on restoring the region's wines to something like their former level of prestige. Its starting point has been to define the type of wine it wishes to offer in terms of must weight, acidity and unfermented sugar. The end result is a medium-dry wine (which to many will taste dry because of the level of acidity) made 100 per cent from Riesling grapes and sold in an embossed bottle, unique to Charta. The association has a strict and effective system of quality control. Whether it is right to describe its firm, steely, medium-dry wines as 'traditional' is open to question, given the fact that German wine has varied in style considerably over the last 200 years. What should not be doubted is the value of the Charta association to German wine as a whole. Its message is simple, received loudly and clearly by the wine-drinker in Germany but only faintly, as yet, elsewhere.

The German wine-producers are not known for mutual understanding, but the commercial difficulties of recent years have encouraged co-operation amongst those with similar aims. However, at trade gatherings the short-term thinking of growers with too much ordinary wine to sell has often predominated, simply because they have been in the majority. Their lack of understanding of the market's possibilities has not helped German wine. The frustration this has caused amongst good estates, and the wish to see a first-class product properly promoted, lay behind the formation of Charta and similar but less well-known groupings. Although some say that the German wine-producing trade should advance not in separate groups but as a body, there are few signs that this is likely to happen. In the meantime, the initiative of the Association of Charta estates is to be welcomed.

RÜDESHEIM TO WALLUF

The 12 largest estates in the Rheingau are based in the 21 kilometres between Rüdesheim and Walluf. They are at: Geisenheim-Johannisberg – G. H. V. Mumm'sches Weingut (54 hectares), Landgräflich Hessisches Weingut (40 hectares), Schloss Johannisberg (35 hectares); Oestrich-Winkel – Gutsverwaltung Wegeler-Deinhard (60 hectares), Graf Matuschka-Greiffenclau'sche Güterverwaltung, Schloss Vollrads (50 hectares), Weingut Fritz Allendorf (37 hectares); Kiedrich – Weingut Dr Robert Weil (36 hectares), Weingut des Reichsfreiherrn von Ritter zu Groenesteyn (32 hectares); Eltville-Hattenheim – Domänenweingut Schloss Schönborn (48 hectares); Eltville-Erbach – Administration Prinz Friedrich von Preussen Schloss Reinhartshausen (67 hectares); Eltville – Verwaltung der Staatsweingüter (136 hectares in the Rheingau), Freiherrlich Langwerth von Simmern'sches Rentamt (38 hectares).

Both Schloss Johannisberg and Schloss Vollrads are defined as *Ortsteile* and are allowed to sell their wines without the qualifying name of a town or village, and all the vineyards of Weingut Dr Weil are at Kiedrich. For the rest, their holdings are spread over a number of villages, with those of Schloss Schönborn running from Rüdesheim in the west to Hochheim in the east. The largest estate, the Staatsweingut or State Cellars, based on Eltville, has holdings that are even more farflung and which, as we have seen, reach from Assmannshausen to Hochheim, and the Staatsweingut in the Hessische Bergstrasse region further south also forms part of its domain. Besides these ten large Rheingau estates there are probably another seventy or so which might all be described as 'well known' in Germany, leaving a further 300 which sell their wine in bottle. Most growers, it is claimed, will have had formal training in vineyard management and wine-making, probably at the local, internationally famous viticultural school at Geisenheim.

Without the 3 million or more visitors that descend on Rüdesheim each year, Geisenheim has a more sober atmosphere. There
is a large, early sixteenth-century church known as the 'Cathedral
of the Rheingau', and also a varied choice of schools and colleges.
Training is important in the life of Geisenheim, but wine keeps the
town in business. It has a number of good sites including the
Rothenberg, whose wines have not been as appreciated as they
might on the export market, perhaps because of their slight *Boden-
ton*, or earthy flavour and smell. Here the preferences of the regular
and the infrequent German wine-drinker go separate ways, with
the latter being rather conservative. A strong flavour is noticeable
in wines from red-coloured soils such as one finds on Geisenheimer
Rothenberg, Traiser Rotenfels in the Nahe, Nackenheimer Rothenberg in the Rheinhessen, or Wintzenheimer Rotenberg in Alsace.
The flavour of the soil is transmitted particularly well by the Riesling vines in which these sites are planted.

One of the earliest-known estate bottlings took place at Schloss
Schönborn about 1750 and samples of the wine, a 1735 Johannisberger Riesling, still exist. (A bottle was auctioned in 1987 for DM
53,000.) At Schloss Johannisberg, overlooking Geisenheim and the
rest of the central Rheingau, bottling started on a regular basis
with the 1775 vintage. Since the mid-1980s Schloss Johannisberg
has followed a clear marketing plan, as a result of which its wines
are either dry or medium-dry, designed to be drunk with food
or, when possible, rich and sweet *Auslesen* and *Beerenauslesen*.
Naturally, on a Rheingau white-wine estate of this calibre, only
Riesling is grown, except for a small area of vines on trial. The
yield at Schloss Johannisberg is kept down to 55–65 hectolitres
per hectare on average, which the flavour, body and undoubted
seriousness of the wines suggests.

From Schloss Johannisberg the *Rheingauer Riesling Pfad*, or
path, which runs from near Lorchhausen to Walluf, follows an old
'ploughman's' route to Schloss Vollrads, another great and even
more ancient estate. In recent years its owner, Erwein Graf
Matuschka-Greiffenclau, has been totally committed to marrying
his wine with food. Besides the Schloss Vollrads annual production
of some 33,000 dozen bottles, Graf Matuschka-Greiffenclau also
sells wine from the estate he leased in 1979, Weingut Fürst Löwenstein. Together, the Graf says, the two properties account for
one-third of all the wines sold under the banner of the Charta

association. Unlike many German estate-owners, Graf Matuschka-Greiffenclau does not believe that statistics and details of the chemical analysis help to promote wine, and so Schloss Vollrads sells on its high quality, elegance and prestige. In the greatest vintages, when the vineyards of less high-lying estates are burnt by the sun, Schloss Vollrads can be quite stunning.

Keeping to the high ground, the *Rheingau Riesling Pfad* climbs behind the village of Hallgarten, where Weingut Jacob Riedel anticipated the future by producing a dry Riesling *Auslese* in 1976, and arrives in the twelfth century at Kloster Eberbach. This complex of monastic buildings belonged to the Cistercians, as did the Steinberg, the best-known vineyard in the Rheinland. Today both monastery and vineyard are owned by the state of Hessen, and Kloster Eberbach is used for tastings and official functions connected with the promotion of wine. The Cistercians laid out the 50-hectare Clos de Vougeot in Burgundy, with which the 30-hectare Steinberg (also encircled since the eighteenth century by a high wall) has something in common. Probably the most significant difference between the two is that the Clos de Vougeot is divided amongst more than seventy growers with varying abilities and aims, while all the wine from the Steinberg is produced in the State Cellars at Eltville. All good Riesling wines need to be aged in bottle but the structure of Steinberger Riesling means that, even in the lower-quality categories, it can be kept with advantage for ten years or more.

From Kloster Eberbach the *Rheingauer Riesling-Route* for motorists leads to Kiedrich, famous for its wine from nearly 180 hectares. Its church, endowed in the last century by an Englishman, Sir John Sutton, has the oldest organ in working order in Germany, and a choir which specializes in plainsong sung mainly in the 'Germanic choral vernacular'. In this village of 3,500 inhabitants, there are eighteen full-time producers and 160 who grow vines on a part-time basis. These figures, which include the Kiedrich holdings of the substantial Weingut Dr Weil and of Schloss Groenesteyn, show that vineyard holdings, even in the comparatively wealthy Rheingau, are still small, and here, as in all the German wine regions, co-operative cellars are essential.

Nearer the Rhein, after Geisenheim, the vineyards of Winkel with its large 100-hectare Hasensprung site, are owned in part by a number of top-quality growers including Johannishof, von Mumm,

Ress and Wegeler-Deinhard. The body and acid levels of the Winkeler wines may vary from one producer to another, but the basic style is very clean, true and direct in flavour. In other words, Winkeler Rieslings are classics, to be recommended to those who do not care for earthy flavours. Oestrich produces wines similar to those of Winkel but perhaps less elegant.

At Hattenheim and Erbach the change of style is more marked. The wines are beauties, with great length of flavour and finesse, and at their best from estates such as von Simmern, Schloss Reinhartshausen and Schloss Schönborn. In an average vintage the Erbacher Marcobrunn is not only the most expensive wine in its quality category in the village or in neighbouring Hattenheim, but also the best. When there is a great vintage and the lesser vineyards are blessed with the warmth which is missing in an indifferent year, the competition becomes much stronger and preference is more a matter of personal choice. What is true is that a top-flight vineyard will produce top-flight wine only in the hands of an outstanding wine-maker. Fortunately, there are a number of them in the Rheingau.

Above Eltville, overlooking the little Sülzbach stream, the Rauenthaler Baiken is one of the vineyards that can claim to challenge Erbacher Marcobrunn for its supremacy in the best vintages. Eltville's own vineyards are not quite in the same class and at this point we could leave the central section of the Rheingau were it not for Weingut J. B. Becker of Walluf. The full, deep-coloured Spätburgunder wines and the dry Rieslings are remarkable and provide a good reason for not driving straight on to Wiesbaden.

HOCHHEIM AM MAIN

Twenty kilometres is a long way in the wine world, and by the time one reaches Hochheim from Niederwalluf, the rivers have changed and so has the soil. The numerous streams that run down to the Rhein through the central Rheingau have helped to create a broad 'palette', made up principally of gravel, sand, loam, clay, marl and loess, not to forget sandstone and slate. The variety makes it difficult to comment on links between specific soils and certain styles of wine. This is particularly true when the impact of the micro-climate and cellar techniques are taken into account as well. Nevertheless, for whatsoever complicated combination of reasons, the banks of the Main produce a more strongly flavoured wine than we usually find in the central Rheingau.

Hochheim sits on an elevated strip of land from which the vineyards fall away gently to the River Main below. They are pleasant to look at, undramatic and, by general agreement, are at their best in the Domdechaney and Kirchenstück sites. Both were originally in ecclesiastical hands, but now include famous estate names such as Aschrott, the State Cellars, Schloss Schönborn and the Werner'sches Weingut amongst the part-owners. More famous outside Germany, but not of the same standing, is another site, once the property of the Church, and now called the Hochheimer Königin Victoria Berg. In 1854 the grateful owner, who had bought the land in 1840, built an 8-metre-high monument in honour of Queen Victoria, who had visited the vineyard nine years before. Although reviled by the Nazis as a 'degeneration of German art', it remains intact. With its inscription in English it is a surprising sight, clearly visible from the air when approaching Frankfurt airport.

In the nineteenth century Hochheim was known in Britain and the USA for still and sparkling wine. Burgeff, the oldest *Sekt* manufacturer in the Rheinland, now owned by Seagram, was able to sell its local 1833 and 1834 sparkling Hochheimer without any effort or advertising, and the demand for Hochheimer was maintained over many years. The shortened form, 'Hock', was used, where English was spoken, as a generic name for Rhein wine until its current meaning was legally established. Nowadays, Hock can be either a table wine from the Rhein region or a quality wine from the same area but bearing the appropriate regional name for quality wine – e.g. Rheinhessen, Rheingau, etc.

Hochheim has not always been regarded politically as part of the Rheingau and it is proud of its independent past. According to a brochure produced by the *Historischer Verein Hochheim* in 1988, nearby Flörsheim supplied Schloss Johannisberg with Riesling vines in 1718, and the Hochheim vineyards were planted solely in Riesling at a time when a mixture of vine varieties was more common. Further, there is documentary evidence to suggest that Hochheim may have picked its Riesling crop late, nearly 300 years before the value of the *Spätlese* harvest was 'discovered' at Schloss Johannisberg in 1775. The best of Hochheimer wines have a weight and style that recall a good Rüdesheimer, but with some of the flavour of a Franken wine.

Today, 10–15 per cent of a Rheingau vintage is made into sparkling wine, and much finds its way to the *Sekt* manufacturers via that important person, the broker. By charging the buyer 2 per cent and the seller 5 per cent, a hard-working broker can make a respectable living, dealing with wine in bulk and bottle. It may be that after a good vintage an estate could easily sell its stock without outside assistance, but the poor vintages demand more effort and so a broker is employed on a contractual basis. When the trade is not interested in a vintage he earns his keep. Throughout France, Italy and Germany the broker finds himself in a worsening financial situation, as large buying organizations trade increasingly and directly with the producer or groups of producers. Although the Rheingau broker feels the results of a changing market, his livelihood seems more secure than that of his colleagues in other German wine regions.

Perhaps, if the international auction houses were able to mount sales in Germany, a more open, lively market would result. The marketing skills of Sotheby's and Christie's might help to uplift the international image of the best German wine. During the last twenty years the locally famous Kloster Eberbach auctions have changed their character. In the past the 'run' of a cask would be put up for sale, and a broker would purchase a lot of seventy-two dozen bottles (i.e. the contents of a 610-litre *Halbstück*), which he passed on to wine-merchants in smaller quantities. Today the broker may bid for as little as eight dozen bottles at one time.

Away from the auction rooms, the consumer is encouraged to buy from the producer. In the Rheingau, of the 380 estates which bottle their wine most sell from the cellar door to anybody who cares to buy. This type of trading is officially encouraged by 'open days' held in the spring and autumn, when estates pull back the cellar doors and tastings are held to attract business.

The Rheingau has all that is necessary to produce fine German wine – a high proportion of Riesling, a number of top-quality wine-makers and a more or less co-operative climate. At its best, it sets a style of Riesling wine which is perfect in its balance. Some would even call it an 'intellectual' wine. If that means that the depth of the bouquet and flavour seem unfathomable in their complexity, then 'intellectual' may be a fair description. In any event, its appeal is unbeatable.

Some recommended producers in the Rheingau

The following are additional to the twelve largest estates listed earlier in this chapter.

Weingut Friedrich Altenkirch, 6223 Lorch, Binger Weg 2: small, high-quality estate, with mainly sloping vineyards.

Weingut Fritz Allendorf, 6227 Oestrich-Winkel, Kirchstrasse 69: large estate with vineyards spread throughout the Rheingau.

Geheimrat Aschrott'sche Erben Weingutsverwaltung, 6203 Hochheim, Kirchstrasse 38: important estate with holdings only in Hochheim.

Weingut J. J. Becker, 6229 Walluf/Rh. 1., Rheinstrasse 5–6: excellent dry Riesling and high-quality Spätburgunder.

Baron von Brentano'sche Gutsverwaltung, 6227 Oestrich-Winkel, Am Lindenplatz 2: elegant Rieslings. Winkeler wines at their best.

Weingut G. Breuer, 6220 Rüdesheim, Grabenstrasse 8: 100 per cent Riesling, 100 per cent professional. Many stylish dry/medium-dry wines.

Weingut Diefenhardt, 6228 Eltville 4, Hauptstrasse 9–11: source of firm, cask-matured Rieslings, made to last, and Spätburgunder.

Weingut Johannishof, 6222 Geisenheim-Johannisberg: extremely elegant Rieslings with a clear, direct flavour.

Weingut Graf von Kanitz, 6223 Lorch. Rheinstrasse 49: organically manured vineyards. Mainly dry and medium-dry Rieslings.

Weingut August Kesseler, 6220 Rüdesheim-Assmannshausen, Lorcher Strasse 16: famous for full Spätburgunders, amongst the best in Germany.

Weingut Freiherr zu Knyphausen, 6228 Eltville, Klosterhof Drais: typical, high-quality Rieslings, from Erbach, Kiedrich and Hattenheim.

Weingut Robert König, 6220 Rüdesheim-Assmannshausen, Landhaus Kenner: 100 per cent Spätburgunder, 250-year-old vine-growing family.

Weingut Hans Lang, 6228 Eltville-Hattenheim, Rheinallee 6: fine, elegant Rieslings, mainly from Hattenheim.

Weingut Dr Heinrich Nägler, 6220 Rüdesheim, Friedrichstrasse 22: 100 per cent Rüdesheimer estate. Stylish, classic Riesling wines.

Weingut Balthasar Ress, 6228 Eltville 3, Rheinallee 7: firm, fresh, high-quality Rieslings from the entire Rheingau.

Weingut J. Riedel, 6227 Hallgarten, Taunusstrasse 1: small, 100 per cent Riesling, 100 per cent Hallgarten estate.

Domdechant Werner'sches Weingut, 6203 Hochheim, Rathausstrasse 30: top-quality, full-flavoured, elegant Rieslings, all from Hochheim.

Weingut Freiherr von Zwierlein, 6222 Geisenheim, Schloss Kosakenberg: well-made, 100 per cent Riesling wines, typical of Geisenheim.

18

Rheinhessen

Area under vine in hectares in 1988: 24,871 ha, planted 22.5 per cent Müller-Thurgau, 12.9 per cent Grüner Silvaner, 9.1 per cent Scheurebe, 8.5 per cent Kerner, 7.9 per cent Bacchus, 7.1 per cent Weisser Riesling, 6.6 per cent Faberrebe, and 25.4 per cent others.

Average temperature during period of vegetation:	14.3°C
Average sunshine hours during period of vegetation:	1,358
Average rainfall during period of vegetation:	315mm
Average annual rainfall:	481mm
Recent vintages in million hectolitres:	1985 1.1, 1986 2.3, 1987 2.1, 1988 2.0, 1989 3.1
Average yield in hectolitres per hectare:	1978–87 94.0 hl/ha

The Rheinhessen produces some of Germany's bestselling wines, which have long been successfully exported throughout the world. In fact, as much as one-quarter of the region's vintage is drunk in the United Kingdom, the USA, The Netherlands, Denmark, Japan, Canada and elsewhere abroad. This shows that the style of Rheinhessen wine is widely liked, and that the wine should be as well placed as any to withstand the competition on a tough international market where supply is greater than demand. However, making the cheap Rheinhessen wine that interests the world's supermarkets and stores has become uneconomic, and many would describe the market for bulk wine in the Rheinhessen as chaotic, or even catastrophic.

The problem lies in the structure of the region's wine trade, and in particular in the overwhelming and increasing strength of relatively few big buyers. They have forced growers who sell their wine in bulk to aim for a large yield of a rather ordinary product.

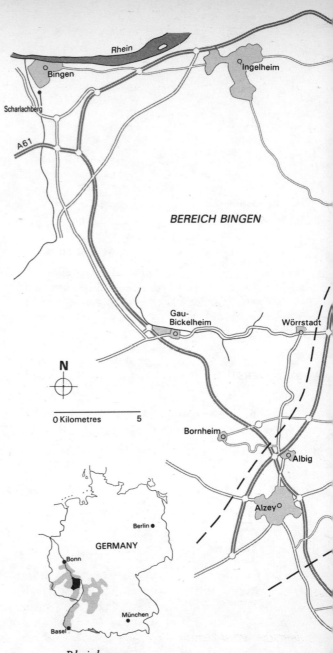

Rheinhessen

MAINZ

Rhein

A3

Bodenheim

Gau-Bischofsheim

Nackenheim

Rothenberg

Pettenthal

Rosenberg
Brudersberg

Findling
Hipping
Ölberg
Kranzberg
Orbel
Nierstein
Bildstock

Selzen

Paterberg

Sackträger
Oppenheim
Herrenberg
Dexheim
Kreuz

Schloss
Dienheim
Falkenberg

Rhein

BEREICH NIERSTEIN

Ludwigshöhe

Uelversheim
Kreuzkapelle

Steig-Terrassen
Bornpfad
Guntersblum

Fischerpfad

Frühmesse
Alsheim

Mettenheim

Bechtheim

Osthofen

Westhofen

BEREICH WONNEGAU

A61

Rhein

Flörsheim-Dalsheim

Worms

Such wine is offered under *Grosslage* names through the grocery stores of Germany and as Liebfraumilch on the export market, both at the rock-bottom prices to which many customers have become accustomed. If it is to make any sense, this type of trading requires the closest possible financial control and is therefore more suited to man-made products, such as beer, where costs can be calculated precisely in advance. It cannot be successfully transferred to wine-making in the Rheinhessen where the quality and size of the grape harvest varies greatly from one year to another. Because its cheap medium-sweet wines have been so well distributed in the last three decades, we have almost forgotten how good medium-price and top-quality Rheinhessen wine can be. As the President of the central co-operative cellars (Zentralkellerei Rheinischer Winzergenossenschaft), Bernhard Zipp, has put it, 'Unless we, in the Rheinhessen, organize ourselves in a more efficient way, the market will do the job for us, mercilessly and unrelentingly.'

That is the gloomy background to Germany's largest wine-producing region in the early 1990s. The Rheinhessen has new marketing ideas of the sort needed to sell wine today, but it will be hard to make them succeed unless the 'reorganization' about which Herr Zipp has spoken takes place. It is probably fair to say that, were the Rheinhessen to shed itself of the 5,000 or so hectares by which it was enlarged between 1970 and 1982, many of the flat vineyards in rich farming land would disappear – and so would the source of much indifferent wine. The dry climate suggests that the region is better suited to growing high-quality grapes on sloping vineyards, particularly on those nearest the Rhein.

Styles of good Rheinhessen wine have become enormously varied in the last fifteen years. Most are now not only drier, but also crisper and more refreshing. The soft wines which, at their best, used to be produced by estate bottlers from Ruländer or Silvaner, are now hard to find and are certainly not in demand. Often they had a vegetal bouquet and were sweet enough to be an enjoyable evening drink, after a meal. Quite possibly when the consumers of good-quality wines have forgotten the reasons why their palates started to turn dry in the 1960s, interest in sweetish wines will be revived. Amongst many outside Germany, particularly in Japan, it still remains.

The Rheinhessen has the largest area planted in Silvaner (3,202 hectares) of any region in Germany and, perhaps, in the world.

The vine's reliable performance recommends it to growers who are looking for a fair but not enormous yield. As a dry QbA, it can be a very good wine to be drunk with a meal and in this guise it is finding new customers amongst all age groups. Research shows that the most enthusiastic consumer of Rheinhessen wine is in early middle age and lives in the densely populated, industrial state of Nordrhein-Westfalen. Whilst wishing to keep his, or her, loyal custom, the Rheinhessen has introduced some attractive wines in recent years, aimed at a more catholic group of people, as will be discussed later in this chapter. In the meantime, the central co-operative cellars at Gau-Bickelheim still processes no less than 39 different grape varieties (many new crossings) each year.

With a modest 7 per cent of the total area under vine, Riesling is not an important force in the Rheinhessen as a whole, but on some estates with holdings in the best sites Riesling accounts for 75 per cent or more. This is especially true of those with holdings on the Rheinterrasse between Bodenheim and Mettenheim.

The growers in the best financial shape are probably those who are also engaged in other forms of farming. Orchards, asparagus, corn or sugar beet bring in a useful, and sometimes the main, income. On the slopes of the Rheinterrasse where grapes are the only crop, wine prices rightly bear a premium. The selling price, however, is often still not sufficient to cover the costs of growing the grapes. According to the large and excellent Weingut Louis Guntrum, they are three times as much as those in the level vineyards away from the Rhein.

Nearly one-third of the region's growers make and bottle their own wine. Tourism is not very developed and so the profitable passing trade is not large. Probably more wine is despatched by carriers to the consumer than is collected from the cellar door. The holdings, although small, are a little larger than those, for example, in Württemberg. The growers cherish their independence and some would regard membership of a co-operative as a loss of freedom. Those who sell in cask or in bottle will continue with their accustomed way of life for as long as possible, but how long that will be nobody can say.

THE RHEINTERRASSE

The most exciting wines in the northern German wine regions today come from two types of producer. In hitherto little-known villages, well-trained, intelligent and farseeing young wine-makers are supplying wines to a far higher standard than their locality might lead you to expect, from low yields of traditional vine varieties. They are making the very best of their fruit and the quality of their wine will be even better in the future as their vines age and their experience increases. They understand that to produce good wine is no longer enough and that, as in other trades, a successful business depends on a well-thought-out marketing position. Besides these welcome arrivals, there are the good and great estates with holdings in vineyards which hundreds of years of vine-growing have shown to be the best in the land. They are concentrated in parts of the Mosel and its tributaries, the Rheingau, the northern part of the Rheinpfalz and in the Rheinterrasse.

By the Rheinterrasse is understood the vineyards on the eroded cliffs of the west bank of the Rhein south of Mainz. They are attached to the villages of Bodenheim, Nackenheim, Nierstein, Oppenheim, Dienheim, Ludwigshöhe, Guntersblum, Alsheim and Mettenheim, a few kilometres north of Worms. More than one-third of the region's Riesling is grown in the 3,500 hectares of the Rheinterrasse, and the Rheinhessen branch of the Verband Deutscher Prädikatsweingüter insists that at least 30 per cent of a member's estate must be planted in Riesling. Besides the right vine variety, the age of the vines and the exposition to the sun, the distance from the Rhein has a marked effect on the micro-climate of a Rheinterrasse vineyard. In the dreadful vintage of 1972 (the worst, with 1965, of the last thirty years) only the Riesling sites nearest the river escaped the serious effects of the mid-October frost, which gave a bitter flavour to so many wines from unripe grapes. The low temperature of the winter of 1979 destroyed many vineyards in Franken but, although in some Rheinterrasse sites it dropped suddenly and rapidly to $-25°C$, its minimum in those nearest the Rhein was $-20°C$. So, if the Rheinterrasse as a whole can be said to be a climatically privileged area, the best vineyards of Nackenheim, Nierstein and Oppenheim might be described as especially favoured.

Over the years one of the most successful Rheinhessen estates in the DLG wine competitions has been the Oberstleutnant Liebrecht'sche Weingutsverwaltung at Bodenheim. Its wines have not only done well but the estate itself has been awarded an *Ehrenpreis* (prize of honour) three times for its overall performance at the DLG competition. About 750 producers on average send their wines to the annual competition and, as only 3 per cent or so are awarded the *Ehrenpreis*, it is valued highly and impresses the consumer. Following the rebuilding (*Flurbereinigung*) of the Bodenheim vineyards between 1967 and 1985, many of the vines are still quite young and it can therefore be expected that the wines will improve further during the 1990s.

Nackenheim is a village a little set back from the over-busy B9 road that follows the Rhein from the French border near the Rheinpfalz to Cologne and beyond. Its small vineyard area of about 150 hectares includes the outstanding Rothenberg site – one of the best in the Rheinhessen. Like others in the neighbourhood it is sloping and shares with some of the best Nierstein vineyards the red, decomposed soil. The largest part of Nackenheimer Rothenberg is owned by Weingut Gunderloch, an estate well known for the elegance of its Riesling wine. Gunderloch has holdings in other sites, but the only wine it sells under a vineyard name is that from the Rothenberg. The remainder are listed either with the estate and vine-variety name, or simply with the village name – an approach modelled on the *Appellation contrôlée* system in France. When all the wines were sold in their various quality categories under a site name, Gunderloch carried out forty bottlings each year. Now there are nine.

The first of the Nierstein vineyards travelling south is immediately adjacent to the Nackenheimer Rothenberg. Niersteiner Pettenthal rises to some 100 metres above the Rhein and in places is as steep as 60 per cent. Its rateable value, the highest of all the 1,000 hectares or so under vine at Nierstein, is eight times greater than that of some of the farming land in which vines were planted in the 1960s, to become part of the *Grosslage* Niersteiner Gutes Domtal – of which more anon.

There are at Nierstein five *Einzellagen* that are exceptions to the rule that all vineyard sites should be at least 5 hectares in size. Amongst them are the 0.6-hectare Glöck, which is known to have been in existence in AD 742, and the steep 1.3 hectare Brudersberg, immediately to the south of Niersteiner Pettenthal. Although

143

separated by the B9 road and the railway from the Rhein, the south-facing Brudersberg is never more than 150 metres from the river. It is one of the best Riesling sites and is owned entirely by Weingut Freiherr Heyl zu Herrnsheim, a leading and very serious estate. Amongst the *Einzellagen* that are known abroad are Oelberg and Hipping. The 60-hectare Oelberg is set back from the Rhein but overcomes any disadvantage by facing south. Many of its vines are old (the site has not yet been reconstructed – *flurbereinigt*) and its ownership is divided amongst a number of growers, including the well-known Weingut Bürgermeister Anton Balbach. This estate produces some 14,000 dozen bottles on average each year, of which over 70 per cent are fresh, lively Rieslings. In the nineteenth century the Balbachs cleared the woods on the slopes near Nackenheim to create Niersteiner Pettenthal. Their descendants through the female line have continued to be leaders in the local community. Niersteiner Hipping, a site in which Balbach has 3 hectares, is a modernized vineyard, producing wines of good weight and style from the red, decomposed soil.

The problem of the 150 growers in Nierstein is not what happens within their own borders but what is going on elsewhere. The excessive production of cheap and ordinary wine in much of the Rheinhessen lowers the whole tone of the region and damages its public image. What is worse for the good growers of Nierstein is that their valuable village name should be legally attached to some of the cheapest wines that Germany can produce. Niersteiner Gutes Domtal is a large *Grosslage*, covering vineyards in about twenty-seven individual sites spread over fourteen villages in the hinterland away from the Rhein. In addition Nierstein itself has a site of 32 hectares (the Pfaffenkappe) which also forms part of Gutes Domtal, and which Nierstein would probably be willing to give away to rid itself of the Gutes Domtal connection.

The legal but otherwise unjustifiable use of the Nierstein name has a long history. In the days before the 1971 Wine Law 'Niersteiner Domthal' was treated with the greatest of imprecision by bottlers in Germany and abroad. The difficulty today is that the consumer who pays a little more than the cost of a kilo of potatoes for a bottle of Niersteiner Gutes Domtal does not understand why he should be charged DM 6.00 for a Niersteiner Spiegelberg Silvaner when bought directly from the producer. Equally, it is said that those with an interest in wine do not travel to Nierstein, believing incorrectly that if they do they will be met with Niersteiner Gutes Domtal. If the law were to be changed in such a way that the community name was dropped from *Grosslage* wines, the matter would be virtually resolved. Piesport, on the Mosel, would be relieved of its Michelsberg connection and Gutes Domtal could go its own way, leaving Nierstein to the Niersteiners. In fact the village's wine-makers are much abused, for not only has their name been debased by poor-quality Gutes Domtal, but it was adopted by an enormous central part of the Rheinhessen in 1971 which became known as the Bereich Nierstein. It is understandable that leading growers with generations of service in the village should say that the Rheinterrasse ought to be made into a separate region. Frankly, a declaration of unilateral independence for Nierstein might not look like an overreaction.

In the same way that some of the best vineyards at Bernkastel form the *Grosslage* Badstube, those at Nierstein are either part of Rehbach or of Auflangen and wines sold under these names should be above average in quality. Wines from the third serious *Grosslage*, Niersteiner Spiegelberg, are likely to be less stylish but distinctly better than anything Gutes Domtal might produce.

In Oppenheim the large *Grosslage* Krötenbrunnen has played the Niersteiner Gutes Domtal role and, therefore, the reputation of the town's wine does not stand as high as it should. Five kilometres of urban development along the Rhein link Oppenheim with Nierstein and their vineyards are contiguous, with the Niersteiner Paterberg and Oppenheimer Schloss sites making the contact. As this is a fine wine-producing part of the Rheinhessen, good-quality wines can be found in most *Einzellagen*. That said, Sackträger and Kreuz in particular can produce beautifully balanced, elegant wines, perhaps less strongly flavoured than some Niersteiners. Amongst the largest producers with holdings in both sites is Weingut Louis Guntrum which owns some 67 hectares spread along the Rheinterrasse. An average yield of a modest 70 hectolitres per hectare no doubt contributes to the quality of its true-to-type wines. Guntrum's clearly defined style is carried over to the merchant side of its business, where the bottlings of lesser wines are enjoyable minor versions of their estate-bottled bigger brothers. The wines of the Oppenheim-based estates of Carl Koch, Sanitätsrat Dr Dahlem, and Friedrich Baumann reflect the demand for dry wine but not to the exclusion of medium-sweet wines. The same can also be said for the wines of the Staatsweingut Oppenheim, an estate of 25 hectares that is part of the Landes-Lehr-und-Versuchsanstalt.

Within the ambit of this teaching and research institute in the older part of Oppenheim (the town was virtually destroyed by the French in 1688), there is a wine museum with a difference. The Deutsches Weinbaumuseum is concerned with the history of vine-growing and wine-making, and the tools of the trade are displayed in a clear and logical order. The museum brings to life the circumstances under which wine was produced in the past, and is instructive as well as entertaining. For the more usual type of wine museum, with displays of ancient wine glasses and artefacts to do with the service of wine, one can visit the Historisches Museum der Pfalz in Speyer, some 70 kilometres south. To feel something of the life of the wine-maker since 1800, it is better to stay in the Deutsches Weinbaumuseum, Oppenheim.

Within this part of the Rheinland, Oppenheim is known for the evangelical St Katharina Church, dating from the thirteenth century but restored in the 1930s. It overlooks the town and is a point of interest in many photographs taken in Oppenheim's 224 hectares of vineyard.

From hereon, moving south, the slopes of the Rheinterrasse start to draw back from the Rhein and by the time Mettenheim is reached, direct contact with the river is lost. Viticulture in Dienheim was flourishing in AD 756, according to records of the monastery of Fulda, and several of the large Nierstein and Oppenheim estates have holdings in Dienheim's 550 hectares under vine. Guntersblum, the immediate neighbour to the south after the little village of Ludwigshöhe, is characterized by what seems an almost excessive number of cellars. *Caves*, the French word for cellars, describes Guntersblum's holes in the hillside well. Some of these cellars date from the sixteenth century and they form an almost unbroken chain, over a kilometre long. It is claimed that there is more Riesling growing in Alsheim than in any other community in the Rheinhessen. Where the soil is light and *phylloxera* does not spread, the vines are ungrafted, as in Weingut Rappenhof's plantation of Riesling in the Alsheimer Fischerpfad site. This 400-year-old, 36-hectare estate makes traditional wines as well as *barrique*-aged Chardonnays and Weissburgunders of great power, some with more than 13 per cent of natural alcohol. It also offers a Blauer Portugieser *en primeur*, shortly after the vintage, and unusually exports its white wine to France.

THE REST OF THE RHEINHESSEN

After Mettenheim the wine villages become less memorable. Some, such as Osthofen, Westhofen and Bechtheim, have a long tradition of good wine-making and will be more widely known when the reputation of the Rheinhessen stands higher in the world. Good wine-makers are not confined to the Rheinterrasse as the Brenner'-sches Weingut and Weingut Jean Buscher at Bechtheim consistently prove. Increasingly, away from the Rheinterrasse it is the name of the producer that counts rather than that of the village in which he makes his wine. An estate-bottled wine from the Rheinterrasse is expected to be good but a wine from the back of beyond which makes the right impression is an unforeseen delight. At this moment, the belief that all German vineyards are capable of producing high-quality wine becomes almost credible.

The son of Pepin the Short, known as Charlemagne, apart from being the greatest European of his day, must also have been a hyperactive viticulturist, so widespread are the legends that link him to the vine. Amongst them is one that tells us that he introduced the first Spätburgunder to Ingelheim in the north of the region. Whether this is fact or myth, an article in the *Frankfurter Allgemeine* in 1983 claimed that the Spätburgunder had been grown in Ingelheim for more than 900 years; the town has built up a reputation for its Spätburgunder over the centuries, similar to that of Assmannshausen across the Rhein. The best-known red-wine estate, Weingut J. Neus, makes its Spätburgunder very much in the traditional German style. That is to say, the average yield is about 75 hectolitres per hectare and the tannin content is low. It is a style of wine that has won many awards and which, at QbA level, commands a price of about DM 1.50 more per bottle than would be asked for a Rheinhessen Riesling.

At Schloss Westerhaus outside Ingelheim, the Rieslings are reminiscent of the Nahe or Rheingau, with a pronounced backbone of tartaric acid. The Schloss, which together with its stud farm is owned by the von Opel family, is in a park overlooking the vineyards. The von Opels' other property, the capsule factory at Nack-

enheim, includes within its precincts the house where Carl Zuckmayer lived. His play *Der fröhliche Weinberg* was at first rejected
by the village, which felt itself caricatured. Later all was forgiven
and, on the principle that there was no such thing as bad publicity,
Zuckmayer was reinstated as Nackenheim's most famous son. In
the meantime the Nackenheimer Kapsel Fabrik has become one of
the largest exporters of capsules in the world.

In the north-west corner of the Rheinhessen, the town of Bingen
faces the Nahe vineyards of Bingerbrück, and is overlooked by the
heights of the Rüdesheimer Berg in the Rheingau. To confuse us
further, Bronner wrote in 1834 that the Scharlachberg site at
Bingen 'supplied the noblest product in the whole of the Nahe'.
Times have changed. Bingen is now anchored to the Rheinhessen
and the reputation of Scharlachberg is not what it was. The quality
of its wine, on the other hand, remains high, and a Binger Scharlachberg Riesling from Weingut Villa Sachsen is an excellent, racy,
often *spritzig* glass of wine. Here the wine-making is highly competent, as it also is in the St Ursula Weinkellerei which distributes
the Villa Sachsen wines outside Germany. The bottlings of the
German export companies show a house style which is followed
by their buyers and wine-makers as closely as vintage variations
allow. The main differences derive from the amount of alcohol,
acid and residual sugar that is wanted in the final blend. At Bingen,
the St Ursula Weinkellerei seems always to have preferred wines
that were well differentiated, true-to-the-vine variety, crisp and
refreshing, and this description fits the estate-bottled wines of Villa
Sachsen equally well.

The export house of H. Sichel Söhne has been established in the
Rheinhessen since the mid-nineteenth century. In its *Kellerei* or
cellars at Alzey, built in 1980, the company bottles its famous *Blue
Nun* Liebfraumilch which, because of its great success based on
good quality at a fair but not cheap price, has suffered more than
most from the debasement of Liebfraumilch in recent years (see
chapter 10). Besides providing a home for Sichel and many small
wine estates, the town of Alzey has its own 15-hectare Weingut,
left to it by a grateful citizen in 1916. There are other towns
which own vineyards in Germany (Frankfurt in the Rheingau,
Hammelburg in Franken, Offenburg in Baden, etc.), but they are
still relatively uncommon and Alzey is proud of its civic involvement in wine-making.

South of Alzey, the 35-hectare Weingut Schales shows a degree of self-confidence in its dealings with the world outside that is often missing on estates in villages more widely known than its own Flörsheim-Dalsheim. It has a range of seventeen vine varieties with Riesling, Silvaner and Weissburgunder slowly replacing some of the plantations of new crossings. The publicity material is of a high standard and includes a summary of vintage reports going back to 1783 – the date of its foundation. Given that the problem of a good Rheinhessen estate comes not from the quality of its product but from the depressing effect, in all senses, of a poor image, the positive and enthusiastic front that Weingut Schales presents to its customers is very welcome.

Equally to be applauded was the arrival in 1986 of 'RS', which admirably meets head-on the accusation that all German wine names are long and complicated. RS stands for Rheinhessen Silvaner. It is a dry QbA with a maximum of 4 grams per litre of residual sugar and a minimum of 5 grams per litre of acid. It is a good-quality, vintage wine, now produced by fifty or more growers to a standard that is so demanding that 35–50 per cent of potential RS wines are rejected by the tasting panel set up to be their judge. The wine bears a yellow-orange and black label, which is common to all its producers. Commercially, it has suffered a bumpy ride so far, but now that it has been agreed that RS will be sold exclusively to quality wine-merchants and the consumer only (not to grocery stores and supermarkets), it is to be hoped that its career will be steadier, based on a retail price of DM 6.50 per 750ml bottle. Other products, such as the medium-dry wine *Der Rheinhess*, or 'Nahesteiner' from the Nahe valley for that matter, have similar aims to RS. However, they are cheaper and sold at the upper end of the German mass market at about DM 4.98 per litre bottle.

Some recommended producers in the Rheinhessen

Weingut der Stadt Alzey, 6508 Alzey, Schlossgasse 14: good Scheurebes and Rieslings and many Huxelrebe *Spätlesen*.

Weingut Arnsteiner Gült, 6522 Osthofen, Friedrich-Ebert Strasse 36: successful Rieslings and Spätburgunders head the list, and are sold directly to the consumer.

Weingut Friedrich Baumann, 6504 Oppenheim, Friedrich-Ebert Strasse 55: stylish wines, fermented and matured mainly in wood.

Weingut Bürgermeister Anton Balbach Erben, 6505 Nierstein, Mainzer Strasse 64: famous Riesling estate. Fresh, true-to-type wines, not matured in wood.

Brenner'sches Weingut, 6521 Bechtheim, Pfandturmstrasse 20: good oak-matured dry wines, much appreciated in Germany.

Weingut Jean Buscher, 6521 Bechtheim, Wormser Strasse 4: award-winning estate with award-winning wines.

Weingutsverwaltung Sanitätsrat Dr Dahlem Erben K.G., 6504 Oppenheim, Rathofstrasse 21–5: good, individually made, stylish wines. Many are medium-sweet.

Weingut Gustav Gessert, 6505 Nierstein, Wörrstädter Strasse 84: high-quality estate, concentrating on Riesling and Silvaner.

Weingut Gunderloch, 6506 Nackenheim, Carl-Gunderloch-Platz 1: low-yield, top-quality estate. Refreshing, beautifully made Rieslings.

Weingut Louis Guntrum, 6505 Nierstein, Wörrstädter Strasse 6: large estate. Excellent, attractive and well-differentiated wines.

Weingut Ernst Jungkenn, 6504 Oppenheim, Wormser Strasse 61: large estate with a good range of typical Rheinterrasse wines.

Weingut Kapellenhof, 6501 Selzen, Kapellenstrasse 18: well-known source of dry and medium-dry wines, sold to the consumer.

Bürgermeister Carl Koch, 6504 Oppenheim, Wormser Strasse 62: traditional, cask-matured wines from dry to sweet.

Weingut Koehler-Weidmann, 6509 Bornheim: good, inexpensive wines from many vine varieties in all quality categories.

Weingut Köster-Wolf, 6509 Albig, Langgasse 62: large estate, with a wide range of interesting, prizewinning wines.

Weingut Kurfürstenhof, 6505 Nierstein, Fronhof 7: award-winning estate. Typically large, Rheinhessen mix of vines.

Oberstlt. Liebrecht'sche Weingutsverwaltung. 6501 Bodenheim, Rheinstrasse 30: modernized estate, classic, long-lived Rieslings.

Weingut J. Neus, 6507 Ingelheim, Bahnhofstrasse 96: famous for traditional German Spätburgunder. Many awards.

Staatsweingut Weinbaulehranstalt Oppenheim, 6504 Oppenheim, Zuckerberg 19: elegant firm wines from many vine varieties.

Weingut Rappenhof, 6526 Alsheim, Bachstrasse 47–9: cask-matured and *barrique*-aged white and red wines. Many styles are represented.

Bezirks-Winzergenossenschaft 'Rheinfront' eG, 6505 Nierstein 1, Karolingerstrasse 6: good source of reliable wines mainly from Müller-Thurgau and Silvaner.

Weingut Schales, 6523 Flörsheim-Dalsheim, Alzeyer Strasse 160: excellent producer of a full range of Rheinhessen wines.

Weingut Schloss Westerhaus, 6507 Ingelheim: stylish Rheingau-like Rieslings, and interesting Burgunder (Pinot).

Weingut Hermann Franz Schmitt, 6505 Nierstein 1, Kiliansweg 2: excellent dry Riesling wines, including *Auslese* quality.

Gustav Adolf Schmitt'sches Weingut, 6505 Nierstein 1, Wilhelmstrasse 2–4: classic wines from 100 hectares, mainly on the Rheinterrasse. Much exported.

Weingut Geschwister Schuch, 6505 Nierstein 1, Oberdorfstrasse 22: full range of Rheinterrasse wines at their best.

Weingut Oberst Schultz-Werner, 6501 Gaubischofsheim, Bahnhofstrasse 10: good, characterful, flavoury wines. Dry for Germany, sweeter for abroad.

Weingut J. u. H. A. Strub, 6505 Nierstein, Rheinstrasse 42: fresh and elegant cask-matured wines, from dry to sweet.

Weingut Villa Sachsen, 6530 Bingen, Mainzer Strasse 184: crisp, lively, beautifully made, balanced Rieslings. Many are dry.

Weingut Eugen Wehrheim, 6505 Nierstein, Mühlgasse 30: individual, elegant, Rheinterrasse wines.

19

Rheinpfalz

Area under vine in hectares in 1988: 22,625 ha, planted 22.3 per cent Müller-Thurgau, 17.3 per cent Weisser Riesling, 11.3 per cent Kerner, 8.9 per cent Blauer Portugieser, 7.9 per cent Grüner Silvaner, 5.9 per cent Morio-Muskat, 5.8 per cent Scheurebe and 20.6 per cent others.

Average temperature during period of vegetation:	15.0 C
Average sunshine hours during period of vegetation:	1,248
Average rainfall during period of vegetation:	385mm
Average annual rainfall:	614mm
Recent vintages in million hectolitres:	1985 1.4, 1986 2.8, 1987 2.3, 1988 2.3, 1989 3.1
Average yield in hectolitres per hectare:	1978–87 116.6 hl/ha

---

A glance at the percentages of the different vines growing in the Rheinpfalz (Pfalz, for short) would not immediately suggest that it was a region dedicated to high-quality wine. Excluding the excellent Scheurebe, nearly 60 per cent of the white-vine varieties are new crossings from which wines of real class are seldom expected. A closer look at the statistics shows that the Pfalz has, after the Mosel-Saar-Ruwer, the largest area under Riesling in Germany. This leads to the correct conclusion that the region's wine can range from very fine to quite ordinary.

The average yield in the Rheinpfalz is even greater than that of the Rheinhessen and the selling price of its wine in Germany is lower than that of any other region. At a local wine-growers' meeting in 1987 the director of the state viticultural teaching and research institute at Neustadt, Dr Adams, reported that to earn enough money to buy a litre of Pfalz wine in 1950 required 1.6 hours of an industrial worker's day. By 1985, sixteen minutes were sufficient. Statistics give us an outline picture of the general health of a region but they are, of course, historical, and fail to show the detail, which in the Pfalz in the 1990s is fascinating.

Until recent years, the only Pfalz wines of real distinction that were widely known came from a few villages between Kallstadt and Ruppertsberg, in the Bereich Mittelhaardt Deutsche Wein-strasse. Here were the homes of the great estates with Riesling vineyards near the Pfälzer Wald or wood. The holdings of the three Bs (Bassermann-Jordan and von Buhl of Deidesheim, and Bürklin-Wolf of Wachenheim) covered nearly 250 hectares, and their wines were recognized as amongst the finest in the land. How pre-eminent they were would doubtless be argued in the region itself, but nobody would question that the number of outstanding estate bottlers has increased throughout the Pfalz in the 1980s. The result is that it has become a very exciting region to visit. As we shall see, high-quality wines from 'traditional' vine varieties are found not only in the famous sites north of Neustadt but also in charming, rustic villages running south to the French border, and even slightly beyond.

The mainly Jewish, good-quality wine-merchants of the Rhein-land were driven out of business in the 1930s and, as in other regions nowadays, most Pfalz estates sell directly to the consumer. The effect of this has been that many German retail wine-merchants concentrate more on foreign wines, rather than risk having their prices undercut by the local estate bottler.

While the region has expanded by one-third since 1964, the percentage share of Riesling has also grown. Silvaner was particu-larly well thought of in Kallstadt and covered 40 per cent of the region twenty-six years ago, but its area is now in a steady decline. The specious charm of Morio-Muskat wine has waned and the planting of red-vine varieties, Spätburgunder and Dornfelder, is increasing quite rapidly.

A quarter of all Pfalz wine is dry. Amongst good wine-makers cask maturation is usual, and *barrique*-ageing is being tried on the Burgunder vine varieties and Dornfelder, in particular. Some producers offer part of their range in bottles of a non-German shape, whilst others seem to have taken their inspiration from the cosmetic industry in search of designs that are different and catch the eye. As always there is much controversy within the region about wine-trade politics, and it could be said that the energy spent on internal fighting might be better saved for making common cause to improve the image of Rheinpfalz wine. As in the Rheinhessen, the albatross of low wine prices hangs round the neck of the Pfalz, as it has done for so many years, and Cyrus Redding's question about Italian wine in 1833 remains valid. 'What object is there for a grower', he asks, 'in labouring to improve that which cannot by improvement turn out of the slightest profit to himself?' To this there has been no answer, particularly if the grower was producing large amounts of inferior grapes, which were giving him a better return than the alternative regional crops of corn, tobacco, sugar beet or potatoes. The effect of the new restrictions on the amount of wine that may be sold in any one year will be interesting, and could have important commercial and social consequences.

From north to south, the vineyards of the Pfalz stretch some 80 kilometres or more. On their western side is the long, unbroken Pfälzer Wald, and from the slopes below the edge of the wood to some 8 kilometres or so to the east the vineyards extend into the plain in the direction of the Rhein. Through the region runs one of the better ideas of the Third Reich. The *Deutsche Weinstrasse* was created in 1936 at a time (yet another) when the region was in financial difficulty. The two large vintages of 1934 and 1935 proved difficult to sell following the demise, enforced by the Nazis, of so many wine-merchants' businesses. The development of the *Weinstrasse* linked together some forty villages and encouraged wine-buying tourists and visitors to the region. The *Weinstrasse* is no longer quite the rural idyll that it briefly was in the 1930s, but the charm of most of its villages has been maintained. The Pfälzers are well aware that, for the customer who comes to the region to buy wine, the beauty of the countryside is a strong attraction and everything possible is done to see that it is not impaired.

BEREICH MITTELHAARDT DEUTSCHE WEINSTRASSE

If a district is called Bereich Nierstein or Bereich Bernkastel, every cheap wine-bottler will make use of the name, but even the German love of length of title is not enough to ensure a general awareness of the Bereich Mittelhaardt Deutsche Weinstrasse. For those that do come across it, the *Bereich* remains the description of an area rather than that of its excellent wine.

The Rheingau probably provides the matrix for perfect Riesling wine, or at least it is easy to believe so until you meet the variations offered by the Mosel-Saar-Ruwer or Nahe. Both lighten the Rheingau style and add their own flavours and bouquets, but the good Pfalz Riesling is different again, with a regional character that is heavier and fuller than anything made further north. In other words, in the Rheinpfalz, and particularly in the Bereich Mittelhaardt Deutsche Weinstrasse, the micro-climate is influenced by the warmth of the Rhein basin, the proximity of the hills of the Pfälzer Wald, and the lie of the land below the woods. The similarity to the Alsatian vineyards at the foot of the Vosges mountains is obvious.

The *Bereich* covers about 47 per cent of the whole of the region. It expanded and blossomed in the early part of the nineteenth century and many of the vineyards date from that time. In some places the landscape was recontoured – a foretaste of the reconstruction of the 1970s and 1980s – and walls were built either to reduce a gradient, or to create south-facing slopes by suitable infilling. Until the start of the twentieth century the way the vines were trained made the use of oxen or horses difficult, and as late as the 1950s much of the heavy work, the removal of eroded earth and the distribution of manure, was still done by hand.

Today less than 10 per cent of those involved on grape-growing in the *Bereich* are employed for more than 200 days per year, and for the majority vine-growing and wine-making are a part-time occupation. The co-operative cellars are well thought of, and process some 40 per cent of the harvest. They are developing their sales in bottle although some are still obliged to sell their wine in bulk less profitably to the trade. The members of the best co-operatives have holdings in sites that are known, even outside Germany. At Forst, for example, nearly 70 per cent of the vineyards supplying the co-operative cellar, the *Winzerverein*, are planted in Riesling, and include the top *Einzellagen* of Kirchenstück, Jesuitengarten, and Ungeheuer, as well as part of the Herrgottsacker site at Deidesheim. The high quality of the wine may be judged, simply and easily, in the wine bar of the *Winzerverein* in the centre of Forst itself.

However pretty it may be, Forst is not the place to start examining

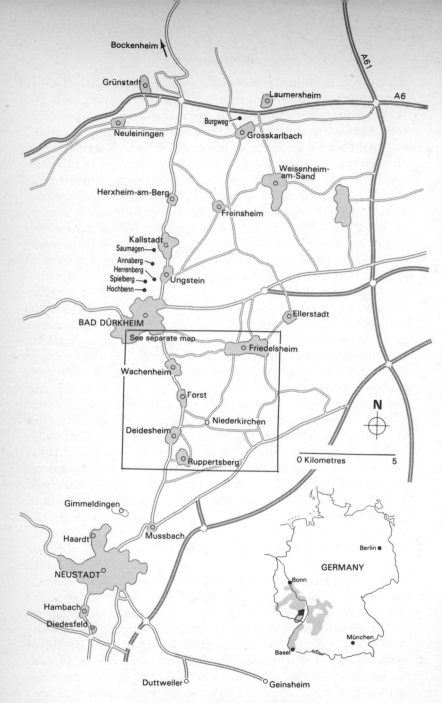

Bereich Mittelhaardt Deutsche Weinstrasse

the district, as further north there are villages which also enjoy an international reputation for their wine. In others, enterprising and skilled growers are setting trends and influencing taste.

Bockenheim at the head of the *Deutsche Weinstrasse* is the first important wine village, travelling south. From here there are long views which on a clear day reach over the closely packed Pfalz vineyards as far as the Odenwald. At Laumersheim, Weingut Knipser makes exciting dry wines. Of its 14 hectares under vine, nearly 5 hectares are planted in Traminer and there are some very impressive wines from Grauer Burgunder and Riesling, many with over 12 per cent of natural alcohol. Knipser is also known for good-quality Dornfelder, and some attractive Blauer Portugieser. So often Portugieser is an apology for a red wine of the most insubstantial sort, but Knipser's wine, from a restricted yield, is charming. This vine interests many lesser growers through its enormous yield (up to 200 hectolitres per hectare), combined with a market price for the wine in bulk often twice that of Müller-Thurgau.

Knipser's holdings stretch to Grosskarlbach, 2 kilometres or so south of the A6 motorway, where Weingut K. & H. Lingenfelder is steadily establishing an international reputation for its Riesling, Scheurebe and Spätburgunder wine. At Grosskarlbach the local climate is drier than that of the region as a whole, so that green manuring in the vineyards (a favourite modern practice) is possible only in a limited way if the vines are not to be stressed in dry weather. The characteristic of Lingenfelder wine that appeals to the export market is that it is well differentiated, clear and direct in flavour. To those who have not met the new style of German Spätburgunder (noticeable tannin and totally dry), the Lingenfelder version is a revelation.

Close to Grosskarlbach are the medieval, walled towns of Freinsheim, and Herxheim am Berg on the *Weinstrasse*. This last is another good point from which to overlook the Pfalz, but perhaps the best of all is Neuleiningen, the ancient, fortified town in an imposing position above the vineyards, near the A6 motorway.

At Kallstadt we have reached the first of the internationally known wine villages. There are many good producers but Weingut Koehler-Ruprecht is particularly well regarded. The wines from the best parts of the variable Saumagen site usually reach the *Spätlese* level of quality and Koehler-Ruprecht's share is planted 90 per cent in Riesling. This estate has also launched a high-quality, *barrique*-aged dessert wine in Bordeaux bottles. Whether this is an enterprising marketing move from a creative mind, or a sad reflection on how difficult it is to sell good German wine at an appropriate price without artificial means of support, is debatable. Weingut Koehler-Rupprecht is a member of the Vereinigung Rheinpfälzischer Weingüter eV, which is itself a part of the Verband Deutscher Prädikatsweingüter (VDP) which we have met in other regions. The Pfalz branch consists of twenty-one members, all of whom have estates in the Bereich Mittelhaardt Deutsche Weinstrasse, and own some 420 hectares of vineyard. Up till recently one of the qualifications for joining the organization was to grow a high proportion of Riesling. This condition has recently been relaxed a little to encourage estates in the Bereich Südliche Weinstrasse to participate. In the south of the Pfalz, Riesling is not so widespread, but there are excellent estates with other traditional vine varieties – the Burgunders and Traminer, for example. All wines that are to be sold under the VDP banner in the Rheinpfalz (and bear the VDP emblem of an eagle with a body formed by a bunch of grapes) undergo a tasting examination. In 1988, 8 per cent failed this test, and the association has strict regulations concerning the membership and the quality of VDP wine. In the large 1989 vintage the average VDP yield in the Pfalz amounted to about 85 hectolitres per hectare with a QmP share of 78 per cent, compared to 51 per cent for the region as a whole. By no means are all good German estates members of the VDP, but most of those that are, are good.

The Kallstadter Annaberg was once one of the best-known sites in Germany and still produces stylish Silvaner, Weissburgunder and Riesling wines, but other sites of similar quality are not hard to find in this privileged part of the region. At Ungstein, nearby, Weingut Pfeffingen has some excellent holdings planted largely in Riesling, but also producing some notable Scheurebe wines.

The spa of Bad Dürkheim with its 18,000 inhabitants is tucked into the foothills of the Pfälzer Wald. In the Winzergenossenschaft 'Vier Jahreszeiten-Kloster Limburg' it has a good co-operative cellar taking in grapes from Wachenheim, Deidesheim, Ungstein and Kallstadt, as well as from Bad Dürkheim itself. The range of vine varieties is wide, with the emphasis being on Riesling, Müller-Thurgau and Blauer Portugieser. The members contract to supply the crop from all their holdings, which avoids any tendency there might be to send only less-good fruit to the co-operative and retain the best for other purposes.

Near the huge Dürkheimer Fass, a cask built to serve as a restaurant in 1934, the over 200-year-old Weingut Fitz-Ritter is one of the town's best-known estates. It has an average annual production of about 16,500 dozen bottles of estate-bottled wine from its vineyards at Dürkheim and Ungstein. The white wines, the Rieslings in particular, retain the freshness which comes from having been stored in stainless-steel vats. The red wines are produced in the old German style and show something of the structure of a white wine, beloved by the conservative local market.

In the Bereich Mittelhaardt Deutsche Weinstrasse the most famous villages and towns by the Pfälzer Wald attract so much attention that it is easy to overlook what is happening elsewhere. Parallel with the *Weinstrasse* and a few kilometres into the Rhein plain, growers such as Lehmann-Hilgard at Freinsheim and Alfred Bonnet at Friedelsheim, further south, make well-defined wines of character and of many different flavours. However, the estate against which others are compared remains Weingut Dr Bürklin-Wolf at Wachenheim on the *Weinstrasse* itself.

The Bürklin-Wolf holdings cover 110 hectares, which probably makes it the largest private estate in Germany. The most important are in seven *Einzellagen* at Wachenheim, four at Forst, four at Deidesheim, and in a further four at Ruppertsberg. Amongst them are unquestionably some of the best sites in the country, so that it can be said that ownership on such a scale carries with it an obligation to produce outstanding, and occasionally great, wine. This Bürklin-Wolf achieves to the benefit of the reputation of German wine as a whole. The characteristic of Bürklin-Wolf's Riesling wine is an intense, clean, full-bodied, elegant flavour. If this description would fit many wines from estates in the region, it is perhaps the degree of refinement that can set the best of Bürklin apart.

Immediately adjoining the vineyards of Wachenheim are those of Forst, a large area of which has been sensitively modernized and reconstructed in the 1980s. Seen from the edge of the Pfälzer Wald, the vineyards at this point are strongly reminiscent of Burgundy's Côte d'Or, with Forst and Deidesheim replacing Meursault and Puligny-Montrachet. The largest *Einzellage* at Forst is the 39-hectare Ungeheuer, but wines from the smaller Kirchenstück and

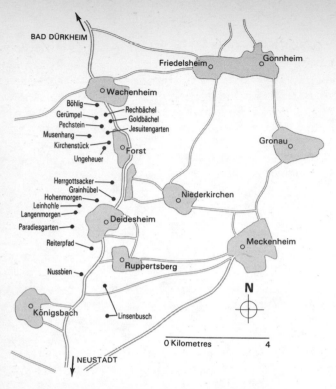

BAD DÜRKHEIM

Friedelsheim   Gonnheim

Wachenheim

Böhlig   Rechbächel
Gerümpel   Goldbächel
Pechstein   Jesuitengarten
Musenhang   Gronau
Kirchenstück
           Forst
Ungeheuer

Herrgottsacker
   Grainhübel
Hohenmorgen   Niederkirchen
Leinhohle
Langenmorgen
Paradiesgarten
                 Deidesheim
Reiterpfad   Meckenheim

Nussbien   Ruppertsberg

                                  N

Königsbach   Linsenbusch

              0 Kilometres   4

NEUSTADT

The Mittelhaardt: Wachenheim to Ruppertsberg

Jesuitengarten sites are usually somewhat more elegant. The famous estates of Bassermann-Jordan and von Buhl have holdings in all three sites. With Bürklin-Wolf these two estates are probably better known outside Germany than the Rheinpfalz region itself.

In the last fifteen years Pfalz wine has lost some of its broad, 'meaty' flavour and has gained more acidity, so that it can now often resemble a wine from the cooler regions further north. On balance the new style is an improvement, although the 'clean as a whistle' approach can sometimes make young dry wines seem ungenerous to an extreme. The Germans have their own appreciative view of such wines which does not always coincide with that held commonly elsewhere. However, there are good producers of both styles, the ultra reductive (absolute minimum contact with the air during maturation) and the very slightly oxidized.

Deidesheim is the base of many leading estates, besides those previously mentioned, including Dr Deinhard, Dr Kern, Kimich and Wegeler-Deinhard and, of course, the excellent co-operative the Winzerverein Deidesheim. It is the oldest co-operative cellar in the region, dating from 1898. That 70 per cent of the members' vineyards are planted in Riesling shows how serious it is.

Deidesheim is also the home of Weingut Menger-Krug, the first German estate to convert all its wine into *Sekt*. In so doing it reflects the lively market for sparkling wines from individual growers. Another sign of the interest in good *Sekt* was the creation of the Vereinigung der Sektgüter der Rheinpfalz in 1988, which has grown to a membership of over forty. Their self-imposed disciplines for the whole production process, from the selection and pressing of the grapes to the maturing of the sparkling wine in bottle, are impressive. Two styles are made, '*brut*' or '*extra brut*', and the *Sekt* may be sold with the association's capsule and bottle tag for up to two years only from the time of the official tasting examination. Freshness, it is thought, is all. Given the enthusiasm of the German market for good *Sekt*, the concept of a Rheinpfalz sparkling wine based on Riesling, Weiss- or Spätburgunder seems thoroughly sound.

Most wine estates go through good and less-inspired periods, but Weingut Müller-Catoir at Haardt, overlooking Neustadt, under the guidance of administrator Hans-Günter Schwarz, is at the peak of its form. Herr Schwarz's method is always to limit yield, never to de-acidify or enrich with sugar, to make late-picked wines really special, and to handle the must and wine as little as possible. Chemistry, according to Herr Schwarz, can produce simple, clean wine, bur complex, great wine comes from experience. This one must believe but Müller-Catoir's first red wine, a 1988 Spätburgunder from young vines, with 13.5 per cent of natural alcohol, is of a sort that nowadays makes a visit to the Rheinpfalz so rewarding. It is not great, but it is very good, and makes one wonder what stunning wines will be produced in ten years' time, when the vines are older and the new styles of wine-making have been practised longer. The advantage of the Rheinpfalz is that it is sufficiently far south to produce full-flavoured dry Burgunder wine, and yet it can also offer racy Rieslings. No other region can do both quite so successfully.

BEREICH SÜDLICHE WEINSTRASSE

Neustadt an der Weinstrasse, with over 50,000 inhabitants, is the largest town in the Pfalz. It is the seat of local government, a centre for the wine trade, and a home for the Rheinland-Pfalz viticultural teaching and research institute which incorporates the oldest wine estate in the region, the Johannitergut, with ecclesiastical origins from the eighth century.

A few kilometres south of Neustadt, the Bereich Mittelhaardt Deutsche Weinstrasse ends and we are in the 12,000-hectare Bereich Südliche Weinstrasse. About a quarter of all Pfalz wine is sold as Liebfraumilch and most of it comes from this southern part of the region. It has long been a district of mass production where much of the crop is delivered to wine-merchants or co-operative cellars. It must be said that in most cases there is a distinct difference between the two, with the co-operatives operating in a more responsible way to build up a reputation for Pfalz wine and increase its profitability. According to Bassermann-Jordan in his *Geschichte des Weinbaues*, the district suffered in the nineteenth century at the hands of powerful outsiders. They bought heavily at the lowest prices and ensured that the reputation of the local wine remained low. The 1988 economic report of the Chamber of Commerce and Industry of the wine-exporting city of Trier shows an interesting picture. Forty per cent of Pfalz wine (and this will mean a high proportion of wine from the Südliche Weinstrasse) is bottled and sold outside the region, and so the Pfalz identity continues to be dissipated.

In the last ten years the quality of wine produced by the co-operative cellars in the Südliche Weinstrasse has improved enormously and a leader in this part of the wine industry is the Gebiets-Winzergenossenschaft Rietburg, a co-operative cellar covering 1,600 hectares from Landau to Neustadt. That good wine does not sell itself, or at least not in large volumes, is a truism; it must be properly packaged and marketed and, with this in mind, the Rietburg co-operative offers under the vine variety name a range (known in Germany as *Die Meisterklasse*) of well-made, attractive wines which omit *Grosslage* and village names. These are the sound-quality, inexpensive wines that the market needs.

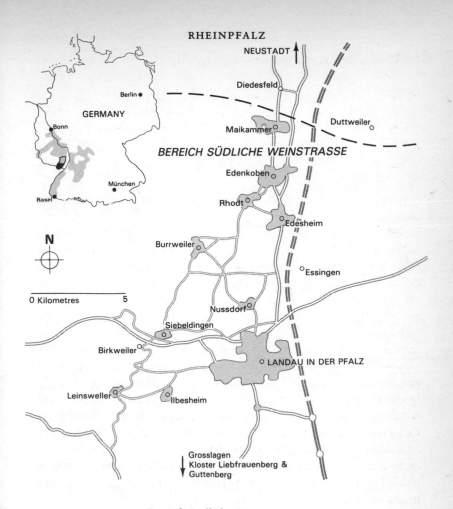

Bereich Südliche Weinstrasse

The Rietburg co-operative lies on the outskirts of Rhodt. It is a charming village, one of a number close to the Pfälzer Wald south of Neustadt, where high-quality private estates nowadays sell almost exclusively to the consumer.

At Birkweiler, on the 10-hectare Weingut Hohenberg, virtually all the wines are dry and mainly from traditional vine varieties, although the holdings include a small parcel of the red St Laurent. This vine was introduced into Germany by Johann Bronner, whose comments on viticulture in the early nineteenth century have often been quoted in this book. Today St Laurent is most widely grown in Austria. Weingut Wilhelmshof is another estate, near Birkweiler at Siebeldingen, which is devoted to dry wines, again from traditional varieties, but perhaps the most famous producer of this little-known but good part of the Pfalz is Weingut Oekonomierat Rebholz. Hansjörg Rebholz says that 'if you are in direct contact with the consumer you cannot allow yourself to make poor-quality wine'. True, but he might have added that if you are trying to sell inferior estate-bottled wine to a serious trade buyer or export house your career is likely to be equally short. Rebholz, however, has no difficulty with its quality. None of its wines is enriched with sugar and none is de-acidified. The result is that with an acidity sometimes every bit as high as that of a Mosel, Rebholz wines need bottle age. They are true to the vine and characterful.

The Bundesforschungsanstalt für Rebenzüchtung, the Federal Research Institute for Vine-breeding, is also established near Siebeldingen, at Geilweilerhof. The Morio-Muskat, Bacchus, Optima and Domina crossings of European vines are its best known offspring. The last named is a red crossing of Portugieser × Spätburgunder, which has established itself more in Franken than anywhere else. The wine has good colour and fairly high acidity. The other three vines have done little for the good reputation of German wine. As always with research institutes, it is not necessarily the final tangible product that is the greatest achievement, and the work of Dr Rapp of Geilweilerhof on the identification of aroma components is discussed worldwide.

The villages in the rolling vineyards along this part of the edge of the Pfälzer Wald are still rural and all the better for it. Leinsweiler is typical. It has been involved in vine-growing for hundreds of years and has an early seventeenth-century, half-timbered town hall and, in Weingut Thomas Siegrist, an outstanding wine-maker. The emphasis in the Siegrist list is on the wine variety, the quality category and the words *trocken* and *halbtrocken*, dry or medium-dry. The 1989 Grauburgunder Spätlese Trocken is a powerful wine with great length of flavour and 14 per cent of natural alcohol. It is well supported on the list by other wines from a low yield. Siegrist also has a number of wines maturing in *barriques*. The young red wines have much tannin and Herr Siegrist is carrying out interesting experiments with alternative forms of cask maturation. His words describe the feelings of many of the new-wave wine-makers in the Pfalz: 'We know what we do not want in red wine, but are not yet certain what we do want.'

The breakdown of the grapes delivered to the large co-operative cellar covering the southern part of the district, the Gebiets-Winzer-genossenschaft Deutsches Weintor, shows no fewer than fifty vine varieties being grown. Müller-Thurgau is the largest supplier followed by Morio-Muskat, Kerner and Silvaner. Thereafter, the tail is long and in terms of 'consumer recognition' almost without meaning. The co-operative cellar sells 80 per cent of its stock (no less than 25.6 million litres) in bottle and the export share of nearly 30 per cent is high. Like its counterpart in the north of the district, the Rietburg co-operative, it is not against using Bordeaux- or Burgundy-shaped bottles for some of its wines. The foreign bottle attracts sales and is certainly more appreciated than the *Pfälzer Löwe*. This is a style of lively, medium-dry wine, produced to an outline recipe agreed by the Pfalz co-operative cellars, and retailed at DM 5.00 per bottle.

When the Bereich Südliche Weinstrasse ends at Schweigen, the holdings of Weingut Leiling and Weingut Friedrich Becker carry on into France. Becker is a young estate producing the new type of Pfalz wine which, some would say, is a return to an older style, mislaid when it became possible to make sweet wine cheaply. In a sense this is true, but the best of today's dry Grau- and Weissburgunders, Traminers and Rieslings from the Pfalz must be more consistent than those of sixty years ago. With this in mind and the continuing improvement in red-wine making, the future of good Pfalz wine looks better in the 1990s than it has done for years.

Some recommended producers in the Bereich Mittelhaardt Deutsche Weinstrasse

Weingut Acham-Magin, 6701 Forst, Weinstrasse 67: Good dry Rieslings in the modern style.

Weingut Gebr. Bart, 6702 Bad Dürkheim, Kaiserslauterer Strasse 42: estate selling QmP only in bottle. Many awards.

Weingut Geheimer Rat Dr von Bassermann-Jordan, 6705 Deidesheim, Kirschgasse 1: famous estate: cask-matured, superb Rieslings. Mainly QmP.

F. u. G. Bergdolt, Klostergut St Lamprecht 6730 Neustadt-Duttweiler, Dudostrasse 17: good range of modern Pfalz wines, some *barrique*-aged.

Weingut Josef Biffar, 6705 Deidesheim, Niederkirchener Strasse 13: ancient Riesling estate. Holdings in top sites.

Weingut Alfred Bonnet, 6701 Friedelsheim: many vine varieties. Wide range of wines, made to last.

Weingut Dr Bürklin-Wolf, 6706 Wachenheim, Weinstrasse 65: top estate. Consistently brilliant Riesling wines from fine sites.

Weingut Arnold Christmann, 6730 Neustadt-Gimmeldingen, Peter Koch Strasse 43: well known for modern style, dry wines and sweet, top category QmP.

Winzerverein Deidesheim eG, 6705 Deidesheim, Prinz-Rupprecht-Strasse 8: top co-operative cellar, bottling wines from famous sites.

Weingut Dr Deinhard, 6705 Deidesheim, Weinstrasse 10: elegant wines, particularly from Riesling and Scheurebe.

Weingut K. Fitz-Ritter, 6702 Bad Dürkheim, Weinstrasse Nord 51: leading estate, fresh, firm Rieslings and cask-matured Spätburgunder.

Forster Winzerverein eG, 6701 Forst, Weinstrasse 57: well-known co-operative. Excellent, inexpensive wines.

Winzergenossenschaft Friedelsheim eG, 6701 Friedelsheim, Hauptstrasse 97–9: good co-operative. Many vine varieties. Good-value wines.

Winzergenossenschaft Herxheim am Berg eG, 6719 Herxheim am Berg: another good co-operative with a wide range of wines.

Winzergenossenschaft Kallstadt eG, 6701 Kallstadt: good range in all the wine quality categories and styles.

Weingut Johannes Karst & Söhne, 6702 Bad Dürkheim, Burgstrasse 15: good medium-sweet 'traditional' Riesling wines, and drier versions.

Weingut Dr Kern, 6705 Deidesheim, Schloss Deidesheim: mainly Riesling estate. Many firm, dry wines.

Weingut Jul. Ferd. Kimich, 6705 Deidesheim, Weinstrasse 54: good dry and medium-dry wines. Many Rieslings cask-matured.

Weingut Knipser, 6711 Laumersheim, Hauptstrasse 47: splendid red and white dry wines. Some *barrique*-aged.

Weingut Koehler-Rupprecht, 6701 Kallstadt: distinguished estate concentrating on drier Riesling wines.

Weingut Lehmann-Hilgard, 6714 Weisenheim am Sand, Friedrich Strasse 21: good, intensely flavoured Riesling wines.

Weingut K. & H. Lingenfelder, 6711 Grosskarlbach, Hauptstrasse 27: excellent Riesling and Scheurebe wines. Top-quality Spätburgunder.

Weingut Georg Mosbacher, 6701 Forst, Weinstrasse 27: good, dry Rieslings from excellent sites. Many top awards.

Weingut Mossbacherhof, 6701 Forst, Weinstrasse 23: 95 per cent Riesling. High-class wines.

Weingut Pfeffingen, 6702 Bad Dürkheim-Pfeffingen: top estate. Many awards. Beautifully made Riesling and Scheurebe.

Ruppertsberger Winzerverein 'Hoheburg' eG, 6701 Ruppertsberg, Obergasse 23: good Rieslings and interesting range of other wines.

Weingut Karl Schäfer, 6702 Bad Dürkheim, Weinstrasse Süd 30: most attractive, flavoury, Riesling wines. Very stylish.

Weingut Eduard Schuster, 6701 Kallstadt, Neugasse 21: well-differentiated, cask-matured Riesling and Silvaner wines.

Winzergenossenschaft 'Vier Jahreszeiten-Kloster Limburg' eG, 6702 Bad Dürkheim, Limburgstrasse 8: sometimes described as the best Pfalz co-operative. Wide range.

Gutsverwaltung Wegeler-Deinhard, 6705 Deidesheim, Weinstrasse 10: elegant, fresh, Riesling wines, made for ageing.

Some recommended producers in the Bereich Südliche Weinstrasse

Weingut Friedrich Becker, 6749 Schweigen, Hauptstrasse 29: dry, well-made wines, some from vineyards across the French border.

Gebiets-Winzergenossenschaft Deutsches Weintor eG, 6741 Ilbesheim: source of good, inexpensive, true-to-type wines.

Weingut Herbert Messmer, 6741 Burrweiler: much Riesling. Prize winning *Auslesen* and wines of higher category.

Weingut Oekonomierat Rebholz, 6741 Siebeldingen, Weinstrasse 54: outstanding estate. Characterful, full-bodied wines. No enrichment.

Gebietswinzergenossenschaft Rietburg eG, 6741 Rhodt, Edesheimer Strasse 50: high-quality, well-made, single vine, good-value wines.

Weingut Thomas Siegrist, 6741 Leinsweiler, Am Hasensprung: fascinating, dry, red and white wines, some *barrique*-aged.

Wein- und Sektgut Wilhelmshof, 6741 Siebeldingen, Queichstrasse 1: still and sparkling wine from limited yields. Skilled wine-making.

20

Franken

Area under vine in hectares in 1988: 5,243 ha, planted 46.8 per cent
Müller-Thurgau, 20.1 per cent Grüner Silvaner, 9.9 per cent Bacchus, 6.4
per cent Kerner, and 16.8 per cent others.

Average temperature during period of vegetation:	14.8 °C
Average sunshine hours during period of vegetation:	1,300
Average rainfall during period of vegetation:	341mm
Average annual rainfall:	590mm
Recent vintages in million hectolitres:	1985 0.07, 1986 0.39,
	1987 0.42, 1988 0.47, 1989 0.79
Average yield in hectolitres per hectare:	1987–87 74.7 hl/ha

Franken is different and proud to be so, for its regional identity is
the strongest in Germany. It lies in the north of Freistaat Bayern,
the largest of the federal states, about the size of The Netherlands
and Belgium put together. Think of Bavaria and we think firstly
of the beer which its inhabitants consume at a rate of 240 litres
each per year. What Bordeaux is to wine, Munich is to beer, but
the city does not have a monopoly on brewing. There are over 800
breweries throughout the state and even in Würzburg, the centre
of the regional wine industry, there is a *Hofbräuhaus*, once the
official Court Brewery. Commercially, the beer and wine of Frank-
en seem to live happily together and both are regarded as utterly
necessary by brewer and wine-maker alike. At a meeting of the
Franken Wine-growers' Association (Fränkisch Weinbauverband)
it was reported that research had shown in 1989 that growers
considered their immediate neighbours to be their greatest competitors. Wine-producers in other German regions came next, followed
by those abroad, but beer was not mentioned.

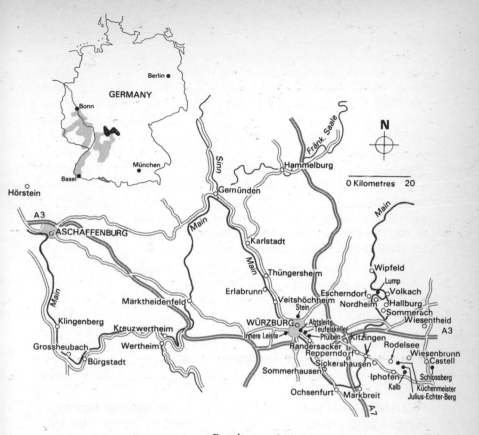

Franken

Beer has one great advantage denied to wine, in that it can be supplied in a steady flow at the pace the market requires, and the supply of Franken wine suffers more than most from a variable climate, as statistics clearly show. Recent extremes in the size of the grape harvest run from a yield of 155 hectolitres per hectare in 1989 to 13 hl/ha in 1985, when even good, south-facing vineyards overlooking the Main were badly damaged. In February that year there were warm sunny days but at night the temperatures dropped to −25 °C. The result was that 2.5 million vines were killed, covering about 19 per cent of the total planted area. The state provided compensation to the growers at a rate of DM 6,700 per hectare, with a maximum of DM 20,000 per estate, but the loss of production in the damaged vineyards for the following three years remained. The details of the 1985 harvest at the district co-operative cellar at Repperndorf, which produces about one-third of all Franken wine, show no crop at all in many places in the southern part of the Bereich Maindreieck, while in the north of the region at Wipfeld the yield rose to 40–50 hl/ha. Big climate variations are characteristic of Franken and the records of the Staatlicher Hofkeller, the former cellars of the prince-bishops of Würzburg, tell us that in 1540 no rain fell between April and October. The vines flowered in May and the grapes were fully ripe by the end of July. Bassermann-Jordan confirms that Franken shared the hot summer of 1540 with the rest of Germany. The dry weather made it possible to cross the Rhein on horseback and cherries produced a second crop in October while, according to records at Bamberg in Bayern, 'water was more expensive than wine'. The climate of Franken remains a difficult partner for the wine industry, and the River Main still freezes over frequently in winter as it has for hundreds of years.

With the effect of the climate in mind, the limit of 90 hl/ha on the amount of wine a producer may sell in any one year from 1990 onwards should not be too burdensome. However, it will oblige a grower who has allowed his Müller-Thurgau vines, in particular, to overcrop to change his ways – as the Franken Wine-growers' Association has recommended for some years.

The Franken vineyard has more than doubled in size since 1964, when Silvaner covered 55 per cent of the area under vine. Although this figure has now dropped to 20 per cent, the plantation of Silvaner has been increasing again since 1986. Its decline coincided with the spread of Müller-Thurgau and to a lesser extent of Bacchus and Kerner, but it has been reversed by the nationwide wish to return to wines from traditional vines. Silvaner is thought to do best on shell lime soils, as at Hammelburg in north Franken, or on keuper, as one finds on the edge of the Steigerwald to the east. Over many years Hammelburger Silvaner has been a good, crisp, full-flavoured dry wine, and the 1983 Iphöfer Kronsberg Silvaner Auslese of Weingut Hans Wirsching at Iphofen in the Bereich Steigerwald is an outstandingly fine wine. It has enormous 'grip' and length of flavour, and will keep well until the year 2000 or later. The range of Silvaner in the region is wide and unrivalled anywhere else in the world. It is said in Franken that you need to be wedded to Silvaner before you can like it. While Franken Silvaner is not a 'beginner's wine' (neither is any Franken wine, outside the region, for that matter), it can often be enjoyed easily by those palates used to the broader wines of warmer climates, and to them it will seem most friendly.

Where Müller-Thurgau does not overcrop, its wine can be much more worthwhile than is usually the case. A good Franken Müller-Thurgau is not as complex as a Silvaner, but in the Bereich Steigerwald its firm structure can make it a thoroughly sound, attractive wine. A Neundorfer Hussberg Müller-Thurgau Trocken QbA from the Castell estate in the indifferent 1984 vintage showed this admirably as late as 1990.

In the early 1980s the Bavarian Ministry of Agriculture proposed that the number of permitted vine varieties should be halved in order to make the total Franken offer more coherent and characteristic of the region. Many of the estates selling directly to the public were not in favour of this reduction as they had developed their own individual markets for wines from the new crossings. The official and understandable view was that growers should concentrate on offering Franken wine as a speciality, and not on specialities from Franken. Today there are about thirty-two named vine varieties in commercial production, of which some twelve are not crossings of European vines. Whilst few would deny that Silvaner and Riesling (on a limited scale) produce the best white wine in the region, some of the new vine varieties make much better wine in Franken than they do elsewhere. This, in addition to the best Kerner and Müller-Thurgau, is certainly true of Bacchus from the Castell estate, which can be an elegant, attractive wine from a yield of about 60 hl/ha.

Some 38 per cent of Franken wine is *Fränkisch Trocken* (contains no more than 4 grams per litre of residual sugar). A further 12 per cent has between 4.1 and 9.0 g/l and, in the eyes of the EC, can still be described as *trocken* or dry. Many would say that, apart from rich wines of at least *Auslese* quality, Franken wine as a type is at its best when dry, with the possible exception of Rieslings. In order to lower the acidity of wines from the Rheinland, Franken wine often used to be added, according to Johann Christian Fischer writing in 1782, and certainly it is the broader structure of Franken wine that makes it a good mealtime drink.

In a report entitled *Die Geschichte der Fränkischen Weinkultur* published in 1860, Sebastian Englerth wrote that in the best sites in Franken, and on the large estates, single vine varieties were planted separately to produce a single vine wine. This was not common practice at that time but it helped to develop clearly defined styles of Franken wine. What united them was the dumpy-shaped bottle with which they had been associated since the early eighteenth century, known as a *Bocksbeutel*. In the 1980s Franken tried to reserve sole use of the *Bocksbeutel* for itself. The local growers and wine-merchants had been concerned since the end of the nineteenth century that foreign wines were sold in their *Bocksbeutel*. Rudolf Friess recorded in his *150 Jahre Fränkischer Weinbauverband*, published in 1986, that many foreign wines were offered for sale in the 1920s not only in the *Bocksbeutel* but also bearing labels and names strongly reminiscent of Franken and the famous Würzburger Stein vineyards. Perhaps the Franconians should have acted much earlier but, be that as it may, in 1984 the European Court of Justice decided that the Bocksbeutel could not be their exclusive property. Within Germany, however, it is now used only for quality red and white Franken wines (QbA and QmP) and for the quality wines of certain villages in the northern part of Baden. Franken has now had to accept that some seventy Portuguese bottlers also put their wines into a *Bocksbeutel*-shaped bottle.

The vineyards of Franken loosely follow the River Main and in so doing form a rather shaky 'W', at the top left-hand corner of which are the vineyards of Hörstein, owned by the Bavarian State Institute for Viticulture and Horticulture, of which the Staatlicher Hofkeller is a part. Aschaffenburg, a city of 59,000 people, has an impressive *Schloss* with its own 0.7-hectare *Einzellage*, the Pompejaner. At Klingenberg, upstream, the town itself has a *Weingut* of 25 hectares which includes parcels of vineyard in several of the neighbouring villages, many on terraced slopes. It is a part of Franken that is well known within the region for red wine. The fame of the expensive Spätburgunder of the Weingut der Stadt Klingenberg is hardly likely to spread much further, however, as it seems to lack the weight of flavour to justify its price.

At Bürgstadt on the south side of the Main, Weingut Rudolf Fürst shows that concentrated, powerful wines can be produced in this part of the region from Spätburgunder and it offers a *barrique*-aged blend of Spätburgunder and Domina (a Portugieser × Spätburgunder crossing) which was particularly successful in the 1988 vintage. The estate also sells a white *Sekt*, made from Spätburgunder, a 'Blancs de Noir'.

This stretch of the Main is attractively wooded, steep-sided and rural. Many of the villages and small towns have interesting old buildings and pleasant places to eat. Preference in everyday food is very much a matter of personal taste, but at the inexpensive restaurant level the standards in Franken seem noticeably higher than they are on the Mosel or in much of the Rheinland. The number of top-class restaurants has greatly increased in Germany in recent years and German chefs are often found in leading positions on the international hotel circuit. For solid, local food, uninfluenced by the notions of *Nouvelle Cuisine*, Franken *Heckenwirtschaft* is unbeatable.

Since the sixteenth century or earlier, a grower has been allowed to serve food with his own wine for a limited number of days each year, on the premises at which he makes his wine. This practice is called *Heckenwirtschaft* in Franken, *Besenwirtschaft* in Württemberg, and *Strauss-* or *Strohwirtschaft* in other regions. To advertise *Heckenwirtschaft* a branch, cut from a hedge (*Hecke*) or wood, is displayed where it will catch the attention of passers-by. The old saying that 'good wine needs no bush' is not really true.

At Kreuzwertheim, the Fürstlich Löwenstein Wertheim Rosenberg'sches Weingut is an important agricultural and forestal estate with 27 hectares under vine, lying on the edge of Franken and, on the banks of the Tauber in Baden, across the Main. Some of the sites are steeply terraced, and known to have been in existence in the twelfth century, but the most famous of the Löwenstein holdings are the 18 hectares in the Homburger Kallmuth – perhaps the steepest vineyard in Franken. In 1971 additional and inferior parcels were added to this site, as happened in many fine vineyards, but the Löwenstein section remains most impressive and produces well-structured Riesling, Silvaner and Traminer dry wines.

From Kreuzwertheim, travelling up the Main, the river turns north to the top of the central part of its 'W' shape. Here the vineyards are sparse, but, as the route descends to Würzburg, it once again passes through important wine villages. At Thüngersheim, the vineyards have been modernized (see chapter 3), with production costs being reduced by up to 40 per cent in the process. Much of the crop is sent to the local co-operative cellar but the great Bürgerspital and Staatlicher Hofkeller estates based on Würzburg also have holdings in the Thüngersheimer Scharlachberg site.

Without a doubt, Würzburg is one of the most impressive wine cities in Europe. In the dying weeks of the Second World War a bombing raid, and the firestorm that followed, destroyed most of the city, but it has been restored or rebuilt with care. The close connection to wine cannot be missed, as vineyards shadow the city on two sides. The most famous is the large Würzburger Stein *Einzellage* to the north. Before the 1971 Wine Law the description *Steinwein* was used with the greatest freedom so that it had become a synonym for *Frankenwein*. That is no longer so, and a Würzburger Stein Riesling from the Juliusspital, Bürgerspital or the Staatlicher Hofkeller is a powerful wine of high quality. A *Spätlese* wine may well cost DM 23.00 per bottle, but if it is as good as the 1988 version from the Juliusspital it is not overpriced. The best Franken wines are never too expensive, but the lesser ones, in comparison with what the Rheinpfalz can offer, sometimes are.

The wine estate of the Bürgerspital zum Heiligen Geist has been endowed with vineyards since the fourteenth century and now has 140 hectares, of which nearly 96 are in Würzburg itself. The rest, with the exception of holdings at Randersacker and Michelau, are downstream from the city. The styles run from the bone-dry to the amazing Würzburger Abtsleite Riesling Trockenbeerenauslese which was picked as early in 1976 as 28 September. It is wine of enormous depth and statistically its 188° of must weight (25.6 per cent of potential alcohol) was only surpassed at a superb tasting in Würzburg in 1989 by that of a 1983 Würzburger Abtsleite Gewürztraminer Trockenbeerenauslese (211° of must weight or 29.3 per cent of potential alcohol) from the Juliusspital.

The Juliusspital complex includes a hospital, an old people's home and the wine cellars, which are supplied by 161 hectares of vineyard, mainly in Würzburg and villages to the east. The third and largest of the estates which add lustre to the city and the whole of Franken is the Staatlicher Hofkeller, whose holdings are spread throughout the region. When the vaulted cellars near the *Residenz*, the former official home of the prince-bishops of Würzburg, are visited by candlelight, with a choir singing melodiously in the background, the effect is magical.

Seven kilometres upstream from Würzburg, the village of Randersacker has 280 hectares of vineyard, including the 40-hectare

Teufelskeller *Einzellage*, as well as the even better, partly Riesling site, Randersackerer Pfülben. As the journey up the Main reaches the lowest point in the central point of the region's 'W', Eibelstadt, Sommerhausen, Frickenhausen and Ochsenfurt are all attractive old places, well worth visiting. Our route from Randersacker takes us across country and away from the river, to Repperndorf, the home of the largest cellar in Bavaria, the Gebietswinzergenossenschaft Franken, or GWF for short.

The list of the *Einzellage* names that appear on the bottles sold by the GWF covers two sides of a computer print-out. Some are well known, such as Escherndorfer Lump, Iphöfer Julius-Echter-Berg, Würzburger Abtsleite, or the charming-sounding Randersackerer Ewig Leben ('Eternal Life'), but many are unfamiliar. Erlenbacher Krähenschnabel ('Crow's Beak') or the local Sickershäuser Storchenbrünnle ('Stork's Spring') have a nice, metrical beat to them, but whether they represent an individual style, or wine worth identification, is another matter. According to the managing director in an interview reported in the magazine *Die Weinwirtschaft*, the GWF produced no fewer than 1,700 different wines in the large 1989 vintage. One can wonder why, but even large co-operative cellars have to reflect the wishes of their members to see their village or vineyard names retained for their wines, rather than meet the needs of a wider market for simpler and fewer designations.

However, about 60 per cent of the GWF wines are sold locally (the equivalent of about 10 million 0.75-litre bottles in an average vintage), and the Franken co-operatives achieve the highest prices for their wines of all the co-operative cellars in Germany.

Three kilometres east of Repperndorf is the town of Kitzingen, where the cellar of a former Benedictine monastery is said to be the oldest in Germany. East of this point, in the Bereich Steigerwald, are three important wine communities. Iphofen is a walled town that has somehow survived the occupation and plundering of foreign forces from the seventeenth century until 1945. Its Julius-Echter-Berg, Kronsberg and Kalb sites are top-quality vineyards with some outstandingly good part-owners. These include the Juliusspital in Würzburg, and Johann Ruck, Ernst Popp and Hans Wirsching in Iphofen itself. Silvaner is widely planted on the slopes of the foothills of the Steigerwald, where Müller-Thurgau also produces fresh, concentrated wines. Between 1980 and 1984, when

Franken and the whole of Germany had two huge vintages in 1982 and 1983, the average Müller-Thurgau yield on the Wirsching estate was 65 hectolitres per hectare. For Silvaner, the figure was 55 hl/ha and for Riesling, 40 hl/ha. A low yield is very much part of Wirsching's and Ruck's success.

Rödelsee lies 4 kilometres north of Iphofen and its best-known site, the 55-hectare Küchenmeister, adjoins the Iphöfer Julius-Echter-Berg. The vines on the edge of the Steigerwald – or, more precisely, on the slopes of the Schwanberg hill – form one consolidated vineyard which amounts to nearly two-thirds of those of the Bereich Steigerwald.

The most powerful single wine-making enterprise in the district is the Fürstlich Castell'sches Domänenamt. The seat of Fürst zu Castell-Castell's family is the seventeenth-century *Schloss* in the middle of the village of Castell. The wines of the estate come from 58 hectares of vineyard and a further 70 hectares are owned by the eighty-eight members of the Erzeugergemeinschaft Steigerwald, the producers' association run by the Castell estate. Up till the end of the 1970s 'export' for Castell meant selling its wine outside Franken, but today it is making serious efforts to sell not only its own but also the similarly labelled wines of the producers' association outside Germany. The range is wide, the quality is good, and the offer is led by Müller-Thurgau and Silvaner, planted in 60 per cent of the estate's holdings.

Schloss Pommersfelden near Wiesentheid, north of Castell, is the very stately home of the von Schönborn family, under whose guidance, and with the help of Balthasar Neumann and other architects, the *Residenz* in Würzburg was built. Over the centuries the von Schönborns have been distinguished churchmen and diplomats, but they are popularly known today for their wine estate in the Rheingau. Near Volkach, north of Wiesentheid, there is another Schönborn property, the Graf von Schönborn'sches Weingut, Schloss Hallburg.

The Main splits west of Volkach and later reunites near Sommerach, to confuse the visitor and create a substantial island of vines. The Winzergenossenschaft Sommerach was founded in 1901, which makes it the oldest co-operative cellar in the region. Grapes are supplied from villages as far away as Iphofen, but with 245 members owning 154 hectares its size is modest. Nordheim, nearby, also has a regionally known co-operative cellar whose members have 300 hectares on all sides of the divided Main, including the village of Escherndorf. Here, as all along this stretch of the river, the vines rise steeply in a continuous sweep of modernized vineyard. The Escherndorfer Lump site, in particular, ripens its grapes well on slopes that reach 60 per cent in places.

Most Franken wine can be described as 'slightly earthy', regardless of whether it comes from mica-schist, variegated sandstone, keuper, shell lime, or alluvial sand types of soil or their many variations. Whether it is the soil alone that so markedly affects the bouquet and flavour of Franken wine, or simply its physical ability to retain moisture and warmth in connection with the microclimate, is a controversial subject that has been examined for some years at the Bavarian State Institute of Viticulture. If final conclusions are reached, they are likely to upset entrenched opinion in many parts of the wine world. Old wine-trade beliefs are not abandoned without a fight.

Some recommended producers in Franken

Bayerische Landesanstalt für Weinbau und Gartenbau, Staatlicher Hofkeller, 8700 Würzburg, Residenzplatz 3.

Weingut Bürgerspital zum Heiligen Geist, 8700 Würzburg, Theaterstrasse 19.

Fürstlich Castell'sches Domänenamt, 8711 Castell, Schlossplatz 5.

Gebietswinzergenossenschaft Franken eG, 8710 Kitzingen/Repperndorf.

Weingut Juliusspital, 8700 Würzburg, Klinikstrasse 5.

Information about the four estates and the co-operative cellar mentioned above can be found in the text of chapter 20.

Weingut Rudolf Fürst, 8768 Bürgstadt, Hohenlindenweg 46: 50 per cent, good, tannic red wine. Fresh Riesling and Müller-Thurgau.

Weingut-Sektkellerei Ernst Gebhardt, 8701 Sommerhausen, Hauptstrasse 21–3: full range of Franken wines, and Sekt from own estate since 1911.

Schloss Saaleck-Städtliches Weingut Hammelburg, 8783 Hammelburg: firm, long-flavoured wines. Bacchus a speciality.

Fürstlich Löwenstein-Wertheim-Rosenberg'sches Weingut, 6983 Kreuzwertheim, Rathausgasse 5: good, dry wines, typical of the region. Mainly Fränkisch Trocken.

Winzergenossenschaft Nordheim eG, 8711 Nordheim: good source of dry and medium-dry award-winning wines.

Weingut Ernst Popp KG, 8715 Iphofen, Rödelseer Strasse 14–15: powerfully flavoured, well-made wines.

Winzergenossenschaft Randersacker eG, 8701 Randersacker, Maingasse 33: good, relatively small co-operative. Mainly dry and medium-dry wines.

Weingut Robert Schmitt, 8701 Randersacker, Maingasse 13: strong-flavoured, fully fermented wines. None is enriched or sweetened.

Weingut Johann Ruck, 8715 Iphofen, Marktplatz 19: top-quality, carefully made wines. No de-acidification.

Weingut Hans Wirsching, 8715 Iphofen, Ludwigstrasse 16: perfectly made wines of depth and character. Great but small estate.

21

Hessische Bergstrasse

Area under vine in hectares in 1988: 389 ha, planted 54.5 per cent Weisser Riesling, 17.2 per cent Müller-Thurgau, 7.7 per cent Rülander, 7.5 per cent Grüner Silvaner, and 13.1 per cent others.

Average temperature during period of vegetation:	15.1 °C
Average sunshine hours during period of vegetation:	1,274
Average rainfall during period of vegetation:	511mm
Average annual rainfall:	756mm
Recent vintages in thousand hectolitres:	1985 24.0, 1986 32.0, 1987 30.0, 1988 31.0, 1989 50.0
Average yield in hectolitres per hectare:	1978–87 77.1 hl/ha

If you wish to taste the wines of Germany's smallest regions, you will almost certainly have to visit them for yourself. The smallest of them all, the Hessische Bergstrasse, is no exception. The Bergstrasse, the mountain road – or, as the Romans called it, *Strata Montana* – runs from Darmstadt east of the Rhein, to Heidelberg in the south and beyond. Since 1971 the vineyards that follow the edge of the Odenwald have been divided in two, with the southern part being included in Baden (the Bereich Badische Bergstrasse/ Kraichgau).

The Hessische Bergstrasse to the north is known locally for its mild climate and the extent of the almond, peach, cherry and apple blossom in spring. The region has its better-known sites, such as the 17.5-hectare Heppenheimer Centgericht, solely owned by the Staatsweingut, but some look more like allotments than commercial vineyards. As in parts of Württemberg, they are dotted with solidly built little huts where the owners store their tools and vineyard equipment.

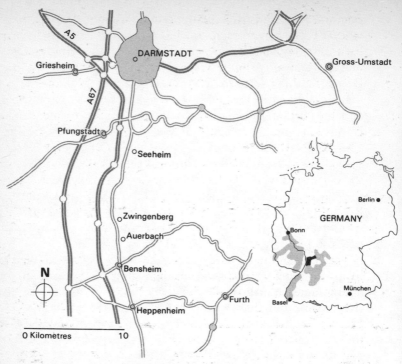

Hessische Bergstrasse

Vineyard reconstruction has been less widespread in the Hessische Bergstrasse than in other regions. (The *phylloxera* pest has not established itself, so perhaps the urgent need to modernize has been missing.) The average annual rainfall is high but the water drains quickly through the varied soils in the steep vineyards. The result, if that is what it is, is a wine with its own regional character. With less acidity than a Rheingau, it develops more quickly and, for those who do not enjoy the very high acid levels of some modern dry wines, the Hessische Bergstrasse version may seem a better choice. It is an excellently flavoured wine, usually without the distinction of the best of the Rheingau, and it can taste well with food.

Yield, that often-discussed theme, is naturally low in the Hessische Bergstrasse and, were it not that the winters are not as unkind as in Franken, the average figure would be even lower. The area planted in Riesling has increased since the early 1960s by 250 per cent and Riesling is still enlarging its share of a slowly expanding vineyard. The new crossings, including Müller-Thurgau, have never been very popular but, as in other regions, Spätburgunder has literally gained ground, with wines made in the 'traditional' German fashion – low in tannin and relatively high in acid.

Besides the easily located vineyards that overlook the Rhein plain and the distant Rheinhessen, there are some isolated sites near Darmstadt and to the east of the city. They form the Bereich Umstadt. Never short of a descriptive phrase, the Germans refer to this outpost of Hessische viticulture as the Odenwälder Weininsel – the Odenwald wine island. The wines are generally light, but when they have a little more weight are said to recall those of the nearby River Main and Franken. This is perfectly plausible, given that wines from near the mouth of the river at Hochheim in the Rheingau also have a distinct flavour of Franken.

The Staatsweingut Bergstrasse, the State Cellars at Bensheim, forms the most famous estate in the region. Today it is an almost autonomous branch of the Staatliche Weinbaudomäne in Eltville (Rheingau), and the managing director of the 37-hectare estate, Heinrich Hillebrand, is the fourth member of his family to hold the post since the start of the century. *Eisweine* are a speciality, and six are included in the 1990 list from the 1987, 1986, 1985, 1983 and 1979 vintages. (One of the two 1985s has added interest, having been picked on 8 February 1986.) For the most part, fermentation at the State Cellars is spontaneous (no added yeast), and this brings out the character of the wine, or so it is thought. Maturation is in 2,400-litre casks and many wines are individually bottled, without being 'equalized', or blended together.

Another Bensheim estate, dating from the turn of the century, is owned by the town itself. The 12 hectares of the Weingut der Stadt Bensheim all lie within the civic boundaries and are planted 73 per cent in Riesling. Amongst the other vine varieties are 1.3 hectares of the late-ripening Rotberger (Trollinger × Riesling – the same parentage as Kerner), which, apart from red and rosé wine, also makes a good *Sekt*. Almost by definition, the Weingut der Stadt is very much a local estate supplying a loyal circle of Bensheim customers.

There is a small co-operative cellar in the Odenwald wine island whose members own 28 hectares of vineyard, but at Heppenheim, south of Bensheim, is the Bergsträsser Gebiets-Winzergenossenschaft (the BGW), a much larger affair dating from 1904. The region has 738 growers, with a low average holding of 0.53 hectares. The BGW has 620 members, some of whom are based in the Badische Bergstrasse at Laudenbach. Much of the production is sold in litre bottles, and it is noticeable that the additional amounts paid to the members for grapes of a higher quality are greater than in many other co-operative cellars. In order to maintain the natural character of the wines, chemical de-acidification is not practised, and a malo-lactic fermentation is encouraged when the level of acidity is too high.

The BGW wines are fairly priced with Spätlese Riesling starting at a little over DM 8.00 per 0.75-litre bottle. The most expensive wine on the list and the star of the show is a 1983 Gewürztraminer Eiswein at DM 55.00 per half-bottle. (The BGW indemnifies its members for the risk involved in leaving grapes on the vine in the hope of making *Eiswein*.) To meet the need for wines with simple names, the BGW launched in the 1988 vintage a range of single-vine QbAs. The Riesling and Grauer Burgunder are dry and the Silvaner is medium-dry. These are simple marketing concepts, which young consumers in Germany are thought to appreciate. The wines can, of course, be supplied in greater volume than would be possible if they came from a single site. It should be repeated that when, perhaps, 80 per cent of the roughly 2,000 *Einzellagen* do not truly represent clearly defined individual styles of wine, there is a strong case for not using their names. Often, the wines are a better proposition when skilfully blended, and sold under an easy-to-remember vine name. A good co-operative cellar is well placed to offer good commercial quantities of such wines.

Some recommended producers in the Hessische Bergstrasse

Weingut der Stadt Bensheim, 6140 Bensheim, Am Ritterplatz.

Staatsweingut Bergstrasse, 6140 Bensheim, Grieselstrasse 34–6.

Bergsträsser Gebiets-Winzergenossenschaft eG, 6148 Heppenheim, Darmstädter Strasse 56.

Odenwälder Winzergenossenschaft eG, 6114 Gross-Umstadt, Riegelgartenweg 1.

Details of the types of wine produced can be found in the text of chapter 21.

22

Württemberg

Area under vine in hectares in 1988: 9,791 ha, planted 24.9 per cent
Weisser Riesling, 21.9 per cent Trollinger, 14.8 per cent Müllerrebe, 9.0
per cent Kerner, 8.9 per cent Müller-Thurgau, 6.1 per cent Blauer Lemberger, 14.4 per cent others.

Average temperature during period of vegetation:	14.3 °C
Average sunshine hours during period of vegetation:	1,227
Average rainfall during period of vegetation:	483mm
Average annual rainfall:	737mm
Recent vintages in million hectolitres:	1985 0.3, 1986 1.2, 1987 0.8, 1988 1.1, 1989 1.7
Average yield in hectolitres per hectare:	1978–87 100.6 hl/ha

---

According to *Württemberg*, published in 1987 by the Verlag
Heinen, Duke Johann Friedrich celebrated his wedding in 1609
with a party for 9,600 guests, each of whom, on average, drank
43 litres of wine. It was a celebration over several days, which
would have contributed handsomely to the annual wine-consumption figure for all Württembergers weaned from their mothers' milk
of 130–50 litres per head. German vine-growing was then at its
peak and the Württemberg vineyards covered over 40,000 hectares.
Today, the area under vine is far smaller than it was 400 years ago,
but wine in Württemberg has remained almost a *Volksgetränk*, an
everyday drink of the people, a characteristic that it had begun to
lose in other parts of Germany by the early 1900s.

Some 80 per cent of Württemberger wine is sold in litre bottles
which then fill neatly the 0.25-litre glass mugs with handles from
which the local wine is drunk. The enthusiasm for wine is such
that of the yearly consumption of 38 litres per head, two-thirds

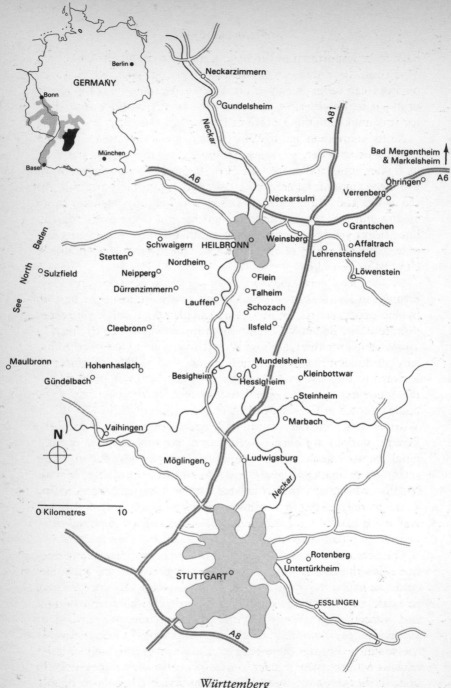

Neckarzimmern

Gundelsheim

GERMANY

Berlin

Bonn

München

Basel

A81

A6

Bad Mergentheim
& Markelsheim

Öhringen

A6

Verrenberg

Neckarsulm

Grantschen

See North Baden

Neckar

Schwaigern

HEILBRONN

Weinsberg

Affaltrach

Stetten

Nordheim

Lehrensteinsfeld

Sulzfield

Neipperg

Löwenstein

Flein

Dürrenzimmern

Talheim

Lauffen

Schozach

Cleebronn

Ilsfeld

Maulbronn

Hohenhaslach

Mundelsheim

Kleinbottwar

Gündelbach

Besigheim

Hessigheim

Steinheim

Vaihingen

Marbach

N

Möglingen

Ludwigsburg

Neckar

0 Kilometres 10

Rotenberg

STUTTGART

Untertürkheim

ESSLINGEN

A8

Württemberg

184

have to be imported into the region, much from outside Germany. This could be a threat to Württemberger red wine, which to an outsider can seem hardly more than a pleasant, uncomplicated drink. It is, however, in the true sense of the word, a speciality, for it is unlike anything produced anywhere else.

A little more than half of Württemberg's vineyard area is planted in red-vine varieties, of which Trollinger has the biggest share. In its Italian homeland in the Süd Tirol, huge clusters of grapes produce large amounts of soft, pale-coloured, agreeable but unserious red wine. The Württemberg version is similarly pale, with more acidity and less alcohol. It too could be said to be over-cropped, but a heavy yield per hectare when weather permits is characteristic of red wine-making in the region. In the large 1989 vintage it climbed to 189 hl/ha.

As has been mentioned, in 1989 the state of Rheinland-Pfalz brought in restrictions on the amount of wine that might be sold by the producer in any one year, calculated on a hectolitre per hectare basis. Baden-Württemberg enforced similar restrictions in 1990, which for the region of Württemberg amount to 110 hl/ha. Any production in excess of these figures will be able to be carried forward to the next twelve-month period, which will be helpful if the following vintage is small but a problem if it is large. The figures quoted at the start of this chapter show that the size of the Württemberg wine harvest can vary widely over the years, and the new regulations are hardly likely to make more than a very marginal improvement in the quality of most wines. As in other regions, the financial reward for making better, but less, wine is usually missing. In the meantime, many Württembergers enjoy some of the lightest red wine in the world, often with enough residual sugar for it to be described as *Halbtrocken* (medium-dry), or even as medium-sweet.

The person who is accustomed to drinking Trollinger daily does not enjoy the greater amount of tannin of a French red wine. He, or she, is happy to pay either over DM 5.00 for a 0.25-litre *Viertele* in a café, or DM 7.30 or so for a litre bottle of similar wine bought in a grocery store. What Trollinger lacks in the view of one of Germany's best-known tasters, the Frenchman Guy Bonnefoit, is 'personality'. For this one needs to turn to other red-wine varieties such as Müllerrebe or Blauer Lemberger (also spelt Limberger). In spite of the fact that a 1988 Fleiner Lemberger QbA was probably the palest, the thinnest 'red' wine that I have ever tasted anywhere, Lemberger is known for wines with noticeable tannin. Faced with overproduction and methods of wine-making aimed at an unusual local market, even Lemberger loses much of its individuality.

Many Germans are gregarious by nature and enjoy sitting in cafés or at home for a long period, talking with friends. In these circumstances, wine becomes a part of the background against which time passes and, like piped music, it is expected to be agreeable but unobtrusive. Much red wine from Württemberg's Weingärtnergenossenschaften (co-operative cellars) is destined to be drunk in this way and its commercial success was such that in the 1980s demand sometimes exceeded supply. On occasions red wine could only be purchased if white wine was also bought. So far, so good, but tastes in Germany can change radically and quickly, and whether the public will continue to want to buy Württemberg red wine from co-operative cellars, at the present rate and price and in its current style, remains uncertain.

Württemberg's white wine, which sells at some 50 Pfennigs per bottle less than the red wine, is an easier product for the foreigner to appreciate. The villages of Lehrensteinsfeld east of Heilbronn, and of Flein a little to the south, are well known for Riesling and, at DM 6.20 or so per litre bottle, it is competitively priced. Screw-top litre bottles are usual, with the space between the wine and the closure receiving a whiff of carbon dioxide to prevent deterioration. As in many other regions, Riesling is increasing in popularity, but its descendant, the Württemberg crossing Kerner, seems to be going out of fashion; perhaps because it has often been prepared as a medium-sweet wine. With a significant proportion of the Württemberg vineyard being less than ten years old (much having been replanted after *Flurbereinigung* or reconstruction), it is difficult to follow quickly and economically the whims of a market when it asks for new or different vine varieties. Changes in styles of wine-making are more easily and less expensively introduced.

Of the 16,492 vine-growers in Württemberg only 2,347 own more than one hectare of vineyard. There are relatively few estate bottlers but amongst them are aristocratic names which even pre-date the eighteenth-century *Gothaischen Genealogischen Taschenführer* and its British equivalent *Debrett's Peerage and Baronetage*. The co-operative cellars, which handle over 85 per cent of the harvest, are obliged to accept whatever grapes members supply. Payment is made based on must weight. What is not taken into direct account is the health of the grapes and how free they are from rot, which, of course, is difficult to quantify. Although some co-operatives do rather more than produce an acceptable drink, the large volume of grapes to be processed does mean that methods of heating the must are adopted, which reduce individuality. In establishments that receive millions of kilos of grapes at the harvest, wine is often made according to a laid-down formula to produce the standard product which the larger customers require.

The main part of the Württemberg vineyard lies on either side of the E70 motorway which runs from Weinsberg, near Heilbronn, to west of Stuttgart. Above this district, known as the Bereich Württembergisch Unterland, and further east there is a *Bereich* named after the three rivers, the Kocher, the Jagst and the Tauber, which borders on Franken. Near Bad Mergentheim (made famous in the nineteenth century by its magnesium-sulphate springs) is Markelsheim, where vine-growing might have disappeared after spring frosts in 1953 had it not been for an extensive *Flurbereinigung* programme. The 136 hectares of weathered chalk soil, planted mainly in Müller-Thurgau and Silvaner, supply private customers and restaurants, via the local co-operative cellar, with concentrated wine from relatively low yields. Moving nearer Heilbronn, the estate of Fürst Kraft zu Hohenlohe-Oehringen has one of the largest 'sole ownerships' in Germany – the 20-hectare Verrenberger Verrenberg site, planted mainly in Riesling. Almost all the wines are fermented out to total dryness and matured in wood. At Neckarzimmern, north of Heilbronn, there is the equally well-known and historic estate of Weingut Burg Hornberg. Until the boundary was moved in 1985, it lay in neighbouring Baden, although the picturesque castle above the vineyards had often appeared on posters promoting Württemberg. Hans-Wolf Freiherr von Gemmingen, whose family bought Burg Hornberg in 1612, is a strong defender of traditional vine varieties, including Traminer and Muskateller. He fears they may suffer from the unpopularity of the scented wines from some of the new crossings. At Schwaigern, west of Heilbronn, Graf von Neipperg has 32 hectares planted in both red and white vine varieties. Tradition is understandably strong on an estate that has been in the Neipperg family since 1200 and the serious red wines have a good colour and body.

These and the white wines are almost all dry. The Baumann family at Schlosskellerei Affaltrach make wine from just over 7 hectares and also from the 126 hectares of a producers' association, which it runs for some 250 local vine-growers. Making sparkling wine has been important to Württemberg since Germany's oldest *Sekt* manufacturer, G. C. Kessler, was established in Esslingen in 1826, and Schlosskellerei Affaltrach expects that if the boom in *Sekt* continues in the 1990s it will soon be selling more sparkling than still wine.

Between the village of Affaltrach and Heilbronn, just south of the E12 motorway, is the town of Weinsberg, famous in the wine world for the State Teaching and Research Institute for Wine and Fruit Growing. The Staatliche Lehr- und Versuchsanstalt, with its 53 hectares of vineyard, is the largest wine-producing estate in Württemberg and the oldest viticultural institute in Germany, dating from 1868. Many vine varieties are grown, with Riesling having the largest share – 22 per cent of the total area. As with the Württemberg co-operative cellars, the red grapes (without their stalks) are heated briefly to 80 °C or so to extract colour, and the wines are encouraged to develop a malo-lactic fermentation to reduce acidity. The results remain a puzzle to the outsider. In the middle of a tutored tasting of rosé-coloured red wines at the Institute in 1988, a frustrated Bremen wine-merchant exclaimed, '*Wann fangen wir mit dem Rotwein an?*' ('When do we start on the red wine?'). He was, it was comforting to note, as much out of his depth as the writer. Even if the Institute tailors its own red wines to the local market, many of its ex-students are making wine of a more internationally recognized style all over central Europe, where Weinsberg and the Austrian Klosterneuburg have much influence.

The co-operative cellar at Grantschen near Weinsberg has recognized a need to offer something more than sound, well-made wine, and has launched a number of interesting products, including a high-quality Dornfelder-Lemberger, cask-matured blend, based on *Kabinett*-quality grapes. It sells at DM 20.00 per bottle, a price at which many of the more recent styles of German wine are offered. They are of great interest and some are of top quality, although the producers admit that, like their colleagues in the newer vineyard areas of the world, they are still developing their wine-making techniques and finding out what suits their particular vineyard environment.

One of the most distinguished wine estates in Germany is Wein-gut Graf Adelmann of Burg Schaubeck at Steinheim-Kleinbottwar, south of Weinsberg. It is well known for full-bodied, tannic red wines made from: Samtrot – a mutation of Müllerrebe, selected at the State Institute at Weinsberg; Clevner (or Blauer Frühburgunder) – a variety of Pinot whose wine sometimes tastes more of Gamay than of Pinot Noir (Spätburgunder); Muskat-Trollinger – a variety of Trollinger with a slight Muskat bouquet, grown at Burg Schaubeck since 1881; Urban – an ancient relative of Trollinger grown at Burg Schaubeck, in a very small area.

The bulk of the red wine, however, is made from the less unusual varieties, Trollinger and Lemberger, but vinification is of the tra-ditional French variety (grapes, sometimes stalks, and must fer-menting together), with a minimum of fining or filtration. Michael Graf Adelmann is a leader in the practice of maturing wine in new wood and he looks for an acidity higher than is usual in Württem-berg in his mainly Riesling white wines (7–8 grams per litre). Perhaps it is significant that over half of Adelmann's wines are sold outside Württemberg. They are widely regarded as amongst the finest of their type in Germany.

In very general terms, there are three sorts of Württemberg vineyard. The first is gently rolling and shares the arable land with various other crops. It is pleasantly rural but makes no special claim for the tourists' attention. The second rises steeply from the edge of a village almost to the brow of a hill, where its ascent is frustrated by a castle surrounded by woodland. The third typical Württemberg vineyard is very steep, terraced and overlooks the Neckar or one of its tributaries. As so often happens, the best sites are the steepest. They are planted with Trollinger or Riesling and because of the angle of the slope the vines grow close together with the branches of one plant being less than a metre from the stock of the next above it. Irrigation is allowed on slopes of more than 30 per cent to strengthen the leaves and so help the grapes to ripen to at least potential QbA level (57° Oechsle or 7 per cent of natural alcohol for Trollinger and Riesling). In the Mundelsheimer Käsberg site overlooking the Neckar, where, incidentally, many of the vines are ungrafted, the vineyard is irrigated by a system that allows water to trickle very slowly into the soil, increasing the weight of the grape juice by a worthwhile 8° Oechsle or so (1.2 per cent of alcohol). To cover costs – or, better still, to make a profit – a grower can either aim for a small crop from which a wine of outstanding quality is produced, as in some of the steep vineyards of the Mosel, or he must look for a larger yield of a lesser wine. With high labour costs any grower who has somewhat ordinary vines growing in steep vineyards is faced with financial difficulties. The growers of Chasselas in the steep vineyards overlooking the Lake of Geneva are in the same position as those with Trollinger in terraced Württemberg vineyards. Both are able to survive for the present through the support of a local market willing to pay more for their wines than the world outside. This was not always so and in the early nineteenth century the British writer Cyrus Redding described Neckar wine as of 'a light red colour, not deep, and of tolerable flavour and bouquet'. He claimed surprisingly that it was made from 'the best French, Hungarian, and even Cyprus vines', but whatever the vine variety, Neckar wine, shipped down the river and along the Rhein to Rotterdam, was better known abroad at that time than it is today.

Stuttgart, the capital of Baden-Württemberg, is a busy city of over half a million inhabitants. In spite of industry and commerce, vines still grow on some of the spurs of land that reach almost into its centre. To the east there are fine-looking, reconstructed vineyards, particularly in the suburb of Rotenberg and in the valley of the Rems.

Of the region's 9,791 hectares under vine some 60 per cent has been rebuilt in recent years and work remains to be done on a further 10 per cent. In about 2,000 hectares either the steepness of the slopes makes reconstruction impractical or the growing conditions are already satisfactory.

At Ludwigsburg, 16 kilometres north of Stuttgart, the eighteenth-century *Schloss* modelled on Versailles includes within its substantial grounds the rococo Schloss Monrepos. The Württembergische Hofkammerkellerei is nearby, but its 38 hectares under vine are spread throughout the southern half of the region on six satellite estates. The yield is restrained, with half the land being planted in Riesling and nearly a quarter in Lemberger. The wines are dry and 90 per cent are sold in Württemberg, mainly to wine-merchants and directly to the consumer.

Württemberg has bred many poets, including Friedrich Hölderlin in Lauffen, the largest wine-producing village in Württemberg, whose light soil is an important source in the region for Schwarzriesling (Müllerrebe) wine. Eduard Mörike was born at Ludwigs-burg, as was Justinus Kerner, after whom the Trollinger × Riesling crossing was named. Best known of all, Friedrich Schiller came from Marbach where *Schillerwein* is produced, as it is elsewhere in Württemberg. In fact, the wine has no connection with the poet and playwright but gets its name from a pink colour which is said to *schillern* or shimmer. It is a QbA, from red and white grapes deriving from the time when different varieties of vine were not grown separately in the vineyard, and their grapes were vinified together, regardless of colour.

Virtually all Marbacher wine is produced by the Württemberg-ische-Weingärtner-Zentral-Genossenschaft at Möglingen, near Ludwigsburg. This large central cellar receives the crop as must or wine from some forty-three smaller co-operatives and a proportion from all the other co-operative cellars in Württemberg. The storage capacity of the central cellar at Möglingen, and its outposts at Maulbronn and Untertürkheim, is the equivalent of about 130 million bottles. Wine in Württemberg is almost a monopoly of the co-operative movement. Such a centralized organization should enable the region to adapt to a changing market in the future, if this becomes necessary.

Some recommended privately owned estates in Württemberg

Weingut Graf Adelmann, 7141 Steinheim-Kleinbottwar, Burg Schaubeck: enterprising estate. Characterful, dry wines. A leader in the region.

Weingut Amalienhof, 7100 Heilbronn, Lukas-Cranach-Weg 5: well known for dry/medium-dry Riesling, and Samtrot, a mutation of Müllerebe.

Weingut Robert Bauer, 7101 Flein, Heilbronner Strasse 56: very successful. Dry, cask-matured red and well-balanced white wines.

Weingut Dr R. Baumann (Schlosskellerei Affaltrach), 7104 Obersulm 1, Am Ordenschloss 15–21: source of stunning *Eiseweine*, and good-quality Württemberg red wine.

Weingut Schozach Graf von Bentzel-Sturmfeder, 7129 Ilsfeld-Schozach, Sturmfederstrasse 4: fourteenth-century estate. Cask-matured Riesling, Spätburgunder, and Samtrot, a mutation of Müllerebe.

Freiherlich von Gemmingen-Hornberg'sches Weingut, 6951

Neckarzimmern, Burg Hornberg: traditional vine varieties and wines. An impressive estate.

Weingut Karl Haidle, 7056 Kernen-Stetten, Hindenburgstrasse 19: concentrated, flavoury wines. Many totally dry.

Weingut Fürst zu Hohenlohe-Oehringen, 7110 Oehringen, Im Schloss: mainly Riesling estate. Good cask-matured Spätburgunder and Lemberger.

Weingut Sonnenhof-Bezner-Fischer, 7143 Vaihingen-Gündelbach, Horrheimer Strasse: mainly traditional vine varieties. Individual, well-made wines.

Co-operative cellars

The following Württemberg co-operative cellars have been particularly successful in the DLG national wine competitions in recent years.

Felsengartenkellerei Besigheim: 350 hectares; 30 per cent Trollinger. Lemberger and Schwarzriesling, 15 per cent Riesling, Kerner and Müller-Thurgau.

Weingärtnergenossenschaft Cleebronn-Güglingen-Frauenzimmern: 270 hectares; 21 per cent Riesling, 15 per cent Schwarzriesling, 15 per cent Kerner, 12 per cent Müller-Thurgau, 11 per cent Trollinger, and 10 per cent Lemberger.

Weingärtnergenossenschaft Dürrenzimmern-Stockheim: 200 hectares; 24 per cent Riesling, 20 per cent Trollinger, 19 per cent Lemberger, and 9 per cent Schwarzriesling.

Weingärtnergenossenschaft Eberstadt: 160 hectares; 30 per cent Riesling, 30 per cent Trollinger, 10 per cent each Lemberger, Schwarzriesling and Kerner.

Weingärtnergenossenschaft Flein-Talheim: 260 hectares; 53 per cent Riesling and 32 per cent Schwarzriesling.

Genossenschaftskellerei Heilbronn-Erlenbach-Weinsberg: 600 hectares; 30 per cent Riesling, 30 per cent Trollinger plus Schwarzriesling, and Kerner.

Weinkellerei Hohenlohe: 260 hectares; 33 per cent Riesling, 15 per cent Silvaner, 15 per cent Trollinger, 10 per cent Müller-Thurgau and 10 per cent Kerner.

Weingärtnergenossenschaft Lauffen: 480 hectares; 70 per cent Schwarzriesling, 7 per cent Trollinger and 6 per cent Riesling.

Winzergenossenschaft Löwenstein: 160 hectares; Riesling, Kerner, Trollinger, Schwarzriesling and Lemberger.

Weingärtnergenossenschaft Nordheim: 180 hectares; 29 per cent Riesling, 18 per cent Schwarzriesling, 12 per cent Trollinger, 10 per cent Kerner, and 10 per cent Müller-Thurgau.

23

Baden

Area under vine in hectares in 1988: 15,000 ha, planted 35.7 per cent Müller-Thurgau, 23.0 per cent Blauer Spätburgunder, 10.9 per cent Rülander, 8.6 per cent Weisser Gutedel, 7.4 per cent Weisser Riesling, and 14.4 per cent others.

Average temperature during period of vegetation:	15.2°C
Average sunshine hours during period of vegetation:	1,411
Average rainfall during period of vegetation:	644mm
Average annual rainfall:	944mm

Recent vintages in million hectolitres: 1985 0.7, 1986 1.4, 1987 1.1, 1988 1.4, 1989 1.7

Average yield in hectolitres per hectare: 1978–87 79.8 hl/ha

Baden stretches 400 kilometres from north to south, with nearly two-thirds of the region lying between the Black Forest and the A5 motorway. The climatic details shown above were recorded at Freiburg, but between the eight wine-producing districts the weather can vary widely. The rainfall in parts of the Ortenau reaches over 1,200mm per year and in the Bereich Kaiserstuhl (the warmest district in Germany) it is less than 700mm, while the Badisches Frankenland in the north has to be satisfied with under 650mm. The extra sun results in a style of wine that is generally more alcoholic than that of any other region in Germany. As explained in chapter 6, EEC legislation puts Baden into what is known for administrative purposes as Zone 'B', alongside various French regions including Champagne, the Loire Valley, Alsace and, perhaps in the near future, Burgundy. However, most Baden producers add less sugar to their grape juice than is usual in France so that many of their wines retain a lightness of style that is essentially Germanic.

Where the vineyards adjoin the Black Forest, they are almost all on sloping ground that rolls sideways from one spur to another. At the edge of the Rhein plain, vines end, as the flat land is at risk from spring frosts.

Yields are relatively low in Baden and from the 1990 vintage onwards the Central Co-operative Cellar, the Badischer Winzerkeller, will pay its members for their grapes at a rate equivalent to a maximum annual production of 72 hectolitres of grape juice per hectare. Any wine in excess of this figure will be carried forward for payment in a later vintage in which 72 hl/ha have not been exceeded. This is a serious limitation and a self-imposed discipline in a large cellar handling about one-third of the Baden harvest. It will reduce its production by 12–15 per cent, assuming the membership (in this case contracted smaller cellars) is not increased, and that must lead to better wine at the lower levels of quality. In fact, basic Baden wine is already very sound, perhaps the best in Germany, which is all to the credit of the co-operative movement which handles 89 per cent of the crop. Middle-price Baden wines are improving rapidly and starting to realize the potential of their climate and soil. The dry wines, sold under the vine variety name, seem destined to help fill the gap between Germany's cheapest medium-sweet QbAs, and the fine estate-bottled white wines. Baden also has its upper-class wines, but these, good as they are, face stiff competition from those of regions further north.

What may be surprising is that Baden grows so much Spätburgunder. Its wine varies from very light and insubstantial to full-bodied, deep-coloured and tannic. The quality of the latter is steadily getting better, with many cellars experimenting with various forms of vinification, and maturation in casks of different sizes, ages and origins. Harvesting with two buckets is common. The first is for clean, healthy grapes to make deep-coloured wine, and the second for those attacked by rot which will produce good *Weissherbst*. In the 1960s Baden tried unsuccessfully to make *Weissherbst* its own exclusive product. Today it is produced as a single-vine rosé wine in all the main red-wine regions in Germany.

Müller-Thurgau is a popular choice of vine in Baden because of its regular crop and a yield which, though less than that in other regions, can still be quite high – up to 144 hl/ha in the Bereich Markgräflerland in the big 1989 vintage. Good-quality Müller-Thurgau can be bought for about DM 6.00 per bottle, and an absolutely top-flight, crisp, firm version from the distinguished Weingut Schwarzer Adler in the Bereich Kaiserstuhl will cost DM 9.00 or so. It will be worth every Pfennig.

The grey Pinot in Baden is a characterful wine. It is usually not so strongly flavoured as an Alsatian Pinot Gris and can, therefore, be enjoyed in rather larger amounts. The Auggen Winzergenossenschaft in Markgräflerland offers a 'Grauburgunder' and a 'Ruländer' *Kabinett* dry wine. The first is picked early and a crisp, dry, flavoury wine is the result. The second is the same vine variety gathered when the grapes were riper. The wine is fuller, and is still dry but it has a different flavour and less acidity. Both styles are very successful and preference for either one or the other is a matter of personal choice. At Auggen, nearly two-thirds of the 250 hectares from which the co-operative draws its grapes are planted in Gutedel, a district speciality which will be discussed in the section of this chapter dealing with the Bereich Markgräflerland.

Riesling is not important in Baden as a whole, but its wine has a considerable reputation at Durbach and elsewhere in the Bereich Ortenau. Here the wine has the grip and refreshing style that it sometimes lacks when grown further south. Similarly, Silvaner might be overlooked were it not for its plantation in the Bereich Kaiserstuhl at Ihringen, Bischoffingen and Oberrotweil.

In Baden we see the advantage of an effective co-operative system. The village co-operatives are often little larger than some of the bigger estates in the Rheinpfalz or Rheingau. The members, usually small growers with perhaps less than a hectare under vine, are contracted to deliver all of their crop to their co-operative. Between the two there is a close contact, and advice on vineyard management is always at hand.

Among the private and state-owned estates, there are some with a reputation that goes well beyond the region. They identify their main competitors on the German market not as their neighbours, or even as the co-operative cellars, but as the French and the Italians. This allows the private estates to work together in Baden with the much stronger co-operative movement in a way that is not found in any other region. Shared tastings and similar wine-trade events show the advantage of making common cause, and the combined effect of four co-operative cellars which market their wines under the title Bad'ner Wein-Cabinet is seen as helpful to all Baden wine-producers.

The region is one of the most interesting to watch in the 1990s and, because of the good organization of its trade, seems likely to be increasingly successful. Perhaps because it is so close to France and Switzerland, it is well aware of the wine trade beyond its borders. Although the top local restaurants have a good range of Alsatian and other French wines, little Baden wine is sold as yet in Alsace, but the Badischer Winzerkeller does have customers in Spain. The structure of Baden wine makes it a natural accompaniment to food, and over 42 per cent (judged by volume) of Baden quality wine which received an AP number in 1989 was dry, and the 'drying-out' process continues.

Looking to the future, it must be assumed that Germany's northern regions will remain absolutely pre-eminent in the production of fine Riesling wine. Where Baden and the Rheinpfalz seem set to forge ahead is with their Burgunder or Pinot wines, which are likely to improve in quality and to become more expensive. As the world appears to be drinking better but less wine, Baden seems to be going in the right direction.

BEREICHE BADISCHES FRANKENLAND AND BADISCHE BERGSTRASSE/KRAICHGAU

Some of the *Bereiche* of Baden are isolated and represent an island of vine-growing in a sea of agriculture or forestry. Others are semi-detached and their wines tend to resemble those of their neighbours. Of such is the Badisches Frankenland, a district of a little less than 700 hectares, which follows the River Tauber downstream until it meets the Main and Franken at Wertheim. Two-thirds of the vineyards are planted in Müller-Thurgau to produce a flowery, earthy wine, very much in the Franken mould. Most of the better-quality versions are sold in Franken's distinctive, dumpy *Bocksbeutel*, and the yield from the sloping or steep vineyards is noticeably lower than in other districts of Germany. (In the large 1989 vintage Müller-Thurgau in the Bereich Badisches Frankenland produced an average yield of 118 hl/ha. In the Mosel-Saar-Ruwer the figure was 191 hl/ha.) Besides Müller-Thurgau, the

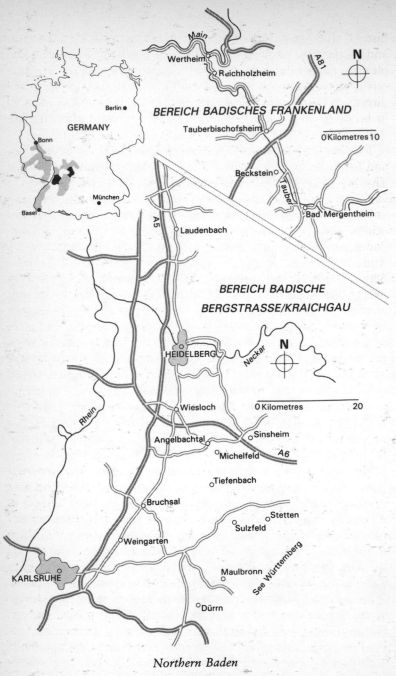

Northern Baden

198

district also has a certain amount of Kerner, Silvaner, Bacchus and Müllerrebe, or Schwarzriesling as it is called. Tourism in this pleasant part of Baden is important and helps a modestly prosperous trade in wine. There is a handful of estate bottlers who sell directly to the consumer, but most of the wine is produced and sold in bottle by the co-operative cellars at Beckstein and Wertheim-Reichholzheim.

The Bergstrasse leaves the state of Hessen south of Heppenheim, and enters Baden as it continues on its way to Heidelberg. Müller-Thurgau predominates, but Riesling is planted in a quarter of the vineyard area which supplies the district central co-operative cellar at Wiesloch. The style of the wines is 'northerly'. They have more acidity and are generally lighter in alcohol than those of south Baden, and the proportion with some residual sugar (medium-dry wines, mainly) at Wiesloch is high. The Winzerkeller Südliche Bergstrasse/Kraichgau, to grant the correct title, is supplied by twenty-one so-called 'dry' co-operative cellars, which are not involved in wine-making. The crop from 4,500 small growers with an average holding of one-third of a hectare, accounts for 75 per cent of the district's total grape harvest. A further 7 per cent is vinified by the Winzergenossenschaft Weingarten in the Kraichgau north of Karlsruhe. Instead of supplying the district central cellars at Wiesloch, some of the villages, such as Dürrn, send their grapes to the regional centre, the Badische Winzerkeller. A 1971 Dürrner Eichelberg Riesling Spätlese tasted in 1990 was still alive, with a dark golden colour and long flavour. Like 'love that's true', well-made wine 'will last for ever'.

The district has only a few private estates of note, amongst which is Weingut Reichsgraf und Marquis zu Hoensbroech at Angelbachtal-Michelfeld. The estate's range of vine varieties is traditional, and the wines include well-structured Weissburgunder with 12 per cent of alcohol or more. At Sulzfeld, almost in Württemberg, the Freiherr von Göler'sche Verwaltung concentrates on Riesling, much of which is sold through the restaurant in Burg Ravensburg. For modern, dry, full-bodied white wines and tannic Spätburgunder, Weingut Albert Heitlinger is one of the best sources in the district. Compared to wines of equivalent quality in, say, Franken, those from the Kraichgau are relatively inexpensive.

BEREICH ORTENAU

Baden-Baden is an elegant spa of 50,000 inhabitants, lying in a deep valley running down from the Black Forest in the direction of the Rhein. Known for its thermal springs since the early third century, and for its casino since the middle of the last, the town is now described as 'international' and 'lavish and worthy'. Such epithets are not acquired cheaply, and neither are the local wines, for the image of the town is not to be maintained by bargain-basement prices, as the estate agents, hotel keepers and restaurateurs understand full well.

South-west of Baden-Baden the villages of Varnhalt, Steinbach, Umweg and Neuweier have an historic right to sell their quality wine in the *Bocksbeutel* of Franken. The percentage of Riesling is high and the 39-hectare Neuweierer Mauerberg knows no other vine, but, for all this devotion to Germany's best vine, the Rieslings from the outskirts of Baden-Baden are not the most exciting. Better examples can be found further south in the Bereich Ortenau.

Vines grow on the south side of the spurs that run down from the Black Forest, and the northern-facing slopes are planted in orchards. At Bühl, Spätburgunder is an important vine variety, and most of the wine is sold by the Affentaler Winzergenossenschaft. The membership is encouraged to produce top-quality fruit by a well-structured scale of payment. An increase of 15° Oechsle in must weight (about 2.3 per cent in potential alcohol) doubles the amount paid for the grapes and further bonuses are given for a delayed harvest. Those wines that have won a Baden quality seal may be sold in a *Buddel* bottle, a variation on the *Bocksbeutel* shape. To win a Baden quality seal (*Badische Gütezeichen*) a wine must have achieved not less than 3 out of a maximum of 5 points at the quality-control (AP) centre. As samples are not examined until after bottling, there is a theoretical risk that a wine might not achieve its minimum 3 points, and therefore become unsaleable in the *Buddel* bottle. This, the cellar master claims, has never happened. Although the 300 hectares of the Affentaler Winzergenossenschaft are probably best known for Spätburgunder, 60 per cent is planted in Riesling, some of which is aged in small casks and sold at a handsome DM 17.50 per bottle.

The importance of Durbach, 6 kilometres north of Offenburg, as a Riesling village dates from the eighteenth century, when Grand

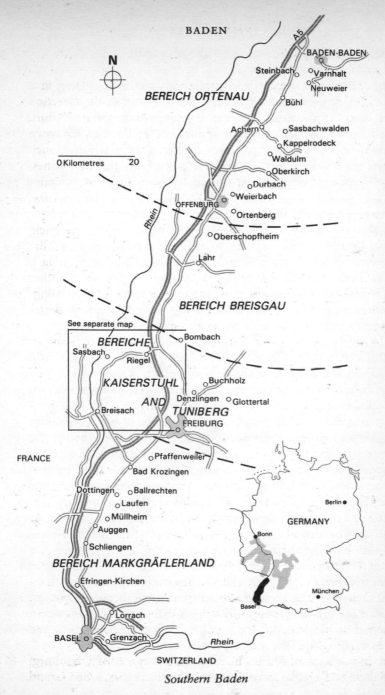

BADEN

N

BEREICH ORTENAU

A5

BADEN-BADEN
Steinbach○ ○Varnhalt
○Neuweier

○Bühl

0 Kilometres 20

Achern○ ○Sasbachwalden
○Kappelrodeck
○Waldulm
○Oberkirch
○Durbach
OFFENBURG ○Weierbach
○Ortenberg

○Oberschopfheim

Rhein

○Lahr

BEREICH BREISGAU

See separate map
BEREICHE ○Bombach
Sasbach○
○Riegel

KAISERSTUHL ○Buchholz
AND Denzlingen○ ○Glottertal
Breisach○ *TUNIBERG*
FREIBURG

○Pfaffenweiler
○Bad Krozingen
Dottingen○ ○Ballrechten
○Laufen
○Müllheim
○Auggen
○Schliengen

BEREICH MARKGRÄFLERLAND

○Efringen-Kirchen

FRANCE

GERMANY
Berlin●
Bonn●
München●
Basel●

Berlin●

○Lorrach
BASEL ○Grenzach Rhein

SWITZERLAND

Southern Baden

Duke Carl Friedrich improved the standard of viticulture. Since the previous century Riesling had been planted, usually as a single vine in the Durbacher Klingelberg vineyard at Schloss Staufenberg. Today Klingelberger is an EC-recognized synonym for Riesling and Durbach has eleven good private estates, including that of Freiherr von Neveu, whose excellent Klingelberger, Spätburgunder and other wines are all bottled and marketed (but not vinified) by the Badische Winzerkeller. Traminer is a speciality in Durbach where it is confusingly called 'Klevner'. (In Württemberg, Klevner is the name used for a mutation of Frühburgunder, and in Alsace for Pinot Blanc, and in parts of Switzerland for Spätburgunder.)

The 36 hectares of Weingut Graf Wolff Metternich make it one of the larger private estates in Baden. The holdings are almost exclusively on the steep slopes above Durbach where it is the sole owner of the Schloss Grohl and Schlossberg *Einzellagen*. At the very top of the vineyards, Schloss Staufenberg looks 25 kilometres east to Strasbourg, and down upon Durbach to the south. This eleventh-century castle is one of a number of estates covering 115 hectares throughout the length of the region, owned by the Markgraf of Baden. Appropriately, Klingelberger predominates in the steep vineyards whose gradient reaches 80 per cent in places, but at the Winzergenossenschaft Durach, Spätburgunder is the leading vine.

The Ortenau villages of Sasbachwalden and Waldulm in the middle of the region are even better known for their red wine. The co-operative cellars at Sasbachwalden receive the grapes from 220 hectares (50 per cent Spätburgunder) and nowadays produce red wine that is serious and internationally acceptable. At Waldulm 85 per cent of the holdings of the members of the co-operative are planted in Spätburgunder, and where the vine is not at home orchards supply the stills with fruit for the refined Black Forest Kirsch and other brandies.

The towns of the Ortenau on the edge of the narrow growing area are linked by the B3 main road, where the dense local traffic encourages the motorist to take to the parallel motorway. Offenburg has its own 30-hectare estate, the St Andreas Hospital Fonds, dating from 1300, where the emphasis is on Müller-Thurgau, Riesling and Spätburgunder. The list offers a wealth of *Trockenbeerenauslesen* from a wide range of vine varieties. The estate of Freiherr von und zu Franckenstein on the north side of Offenburg has all its 14 hectares in the Abstberg *Einzellage* at Zell-Weierbach. The 'take-home trade' in Spätburgunder is important at the local *Winzergenossenschaft*, and the Franckenstein estate is known for its dry wines, which are sold mainly through retail wine-merchants, and in the good-quality restaurants which are a feature of southwest Germany.

BEREICH BREISGAU

Freiburg is the impressive capital of the Black Forest and of the Bereich Breisgau. It is a city of 178,545 inhabitants, whose centre was destroyed in an air raid in 1944 but which has been painstakingly restored. Besides being attractive to the tourist, Freiburg is also a focal point for the wine trade of the whole of the region.

Nearly 700 hectares fall within the city's viticultural boundaries. They stretch east into the Bereich Tuniberg, south to the Bereich Markgräflerland, and north to the Bereich Breisgau. There is a vineyard within the *Altstadt* (the 'old town') but serious Breisgau vine-growing starts at Denzlingen and in the Glottertal, a beautiful Black Forest valley in which the television series *Black Forest Clinic* was filmed. The Breisgau vineyards, planted 46 per cent in Müller-Thurgau, 26 per cent in Spätburgunder and 16 per cent in Ruländer, usually produce wines that are similar to those of the Bereich Kaiserstuhl, but with more acidity. The vines grow at a height of 200–300 metres above sea-level, but in the micro-climate of the Glottertal they reach up to 500 metres. (The rule of thumb in Germany is that for every 100 metres above sea-level the average annual temperature drops by 0.6° C.)

The state viticultural institute in Freiburg (the Staatliches Weinbauinstitut) and the Stiftungskellerei have small holdings in the Freiburger Schlossberg site in the Breisgau, but the district has few private estates.

A little to the north of Denzlingen, at Buchholz, Spätburgunder is grown on the Italian pergola system, with the picker walking under the vine to harvest the grapes that hang down from above. (It is probably coincidence that one of the Italian Süd Tirol's most famous villages for Spätburgunder grown on the pergola system is also called Buchholz.) Further north, at Bombach, the 17-hectare Weingut Kirchberghof is the largest private estate in the Breisgau.

Most of its wines are not only dry in the eyes of the EC, but have less than 2 grams per litre of residual sugar, making them even more interesting to the modern German wine-lover.

It has been suggested that if the Breisgau lacks an 'identity', it may be because there is only one village co-operative that actually bottles its wine. All the rest pass the crop to the Badische Winzer-keller for processing in Kaiserstuhl. In spite of this, or perhaps because of it, two Breisgauer 1988 wines, a Müller-Thurgau and a Spätburgunder, bottled by the Badische Winzerkeller, were any-thing but retiring or lost in a tasting in 1990. They were from vines of twenty or more years, and showed the concentrated flavour and, in the case of the Spätburgunder, the complexity that comes from a low yield. In those cellars where Spätburgunder is allowed too large a crop, the wine is pleasant but lacks any character. It then needs an addition of wine from a grape with much colour, to hide the effect of dilution.

BEREICH KAISERSTUHL

In 1990 Kaiserstuhl left its small neighbour, Tuniberg, and became a single *Bereich* of some 4,000 hectares. Its boundaries are easily defined for they end at the point at which the slopes of the hills touch the Rhein plain. The contours of Kaiserstuhl were created by volcanic activity 10 million years ago, but they have been adjusted in the twentieth century by *Flurbereinigung*. Huge ter-races, with a slight reverse slope towards the hillside, have been excavated in the interests of economic vine-growing. It has to be said that in winter these earthworks look stark and unfriendly, but leaves on the trees and vines in summer soften the effect to good purpose. The hills of Kaiserstuhl rise to a peak of 557 metres on the grimly named Totenkopf (Skull and Crossbones), and below it to the west and south are some of the best wine villages of Baden.

According to the *Geschichte des Weinguts Freiherr von Gleich-enstein*, written to celebrate the 250th anniversary of the estate in 1984, quality wine-production started in Kaiserstuhl at the end of the eighteenth century. Until then, wines had been grown on loess, but in 1813 what are now called traditional vine varieties were planted in Ihringen on volcanic soil. With the help of explosives, the Ihringer Winklerberg was created between 1842 and 1844 and

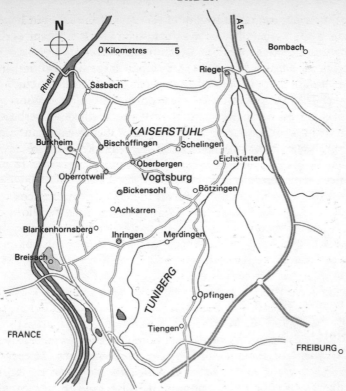

Bereiche Kaiserstuhl and Tuniberg

the new vineyard was filled with 'Rheingau Riesling, Deidesheimer Traminer, and Spätburgunder from Clos de Vougeot'.

Two of Kaiserstuhl's best private estates have holdings in the Winklerberg. Weingut Dr Heger produces top-quality, *barrique*-aged Spätburgunder and some of the best Silvaner in Germany. Weingut Rudolf Stigler has a range of characterful red and white wines with an unusually high proportion of Riesling. Wines from the private estates and from the village co-operative can almost always be bought directly from the cellar door. Much is sold in this way in Kaiserstuhl, particularly to Germans who break their journey north after a Mediterranean holiday by spending a night in the district.

On the outskirts of Ihringen at Blankenhornsberg, the state has a viticultural station and the solely owned Doktorgarten *Einzellage*.

Most of the wines are not sold with a site name but simply as Blankenhornsberg. Ihringen is the warmest village in Germany and with nearly 600 hectares is one of the bigger wine communities. At the good and large *Winzergenossenschaft*, nearly half the production is in Silvaner – the local speciality.

Although the private estates are more strongly represented in the restaurants, the village co-operatives are well regarded and receive grapes from some of the best, as well as from ordinary, vineyards. The Winzergenossenschaft Bickensohl has an excellent Grauburgunder, a good, solid, flavoury QbA, which is sold with the vine variety emphasized on the label.

At Oberbergen, the famous Schwarzer Adler restaurant has a fascinating wine list (it includes a host of Sauternes and other French wines). The owner's approach to his own 6 hectares of vineyard is French-influenced and scorn is poured copiously upon the merest suggestion of residual sweetness that is not the result of a natural halt to fermentation.

Weingut Salwey at Oberrotweil has nearly 4 hectares in the Glottertal in the Bereich Breisgau, and is much admired in Germany for its dry, *barrique*-aged Burgunder wines. The list of vine varieties covers those that are traditional to Kaiserstuhl, plus Muskateller. This is a wine that has a small, but justified, place in the offer of German wines, as a minor speciality in Baden-Württemberg. It is usually light and stylish – much more so than Morio-Muskat – and can either be sold as a single vine wine or used to titivate a blend.

Barrique-ageing is a speciality, if not an obsession, of Karl Heinz Johner at Bischoffingen, whose *curriculum vitae* includes a long spell at Lamberhurst vineyard in England. His casks of some 225 litres have been stored beneath his house and in garages in the village, but a new *Kellerei* is under construction. Here his powerful, concentrated wines will be able to be lodged and tasted in more likely surroundings. At Bischoffingen there is also a large co-operative cellar supplied by 264 hectares, mainly with Müller-Thurgau, Spätbunder and Ruländer.

Burkheim, a few kilometres west of Bischoffingen, has a charming, picturesque centre that is reached through an old town gate. There is a good private estate in Weingut Bercher, devoted to dry, cask-matured Burgunder of real substance and worth. The *Winzergenossenschaft* at Sasbach in the north-west corner of the district is another nearby source of exciting, serious, red and white wines, but, in Kaiserstuhl, these are not hard to find.

In the north-east corner of the district, a kilometre or so from the A5 motorway to Basel, all the grapes from Riegel are sent to the Badische Winzerkeller. The town is perhaps best known for its splendid beer and an impressive town hall, dating from 1784.

At the opposite end of Kaiserstuhl, Breisach sits on its hill with the restored St Stephanus minster looking a few hundred metres over the Rhein to France. In the opposite direction is the Ihringer Winklerberg with the important Badische Winzerkeller in the middle distance.

THE BADISCHE WINZERKELLER AND THE BEREICH TUNIBERG

The Badische Winzerkeller receives all the grapes from forty-nine co-operative cellars and part of the crop from a further forty-five. Its impressive statistics include a storage capacity of 160 million litres (equal to nearly 18 million dozen 750ml bottles) and a stock holding after the large 1989 vintage equivalent to four years' sales. Much is sold in bulk to the wine trade, but the share of the more expensive wines in 750ml, as opposed to litre, bottles is growing. The Badische Winzerkeller is taking part in all the current search for newer ways of presenting wine in Germany. They include *barrique*-ageing, environmentally friendly vine-growing, the limited use of Bordeaux-shaped bottles, and 'light wines'. Amongst these newer concepts is the Müller-Thurgau with 9.5 per cent of alcohol, sold under the alternative grape name of Rivaner in a slim green bottle. Historically, Baden wine has been bottled in both green and amber-coloured glass, but the use of amber in the region has become associated with medium-sweet wine and is probably now in decline.

The cellars offer over 800 different wines but more than 50 per cent of the volume turnover is in twenty lines only. According to Armin Göring of the Badische Winzerkeller board, the three items of information that attract the customers are the name of the region, the vine variety and the word *trocken* or dry. It is upon these that many of the Badische Winzerkeller labels concentrate. In addition to the cheaper ranges, there are the wines made from vines that are over twenty years old, as already mentioned, as well as those from the von Neveu estate in Durbach. This upper-class end of the range is likely to expand to meet the demand for less, but better, wine.

Besides its still-wine range, the Badische Winzerkeller also produces sparkling wines through a subsidiary organization in Breisach, the Gräflich von Kageneck'sche Wein und Sektkellerei mentioned in chapter 12. They are made exclusively from Baden base wine, with the members' grapes being picked at the right moment to retain the acidity that is essential to all good sparkling wine. Some of the wines develop their sparkle in vat and others in bottle, but all are sold as a single-vine wine. Those at the top of the range, the Kageneck Grauer Burgunder and Riesling (both are *extra brut*) at about DM 17.00 per bottle, are refined and true to the vine variety.

Baden used to describe its wines as 'spoilt by the sun' – meaning, it must quickly be added, blessed by much sunshine. A 1964 Niederrimsinger Rotgrund Ruländer Auslese from the Bereich Tuniberg, tasted at the Badischer Winzerkeller in 1990, showed the benefits and strength that comes from extra sunshine. The wine, which was made from healthy but shrivelled grapes (little noble rot in 1964), had about 16° of potential alcohol. If the new-style Grauburgunder is attractive and supposedly geared to modern living, well-made, heavy Ruländer in the old style is also easy to justify.

The Bereich Tuniberg is in some ways a small-scale version of Kaiserstuhl. It rises in a similar way from the Rhein plain, but only to about 100 metres above river level. The climate is a shade less warm and the rainfall is a little heavier. The choice of vine varieties grown in the modernized vineyards is the same as in Kaiserstuhl and the co-operatives deliver all their crop to the Badische Winzerkeller. There are, in addition, a few small private estates. The countryside is rural and rolling, the villages attractive and well restored after the damage of the last and previous wars.

BEREICH MARKGRÄFLERLAND AND THE BEREICH BODENSEE

Markgräflerland is a pleasant, hilly district whose vineyards cover just under 3,000 hectares. They stretch from the outskirts of

Freiburg in the north to the industrial town of Grenzach-Wyhlen, east of Basel. 'Gentle' seems the right word to describe the scenery until it quickly and surprisingly changes as one climbs east towards the Münstertal. Here, the sparsely clad and often wet mountains would not look out of place in Scotland, but the warmth and the rain in the western foothills suit the Gutedel vine well. It covers 43 per cent of the vineyard area and it was the Markgraf of Baden who, as with Riesling at Durbach, promoted the growing of Gutedel as a single vine. Its wine, in Markgräflerland, is a sound, simple, balanced white wine which at DM 6.00 or so for a QbA ranks a little higher than a Müller-Thurgau QbA. In price ascending order after Gutedel, the next QbA on a co-operative retail list will be Silvaner, followed by Weissburgunder, perhaps Riesling, then Grauburgunder, Spätburgunder and finally Gewürztraminer. The villages of Markgräflerland are proud of their local co-operative cellars. The *Winzergenossenschaften* are not as well known outside their district as some in Kaiserstuhl or the Ortenau, but they offer good, true-to-type, dry wine at a reasonable price. Some of the best are listed at the end of this chapter.

There is a district co-operative, the Bezirkskellerei Markgräflerland at Efringen-Kirchen, 14 kilometres north of Basel. In spite of its name, only villages in the south of the district deliver their grapes for processing, and those in the north without a wine-making co-operative of their own send their crop to the Badische Winzerkeller.

There are a few private estate bottlers, including the 7-hectare Weingut Hartmut Schlumberger at Laufen near Müllheim. It has the usual range of traditional Baden and Markgräflerland vine varieties with the emphasis on Gutedel.

Weingut Hermann Dorflinger of Müllheim has also long been a source of successful dry wines.

Blankenhorn is a name that appears often in the history of south Baden wine-making, and at Schliengen there is not only the oldest co-operative cellar in the district but the 17.5-hectare Weingut Blankenhorn. The estate also has a separate wine-merchants' cellar which buys grapes from smaller growers in the manner of houses such as Trimbach and Hugel across the Rhein in Alsace. Yields are low at Weingut Blankenhorn, even though the mix of vine varieties includes the fruitful Müller-Thurgau and Gutedel.

One hundred slow kilometres east of Basel, Baden has a *Bereich* of over 400 hectares near the Bodensee. Curiously, so do Württemberg and the state of Bavaria, but Baden's holdings are the most important. The Staatsweingut Meersburg is one of the few state-owned wine-producing enterprises in Baden-Württemberg to make a profit. It has 62 hectares, mainly at Meersburg (46 per cent Spätburgunder, 34 per cent Müller-Thurgau), with isolated vineyards elsewhere, including Germany's highest vineyard (552 metres above sea-level) at Hohentwiel west of the Bodensee. In this little district there is a strong risk of late spring frosts, and the heavy rainfall can produce *botrytis* rot too soon in the autumn. The setting of the early eighteenth-century buildings of the Staatsweingut, separated from the Bodensee by steep vineyards, is immensely impressive and brings this chapter on Germany's longest region to an end.

Some recommended estates in Baden

Weingut Bercher OHG, 7818 Burkheim, Mittelstadt 13: fully fermented wines up to *Auslese* level. Good, tannic Spätburgunder.

Weingut Blankenhorn, 7846 Schliengen, Basler Strasse 2: concentrated, fresh white wines and supple, gentle reds.

Weingut Hermann Dorflinger, 7840 Müllheim, Mühlenstrasse 7: cask-matured Spät- and Grauburgunder. All fully fermented.

Weingut von und zu Franckenstein Rentamt, 7600 Offenburg, Weingartenstrasse 66: fresh, dry Rieslings and full-flavoured Spätburgunder.

Staatliches Weinbauinstitut Freiburg, Versuchs- und Lehrgut Blankenhornsberg, 7817 Ihringen: high-quality wine-making. Traditional and new varieties.

Stiftungskellerei Freiburg, 7800 Freiburg, Deutschordenstrasse 2: stylish, concentrated wines, excellent wine-making.

Weingut Freiherr von Gleichenstein, 7818 Oberrotweil, Bahnhofstrasse 12: cask-matured, tannic Spätburgunder. Well-made dry white wines.

Freiherr von Göler'sche Verwaltung, 7519 Sulzfeld, Hauptstrasse 44: full, slightly earthy but elegant white wines, and Lemberger red.

Weingut Dr Heger, 7811 Ihringen, Bachenstrasse 19–20: perhaps the finest wine-maker in Baden.

Weingut Albert Heitlinger, 7524 Oestringen-Tiefenbach, Am Mühlenberg: good, tannic but fruity dry red wines.

Weingut Reichsgraf und Marquis zu Hoensbroech, 6921 Angelbachtal-Michelfeld, Hermannsberg: firm, dry, solid, high-quality white wines. Excellent Weissburgunder.

Schlossgut Istein, 7859 Efringen-Kirchen: full-bodied dry white wines, some with high alcohol.

Weingut Karl H. Johner, 7818 Bischoffingen, Gartenstrasse 20: characterful, and intense, *barrique*-aged red and white wines.

Weingut Kirchberghof, 7832 Bombach: good, dry, 'modern' white wines. Serious reds.

Weingut Heinrich Männle, 7601 Durbach, Sendelbach 16: fresh and crisp white wines, good, cask-matured reds.

Graf Wolff Metternich Weingut, 7601 Durbach: top-quality white wines with excellent body, grip and flavour.

Weingut Freiherr von Neveu, 7601 Durbach: true to type Rieslings, and impressive Spätburgunders.

St Andreas Hospital Fonds, Weingut der Stadt Offenburg, 7601 Ortenberg, Steingrube 7: full range of mainly white wines. Many QmPs.

Weingut Salwey, 7818 Oberrotweil, Hauptstrasse 2: dry, cask-matured (some *barrique*-aged) wines. Great reputation.

Markgräflich Badisches Weingut Schloss Staufenberg, 7601 Durbach: elegant, dry Rieslings with refreshing acidity and good body. Baden classics.

Weingut Hartmut Schlumberger, 7811 Sulzburg-Laufen, Weinstrasse 19: dry wines, some *barrique*-aged, and softened by malo-lactic fermentation.

Weingut 'Schwarzer Adler', 7818 Oberbergen, Badbergstrasse 23: absolutely dry, concentrated, firm, cask-matured, top-quality wines.

Staatsweingut Meersburg, 7758 Meersburg, Seminarstrasse 6: lively, firm white wines, some excellent Spätburgunder.

Weingut Rudolf Stigler, 7817 Ihringen, Bachenstrasse 29: source of fascinating, well-differentiated wines. Riesling specialist.

The following co-operative cellars in Baden are known for the quality of their wine

BEREICHE BADISCHES FRANKENLAND AND BADISCHE BERGSTRASSE/KRAICHGAU

Winzergenossenscraft Badisches Frankenland: 337 hectares; 78 per cent Müller-Thurgau, 8 per cent Kerner, and 6 per cent Silvaner.

Winzergenossenschaft Beckstein: 320 hectares; 75 per cent Müller-Thurgau, 10 per cent Kerner, and 5 per cent Bacchus.

Winzerkeller Südliche Bergstrasse/Kraichgau: 1,500 hectares; 42 per cent Müller-Thurgau, 25 per cent Riesling, and 9 per cent Weissburgunder.

Winzergenossenschaft Weingarten: 140 hectares; 54 per cent Müller-Thurgau, 11 per cent Weissburgunder, and 9 per cent Ruländer.

BEREICH ORTENAU

Affentaler Winzergenossenschaft Buhl: 280 hectares; 60 per cent Riesling, 25 per cent Spätburgunder, and 12 per cent Müller-Thurgau.

Winzergenossenschaft Durbach: 305 hectares; 33 per cent Spätburgunder, 27 per cent Müller-Thurgau, and 16 per cent Riesling.

Winzergenossenschaft Kappelrodeck-Waldulm: 110 hectares; 85 per cent Spätburgunder, 10 per cent Müller-Thurgau, and 4 per cent Ruländer.

Winzergenossenschaft Renchtäler: 452 hectares; 32 per cent Spätburgunder, 29 per cent Müller-Thurgau, and 23 per cent Riesling.

Winzergenossenschaft Sasbachwalden: 220 hectares; 50 per cent Spätburgunder, 20 per cent Riesling, and 20 per cent Müller-Thurgau.

Winzergenossenschaft Waldulm: 110 hectares; 85 per cent Spätburgunder, and 10 per cent Müller-Thurgau.

BEREICH KAISERSTUHL

Winzergenossenschaft Bickensohl: 170 hectares; 30 per cent Müller-Thurgau, 25 per cent Ruländer, and 20 per cent Spätburgunder.

Winzergenossenschaft Bischoffingen: 260 hectares; 31 per cent Müller-Thurgau, 29 per cent Ruländer, and 24 per cent Spätburgunder.

Winzergenossenschaft Burkheim: 135 hectares; 40 per cent Müller-Thurgau, 25 per cent Spätburgunder, and 23 per cent Ruländer.

Kaiserstühler Winzergenossenschaft Ihringen: 420 hectares; 37 per cent Silvaner, 23 per cent Spätburgunder, and 22 per cent Müller-Thurgau.

Kaiserstühler Winzerverein Oberrotweil: 342 hectares, 31 per cent Müller-Thurgau, 28 per cent Spätburgunder, and 27 per cent Ruländer.

Winzergenossenschaft Sasbach: 100 hectares; 40 per cent Spätburgunder, 33 per cent Müller-Thurgau, and 16 per cent Ruländer.

BEREICH MARKGRÄFLERLAND

Winzergenossenschaft Auggen: 216 hectares; 60 per cent Gutedel, 20 per cent Müller-Thurgau, and 10 per cent Weissburgunder.

Winzergenossenschaft Ballrechten-Dottingen: 120 hectares; 38 per cent Müller-Thurgau, 34 per cent Gutedel, and 10 per cent Spätburgunder.

Bezirkskellerei Markgräflerland Efringen-Kirchen: 320 hectares; 52 per cent Gutedel, 26 per cent Müller-Thurgau, and 12 per cent Spätburgunder.

Markgräfler Winzergenossenschaft Müllheim: 100 hectares; 35 per cent Gutedel, 30 per cent Müller-Thurgau, and 12 per cent Spätburgunder.

Winzergenossenschaft Pfaffenweiler: 135 hectares; 36 per cent Müller-Thurgau, 32 per cent Gutedel, and 17 per cent Spätburgunder.

Erste Markgräfler Winzergenossenschaft Schliengen: 160 hectares; 41 per cent Gutedel, 23 per cent Müller-Thurgau, and 19 per cent Spätburgunder.

24

Eastern Germany

'Les environs de cette ville sont presque tous vignobles. Je ne sais pas pourquoi, car le vin y est détestable.' Those harsh words from the *Mémoires du Baron de Pöllnitz*, published in 1734, describe the wines of Naumburg in what, at the time of writing, is still the German Democratic Republic. Whatever the quality, documentary evidence dating from no less a year than 1066 shows that Naumburg shares with other towns and villages in the valleys of the Saale, Unstrut and Elbe rivers a long history of wine-making.

According to Basserman-Jordan, in the thirteenth century vines were grown as far north as Tilsit (Sovetsk) which, like Newcastle upon Tyne, lies on the 55° of latitude, and viticulture extended to the monasteries of Denmark. Two hundred years later there were ninety-two vineyards in Berlin and at the end of the eighteenth century Potsdam was noted for its red wine.

Although some vineyards remain in the south of eastern Germany, those in the north started to disappear in the sixteenth century when German viticulture was at its peak. The storehouses of the Hansa Trading Association began to be filled not just with wines from the Rhein but with those from France and Spain as well. In comparison, the north German wines would have seemed light and thin. The reformation and the dissolution of the monasteries, plus some particularly cold winters, helped to bring vine-growing in north Germany to an end, and severely reduced the size of the vineyard of the Kingdom of Saxony to the south.

In the 1950s the vineyards of the Deutsche Democratische Republik shrank to less than 200 hectares, but since then they have expanded once more and it is the aim that they should cover 1000 hectares by 1995. Recently people from many different occupations have taken to vine-growing as a hobby that produces an additional, and untaxed, income. A report in the *Rhein Zeitung* in 1990 explained that wine had become a useful item of barter, to obtain goods that were not available for cash. Those who had been barred from advancement because of their political views had found comfort in tilling the vineyard soil.

There are four wine-making cellars in eastern Germany, run on co-operative lines in two vine-growing regions. Along the Elbe between Dresden and Neuseusslitz, north of Meissen, are some 300 hectares under vine, and further west, near the River Saale and its tributary, the Unstrut, there are a further 400 hectares. In both regions, the vineyards are mainly sloping and often terraced. The climate is very continental with temperatures in the winters of 1985, 1986 and 1987 dropping to $-25°C$, $-28°C$ and $-30°C$ respectively. In fact, the extreme cold of early 1987 almost prevented any wine from being made, and the Winzergenossenschaft Meissen, which normally processes 400,000–500,000 litres, could produce 16,000 litres only. The annual rainfall of 500mm is low and in many respects the climate is similar to that of Franken, with whose wines eastern Germany's are sometimes compared.

Müller-Thurgau covers 50 per cent of the total area under vine, Weissburgunder 13 per cent, Silvaner 9 per cent, Traminer 10 per cent, Gutedel 6 per cent, Riesling 5 per cent, Ruländer 3 per cent, Portugieser and Spätburgunder 2 per cent each. For the most part, wines sold with an indication of a vine variety are dry, and the rest are medium-dry or medium-sweet. Vines are grown and wines are made largely according to legislation created before 1939. The lowest quality level is simple table wine; then come quality wine and wine from *Spätlese* grapes. These last have to be gathered after a fixed date, but are not required to reach any particular concentration of sugar. Very occasionally an *Auslese* crop is picked, or even a *Beerenauslese* (see chapter 4) in an exceptional year like 1983.

Of all the vine varieties, perhaps Ruländer and Traminer from the Elbe valley are the most successful as single-vine wines. Traminer, Riesling (of course) and Weissburgunder can be harvested late in the season. In eastern Germany wines from the last two vines are said to develop well in bottle.

The lack of clear distinction between *Einzellage* and *Grosslage* wine names in western Germany is almost mirrored in the east. A Meissner Domprobstberg is a wine from a single site, but a

Meissner Domherr is a medium-sweet brand wine from co-operative cellars at Radebeul and Meissen, based on Traminer, Weissburgunder, Riesling and Morio-Muskat. Other brand wines, similarly named, add to the possible confusion. Meissen is one of the few familiar wine names in the Elbe valley and to make use of this point of recognition, any wine from the region may be sold as 'Meissner'.

The unification of Germany should make a great difference to wine-production in eastern Germany. It is short of all materials, from simple vineyard tools such as hand shears to vines themselves. The wine-makers also speak of a lack of good training facilities and a shortage of wine literature. They look for help to western Germany, which, in turn, sees the east as a market for her own wine. The idea developed by the *Reichsnährstand* in the mid-1930s of linking wine-producing villages with large centres of population away from the vineyards is being revived by a number of western German co-operative cellars looking to the east. What effect there will be in eastern Germany of an influx of west German wine is not clear. At present both east and west consume a similar amount of beer per head of the population (144 litres in the west per annum and 141 litres in the east), but the east German drinks half as much wine and sparkling wine as the west German. Total wine imports into eastern Germany amount to about 1.5 million hectolitres, of which only 35,000 hectolitres came from west Germany in 1988. It may be possible to expand the east German wine-production of 27,000 hectolitres per year when both the vineyards and the trade itself have been rebuilt, but that may be difficult, as the European Community is looking to reduce, rather than increase, its area under vine in the 1990s. As a number of western German firms have realized, eastern Germany offers not just a new and welcome extension to the home market, but a platform from which to set off for the rest of Eastern Europe.

APPENDIX I

Average Annual Wine-production
1978–1987

	1,000 hectolitres
France	69,207
Germany, West	9,289
Luxembourg	128
Italy	74,118
Greece	4,949

Source: Deutscher Weinbauverband

The average annual wine-production in the EC leads to a surplus. Its main sources are France and Italy, with West Germany only a relatively minor contributor, as the figures in 1,000 hectolitres show overleaf:

	Production 1987/88	Imports 1987/88 Ex-EC	Ex-elsewhere		Exports 1987/88 To EC	To elsewhere	Consumption 1987	Surplus as percentage of production
France	68,950	3,930	500		9,427	3,750	41,900	= 18,303
					(19.1% of production)			= 26.5%
Germany Western	8,623	8,735	1,065	LESS	1,890	720	15,614	= 199
					(30.3% of production)			= 2.3%
Italy	72,400	400	50		8,500	3,000	40,135	= 21,215
					(15.9% of production)			= 29.3%

Percentage of production exported to 'elsewhere' (third countries):

France	5.4%
Germany Western	8.3%
Italy	4.1%

Source: EC Commission/Deutscher Weinbauverband

APPENDIX II

Average Size of Planted Vineyard per Producer

	Hectares
France	4.36
Germany, Western	1.05
Luxembourg	1.04
Italy	0.86
Greece	0.52

Source: Professor Dr Kalinke, Geisenheim

When the results of the latest census are published, it is likely that the average size of planted vineyard per producer in western Germany will be seen to have increased. If this is so, it will be mainly the result of a concentration of ownership during the difficult trading conditions of the 1980s.

APPENDIX III

Ownership of Vineyards as a Percentage of Total Number of Producers

	Under 1 ha	1 to less than 5 ha	5 to less than 10 ha	10 ha or more
France	32%	35%	23%	10%
Germany, Western	72%	24%	4%	under 1%
Luxembourg	66%	34%	under 1%	under 1%
Italy	77%	21%	2%	under 1%
Greece	85%	15%	under 1%	under 1%

Source: Figures prepared by Professor Dr Kalinke, Geisenheim

APPENDIX IV

Minimum Natural Alcohol Content

The official quality categories are based on a scale, varying according to vine variety and region, of the potential alcohol content of the must. The minimum figures for Riesling (percentage by volume) are as follows:

Region	QbA	Kab	Spät.	Aus.	B. Aus./ Eis.	TbA.
Ahr, Mittelrhein, Mosel-Saar-Ruwer	6.1	8.6	10.0	11.1	15.3	21.5
Nahe	7.0	9.1	10.3	11.4	16.5	21.5
Rheinhessen, Rheinpfalz	7.5	9.5	11.4	12.5	16.5	21.5
Rheingau, Hess. Bergstrasse	7.0	9.5	11.4	13.0	17.7	21.5
Baden except Ber. Bodensee & Bad. Frankenland	7.5	10.0	11.6	14.8	18.1	22.1
Ber. Bodensee, Bad. Frankenland	7.5	10.0	11.4	13.4	17.5	21.5
Württemberg except Ber. Württemb. Bodensee	7.0	9.4	11.4	13.0	17.5	21.5
Franken, Ber. Württembergischer Bodensee	7.5	10.0	11.4	13.8	17.7	21.5

Vintages in the 1980s

The quality of a vintage can be judged rather broadly by the proportion of QmP it produces. The figures below are based on those officially recorded at the harvest, and published by the trade magazine *Die Weinwirtschaft*. They express the approximate amount of QmP as a percentage of the total yield.

The first row of figures shows the size of the harvest in each year in million hectolitres.

	1980	1981	1982	1983	1984	1985	1986	1987	1988	1989
	4.5	7.3	15.8	13.4	8.0	5.3	10.2	8.7	9.2	13.4
	%	%	%	%	%	%	%	%	%	%
Ahr	50	46	25	43	2	45	3	8	34	16
Mittelrhein	20	40	36	67	–	44	11	18	54	58
Mosel-Saar-Ruwer	16	37	36	51	1	37	14	6	51	40
Nahe	34	46	30	48	1	43	18	8	49	66
Rheingau	16	27	26	70	2	60	32	9	71	60
Rheinhessen	43	46	26	46	8	62	20	16	49	62
Rheinpfalz	33	46	16	42	9	53	12	15	40	51
Franken	36	32	21	37	–	74	22	6	48	19
Hessische										
Bergstrasse	30	41	43	54	2	71	22	11	44	62
Württemberg	11	35	2	12	2	38	2	6	9	39
Baden	55	22	8	48	4	39	9	26	23	39

Additional source: 1989 statistics only – Sichel report

Throughout the world it is accepted that wines that take a long time to reach maturity are often the best. In Germany a most important aid to longevity in wine is a high level of acidity – particularly of tartaric acid. Thus Rieslings and Scheurebes are known to be long-lasting, and theoretically Müller-Thurgaus and Silvaners develop more quickly. That broad statement is sometimes proved wrong when the structure of a full-bodied but relatively soft wine enables it to taste fresh for many years. This can easily happen with wines from Gewürztraminer and Ruländer.

Over the last sixty years the finest Rieslings lingered on their high plateau of quality not simply because they were strong in acid, but also thanks to their unfermented sugar. Even with wines of middling quality, sweetness helps to delay the effects of increasing age. In the 1990s many of the better Riesling wines are being bottled dry and producers do not yet have the experience to say for how many years these new wines will be at their best. The feeling is expressed that, although the dry wines need bottle age, they will not require as much as the medium-sweet versions of the post-Second World War period. A suggested rule of thumb for all dry German wines would be that they should be drunk within eight years of the vintage, but this cannot be more than a suggestion. A harvest of clean, healthy, ripe grapes with adequate acidity is the point of departure for all the best German white wines, but careful grape selection in somewhat ordinary vintages can also result in wines of character as 1987 and 1984 showed us.

In the regions where Riesling plays an important role, there have been vintages of outstanding quality in 1989, 1988, 1983, 1979, 1976, 1975, 1973 and 1971, and good wines in 1986, 1985 and 1981.

Riesling *Auslese* occurs infrequently on the Rhein but when it does, the sweeter versions can be kept for ten years or more after the vintage. Fifteen years is not too long to store the even rarer Riesling *Beerenauslesen* and *Trockenbeerenauslesen*; and for Riesling *Eisweine*, with their very high acidity, fifteen years' development is about the minimum required.

Wines from other traditional vine varieties would normally be expected to mature perhaps 30 per cent more quickly than Rieslings of an equivalent quality category.

APPENDIX VI

Dry Wine

The chart below compares the amount of dry quality wine which received an AP control number in 1985 with that of 1989, and relates it to the total volume of wine to gain an AP number in both years. The move to dry wine continues, but at a pace that varies from one region to another. Baden and the Rheinpfalz are the largest suppliers, but both in Franken and the Rheingau the percentage of dry wine is also high.

	1985		1989	
	Dry wine as percentage of total	Amount of dry wine in hl	Dry wine as percentage of total	Amount of dry wine in hl
Ahr	20	6,529	25	8,038
Mittelrhein	22	5,164	26	7,581
Mosel-Saar-Ruwer	6	68,199	10	109,703
Nahe	13	35,625	22	57,942
Rheingau	28	44,840	40	75,052
Rheinhessen	7	118,481	11	212,742
Rheinpfalz	18	331,478	23	474,067
Franken	36	149,744	50	233,390
Hessische Bergstrasse	27	8,185	37	9,907
Württemberg	15	140,570	26	275,609
Baden	31	326,000	43*	478,300*

*Approximate figures.
Source: Die Weinwirtschaft

Per Capita Drink Consumption in Western Germany

The figures given are litres.

	1980	1989
Still wine	21.4	21.1
Sekt	4.4	5.2
Beer	145.9	142.9
Spirits	8.0	6.2
Mineral water	40.2	81.8
Soft drinks	72.0	82.0
Fruit juices	19.4	36.2
Coffee*	158.8	190.5
Instant coffee	8.9	8.8
Tea†	26.8	25.1

* calculated at 35 grams of roast coffee per litre.
† excluding herbal teas.
Source: Ifo-Institut

Still wine consumption in western Germany remains virtually constant, but the sales of *Sekt* steadily increase. The consumption of beer has declined slightly and that of spirits considerably. Of the 21.1 litres of still wine drunk by the Germans each year, approximately half is imported.

The West German per capita consumption of wine and *Sekt* taken together, is the twelfth largest in the world as the figures below show:

Per capita consumption: wine and sparkling wine 1987 in litres

Italy	79.0	Switzerland	49.5
France	75.1	Chile	35.0
Portugal	64.3	Austria	32.1
Luxembourg	58.5	Greece	31.8
Argentina	58.1	Romania	28.0
Spain	54.0	West Germany	25.8

Source: Produktschap voor Gestilleerde Dranken

APPENDIX VIII

Production and Export of Wine from Germany 1979–1989

———

	Harvest in million hl*	Exports in million hl	Exports as percentage of harvest
1979/80	8.3	1.7	20
1980/81	4.5	1.9	42
1981/82	7.3	2.0	27
1982/83	15.8	2.4	15
1983/84	13.4	2.9	22
1984/85	8.0	2.7	34
1985/86	5.3	2.3	43
1986/87	10.2	2.5	24
1987/88	8.7	2.6	30
1988/89	9.2	2.6	28

* The figures for the harvest are those recorded by the producers immediately after the vintage. They refer to the year in which the twelve-month 'campaign' started.

Source: Die Weinwirtschaft and the Verband Deutscher Weinexporteure

APPENDIX IX

Export of Wine from Germany to the Ten Largest Importing Countries

---

Exports in hectolitres in 1979, and their performance in 1989

	1979	1989	Variance
United Kingdom	456,052	1,523,523	+234%
USA	413,508	196,152	−53%
Netherlands	136,695	224,373	+64%
Denmark	99,860	90,623	−9%
Canada	97,569	92,403	−5%
Belgium/Luxembourg	69,569	43,411	−38%
Sweden	50,213	87,207	+74%
Japan	46,991	134,998	+187%
France	26,655	17,861	−33%
Australia	22,387	9,155	−59%

In 1989 Norway (59,123 hl) and Mexico (40.223 hl) were among the ten largest importing countries of wine from Germany. They had replaced France and Australia.

Total exports of wine from Germany amounted to 1,502,087 in 1979 and 2,625,777 in 1989 – an increase of 75 per cent.

Cheap white wine accounts for the large increase in exports to the United Kingdom. Trade sources suggest that exports of medium-price branded wine to the United Kingdom have declined considerably, and that those of estate-bottled wine have also decreased.

Ignoring sales to the United Kingdom, exports of wines from Germany rose from 1,046,035 hl in 1979 to 1,102,254 in 1989 – an increase of 5 per cent.

Source: Verband Deutscher Weinexporteure

APPENDIX X

High Quality Vineyards Well Known Outside Germany

The name of an individual vineyard site can be taken as in indication of quality in wine only when it is linked to that of a good bottler. This may be an estate or a co-operative cellar. Many of the producers listed at the end of each chapter describing a wine region, own the free- or leasehold of the better parcels of land within the individual sites. However, these sites have not always been of their present size. The famous Wehlener Sonnenuhr covered 10 hectares at the start of the twentieth century, was increased to 35 hectares in 1953 and later again to 58 hectares, only to be subsequently reduced to 47 hectares. The Bernkasteler Doctor has expanded and contracted in a similar but smaller way. Some wines from well-known vineyards, such as the Zeltinger Himmelreich, are estate-bottled, but others from the same site are sold in bulk on the open market, to be bottled separately or to become part of a commercial blend. Therefore, in most cases it would be very unsafe to say categorically that a particular vineyard always produced better wine than another. However, if wines from the following individual vineyard sites (*Einzellagen*) are estate-bottled by the producers mentioned in this book, they should be good representatives of their type and some of the greatest German wines are likely to be found amongst them.

Where a vineyard is solely owned by one estate as indicated by an asterisk, most of the complications described above no longer apply.

MOSEL-SAAR-RUWER

Bernkasteler Doctor
Bernkasteler Graben
Brauneberger Juffer
Brauneberger Juffer Sonnenuhr
Eitelsbacher Karthäuserhofberg*
Erdener Prälat

Erdener Treppchen
Graacher Domprobst
Graacher Himmelreich
Graacher Josephshöfer
Kanzemer Altenberg

Maximin Grünhäuser Abtsberg*
Maximin Grünhäuser
  Herrenberg*
Ockfener Bockstein
Piesporter Goldtröpfchen
Scharzhofberg

Uerziger Würzgarten
Wehlener Sonnenuhr
Wiltinger Braune Kupp
Zeltinger Himmelreich
Zeltinger Sonnenuhr

NAHE

Dorsheimer Goldloch
Kreuznacher Krötenpfuhl
Kreuznacher Brückes
Niederhäuser Hermannsberg

Niederhäuser Hermannshöhle
Schlossböckelheimer Felsenberg
Schlossböckelheimer Kupfergrube
Traiser Bastei

RHEINGAU

Erbacher Marcobrunn
Erbacher Siegelsberg
Geisenheimer Kläuserweg
Geisenheimer Rothenberg
Hattenheimer Nussbrunnen
Hochheimer Domdechaney
Hochheimer Kirchenstück
Hochheimer Königin Victoria
  Berg*
Johannisberger Klaus
Kiedricher Gräfenberg

Kiedricher Sandgrub
Kiedricher Wasseros
Oestricher Lenchen
Rüdesheimer Berg Rottland
Rüdesheimer Berg Roseneck
Rüdesheimer Berg Schlossberg
Schloss Johannisberg*
Schloss Vollrads*
Steinberg*
Winkeler Hasensprung

RHEINHESSEN

Binger Scharlachberg
Nackenheimer Rothenberg
Niersteiner Hipping
Niersteiner Orbel
Niersteiner Oelberg

Niersteiner Kranzberg
Niersteiner Pettenthal
Oppenheimer Kreuz
Oppenheimer Sackträger

RHEINPFALZ

Deidesheimer Grainhübel
Deidesheimer Herrgottsacker
Deidesheimer Hohenmorgen
Deidesheimer Leinhöhle
Grosskarlbacher Burgweg
Kallstadter Annaberg
Forster Kirchenstück

Forster Jesuitengarten
Forster Ungeheuer
Ruppertsberger Linsenbusch
Ruppertsberger Reiterpfad
Wachenheimer Böhlig
Wachenheimer Gerümpel
Wachenheimer Rechbächel*

FRANKEN

Casteller Schlossberg*
Escherndorfer Lump
Iphöfer Julius-Echter-Berg
Iphöfer Kalb
Randersackerer Pfülben

Randersackerer Teufelskeller
Rödelseer Küchenmeister
Würzburger Abtsleite
Würzburger Innere Leiste
Würzburger Stein

APPENDIX XI

The German Label

'Detailed Rules for the Description and Presentation of Wine' tell us what has to appear in one field of vision on a wine label. This obligatory information identifies the wine, and to it may be added certain optional information, indicating some of the particular characteristics of interest to the consumer. The regulations state how the characters used on the label must relate to each other. As their title claims, they are 'detailed', and like all wine legislation within the EEC work on the principle that unless whatever is proposed is expressly allowed, it is forbidden. (The German Wine Law before 1971 took the opposite view that everything was legal unless regulations instructed otherwise.)

The German label designer is becoming increasingly skilled in combining the requirements of the law with the marketing wishes of his clients. Striking modern labels are as common in Germany as they are in Italy, but most estate bottlers prefer to adjust their existing designs rather than change to a completely new concept.

The simplicity of the 1865 Marcobrunner label has its charm, but that of Weingut Kühling-Gillot in the Rheinhessen observes today's legal requirements without disturbing the estate's customers.

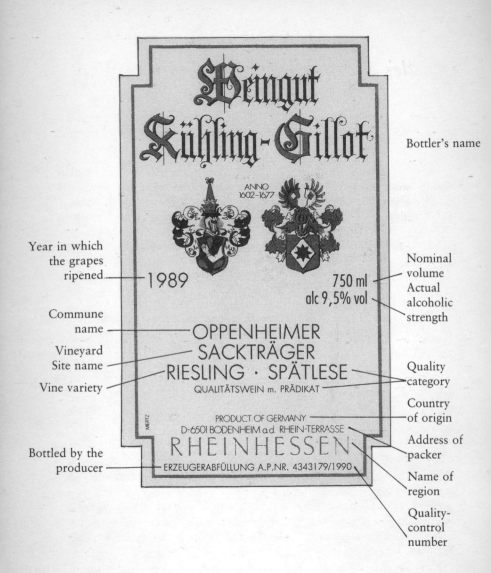

Bottler's name

Year in which
the grapes
ripened

1989

Commune
name

OPPENHEIMER

Vineyard
Site name

SACKTRÄGER

Vine variety

RIESLING · SPÄTLESE

QUALITÄTSWEIN m. PRÄDIKAT

750 ml
alc 9,5% vol

Nominal
volume
Actual
alcoholic
strength

Quality
category

PRODUCT OF GERMANY
D-6501 BODENHEIM a.d. RHEIN-TERRASSE

RHEINHESSEN

Bottled by the
producer

ERZEUGERABFÜLLUNG A.P.NR. 43431 79/1990

Country
of origin

Address of
packer

Name of
region

Quality-
control
number

ANNO
1602-1677

MERTZ

APPENDIX XII

Bottles and the Service of German Wine

About two-thirds of all German wine sold in bottle is distributed in the 0.75-litre size. The green litre bottle accounts for most of the remaining third, with a small amount being filled into the other sizes allowed by the EC.

The only bottle reserved for wines from specific geographical areas is the green, or amber, flagon-shaped *Bocksbeutel* (see chapter 20). Mosel-Saar-Ruwer wines are offered in the slim, tall, green bottle, as are many wines from Württemberg and Baden. Rheingau, Rheinhessen, Nahe and Rheinpfalz wines are sold mainly in amber glass, and many red wines in all regions are filled into an amber Burgundy-type bottle. The colour of German wine bottles is a matter of tradition and availability, not of legislation. Some bottlers are now using green glass for drier, and amber for sweeter wines, but this is an individual commercial decision. Others choose bottles of foreign, often Italian, origin to meet, as it is thought, the expectations of a particular sector of the wine market. The choice and use of bottles of varying colours and shapes has probably never been greater than it is in the 1990s.

The service of German white wine is no different to that of any other white wine. That is to say, a dry or medium-dry wine should be drunk slightly chilled, with the sweeter wines being served a little cooler. In practical terms, an hour or so in a domestic fridge should be sufficient to make the wine pleasantly cool, without having its flavour hidden by being over-chilled. If a sweet wine is transferred from the fridge to the freezing compartment for the last 15 minutes before being served, it should be at the right, refreshing temperature when drunk from the glass.

Traditional German wine glasses are not designed to make the best of the most delicate, refined wines in the world. The 0.20 or 0.25-litre rummer with its robust green or amber stem, placed on the table with a '*zum Wohl*' ('cheers!') from the waitress, is the standard café glass. In the increasing number of high-quality restaurants the glassware is international in origin and design, and reflects the quality of the wine, and of the food which it is to accompany.

In *Germany and the Germans*, John Ardagh wrote that once the Germans 'discover a cause, then they go for it twice as hard as anyone else'. With all the zeal of the recently converted, the Germans discuss which wine will most perfectly consummate the multi-faceted flavours of their new and excellent kitchen, or vice versa. Of course, German wine can be drunk every bit as satisfactorily with food as wine from elsewhere, providing the universal ground rules are observed. To be fair, the German insistence that body and structure in wine are as important as colour when selecting a wine for a particular dish seems technically absolutely correct. Equally true is their claim that the sweetness in some sauces served with meat is best offset by a certain amount of residual sugar in an accompanying wine. But many of the sweet and fine German wines, particularly Rieslings, are so complex in flavour, and so elegant that, as ever, they are best enjoyed without food.

Glossary

ABFÜLLUNG: bottling.

ALCOHOL, ACTUAL: the alcohol present in a wine.

ALCOHOL, NATURAL: alcohol derived solely from the sugar of the grape.

ALCOHOL, POTENTIAL: the alcohol that would be produced by fermenting all the sugar in the wine.

ALCOHOL, TOTAL: the sum of the actual and potential alcohol.

AMTLICHE PRÜFUNG: Official quality examination for wine, unique to Germany.

ANBAUGEBIET: a specified region for producing quality wine, e.g. Rheinhessen.

AUSLESE: a wine of *QmP* quality, usually at its best when the result of careful grape selection.

BARRIQUE: cask of about 225–8 litres, used when it is still young to impart tannin to a wine in Germany and, more often, abroad.

BEERENAUSLESE: a *QmP*, produced from overripe grapes, probably affected by *botrytis cinerea*.

BEREICH: a district for producing quality wine, e.g. Bereich Bernkastel.

BEZIRK: district – not an official EC designation.

BOTRYTIS CINEREA: a fungus that can much increase the sweetness of grapes that are already ripe.

BRUT: describes a dry-tasting sparkling wine with up to 15 g/l of residual sugar. '*Extra brut*' corresponds to a maximum of 6 g/l.

EDELFÄULE: describes the quality enhancing rot caused by *botrytis cinerea*.

EINZELLAGE: a single vineyard site, the smallest geographical unit in which grapes are planted in the EC.

EISWEIN: high-quality wine produced from must of a certain minimum concentration, from frozen grapes.

ENRICH: EC term for the addition of sugar to must or wine to make it more alcoholic.

ERZEUGERABFÜLLUNG: bottled by the producer.

ERZEUGERGEMEINSCHAFT: agricultural or viticultural producers' association.

FASS: cask.

FLURBEREINIGUNG: the reconstruction, modernization, and reallocation of farming and vine-growing land.

FRÄNKISCH TROCKEN: describes a Franken wine with less than 4 g/l of residual sugar.

FUDER: cask of about 1,000 litres, particularly associated with the Mosel-Saar-Ruwer.

GEBIET: district – not an official EC designation.

GROSSER RING: association of high-quality estates in the Mosel-Saar-Ruwer region, all members of the *VDP*.

GUT: an estate.

HALBFUDER: cask of about 500 litres.

HALBSTÜCK: cask of about 610 litres.

HALBTROCKEN: medium-dry.

HOCHGEWÄCHS: description given to a Riesling *QbA*, of a superior standard.

HOCK: a quality wine from the Ahr, Hessische Bergstrasse, Mittelrhein, Nahe, Rheingau, Rheinhessen or Rheinpfalz, or a table wine from the sub-district, Rhein. A description used only in English-speaking countries.

JAHRGANG: vintage, meaning the wine of one year rather than the grape harvest.

KABINETT: first category of *QmP*.

LANDWEIN: a superior form of table wine. Cannot be sweeter than medium-dry.

LEHRANSTALT: teaching institute.

LESE: the harvest.

LIEBLICH: medium-sweet.

MALO-LACTIC FERMENTATION: makes a wine taste softer.

NEUZÜCHTUNGEN: crossings of the European vine *vitis vinifera*.

OECHSLE: scale, named after its inventor, for the measurement of the specific gravity of must.

OIDIUM: powdery mildew.

ORTSTEIL: part of a larger community.

PERONOSPORA: downy mildew.

PHYLLOXERA: disease caused by an aphid.

PLASMOPARA VITICOLA: fungus causing downy mildew (*peronospora*).

POKAL: traditional German wine glass of 200 or 250ml content.

QbA: quality wine from a single *Anbaugebiet*.

QmP: quality wine with the added distinctions, *Kabinett, Spätlese, Auslese, Beerenauslese, Eiswein* or *Trockenbeerenauslese*.

RESTZUCKER: residual and therefore unfermented sugar.

RÖMER: a rummer, a specific type of glass.

ROTLING: a rosé wine blended from red and white grapes or their pulp.

SCHLOSS: castle or palace.

SEKT: quality sparkling wine.

SIEGEL: a seal, used to indicate wine of superior quality.

SPÄTLESE: a wine of *QmP* quality made from late-picked grapes.

SPRITZIG: describes a wine with a small amount of noticeable carbon dioxide.

STÜCK: cask of about 1,200 litres.

SÜSSRESERVE: unfermented grape juice used to sweeten wine.

TABLE WINE, TAFELWEIN: the lowest category of wine made in the EC.

TROCKEN: dry.

VDP: Verband Deutscher Prädikatsweingüter – an association of German top-quality wine estates.

VERBAND: an association.

VEREIN: a union.

VERSUCHSANSTALT: experimental institute.

VERWALTUNG: administration.

VORLESE: a picking of grapes before the start of the main harvest.

WEINGÄRTNERGENOSSENSCHAFT: name used in Württemberg for a *Winzergenossenschaft*.

WEISSHERBST: rosé *QbA/QmP*, from a single vine variety in all regions other than Mosel-Saar-Ruwer, Mittelrhein, Nahe and Hessische Bergstrasse.

WINZERGENOSSENSCHAFT: a co-operative cellar.

WINZERVEREIN: alternative name for a *Winzergenossenschaft*.

Bibliography

Adelmann, Raban Graf, *et al. Württemberg*, Stuttgart: Seewald, 1981

Ambrosi, Hans. *Wo grosse Weine wachsen*, Munich: Gräfe und Unzer, 1975

– Helmut Becker et al. Der Deutsche Wein, Munich: Gräfe und Unzer, 1978

– and Bernhard Breuer. *Die Ahr*, Stuttgart: Seewald, 1978

– and Bernhard Breuer. *Franken*, Stuttgart: Seewald, 1981

– and Bernhard Breuer. *Der Mittelrhein*, Stuttgart: Seewald, 1979

– and Bernhard Breuer. *Die Nahe*, Stuttgart: Seewald, 1979

– and Bernhard Breuer. *Der Rheingau*, Stuttgart: Seewald, 1979

– and Bernhard Breuer. *Hessische Bergstrasse*, Stuttgart: Seewald, 1981

Andres, Stefan. *Die Grossen Weine Deutschlands*, Berlin: Ullstein, 1960

Ardagh, John. *Germany and the Germans*, London: Penguin, 1988

Arntz, Helmut. *Chronik der ältesten rheinischen Sektkellerei Burgeff & Co*, Wiesbaden: Wiesbadener Grapische Betriebe, 1962

– *Deutsches Sektlexikon*, Wiesbaden: Wirtschafts Verlag, 1987

Badischer Weinbauverband. *Baden und seine Burgunder*, Freiburg: Rombach, 1981

– *Der Gutedel und seine Weine*, Freiburg: Rombach, 1982

– *Riesling, Silvaner, Müller-Thurgau*, Freiburg: Rombach, 1983

– *Traminer, Gewürztraminer, und Muskateller*, Freiburg: Rombach, 1982

Bassermann-Jordan, Dr Friedrich. *Geschichte des Weinbaues*, Frankfurt: Heinrich Keller, 1907

Becker, Werner, *et al. Wegweiser durch das Weinrecht*, Bingen: GEWA-Druck, 1983

Bronner, Joh. Ph. *Der Weinbau am Haardtgebirge von Landau bis Worms*, Heidelberg: C. F. Winter, 1833; reprinted Neustadt: M. Birghan, 1981

– *Der Weinbau in der Provinz Rheinhessen, im Nahetal und Moselthal*, Heidelberg: C. F. Winter, 1834; reprinted Neustadt: M. Birghan, 1981

Currle, Otto, and Otmar Bauer. *Rheinhessen*, Stuttgart: Seewald, 1981

Dahlen, H. W. *Beiträge zur Geschichte des Weinbaues u. Weinhandels im Rheingau*, Mainz: Ph. v. Zabern, 1896

Dietzel, Andreas. *Geschichte des Weinguts Freiherr v. Gleichenstein*, Vogtsburg-Schelingen: Hermann Delabar, 1984

Dochnahl, Friedrich Jakob. *Katechismus des Weinbaues, der Rebenkultur und der Weinbereitung*, Leipzig: J. J. Weber, 1896

Dohm, Horst. *Sekt zwischen Kult und Konsum*, Neustadt: Meininger, 1981

– *Weingüter in Deutschland*, Neustadt: Meininger, 1985

Duff, David. *Victoria Travels*, London: Frederick Muller, 1970

Friess, Rudolf. *150 Jahre Fränkischer Weinbauverband*, Würzburg: Fränkischer Weinbauverband, 1986

Fuchss, Peter, and Klausjürgen Müller. *Rheinpfalz*, Stuttgart: Seewald, 1981

Geiger, Michael, *et al. Die Weinstrasse Porträt einer Landschaft*, Landau i.d. Pfalz: Pfälzische Landeskunde, 1985

George, Harry. *George's Weinführer*, Waldkirch: Waldkircher Verlag, 1989

Goldschmidt, Dr Eduard. *Deutschlands Weinbauorte und Weinbergslagen*, Mainz: Verlag der Deutschen Wein-Zeitung, 6th edn, 1951

Goldschmidt, Fritz. *Das Weingesetz*, Mainz: Verlag der Deutschen Wein-Zeitung, 1930

Grunberger, Richard. *A Social History of the Third Reich*, London: Penguin, 1987

Hallgarten, S. F. *Rhineland Wineland*, London: Arlington Books, 4th edn, 1965

Harenberg. *Deutsche Weinführer*, Dortmund: Harenberg Kommunikation, 1987

Heinen, Winfrid. *Baden*, Trittenheim: Heinen, 1987

– *Württemberg*, Trittenheim: Heinen, 1987

Hillenbrand, Walter. *Weinbau-Taschenbuch*, Wiesbaden: Dr Bilz & Dr Fraund, 1978

– *et al. Taschenbuch der Rebsorten*, Mainz: Dr Fraund, 1990

Historischer Verein Hochheim am Main eV. *Hochheimer Spiegel Nr 2*, Hochheim, 1988

Hyams, Edward. *Dionysus – A Social History of the Wine Vine*, London: Thames and Hudson, 1965

Jakob, Dr Ludwig. *Lexikon der Oenologie*, Neustadt: Meininger, 1979

– *Taschenbuch der Kellerwirtschaft*, Wiesbaden: Dr Bilz & Dr Fraund, 1977

Jamieson, Ian. *The Mitchell Beazley Pocket Guide to German Wines*, London: Mitchell Beazley, 2nd edn, 1987

Johnson, Hugh. *The Story of Wine*, London: Mitchell Beazley, 1989

Kähni, Otto, *Der Ortenauer Weinbau und das St Andreas-Weingut der Stadt Offenburg in Vergangenheit und Gegenwart*, Stadt Offenburg, 1969

Langenbach, Alfred. *The Wines of Germany*, London: Harper & Co., 1951

Leenaers, Robert, and Hans Jorissen. *Atlas van Rijn & Moezel Wijnen*, De Meern: Het Spectrum, 1986

Pigott, Stuart. *Life beyond Liebfraumilch*, London: Sidgwick & Jackson, 1988

Pilz, Hermann. *Sekt aus Moselwein Herstellung und Vermarktungsorganisation*, Münster-Hiltrup: Landwirtschaftsverlag, 1987

Redding, Cyrus. *A History and Description of Modern Wines*, London: Whittaker, Treacher, & Arnot, 1833; reprinted 1980

Rudd, Hugh R. *Hocks and Moselle*, London: Constable, 1935

Ruthe, Dr Wilhelm. *Der Deutsche Wein*, Munich: F. Bruckmann, 1926

Scheuermann, Mario. *Deutsche Spitzenweingüter*, Düsseldorf: ECON, 1989

Schoonmaker, Frank. *The Wines of Germany* (revised by Peter Sichel), London: Faber and Faber, 1983

Seward, Desmond. *Monks and Wine*, London: Mitchell Beazley, 1979

Siefert, Fritz. *Das deutsche Städtlexikon*, Stuttgart: Füllhorn-Sachbuch, 1981

Simon, André. *The History of the Wine Trade in England*, London: Wyman & Sons, 1906

Stabilisierungsfonds für Wein. *Deutscher Wein Atlas*, Mainz: Deutsches Wein-Institut, 1988

Stadt Alzey. *60 Jahre Weingut der Stadt Alzey*, Alzey: Stadt Alzey, 1976

Stöhr, Wolfgang, *et al*. *Mosel-Saar-Ruwer*, Stuttgart: Seewald, 1981

Sturm, Joh. Bapt. *Rheinwein*, Frankfurt: C. Naumann's Druckerei, 1882

Tiltz, Werner. *Einkaufsreise in die deutschen Weinschatzkammern*. Munich: Steinheim, 1984

Troost, Gerhard. *Technologie des Weines*, Stuttgart: Eugen Ulmer, 1980

Verein der Absolventen der LLFA. *50 Jahre Deutsche Weinstrasse*, Neustadt, 1985

Vizetelly, Henry. *Facts about Champagne and Other Sparkling Wines*, London: Vizetelly, 1879

Weinbauverein Walluf. *1200 Jahre Wallufer Wein 779–1979*, Walluf: Winzerverein Walluf, 1979

Index

Note: Where a geographical name appears on a map, a * is placed after the appropriate page number.
The following abbreviations are used in the index: 'Wgt' for 'Weingut', 'Wzg' for 'Winzergenossenschaft'.

241